Vendetta

Vendetta

Paul Henke

METHUEN

Published by Methuen 2021

1

Methuen & Co
Orchard House
Railway Street
Slingsby
York YO62 4AN
www.methuen.co.uk

Methuen & Co Limited Reg. No. 5278590

A CIP catalogue record for this book is available from the British Library

ISBN 978 0 413 77856 7

Typeset by SX Composing DTP, Rayleigh, Essex
Printed and bound in Great Britain by
Clays Ltd, Elcograf S.p.A.

Vendetta

Prologue

The six men were on their knees, facing Mecca, their foreheads on the ground. They were reciting the Maghrib, the fourth prayer of the day, at the correct time, which was just after sunset.

When they finished they stood up and exchanged smiles and high-fives. The men were in their late twenties, early thirties. They were of medium height and weight and each of them would be lost in a crowd of two. As it was they wore typical Arab garb - a thawb and a keffiyeh and hence stuck out like sore thumbs. They quickly pulled off their clothes and put on jeans and shirts. Reluctantly, a few weeks earlier, they had shaved their beards, seeing their naked faces for the first time in many years.

In the name of Allah and the prophet Mohammed they wanted the world to know what they were doing. Or in this case what they had done. Broadcasts on social media would ensure that happened.

They were determined to make the West pay for its crimes against Muslims and Islam.

This would be a glorious day. Appropriately, the day was known as Isra and Miraj or the Miraculous Night Journey. It was the day the Prophet Mohammed, in one night journeyed from Makka to Jerusalem and then ascended to the heavens. On this night Muslims the world over celebrated the occasion by offering optional prayers and lighting up villages, towns and cities with candles and electric lights. For the six men they would celebrate with a devastating blow against the non-believers along with their own martyrdom. Ironically the day coincided with the Christian

1

festival of Easter, the day the false prophet arose from the dead, a day seeped in blasphemy. But that day would go down in history. The planned attack, though not on the scale of 9/11, would be highly significant and would show the West that nobody was safe.

Their plan was simple. They would take different positions at the Union of European Football Associations' final match. The stadium would be packed. It was the big one. Spain versus Germany, each with three titles to their name. They would explode their suicide vests simultaneously. They would watch the chaos from their privileged positions at the gates of Jannah where God and the prophet, peace be upon him, resided.

They had discussed endlessly by which of the eight gates leading to paradise they would enter. They had finally decided it would be the gate known as Baab Al-Jihad. The gate reserved for those who died in the defence of Islam. The irony that the Qu'ran (2:193) stated "Let there be no hostility except to those who practice oppression," was lost on these men as it was on all fanatics.

They were excited at the thought that they would become holy martyrs doing Allah's work.

The next stage in their preparations was to take their suicide vests and put them on, using Velcro to secure the vests in place.

'Remember my brothers, once you press the thumb switch its release will set off the explosion. If we are killed we will take many of the infidels with us.' The speaker was Abdul-Hameed Saud, the eldest son of a Saudi Prince after whom he was named. His hatred of all things Western was well known by his circle of friends. He often boasted about it, sometimes to the wrong people. People he knew who loved their religion and hated what was happening to it. They were vital in the war against the West.

The weather was perfect. Allah was smiling on them. It was cold with a light wind from the north-west bringing clouds with it, making it judicious to wear a waterproof jacket. They pulled on cagoules, a thin, loose fitting, nylon cover that reached their knees. Their arms and hands were inside, mere inches from the detonator switch.

The team leader spoke into his mike. 'Alpha 1 you copy?'

'Loud and clear, Alpha. The information was accurate.'

'I concur,' said Alpha.

Alpha was sitting in a Ford Transit van about 350 metres away from the target building. He had on a pair of earphones and was listening to the terrorists praying before preparing to leave.

They had discussed taking the targets out whilst in the building but taking all six in one hit was problematical and if they had enough explosives one vest could set off the other five. The team would die with the jihadists. They put their lives at risk on a regular basis. It was their job. But not needlessly; hence the reason they had decided on their current strategy.

'Good. We know there are six of them and they will be exiting in intervals starting in about two minutes I would guess.'

'I'm now in place,' said Alpha 3, 'the south window is covered.'

'Alpha 4?'

'Ditto to the north.'

'Alpha 2?'

'In position at the rear.'

'Okay. I can hear them saying their farewells and how they will all meet again in paradise.'

The jihadists were in a large, derelict industrial unit on the outskirts of Berlin. The building they were using was in better condition than the others with some of the windows still intact. The Alpha team knew the jihadists had been there for two days, planning and praying. And, the team members suspected, building up the courage to die. Now they were ready.

One of the terrorists said, 'Over 100,000 people are expected in the stadium to watch the match. There will be hundreds of deaths and injured. Allamdulillah.'

'Praise be to God I don't think,' muttered Alpha 2 into his microphone.

None of the others bothered to reply. They'd heard it all before.

The team knew the level of devastation, death and injuries that would be inflicted if six high explosive vests erupted in the middle of the crowd. It didn't bear thinking about. They were there to ensure it wouldn't happen. And it wouldn't. This op was a milk run compared to most of the jobs they were asked to do.

Outside the front of the building three motor scooters were parked while a fourth was in the rear. They made ideal transport in the congested city. Weaving in and out of the traffic ensured the jihadists arrived at the stadium in plenty of time.

Alpha transmitted, 'Heads up. The first man is on his way. He's coming out the front. Wait, another one is coming your way Alpha 2.'

'Roger that. He's coming out now. He's walking this way towards the scooter.'

Alpha 2 was hiding next to a rubbish skip beside the scooter. He waited until the terrorist reached the scooter which put him three metres away before standing up. The man jerked half a step backwards before Alpha 2 fired two rounds from a silenced Glock 40 Gen 4. The 6 inch barrel, with its improved velocity and 15 rounds was a formidable and accurate pistol. In the hands of an expert it was about the finest automatic available and Alpha 2 was an expert. He ducked down behind the heavy metal skip and waited a few seconds. Nothing happened. 'Two in the head. As dead as a dodo.'

'Alpha 1?'

'I've got him in sight boss.'

Alpha 1 was using a British army L115A3, part of the Sniper System Improvement Programme (SSIP). It hadn't been possible to get close to the building in the front so the sniper was about 150 metres away.

Alpha 1 watched as the man climbed onto the scooter, started it up and drove sedately away. His closest point of contact with the sniper was about 100 metres. That was when Alpha 1 took the shot and blew the man off his scooter. The heavy calibre round had taken away most of the target's head. The silencer attached to the weapon was highly effective.

'He's down.'

4

'Alpha,' Alpha 2 broadcast, 'I've dumped the body in the skip. The IED vest is basic. I've removed the det.'

'Roger that. We should have another target in a couple of minutes. There are four left and as far as they know two bikes. So presumably they'll come out in pairs. Yes. Two coming out the front now.'

'I've got them,' said Alpha 1.

He watched as the two men climbed onto one of the scooters and headed towards the sniper. They were travelling slowly, wobbling slightly, as though the driver was unused to the machine.

Suddenly the scooter swerved and tipped over. The two men hit the ground and a second later there was a massive explosion. The bodies were shredded into tiny parts, the round pellets flew with considerable force in all directions while the noise reverberated around the area.

'Damn,' said Alpha.

'Can you hear anything from inside the building?' Alpha 2 enquired.

'Yes. They're arguing with each other about what's happened. They're sure the police must be outside.' After a few minutes Alpha said, 'They've convinced themselves that it must have been an accident. Perhaps one of them was fiddling with the switch. If it had been due to the police they would either have been attacked or the police would be outside demanding that they surrender. They're nervous. One of them is telling the other to take the scooter and go. That he will go through one of the windows. They've just exchanged *Inshallahs*. Looks like they are on their way.'

'Someone is at the south window,' said Alpha 3.There came the faint tinkling of breaking glass. 'Yep, he's coming this way.'

'The other one isn't taking the scooter and is walking towards me,' said Alpha. 'You got a shot Alpha 1?'

'Negative.'

'Then he's mine.'

'Mine's down,' announced Alpha 3.

Alpha stepped down from the van about 15 metres in front of the terrorist. The man stopped in surprise but before he could react Alpha lifted his Glock in a two handed grip and blew the man's head apart. As he fired he ducked down behind the van. Nothing happened. Alpha approached the body and tentatively lifted the corpse's nylon cagoule. One glance was enough. There were two reasons the vest hadn't exploded. One was obvious and hence the requirement for head shots. The other was perplexing. The vest was a dummy.

Alpha 1 approached. 'We've made the other vests safe, boss, what about this one?'

'It's a dummy.'

'Another holy warrior not prepared to make the sacrifice.'

'You've got it. I suspect he saw himself as too important to die just yet but needed to ensure the others did as they were told.'

'I guess this one must be the Prince's son.'

'I guess so as well.'

The dead men were later identified as Saudi Arabians. They had entered Europe on forged passports bought for US$ 5,000 each from a lawyer living on Malta. Jihadists the the world over knew such an amount to be a mere bagatelle for the financiers of Islamic jihad who dreamt of a worldwide caliphate ruled by an elite based in the kingdom of Saudi Arabia. The caliphate would be cemented in Wahhabism, the puritanical form of Sunni Islam practiced in Saudi Arabia and Qatar. It was oppressive in the extreme and responsible for the stoning, beheading and murders of thousands of people of all faiths. All had deserved to die. If it took a thousand years to achieve their dream it didn't matter. While the West thought in terms of immediate gratification the Wahhabis thought in terms of centuries.

The team left before the police arrived. The paperwork and removal of the corpses was to be left to the authorities who could even claim the credit for the operation, which was preferable.

What none of the Alpha team could know was that their actions were to have dire consequences.

1

Nicholas David Hunter, GM, RN was enjoying a pint of real ale in a bar in Cardiff. The room held over 60 wooden tables, the bar was long, wooden and had an array of pump handles in clusters of three. The customers scattered around the room were laughing and joking, enjoying themselves. On a warm Friday afternoon in August the place was busy but not yet packed. Escapees from a hard week's work were beginning to arrive, filling up the place.

Hunter had a few days off from his own hectic life as a senior officer at TIFAT, The International Force Against Terrorism. It was an unusual posting for a man of his specialisation. He had started his military career as a naval officer, entering Dartmouth at the age of 18. After his initial training he went on to become an MCDO, a Minewarfare and Clearance Diving Officer. In essence an expert diver as well as being pretty adept at dealing with certain types of mines and bombs.

In spite of having command of a Royal Navy minehunter for 15 months the problem he had faced, like so many of his compatriots, was the shrinking of the Royal Navy and a sharp reduction in promotion prospects. Like others serving their country he had found it was shameful that the Royal Navy was now smaller than the French Navy.

He had been invited to join TIFAT and when he was promoted to Commander he had relinquished his military career to become the operations director at TIFAT. This meant he coordinated and ran operations though he was also active on the frontline.

He was 6ft 2ins with black hair, blue eyes, a determined chin and aquiline nose. Built like an athlete with narrow hips and broad shoulders he wouldn't disgrace himself running a marathon. Right then he was dressed in black jeans, a blue shirt and a cream coloured safari style jacket. He liked the extra pockets it sported.

He was pondering his reasons for being in the city. For quite a while he had been meaning to visit the area, particularly the valleys where his family on his mother's side came from. The story of the family's rise from relative poverty in a mining village called Llanbeddas to significant wealth in a single generation was well documented, beginning with the book *A Million Tears*. His father had been the journalist who had written it while at the same time meeting Hunter's mother. The rest, as it was said, was history though not necessarily love at first sight.

The reason for delay was typical of many people, life and events got in the way. However, having completed an operation in London where a team of three terrorists had been eliminated, he had decided he was close enough to South Wales to spend a few days exploring the villages and valleys.

But two days had been enough and he was now booked to return to Scotland on that evening's flight.

The pub he was in sold some of the best ales in the UK and he was savouring the taste of a locally brewed beer when he saw the two men. As usual he was sitting at the back of the room, near a "staff only" door. He had already noted there were three public entrances/exits and two for staff. One was via the kitchen while the other lead to a short corridor with storerooms, a staff room and a door at the end leading to a courtyard. Thanks to the warm afternoon the door was wide open.

On the whole, the customers were having a good time except for the two men who had entered 10 minutes earlier. They both had drinks of what looked like lemonade, though it might have been sparkling water. So far they had spent their time looking nervously about the place. Then one of them had nodded in his direction. It was an action more imagined than real. But then both seemed to take an undue interest in him and alarm bells were sounding in his head.

Normally he would be armed but following the London operation and having decided he would fly back to Edinburgh he had left his automatic pistol with the team. Though in the circumstances it wouldn't be much use. What was he going to do if he had been armed? Shoot some men for looking at him strangely?

He glanced around, not looking directly at them. They were no longer looking his way so maybe he was just being paranoid. He sipped more beer and followed it with a few salted peanuts. His peripheral vision told him that he was fully justified to be feeling paranoid. They were looking his way again.

He took an inventory of the men. Late twenties possibly early thirties, slim, thin faces, clean-shaven, dark hair and swarthy complexions. They had the indelible look of being from the Middle East, possible North Africa or at a stretch even Greece. It didn't mean they weren't British, only their ethnicity was debatable.

An American SEAL, a close friend of his, had once said, 'Nick, if you're not Islamophobic then you don't understand what's going on in the world. Not all Germans were Nazis, not all Russians were Stalinists, not all North Vietnamese were Communists and not all Chinese were Maoists. But look what the few who were did to the world. It's the same with Muslims. A few people are wrecking a great religion and heaping untold misery on fellow Muslims as well as the West. A third world war has already started our politicians are too gutless to say so.'

His friend, Colonel Hiram Walsh, had been correct. It was why the security services of every nation in the democratic world felt as though they were fighting with two hands tied behind them. That had been the reason why TIFAT had come into existence. His boss, General Malcolm Macnair, had written a hard-hitting paper on the subject that had resulted in an organisation with the mandate to take the fight to the terrorists. It ensured there was little delay in reacting to a terrorist incident and as often as possible it meant no prisoners, like the recent London op. The terrorists had been killed and the world was a safer place. While he pontificated on the reality of what the West faced his next move was decided for him.

He saw one of the men reach into a bumbag at his waist and take out what looked like an automatic. Most people would freeze at that point while the brain interpreted what the eye was seeing. This reaction was normal denial at the events unfolding. It was a question of it being impossible - unless you were trained to expect the unexpected and to react instinctively.

Hunter didn't know if he was suddenly the target or if the men were going to open fire on the customers. What he did know was that he wasn't able to get to them before they started shooting with himself as the first casualty. He needed to escape and return, preferably armed even if it was only with an empty bottle, though he would prefer something more deadly like a chef's knife.

Hunter didn't hesitate. The men were about five metres away, the floor between him and them was devoid of tables but with customers passing back and forth. Hunter launched himself out of his chair and through the "staff only" swing door leading to the short corridor and the outside world.

He knew that he would be in a large courtyard with a high wall and a double wooden gate. He also knew that there were four industrial size waste bins on the right as he exited the building. To the left was the backdoor to the kitchen which was wide open. It also had two young people standing outside having a cigarette. They were dressed in white smocks and white porkpie hats. The boy and girl were kitchen staff who looked at Hunter in complete surprise.

'Go in! Now!' Hunter yelled. As he half expected neither moved. Hunter grabbed both by their jackets and virtually threw them through the door and into the kitchen. As the two youngsters began to protest Hunter said, 'Call the police. Two men with guns are in the courtyard.'

There were six or eight in the kitchen and they were in a frozen tableau staring at Hunter. Most were young except two of the women, who were older than the others.

'Phone the police!' Hunter spoke harshly. 'Now!'

'Oi, you can't come in here,' said one of the older women.

There was a rack of kitchen knives on a stainless steel counter to his left and he grabbed one. It had an eight inch blade and a stout handle.

'Just call the police!'

Stepping around a large central work station he reached the door back into the corridor. So far he had taken less than three seconds from shoving the kids into the kitchen to reaching the door. There was no time for subtlety. Men with guns amongst innocent civilians spelt trouble. From the way they were acting he had appeared to be the target but that made no sense. They couldn't have known he was going to be there and he was sure he hadn't been followed. Making sure he had no one on his tail was second nature to him as it was for the rest of the TIFAT team. He may have become the target but he was positive it hadn't started that way. If he didn't stop them he figured a lot of innocent bystanders were going to die or be injured. That was something Hunter knew the terrorists were particularly good at. They enjoyed killing innocent men, women and children in pursuit of their aim to create a worldwide caliphate.

He entered the corridor. Two paces away was the back of one of the gunmen. He couldn't see the other. The man was hesitating in the doorway. Hunter didn't. He stepped up to the man who was holding an automatic in his right hand, dangling down by his side. A glance showed Hunter that the man had his finger on the trigger. He figured the safety was off and so a reflex action by the gunman could fire a round and although the weapon was pointing at the ground the bullet could ricochet off the concrete and hit Hunter.

The man must have sensed his presence because he began to turn around. For Hunter things slowed down. Continuous training mixed with superbly honed reflexes stood him in good stead. Hunter wrapped his right hand around the gunman's fist gripping the gun and bent it inwards towards the man's thigh. The gun went off with a heavy cough its silencer doing the job for which it was designed. The bullet hit the man in the middle of his thigh, shattering his femur. Before the man could scream Hunter hit him hard on the side of his forehead with the base of the knife handle. The man dropped to the ground, unconscious. Hunter just hoped the man wouldn't bleed to death as he wanted to question him before he died. Hunter twisted the pistol out of the man's hand, deliberately bending the man's index finger backwards, breaking it at the joint.

Looking at the amount of blood already pooling next to the body meant the man would bleed out sooner rather than later.

The second man was five paces away, standing still, hesitating, nervous, looking around him with jerky movements. The gentle cough of the gun and the sound of the body dropping had caused him to jerk his head around. Hunter figured the gunman hadn't expected him to be standing where he was so the man's response was slower than Hunter's. However, the gunman was bringing his automatic to bear even as Hunter fired a snap shot and hit the man in the right shoulder, sending him staggering backwards. Unfortunately it was the wrong shoulder. The man was left- handed and had the presence of mind to continue to bring his pistol up. Like many of his kind not only was he utterly ruthless but he was also incredibly tough. His religious belief helped to reinforce that toughness.

If he hadn't moved Hunter would have been in serious trouble. However, he was throwing himself to the right, even as the other man fired a shot. The bullet passed harmlessly over Hunter's head only to hit a window behind him. There was a scream. It sounded as though someone in the bar had been shot.

Unfocused anger made you careless. Hunter knew that. Focussed anger and hatred was a great help in dealing with the enemy. It meant there was no hesitation, no wondering if he was doing the right thing. There was only action and reaction until the few seconds needed to complete the move were over.

As he fell to the ground he pulled the trigger twice. The first shot hit the target in the right knee, blowing it apart while the second shot hit the man in the left elbow, his weapon thrown from his hand.

The man was knocked to the ground and was silent for a few seconds before he began to moan. Hunter stood up and approached the man who was now gasping, his eyes tightly shut, unable to move.

'Saa'idnee! Saa'idnee!' The man spoke in Arabic.

'You can plead for help all you like but you won't get it,' Hunter said, in the same language.

'You speak Arabic?' The man gasped.

'Some.' In reality he was fluent after nine months of intensive learning and although he couldn't read or write the language his accent was good enough for him to be mistaken for an Arab.

The man switched to English. 'Help me! Please, please help me.' The man moaned, tears streamed from his eyes and down either side of his face.

Hunter knelt beside the man and pointed the automatic at his temple. 'Why should I?'

'It…It is your duty. I am injured.' The man gasped in pain and then said, 'Oh, God.' He moaned again.

'Mine or yours?'

'What do you mean?'

'My God is a loving God while yours is a coward who says you should kill innocent men, women and children.'

'I am fighting for Islam. For the one true God. The one true prophet, Mohammed, peace be upon…' he gasped. 'Help me.' The man closed his eyes.

'I will but only after you answer some questions. I have morphine available which will stop the pain immediately,' he lied.

'Anything, anything.' The man moaned again. His wounds must have been agonising with a shattered knee, elbow and a bullet in the shoulder. They were bleeding a fair amount but not as badly as they would have been if an artery had been hit. First aid would more than likely save the man's life though there was little chance of that happening.

'You were looking at me. You know who I am. Was I your target?'

There was no answer. Hunter reached down and gripped the man's shattered elbow. The man screamed loudly, opening his eyes.

'Was I your target?'

'No! I recognised you!' Gasping, the man added, 'We were going... going to attack the people in the room. But...but if you had a weapon then you would have stopped us. So...so we had to take care of you first.'

All of which made sense to Hunter. Unluckily for the gunmen, he had been in the right place at the right time to stop the attack.

There was another gasp and more tears oozed out of the terrorist's eyes. 'Please, the morphine.'

Hunter heard a sound behind him and looked over his shoulder. A couple of the braver customers were looking out of the door while a face appeared in the doorway to the kitchen.

'Don't come out! It may be too dangerous.'

A young female voice called, 'We've sent for the police.'

'Good.' He didn't really mean it in spite of yelling at them to do so. Once the police arrived the interrogation by necessity would be over. He heard sirens in the distance approaching fast. It was over but he faced a dilemma. If he let the terrorist live he knew there would be all sorts of problems. The man would claim innocence, that he had been tortured. That Hunter had planted the gun on him. It would mean appearing in court and being cross-examined. It would mean publicity and an intrusion into TIFAT's activities. A dead terrorist ensured none of that happened. It would all be short-lived instead of trouble being dragged out for weeks. Hunter knew all this. With his back to the building he reached out and placed his left hand around the man's neck and was about to squeeze when the man gasped and died.

It was at that moment a stentorian voice called out. 'You, drop your weapon and lay on the ground, legs and arms spread.' An Armed Response Unit had arrived.

Hunter was aware of how nervous those police units were. They may have practiced the drill regularly but probably had never carried out a real operation. In fact, if they were lucky, they never would in their entire careers. Hence the only thing to do was to obey.

He had his back to the voice and he put his arms out straight. The gun dangled from the forefinger of his right hand and he placed it on the ground before lying out flat precisely as he had been ordered.

He heard footsteps approaching and then was prodded hard in the back by a boot.

'Put your arms behind your back,' a voice snarled.

'No. Reach inside my jacket...' he got no further. This time the prod was much harder. Hunter gritted his teeth. 'I said...'

'And I said put your hands behind your back!'

Hunter did as he was told and turned his head to look at the man giving the orders. He was a Sergeant, fully kitted and spurred in protective uniform and carrying an H&K MP5SF – the 9mm single-fire version.

'Listen to me carefully, Sergeant, if you put those cuffs on me I will have your stripes, maybe even your job.'

There was a second man with him, a constable. Two others approached. From the insignia on his shoulders one was an Inspector.

'I told you to handcuff this man,' said the Inspector. He was a little man with a loud voice.

Hunter rolled over. Whatever they did, they wouldn't shoot him. He was now unarmed.

'Stay still,' barked the Inspector.

2

'I told your Sergeant to look inside my pocket for my ID. When you have read it I will stand up and you will treat me with courtesy as is due my rank. Do I make myself clear?' Hunter's tone was as cold as an Arctic frost.

The four men exchanged looks. Uncertainty was written across their faces.

'My name is Hunter, Operations Director at TIFAT.'

'What's that supposed...' the Inspector began but stopped when the Sergeant put a hand on his arm.

'Sir,' he addressed Hunter, 'I apologise.' He reached out a hand to help Hunter to his feet. Hunter grasped it and stood up.

The Inspector looked as though he was about to have apoplexy. 'How dare you Sergeant! What do you think you're doing?' The Welsh lilt came across strongly, agitation strengthening his accent.

Instead of answering, the Sergeant spoke to Hunter. 'Please excuse the Inspector, sir, he has only just been attached to the unit.' He then looked at his senior officer. 'Sir, this man is Commander Nick Hunter, of The International Force Against Terrorism.'

If Hunter was surprised that the Sergeant knew his name he didn't show it. Instead, he looked at the Inspector.

'What are you talking about man? What is this force you're talking about?'

Hunter smiled, reached inside his jacket pocket and extracted a leather folder containing his TIFAT identity card and gun permit.

He handed it to the Inspector. The man took it, looked at the photograph, rank and title and then thrust it back.

'This means nothing,' he sad. 'It could be off eBay for all I know. Until I ascertain what is going on you will be kept under arrest.'

While he was speaking Hunter had removed his mobile. 'I'll just phone your assistant chief constable and he can settle matters.'

'Yes, do that,' said the Inspector, 'as if you're likely to know the ACC.' There was no mistaking the sarcasm in the Inspector's voice then he snapped his fingers. 'Oh, you lot. You're the people who write those reports on international terrorism. I've skimmed a few. They're just pure sensationalism at best. Anyone would think you were writing a precis for a spy thriller.'

As a cover for their activities TIFAT produced in-depth reports dealing with international terrorism as well as analysing the activities of certain governments. Top of the rogue governments' list was North Korea, whose leader seemed to be enjoying himself jerking the chain of the US President. The Western intelligence world knew the North Koreans were pursuing the manufacture of nuclear weapons. The problem was the US President didn't want to acknowledge the fact.

TIFAT had a network of people able to write such reports that were deemed highly classified and for the eyes of certain individuals only. The less scary were passed down the line to more junior ranks if the report was applicable to their operational requirements. The Inspector would have seen one or two, maybe more, depending on his previous job.

TIFAT was in reality a proactive organisation taking the fight to the enemy. The report writing was a smokescreen that enabled TIFAT to deny being involved in certain operations though the story was wearing a bit thin.

Hunter did know the Assistant Chief Constable having met him at an anti-terrorist symposium, hosted at TIFAT HQ in Scotland. The two men had hit it off in spite of their age difference of nearly 20 years. In Hunter's mobile was the telephone number of every police HQ in the UK. He scrolled down to the Cardiff number and speed dialled.

'Assistant Chief Constable Davies, please. Tell him Commander Nick Hunter is on the phone. Yes, that's right, TIFAT.' The delay was only seconds. 'Dan?'

'Hello, Nick. This is a pleasant surprise. At least I hope it is.'

The Inspector was making frantic signals and said, 'All right. All right. You can stop the call.'

'Dan, have you heard about the incident in the pub?'

'No what...Hang on a moment,' he trailed off. 'Thanks.' He was obviously speaking to someone else. 'Possible gunshots. An ARU deployed. You there?'

'Yes, right in the middle of it. I'm with an Inspector who seems to doubt my credentials.' Hunter was in no mood to be magnanimous.

'Put him on.'

Whatever the ACC said, the man sheepishly handed the mobile back to Hunter with, 'The ACC would like a word.'

'What's going on, Nick?'

Hunter explained briefly while the others listened in. By now a few more customers from the pub were making their way into the courtyard. One was using his mobile and was obviously taking photographs or video.

Hunter broke off from what he was saying and addressed the Inspector. 'Get rid of those people and stop that man from taking photos for Christ's sake and get this area sealed off.'

'Nick, I heard that. I'll be there in ten minutes.' The ACC broke the connection.

Whatever Davies had said to the man it had been highly effective. In many respects the Inspector had been following protocol. The problem was the protocol came from an inflexible operations manual that was less than adequate when dealing with modern problems such as terrorism, now acknowledged as the greatest scourge of the twenty-first century. Any slip-ups in procedure often meant the guilty going free on a legal technicality, laughing their heads off at the police though sometimes at MI5 as well. Certain solicitors and barristers were particularly adept at the practice. They weren't concerned whether or not their clients were innocent or guilty or a future threat to the public, only that the minutest interpretation of the law was followed.

'Thanks,' Hunter said to the Sergeant.

'That's okay, sir. You must forgive the Inspector. He's new, young and,' he looked around but the others had followed the Inspector to the corpse next to the backdoor, 'out of his depth. A fast tracked officer out of university.' The man shrugged. 'You know how it is.'

Hunter nodded. The armed services worked the same way. Except junior officers had it instilled into them that NCOs were to be listened to and obeyed, although the orders were usually given in the form of suggestions.

Hunter knelt next to the dead man, reached inside a pocket and removed a wallet and a passport. The passport was Saudi Arabian. In another pocket he found a mobile phone. He heard heavy footsteps and the Inspector approached.

'Care to go through it all again?' The Inspector asked.

By way of an answer Hunter asked, 'What's your name?'

'Inspector Jones. Phil Jones.'

Hunter held out his hand, the other man hesitated and then shook it. 'Nick Hunter.'

Hunter guessed Jones was around thirty, maybe even younger, fast tracked on his way to the top provided he kept his nose clean.

'We need to check the pockets of the other man,' said Hunter.

'I thought we should wait for forensics.'

'What for? They're dead and I killed them.' Keeping his head bent down and looking at the ground Hunter approached the second body. He felt inside his pockets, extracting a passport, wallet and phone.

'I'd better take those,' said Jones.

Hunter shook his head, still looking downwards. 'Speak to the ACC when he gets here. You'll find he'll be more than happy if I take them. We'll process them more quickly and far more effectively than you can.'

'I'm not sure…'

Turning his back to the building Hunter walked away, the Inspector following. There was a slight commotion at the door and the Assistant Chief Constable arrived. Jones turned, drew himself up and threw a salute at the senior officer. Hunter kept turned away until Davies came up to him and the two men shook hands warmly.

The ACC was a big man. At 6ft 6ins, heavy set with a red, florid face he radiated bonhomie. The reality was something different. Behind his hail-fellow-well-met exterior was a sharp mind combined with a wide ruthless streak down his back. He played by the rules but was forever nagging politicians, in particular the Home Secretary, to bring in tougher, more stringent laws that would enable the police to do a better job. To date he hadn't got very far but that didn't stop him trying.

'Dan, I was just telling Inspector Jones that I would take the passports, wallets and phones. We can process them far more effectively at Rosyth.'

'Yes, of course. Once you have, send us what you find and we'll follow up on next of kin and so on, in case they have family here.'

'I doubt it,' said Hunter. 'They're travelling on Saudi passports.'

'Why am I not surprised?' The ACC asked rhetorically.

A forensics contingent arrived, dressed in their white coveralls.

'You're not needed,' said Dan Davies.

'But, sir...'

'Just have the bodies taken away, through the gate,' he pointed at the rear wall. 'It's up to you but I wouldn't waste my time on any form of autopsy. We know what happened and how they died.' He smiled at Hunter. 'Good job, by the way.'

'Thanks, Dan.'

By now the courtyard was empty of rubberneckers though Hunter was sure those who had been there were even now sending video and photographs out via the internet and various social media. It was why he had kept his head down and his back to the building as much as possible. He didn't want to be recognised if he could help it. There were enough people in the world who knew who he was. Quite a few were his enemies who wanted him dead along with the others at TIFAT.

The dead man had said they had wanted to kill him to stop him interfering in their attack but reality could have been something else. It was conceivable that he may have been the target but somehow he didn't think so. It really was just one of those strange coincidences.

The ACC broke in on his thoughts. 'What are your plans? Are you staying here? Actually, why are you here?'

'Old family business from about a century ago. This is where we came from and I decided to come and take a look at the area.'

'First time?'

'Yes. I thought I might have an affinity for the area but it's just another village and another valley.'

'Where?'

'Llanbeddas, just north of Pontypridd.'

'Not the most attractive area we have to offer.'

'No, but none of the old mining villages are.'

'Point taken. Care for a spot of dinner?'

'Sorry, Dan, the General is expecting me back in time for morning prayers tomorrow.'

'Morning prayers? You mean you say a prayer to our Maker?'

Hunter couldn't help grinning at the notion. 'No. It's what we call a heads of department meeting. Although nowadays we involve the teams as well. It used to last about forty minutes or so and now we're lucky to be done in an hour and a half.' His eyes were bleak when he looked at the ACC. 'It's getting worse, Dan, a hell of a lot worse.'

'Tell me about it. When will it end and we can go back to good old fashioned policing?'

'It won't. Not in my lifetime, at least.'

'Nor mine, that's for damned sure. Hell Nick, you know what it's like. The number of reports we're getting from across Europe is about terrorist attacks increasing while our political masters are like rabbits caught in the headlights of a speeding truck.'

'There isn't much we can do except keep pushing back.'

'Easier said than done. For the first time in my life I'm looking forward to retirement.'

'Retirement? You? I thought you'd be in line for the top job.' There was no hiding the surprise in Hunter's voice.

'I am. I've been told on the grapevine that it's mine for the asking following procedures.'

'You mean interviews, a short list and then a job offer?'

'Precisely. But I'm not sure I want it. I'm at the top operationally. The next step-up means budgets, manpower and politics. Oh, and PR as well. Something I'm not very good at. Talking of which, the press are already gathering like vultures. We've detained a few people who took video and photos using their mobiles but some will have got out. I noticed you keeping your head down as much as possible.'

'Yeah. You can have the glory.'

'Thanks.'

'Where's your CC? Shouldn't he be here?'

Davies shook his head. 'Gardening leave, retirement in a couple of months. After that fiasco a few weeks ago.'

There was no need to expand that remark. Three men had attacked the Welsh Assembly and taken a number of politicians hostage. They made ludicrous demands along the lines of all Western countries should pull their troops out of Iraq. The Chief Constable had called it wrong. He thought that he could end the situation quickly and with the minimum of bloodshed. His negotiating skills were poor to say the least. It resulted in one Assembly Member being shot dead with a bullet in his skull. Then the CC made his second disastrous decision.

He panicked and sent in an ARU in spite of Dan Davies arguing against it. An ARU is not the answer against terrorists in a hostage situation unless they're properly trained. The SAS or TIFAT were what was needed. The SAS was stretched to breaking hence Hunter and a team had been dispatched from Rosyth to Cardiff and had arrived at the airport 16 hours after the whole thing kicked off. They were getting kitted and spurred when they were told to stand down.

The three men had managed to escape the building and were on the run with a fleet of police cars chasing them. They were north of Brecon with further units closing in when what happened next came under the heading of textbook cock-up. The three men took over a farmhouse with an elderly couple as hostages. Again, the CC didn't wait but sent in an ARU. Two of the terrorists were killed, one was taken prisoner, the old man was shot and killed while his wife of 56 years died from a heart attack. The preliminary enquiry was damning of the CC's decisions and it was acknowledged that he had been out of his depth. The newspapers had also identified the man as being a political appointee being a well-known supporter of Welsh independence, though he had claimed that had been in his youth. The man had been appointed by the Police and Crime Commissioner, a crony of the leader of the Welsh political party, Plaid Cymru. As was often the way in such cases nepotism wasn't far beneath the surface. The three men had been friends at university. Luckily for the UK such cronyism was rare though not unknown.

'I'm acting CC which has helped to convince me I don't want the job.'

'I wouldn't want the General's job for all the tea in China so I get where you're coming from,' said Hunter, referring to his boss, General Malcolm Macnair.

'Malcolm isn't thinking of retirement, is he?' There was genuine shock in the ACC's voice.

Hunter chuckled. 'No. He'll have to be prised out of there or shipped out in a wooden box.'

'Thank God for that.'

'By the way, I heard a scream from inside the pub. Anyone hurt?'

'No. A bullet went through a window narrowly missing some woman who went into a spasm of hysterics.'

'I can't say I blame her,' said Hunter.

'Neither do I. There are a lot of lucky people in there today. Nick, I'm not an idiot.'

'Good lord, Dan, I don't think you are for a second.'

23

'Figure of speech. You were the target. Any idea why?'

Hunter shook his head. 'That's what I thought as well. However, the man over there,' he jerked his head at the body, 'said he had recognised me and wanted to take me out before attacking people in the bar.'

Frowning, the ACC said, 'I guess that makes sense. Do you believe him?'

Hunter shrugged. 'Unless shown otherwise I guess I've no choice. The problem is I don't like being recognised by a Saudi terrorist.'

Davies nodded in a sympathetic attitude. 'It can't be helped. You've been very effective in any number of high profile operations and so there are those in some quarters who must inevitably know who you are.'

'I guess so. But I don't like it one iota. If I lose my anonymity my effectiveness could be seriously compromised.'

'Nick, there's no answer to that. For them you were in the wrong place at the wrong time. In turn, that means for us you were in the right place at the right time. One man recognised you. It doesn't, on the face of it, matter that much.'

'I guess you're right.'

An ambulance backed up through the wooden gates and the two bodies were placed on a couple of stretchers and wheeled into the vehicle. The doors were slammed and the ambulance drove away. It went quietly. Sirens and lights were unnecessary for the dead. Two constables on either side of the gates closed them in the faces of the paparazzi whose cameras were flashing nonstop. Hunter kept his back to them.

'Dan, tell the reporters your officers dealt with the problem. The usual.'

'I'll keep your name out of it but you know how it is. It's a question of careless talk costs lives. If any one of my men here tells a friend or a colleague about what happened they could pass your involvement on to the press.'

'That can't be helped,' Hunter said.

'It's happened before.'

'But I'm quickly and easily forgotten,' grinned Hunter.

'You wish. How many medals do you have, Nick?'

Hunter looked uncomfortable.

'I'll tell you. A George Medal and bar and a number of mentions.'

A mention in dispatches was one below an actual piece of silver, none of which Hunter had relished receiving. General Macnair had pushed operational reports further up Naval Command in case Hunter decided to return to General Service from TIFAT. Recognition of his exploits wouldn't go amiss. However, he had made it clear he wouldn't be returning to the RN, not now nor any time in the future. By way of confirmation, he had resigned his commission.

'I've told the General I want a lower profile. Any medals are to be given to the others. They deserve them.'

'And they've had them. Less of the modesty, Nick. At my level throughout the police, the special ops world and the security services your name is known. The only way to keep a lower profile is to quit.'

Hunter gave a wry smile.

'Exactly. There isn't a dog's chance of that happening. Just be careful.'

3

Ruth Golightly recognised the four men as they approached her. They all looked the same - of medium height and weight, bearded and with Middle Eastern complexions. The names they used were aliases, a necessity in their line of work, as members of Mossad, the Israeli secret service, renowned for its ruthlessness.

On this occasion their first names were Abdul-Mutaal (known as AM by colleagues and friends), Anas, Omran and Majdy. All were in their late twenties and, with their pious attitude and subservient manner, easily passed as young, innocent Muslim men.

Mossad's main purpose was to protect Israel from her enemies of which there were many. Its motto, "By way of deception thou shalt do war" gives a clear indication of its modus operandi.

The four men had established themselves in Iran but were using their fake identities for this new mission. Ruth Golightly had summoned them to a meeting in Moscow. Thanks to the cordial relations that existed between Iran and Russia flying back and forth was easy with the right paperwork.

The meeting was to take place in a safe house on the outskirts of the city. The location was a ground floor apartment with a basement and had been owned by the Israelis for more than two decades. During that time many alterations had been undertaken. The doors front and back were made of reinforced steel with a wooden veneer. The windows were bullet proof with the added facility of steel shutters if needed. These precautions were typical of the planning the Israelis put into any operation, particularly a long term one. They would not stop an attack by Russian security forces for long. However, they would give anyone in the house time to get to the basement and escape through an underground passage that led to the nearest Metro station. At the end of the 250 metres long tunnel was a door leading to the corner of platform 1 and hidden behind a pillar. A key to the door hung alongside it. The lock was oiled every few months. The whole setup showed how thorough the Israelis were when it came to protecting the lives of its frontline operatives.

Since the fall of the Soviet Union, Iran and Russia had become close strategic allies forming an axis in the Caucasus with Armenia. Because of economic sanctions imposed on Iran by the West, Russia was now its most important trading partner. This close relationship was enhanced thanks to the massive oil reserves in Iran, sold to Russia on very favourable terms. Iran was the only country in Western Asia to have joined the Russian equivalent of NATO, known as the Collective Security Treaty Organisation – CSTO and arms for their military were provided mainly by the Russians.

The meeting that was about to take place was of important strategic value to Israel. That information was being passed to the four men in person demonstrated Mossad's mistrust of electronic transmissions. Even with encrypted information, security was not guaranteed. The Israelis and Mossad in particular, trusted nobody unless trust had been earned and Israelis always acted through a thick veil of paranoia. It was safer that way.

There was little danger of anything going wrong with meeting in Moscow at that time. There was a huge trade exhibition involving Russia, Iran and China with people arriving and leaving the country by the planeload. All four men had good reason to be in Moscow thanks to their jobs in real companies in Tehran. They looked what they were – junior executives in successful companies. Hence the four of them were wearing dark suits with white open necked shirts, all very respectable.

To date they had spent over four years in enemy territory – too long, in fact. They had no illusions as to what would happen if their cover was blown. Their deaths would be particularly unpleasant. The dilemma for the Israeli hierarchy and those charged with protecting the country was that the four men were doing such a good job so any suggestion that they be moved to a fresh assignment was met with reluctance. To date their achievements included identification of five Iranian missile sites that Israeli planes had destroyed and the prevention of three planned attacks on Israel.

The room they would be using was situated at the back of the house. It was a large kitchen/diner with a scarred wooden table with seating for eight. The sink was old stainless steel, the plumbing was 1950s Soviet and the electric wiring was probably unsafe. The electric cooker had three hot plates of which only two worked and an oven that worked in fits and starts. Blown fuses were common. The walls were an indifferent cream colour and had long lost their shine. The only redeeming feature was that the room was clean and tidy.

The couple who lived there were Russian Jews who had supported Israel all their lives. Now in their early seventies they had made a request to Mossad. They wanted to live out their days in the country they had striven so hard to protect. Their request along with a guaranteed pension and apartment had been granted. They would be leaving Russia in one week. For both their departure couldn't come soon enough.

The information about the men and the meeting swirled through Ruth Golightly's mind as she sat at the table with a mug of hot tea at her elbow.

She was an attractive woman, tall and slim, with black straight hair to her shoulders, parted in the middle. Her eyes were brown, her nose straight and her mouth wide when she smiled. She was dressed in a dark blue business suit with a cream blouse. She looked every inch the businesswoman she pretended to be though her actual job was far different.

She wasn't smiling at that moment as she was preoccupied with personal thoughts. Three months ago she had divorced her husband after only 11 months of marriage. He was a professor of history at Tel Aviv University, tall, distinguished but a womaniser. His preferred prey were undergraduates dazzled by his position, coupled with their belief that having sex with him would help them to a higher degree. It did. When Ruth Golightly had left her husband the last thing she did was hit him on the nose with the palm of her hand. It was a straight blow that broke the cartilage and disfigured his nose making him look like a failed boxer. She had warned him that if he caused any trouble over their divorce she would put him in hospital for six months. He believed her. She had immediately resorted to her maiden name and expunged the memory of her disastrous marriage from her mind. It usually worked but not always.

She had rejected the only man she had ever really loved and to this day she had doubts about the decision she had taken. She picked up her mug of tea, took a sip, grimaced and replaced it on the table. It had gone cold.

Unconsciously she massaged her left knee. It had been crushed when a rock had fallen on it during an operation in Columbia. The Columbian operation had been to destroy a massive shipment of cocaine. It had been successful and she had been the only one injured. It had been touch and go as to whether or not she lost her leg but thanks to the rapid response of the TIFAT team she was working with and the skill of the American doctors on a US aircraft carrier, her leg had been saved.

Ruth stood up and walked across to the sink where she ditched the tea and swilled the mug under the tap. The water was barely lukewarm, a further testament to life under communism. The tea was like acid in her stomach. She sat back down, her hands on the table, her fingers beating an irregular tattoo, the only sign of her stress.

Her job at Mossad was as a unit leader and the four men she was about to meet were part of her team of officers. She was fanatical in her efforts to keep her people safe and moved heaven and earth when necessary to protect them from harm. On occasion she failed with dire consequences. In their line of work it wasn't a case of losing your job but your life. So far she had lost two agents in separate operations. As a result she took even greater care of her people. Her actions had led to a number of arguments with her bosses but to date she had prevailed. Among her peers she was known affectionately as "mother hen", a sobriquet she accepted with good grace.

This time it was different. It had been made clear to her in no uncertain terms that the information needed was vital. The risks to the team were of secondary importance when compared to the benefit of knowing if the report Mossad had received was true. She hadn't liked it, protested and been threatened with immediate dismissal if she couldn't do her job. Reluctantly she had given in, acknowledging the importance of the operation.

The four men began to assemble. Each of them had spent time looking for any potential threat to their safety but nothing seemed amiss.

When Anas, the third man, arrived Ruth greeted him with an apology. 'Sorry, Anas, the coffee is undrinkable and the tea isn't much better.' She knew his penchant for a decent cup of tea.

Smiling, Anas reached into a bag and removed a packet of Typhoo tea bags. Tossing it in the air, he said, 'Not to worry, I brought my own. Also,' he put his hand back into the bag, 'I've brought milk and sugar.' He smiled in triumph. 'The English solution to all problems from insomnia to…to bereavement.'

AM and Majdy smiled and clapped their hands together silently, in tribute to his forethought.

'Good one,' said Ruth. 'Well done. I'll boil the kettle while we wait for Omran.'

Although they were off the grid they still used their aliases. Interchanging from their birth names to their pseudonyms could become confusing even for the most experienced agent so once in character it was deemed safer to stay that way.

Finally, Omran walked through the door.

'Everything okay?' Ruth greeted him.

'Yes,' he smiled in return. 'I couldn't see anyone taking an interest in this place but,' he shrugged, 'you never know. The Russians are very good at surveillance.'

Ruth nodded. Mossad had lost a number of agents in the new Russia for one reason or another. The problem was becoming worse. The problem was Russia's support of Iran. The clerical despots in Iran had declared that Israel should not be allowed to exist and that all good Muslims should help to wipe the nation off the planet. Israel, as always, was prepared to fight fire with fire. For every bomb or missile directed at Israel by Iran the Israelis would deliver two.

The Jews of Israel did not believe in turning the other cheek. They had done so in the 1930s and had paid an appalling price. It would never happen again. At the forefront of their war to survive was Mossad.

They exchanged gossip while waiting for the kettle to boil. Finally it was ready and Ruth busied herself making the tea. For the men it was milk and two sugars, for Ruth it was no milk and no sugar.

'Okay, now we have our teas we can begin,' said Ruth. 'The reason I called this meeting was to personally brief you on some information that has come our way. If it is true then we need to take urgent action. There are two aspects to this operation, the first is to confirm the intelligence and the second is to destroy the target if necessary.'

'What's the target?' Majdy asked raising his hand as though he was at a college tutorial.

'I'll come to that. We have it on good authority that the Iranians have developed an enhanced form of PE.' She paused then added, 'The reports we've received suggest it is at least twice as powerful as anything currently available.'

Ruth continued. 'The targets are not specific. However, it means less explosives to achieve the same result. It will be more easily smuggled onto a plane or into a crowded space such as happened in Manchester.' Ruth was referring to the suicide bomber who had killed and injured dozens of mainly young people who had attended a pop concert in Manchester, England. Lives had been ruined as well as lost. If the intelligence about the new explosive was true then such incidents could escalate significantly. 'It goes without saying that any attacks will be aimed at us.'

Her hatred of the people who committed the atrocities kept Ruth focused and determined to stop them at all costs.

'Where did the information come from?' Omran asked.

Ruth glanced at all four men before replying. 'Sorry but that's classified.'

They nodded in unison. Ruth was aware that they thought there was a senior official in Iran who fed information to Mossad. What they didn't know and would be less sanguine about was the fact that the information was being paid for. This made the informer less reliable than if he had been loyal to Israel. It was a business transaction pure and simple. Ruth also knew that her source was on the point of abandoning Iran for the West. She had tried persuading him to stay longer using the best method she knew – bribery. But it was to no avail. The man had decided that he had used up his luck and it was time to get out while he could. She didn't blame him. If he was caught he would be put to death in a very unpleasant way.

Ruth had never been able to make up her mind whether or not to despise the man as a traitor to his country or honour him. There was little doubt that he had helped to keep Israel safe.

Sometimes she was able to double-check the information, at other times she had to accept it at face value. To date, and to the best of her knowledge, she had not been let down. However, there was always a first time. When she was first approached by the Iranian she'd had her doubts. Trust wasn't something that came easily to anyone in her position. It had to be earned. She had tested him a number of times, seeking information she had already verified. She was fully aware that good intelligence was beyond price but if bad or fabricated it could spell disaster. She hadn't rushed the process. It had taken six months but finally she reported to her bosses that the man appeared to be trustworthy. There had been only one blot on his record. She had discovered that while he sold information to the Israelis he was also selling information to the Saudis.

She had consulted her boss, the Director of Mossad, about the conflict of interest and they agreed to let the op run as it was.

She knew that the Saudis hated the Iranians and wanted nothing more than to wipe the country off the face of the earth. If they tried they knew the reverse would happen so the Saudis blustered and threatened but didn't actually do anything. She knew this to be a typical reaction by the Arabs and part of their national character, all talk and no action.

The Arab hatred stemmed from the fact that Iranians were Shia Muslims and the Saudis Sunni. The modern day situation could be traced back decades to the 1930s or 40s though the hatred had its roots much earlier. As always in such cases, where religion was involved, none of it made any sense. Most university scholars had been trying to unravel the mess and find some sort of answer without success.

Ruth didn't know the name of the Saudi who was the recipient of the info from her spy but she would find out. That name would be the price her informant would have to pay if he wanted Mossad to help him escape the clutches of the Iranian secret police. He would need a new ID and passport, something she had already agreed to. He would become an American, the preferred nationality of all traitors from the Middle and Far East. When she knew the name of the recipient she would try to coerce him into supplying her with information, for a price.

'What do you want us to do?' AM asked.

Opening her laptop she placed it on the table facing the four men and pointed at a photograph. 'This is Naseri Street, The Vanak Apartment Hotel. It is part hotel for short stay visitors and long term lets on the second, third and fourth floors. The apartments are ninety percent occupied, the hotel rooms virtually empty, which is an indication of the collapse of Iran's tourist industry. In its heyday the hotel was busy with a first class restaurant and bars selling more different flavoured tea than just about anywhere in the Middle East.

Of course, there was no alcohol sold on the premises. As you all know, Sharia law reigns supreme.'

'They're all hypocrites,' said Anas.

They all knew what he meant. Whether Saudi or Iranian, whenever they arrived in a non-Islamic country they immediately hit the booze. The women wore burkas at home and dressed like glamorous models when abroad. Many, especially the Iranian women, were very attractive and deserved more than a passing glance.

'You're right. In the basement are a series of large rooms. They house a kitchen that is no longer used, storerooms and a laundry room. We have it on good authority that the kitchen is being used to create IEDs with a new means of delivery.'

'Do we know what that is?' Omran asked.

Shaking her head Ruth replied, 'No. At least we don't think so. This is where the information gets a bit wonky.'

'Wonky? How?' Majdy asked.

'According to our informant the material is being placed in balls. What type of balls we're not sure.'

'You mean like footballs or something as small as tennis balls?' Anas asked.

'The intel we have is tennis balls or cricket balls.

'Why?' AM asked.

'Why what?' Ruth replied.

'Why stuff the explosive into a ball?'

'To smuggle onto a plane or some other target where there's security.'

'How is that meant to work?' Majdy asked.

'We've wondered the same,' replied Ruth. She flicked her hair behind her left ear and frowned. 'The only thing that makes sense is that they somehow openly take the balls through security. ' She shrugged. 'But even that's nonsense. The x-ray machines would pick them out as being packed with explosives. The new computed axial tomography is virtually infallible. Especially when combined with IMS.' She was talking about the ion mobility spectrometer, a system none understood but were aware that it worked in the detection of explosives.

'The problem is,' said Anas, 'the kit is expensive to buy.'

Ruth shook her head. 'Not when compared to the price of a plane being blown out of the sky or an attack on a crowded train or in a building.'

'So why aren't there more?' Anas spoke with scorn in his tone.

'I don't know except to say the equipment is highly sophisticated and it takes time to train the operators to a level of proficiency that is of any value.'

'So train them,' said Anas.

'Anas drop it. Take it from me it's easier said than done.'

Anas nodded. Mossad was renowned for being the most effective security organisation in the world, dollar for dollar more effective even than the American CIA. However, with a budget of $2.8 billion and a staff of 7,000 it was also the second biggest in the world.

Ruth belonged to a unit tasked with information gathering. Spying in other words. From time to time an operation meant killing the enemy but she had no problem with that. She had carried out wet work on numerous occasions in the past, as the situation demanded.

Mossad had an advantage over other security services. It was exempt from the constitutional laws of the state of Israel. In other words it was free to operate anyway it chose as long as it fulfilled its mandate, which was to keep Israel safe.

Majdy said, 'Maybe the Iranians have invented some sort of covering that prevents the x-ray machines seeing inside the balls. Of course, if they have then it needn't be balls but some other shaped mechanism.'

'It's possible,' said Ruth, 'but that's why I called you here. We have a number of questions and very few answers.'

'How urgent is this op?' Omran asked. 'What about prep time including surveillance.' He snapped his fingers, 'And let's not forget the escape plan should it all go tits up.'

'Our informant told us that they are almost ready to deploy the balls. If what he tells us is true then there could be a spate of attacks both in Israel and in other parts of the world.'

'Other parts of the world are not our concern,' said Omran.

Ruth sighed. 'I've told you before Omran, it is our concern. If something goes wrong and our allies learn that we knew something was going to happen and we didn't tell them we'd be even more isolated than we are now. Anti-Semitism is on the rise across Europe and especially in Britain thanks to the Labour Party being infiltrated by left-wing fanatics. In a nutshell we need all the friends we can get. The situation with the Palestinians is worsening by the day. Russia, Iran and Syria are stirring the pot and adding chemical weapons into the mix. High-powered explosives will add to the problem in no uncertain terms. The bottom line is we need to investigate and we need to do so sooner rather than later.'

'Why make high explosive balls the size of tennis balls?' Omran asked, looking pensive. 'Why not something bigger like a football?'

Ruth replied, 'Maybe deploying them is easier. They could be thrown or even fired from a slingshot. We don't know. But it's all we've come up with to date.'

There were gloomy nods from the other four.

Majdy spoke. 'It's as good a reason as any, I suppose. If the terrorists have found a way to make a powerful explosive easily and cheaply then we could be heading for some real trouble.'

'Amen to that,' said AM. He didn't need to add that they had enough trouble as things stood but that was usual for Israel.

'Why are we meeting here in Moscow?' asked Majdy.

'We think this is too important to wait. We knew you were all coming here for the exhibition so it was convenient to meet here.'

'How many people can we expect?' Anas asked.

'The best estimate we have is between seven and ten.'

'Based on what?' Again it was Anas who asked the question.

'Same source. He's been there twice. The first time there were ten people the second time there were seven.'

'I take it you want the facility destroyed?' Omran asked. He was the explosives expert amongst them though the other three were equally competent.

'Correct, destroyed so it can never be used again.'

'What about the apartments and hotel?' Anas asked.

'We all know the propensity for the Iranians, Iraqis and other Middle Eastern countries to hide their deadliest secrets amongst the innocent. And the more innocents involved the better the regimes like it.'

'So what are you saying?' Omran asked.

'Do your best to destroy the basement but leave the building standing. If it's too difficult please remember destruction of the basement is the most important. If the Iranians want to hide an explosives factory in such a delicate position then it's down to them. Whatever the consequences it will be their fault.'

'The rest of the world won't see it that way if we are identified as the perpetrators and innocent people are killed,' said Anas.

'Very probably,' said Ruth. 'In the past when we've proved our innocence we've still been branded as guilty by much of the world's press.'

Orchestrated ruthlessly by certain organisations and countries Israel was the scapegoat for many of the world's ills. Or so it seemed to the Israelis in particular and to Jews in general.

'I understand you're leaving tomorrow,' said Ruth.

'That's right,' said Anas. 'Our flight to Tehran is at fourteen hundred.'

'Good.' Ruth nodded her satisfaction. 'You know the objective. As usual you're on your own so be careful. I leave it to you to plan your actions and how you'll carry them out. Just bear in mind that time is of the essence.'

'We understand. Are we done?' Anas enquired.

'Yes,' Ruth replied. 'Anas you go first. We'll follow at five minute intervals.

After the four men had left Ruth sat for a few minutes with her head in her hands. Innocent Iranians didn't deserve to die but the explosives had to be destroyed at all costs.

4

The four Israelis stayed clear of each other in the hotel that evening. Whilst the Russians had a well-publicised ethos for hard liquor the Iranians pretended the opposite. Typical of their culture they were unable or unwilling to recognise the hypocrisy of their attitude and cultural mores. As it was, with their departure back to Iran less than 18 hours away the Iranian delegates were drinking very heavily. The copious amounts of vodka they were drinking were mixed with some sort of sweet cordial or juice. It was the only way that most of them could drink the stuff. Anas looked around the room with a blank expression on his face and contempt in his heart.

He hated them with every fibre of his being. Just a degree or two lower was his dislike of Russians. Not the people but the hierarchy. As far as he was concerned the majority of people were like docile rabbits, doing as they were told. On the whole they lived just above the poverty line while the oligarchs, led by the political elite, grew richer by the day and enjoyed extravagant lifestyles anywhere but in Russia. Life there was too depressing and little changed from its communist past.

The Russians thought of themselves as a first world country but in reality it was barely second world and parts of it were even third world. The Russians flexed their military might in the Middle East but the cost to the man in the street was massive. Bullets, bombs and military hardware came at a heavy price. But for some reason, unfathomable to the West, Russia chose to support the Iranians and Syrians. This was in spite of the atrocities being committed by the

Assad regime. But the West also had a dilemma that was neatly summed up by a British politician. Choosing between Assad and the rebels was like choosing between a monster and a madman. The dilemma was the rebels were members of ISIS who were at war with the West.

So, thought Anas, it went round and round. The world was mad so on that despondent note, Anas took himself to his room. In spite of his thoughts sleep came easily. He had spent so long in fraught and dangerous situations they no longer bothered him. What would be would be. Inshallah in Arabic or "if God wills it" in English meant there was little he could do if anything went wrong. The only problem he had was his lack of belief in any sort of God. If there was one the eternal question that needed answering was why did God allow the world to get in such a mess? A question that defied any logical answer.

The flight back to Tehran was a scheduled five hours and thirty-six minutes. However, according to the plane's captain there was a delay due to air traffic control and they sat forlornly in the aircraft for the best part of ninety minutes. Being Air Iran there was no alcohol on offer, which just added to the misery of the passengers. The four men sat apart in different areas of the cabin and avoided any contact.

When the plane landed at Tehran they disembarked, passed quickly through immigration and customs and made their way outside. Now it was every man for himself as they hailed taxis and gave addresses. Anas lived in a one-bedroom apartment on Motahhari Avenue and having used Google Earth knew he was 6.35 kilometres from their target.

In the course of the next hour the other three arrived at his apartment. They were greeted with a selection of teas but all chose Earl Grey.

They didn't talk business. They were too experienced for that. First of all they swept the apartment for bugs but found none. Next, they closed the blinds. These had been manufactured in Israel and prevented eavesdropping from a parabolic microphone. They also switched on a radio broadcasting a speech by the Ayatollah. They were used to it and mentally tuned out the noise.

'I've been into the municipality's computer and downloaded a plan of the building,' said Majdy. He was the most computer savvy of the four and would command a very high salary if he was working for a Western company. As far as he was concerned his passion for Israel was reward enough. 'I've just e-mailed it to your iPhones. Also here are a few tourist brochures describing the place.'

'Where did you get them from?' AM asked.

'The tourist information office at the train station.'

They each took a brochure and glanced through it. In spite of the efforts of the cameraman the building looked drab and uninviting. In reality it was typical of many other buildings to be found in Iran.

'The rooms look big and inviting,' said AM, 'which they may very well be.'

That raised a few chuckles mixed with shaking heads.

'By the standards in this lousy country,' said Anas, 'it doesn't look too bad. There's a tea bar and a restaurant both of which look welcoming.'

Majdy said, 'From the plans there appears to be thirty-eight one and two bedroomed apartments while on the ground and first floor there are sixty-six bedrooms all purporting to be en-suite.'

The others knew what Majdy meant. Many hotels had en-suite facilities that didn't work properly for the simple reason there was insufficient water flowing through the pipes. It sometimes left toilets smelling and it wasn't of roses.

'It's possible,' said AM, 'that the guards and people making the explosives live there as well.'

'More than likely,' Anas said. It would avoid wasting time travelling back and forth, which means more time on the job. However, let's not jump ahead of ourselves. The explosive may not be manufactured there only packed into the balls, if they exist that is.'

'Why shouldn't they exist?' Majdy asked.

'You know as well as I do there's always room for error with Intel.'

They all nodded and exchanged gloomy looks. He was right. They'd been let down often enough in the past.

Majdy said, 'Take a look at the fourth page of the plans.' He waited while the other three downloaded their e-mail, opened the attachment and changed their screens. 'As you see there are two stairwells, one from the hotel lobby and one from the corner at the rear of the building.'

The other three nodded.

'Time is short so we can't set up a surveillance post even for a few days.'

'What about the hotel lobby?' AM asked.

Anas shrugged and answered. 'I doubt they'll be using it. If people are coming and going they wouldn't want to draw attention to the stairwell. Someone might become too nosy. I figure they'll use the one on the corner to access the basement but use the main door like anyone else to access their rooms. That is, assuming they live there.'

'I think you're right,' said AM, 'and we should take a look. When?'

'No time like the present,' Omran replied.

None of them was happy but what choice did they have? Ruth had made it clear that time wasn't on their side. The more bombs made and dispatched the more lives were put at risk and the chances were they would be Israeli lives.

'Are we tooling up?' Omran asked.

Majdy answered. 'Yes. If we're stopped by cops and arrested even on grounds of suspicion we'll be in the clutches of the SAVAMA so quickly our feet won't touch the ground. In my case I'll be dead. I won't be surrendering, that's for sure.'

The others all agreed.SAVAMA was the Ministry of Intelligence and National Security of Iran. The organisation was well known to have cellars where state sponsored torture and executions took place. 'Innocent until proven guilty' did not exist in Iran. Even if you could prove yourself innocent of any crime, once in the clutches of SAVAMA the chances of ever seeing the light of day again hovered somewhere between nil and remote.

'The same goes for all of us,' said AM.

They agreed they would be armed with silenced automatics. At least the weapons were the finest found anywhere in the world. They were of American design, stolen by the Israelis. If there was one thing the Israelis were good at it was stealing useful technology from her friends, usually America. This was made possible by the large network of Israeli supporters to be found in the USA, starting with members of the Senate and Congress to media moguls who supplied the overt propaganda support. These were followed by people working for companies in the design world of technology where in spite of signing confidentiality contracts they had a greater loyalty than that owed their companies, which was to Israel. It enabled the country to keep abreast of new technology at very little cost. Israel's activities against their best friend the USA, were investigated by a congressional committee who were scathing in their damnation of Israel, the only true ally the West had in the Middle East. Israel's relationship with the democratic Western world was a fine balancing act often violated by the Israelis and tolerated by the West.

The problem was the West needed Israel more than ever. This was especially true as Iran was flexing its muscles in the region and interfering where it shouldn't.

'What are those?' Anas pointed to a series of parallel lines that appeared to be about a metre apart.

'A disused underground water pipe,' said Omran.

'How do you know?' AM asked.

Omran shrugged. 'I was in a museum in Tehran a few months ago,' he began.

'What were you doing there?' Majdy asked before adding, 'You don't normally frequent places of intellectual stimulus.'

They all grinned. It helped to ease the tension in the room.

'I was meeting someone.'

'Who?' AM frowned.

'A girl if you must know.'

'Oh hell, Omran,' said AM, 'you haven't gotten yourself involved with an Iranian woman have you? Please say you haven't.'

Omran squirmed uncomfortably. 'I have. She's a Christian, beautiful and intelligent.' He spoke defiantly.

'Huh,' said Majdy, 'she can't be that intelligent if she fancies you.'

'Does control know?' AM asked.

'Yes. I told her when we were in Moscow.' Sighing, he went on, 'This is my last op. I'm out of here and back to Israel.'

'What about your girlfriend?' Anas asked.

'She's already there. When her parents learned about me and the fact that I am a Jew she was given an ultimatum. Give me up or leave Iran.' Shrugging, he added, 'She chose me.'

'Obviously proof of her deranged mental state,' said Anas, then he grinned. 'But way to go bro, way to go.'

They high-fived while the other two nodded.

'Okay,' said AM, 'it's coming up to five o'clock. The roads and pavements will be busy so now is a good time to scope out the area. Anas and I can take the bus and walk around while you two take the scooters.'

Outside it was hot and humid. The pavement was jam-packed and the traffic bumper to bumper. A cloud of toxic diesel fumes hung over the city despite efforts to improve the sir quality. Respiratory problems were common in the country.

The bus AM and Anas climbed into was beginning to look dilapidated. Not on its last legs, but close. It was lopsided due to collapsed springs on the near side front and rear as well as worn tyres all around. At first, sanctions on Iran by the West had affected the country's economy sufficiently to convince its rulers that giving up its nuclear weapons programme was preferable to economic decline and potential collapse. A starving population could easily whip itself into a frenzy sufficient to bring down the government. Such an event did not suit Iran's rulers. They enjoyed their state sponsored lifestyle too much.

But now things were about to get even worse. The Iranian leadership had decided that action taken by the Americans was an insult and so had decided to restart enriching uranium to weapon grade standard. So sanctions, which had been easing, were being re-introduced at an alarming rate. Unemployment had peaked at 15.3% only months earlier but was now on the rise again, hitting 16.8% the previous week.

There was a great deal of unrest in the country and demonstrations, marches and in some cases riots were now a regular occurrence. The government's reaction in all cases was heavy-handed resulting not only in serious injury but deaths to protesters who just wanted a regular life. This meant a family life with work, food and a safe place to live. Education and medical facilities would naturally follow. Iran had been a civilised nation while people in the West were still living in caves. They had led the known world in architecture, the arts, education, inventions and many other things. Now Iran was described as a 'basket case' rather than a civilised country.

The bus was packed and its air conditioning was fighting a losing battle. Anas and AM were at the front, next to the door, barely able to stay upright as they gripped worn nylon straps hanging along a rail each side of the passageway, the bus lurching forward, alternating between slow and stop.

After 10 minutes Anas spoke. 'Let's get off and walk. This is ludicrous. We'll get there faster on foot.'

'Agreed.'

At the next stop they climbed down from the bus with sighs of relief. Their shirts were sodden with sweat and sticking to their bodies. They ambled away, keeping pace with the bus but with greater comfort. They dodged in and out of the teeming crowds most of whom were heading home after a day's toiling in badly air-conditioned offices where the electricity was prone to die at any moment.

'The trouble with sanctions,' said AM, 'is that they hurt ordinary people.'

'Are you going soft?'

AM glanced at his friend and shrugged. 'Maybe. We've been here long enough to get to know some nice, ordinary and dare I say it, good people. They don't deserve all this.' He waved his hand around him.

'You're right of course but the solution lies in their hands.'

'Easier said than done.'

'Most things are.

On that philosophical note they dropped the subject. Both men hated the regime but quite liked ordinary Iranians.

The regime could ease the problem by allowing weapons inspectors access to Iran's nuclear facilities to ensure enriched uranium wasn't being produced. Further, if the country stopped its regional proxy wars all sanctions could also be lifted and the country could get back to normal. What was known as the Saudi Arabia – Iran Cold War was in danger of hotting up. As it was both sides provided support to opposing factions in the civil wars in Iraq, Yemen and Syria. Their support also extended to further wars penetrating as far south and west as Nigeria. Hidden behind the curtain of religion was deep-seated hatred and greed.

The two men arrived at their destination 20 minutes later and stood on the opposite side of the road to the concrete monstrosity.

'What do you think?' Anas asked.

'Did you see the camera?'

'On the opposite building pointing at the steps. There's a second one on the other building next door. Between them they probably cover a wide arc.'

'I saw it,' said AM with a frown. 'Do we cut the power to the buildings?'

'I guess that could work. With the outages around here it's possible nobody will notice anything wrong long enough for us to get the job done. Let's go in here.'

They went into a coffee shop where the air-conditioning was working. It was a relief to get out of the cloying heat.

'It's popular,' said AM, 'and reminds me of an English pub only with one huge difference.'

The tables were full and there were men standing two deep at the bar. The volume of noise meant leaning close to talk and be heard.

'Yeah, I know. No women except those few in the corner looking like scarecrows.'

'Now, now,' said a smiling AM, 'no insulting their national costume.'

The four women sitting alone at a corner table all wore the niqab, looking at the tabletop or each other, keeping their eyes averted from the men in the room. One lifted her face veil and sipped her drink.

'I need to get out,' said AM.

'We only just got here. At least have something to drink.'

'I mean this country. I hate it.'

'You and me both. Ruth has agreed this is our last job. There's a limit and I'm at it. I want an open society where we can buy a beer or a glass of wine, where we can ogle the girls, chat them up and live like reasonable human beings. This country is like a prison without the bars.'

'At least it's not as bad as Saudi,' said AM.'

'Nowhere on earth is with the probable exception of North Korea.'

The two men had managed to get to the bar. AM ordered lemon teas, which were promptly served. They managed to move to a corner of the room away from the bar. In the heat and dust lemon tea was ideal for quenching one's thirst. They both took an appreciative sip.

Anas leant closer to AM and said, 'According to the municipality plans the main junction box is in the basement. We want to take out the power so that we have an advantage against any guards. If the cameras are a live feed and are being monitored then the loss of the picture will alert SAVAMA that something is up. That could lead to them coming to investigate. From their HQ to here is only about 20 minutes.'

'If the site is that important I think they'll have an observation post somewhere close. Maybe in the hotel or in one of the buildings across the road.'

'You could be right.' Anas scratched his upper lip with the forefinger of his left hand, a subconscious habit he had when pondering a quandary. 'If we alert them to something going on will we have time to destroy whatever we find?'

'Maybe. But I was also thinking along the lines of getting away with our lives as well as doing the job. For some reason I find that's important to me.'

'Me too. If there are police or SAVAMA watching would they react should their monitors go down? The answer is no. It must happen regularly.'

'The cameras and monitors could have battery backup.'

'Is that likely?' Anas asked, sipping his tea.

AM shook his head. 'Highly doubtful but not impossible.'

'You know what they're like. They think that being in their own country they're safe. After all, when was the last time there was an attack on Iranian soil?'

'I can't remember one. Okay, so what you're saying is that we should have time to get in, take a look and if there is a problem deal with it.'

'Yeah. Forget any further surveillance. Let's get the job done and dusted.'

AM said, 'I agree. Let's go.'

It took nearly an hour before the four of them reconvened at the apartment. There followed a further hour of discussion. They had actually identified four cameras in total, two aimed at the steps to the basement and two located about 100 metres either side of the road. Anyone in the area would be on camera.

'Are they live feeds and if so who will be watching in the middle of the night? If they are recording the area then there's no problem,' said Majdy.

'Only so long as we can get to the building without being spotted,' said Omran. 'Did any of you notice cameras at the door so any visitor can be checked before the door is opened?'

They shook their heads.

'I suspect cameras would draw attention to the doorway which is not something the regime would be keen on,' said Omran.

'I went inside the hotel and wandered around,' said Majdy. 'Where the door to the basement should be has been bricked over. If you look closely you can see a faint outline of the doorway. Which means there is only one way in.'

'And out,' said Omran.

Majdy shook his head. 'No. That's where you're wrong.'

'You just said…' began Anas.

'I know what I said. Only there is another way and that's through the underground waterway.'

'Is it possible?' Anas sounded dubious.

'Yes. There are large chambers where water can accumulate in the event of possible flooding and they have manhole covers allowing inspections. The city is short of water and so I suspect the system hasn't been used in a very long time,' said Majdy. 'Worse case is we might have to swim.'

AM said, 'I like it. We could also booby trap the front door. We do that as soon as we go in.'

'Sounds good,' said Omran. 'Once we're out where are we headed?'

'For the border,' said AM. 'Collect your passports and anything of value and meet back here,' he looked at his watch, 'between eleven and midnight. We'll hit the target at two thirty or thereabouts. Lowest ebb and all that.'

'Are we clear?' Majdy asked. 'We need to take out the electricity so we have an advantage using our NVGs and hope there is nobody watching the monitors 24/7. All in all it means speed is of the essence.'

'If it's live observation?' AM asked.

'If it's to the nearest police station then we'll have 10 to 15 minutes before they get there. Enough time to do the job,' he spoilt the observation by adding, 'with luck.'

'And time to get away? Omran asked.

'Using the water pipe I think we can manage it.'

There was a heightened tension in the air as three left and Anas was alone with his thoughts. It was time to get out. He'd had enough of Iran and the constant fear engendered just by being in the country.

He was always looking over his shoulder, wondering when the tap would come and he would be dragged away. Or arriving at his crummy apartment to find it's already occupied by the enemy. An enemy who hated him as much as he hated them, which was saying a lot. Iran was a backward looking theocracy that had no place in the 21st century. Oppression was worse than it had been in the Soviet Union in the bad old days of Stalin and his thugs and on a par with Iraq, Syria and Libya. The West should have left the dictators alone. They at least knew what was necessary to maintain law and order even if it did come at a high price. That price was nothing compared to what was being paid throughout the region by dispossessed people whose lives had been destroyed. The unspoken reality was the West had been responsible with the misguided notion that they could impose democracy.

He couldn't see an end to the fighting and deep hatred that was the primary emotion to be found in the Middle East.

The other three trickled in just before midnight.

'We'll check the gear one more time,' said AM. No one objected and no one groaned. It had been drilled into them that checking gear right up to the time of the op was a way to ensure nothing was forgotten and nothing was missing. It also helped to take their minds off what was ahead; death or capture were two possible out-comes.

They each had a silenced automatic, courtesy of the Italian arms manufacturer Fabbrica d'Armi Pietro Beretta. The guns were compact and easy to carry.

They had explosives as well as thermal bombs. The latter could be pasted on the hinges of a door or lock, using a highly effective glue and when detonated emitted a powerful flash of intense heat. It was sufficient to destroy the toughest hinge or lock without the telltale bang of an explosion.

'Ready to go?' AM asked.

There were nods all round. If any of the men were nervous they didn't show it.

Outside they dumped their bags into the trunk before climbing into an Iranian built IKCO Samand 4-door. It was white, 15 years old, battered and rattled as it rolled.

'Are you sure this wreck will get us where we're going?' Majdy asked.

AM, behind the wheel, replied haughtily, 'There's still plenty of oomph in her when called upon.' As if to prove it he accelerated for a few hundred metres before relaxing his foot. The old crate had wound up to 60 kph without any sign of distress. 'See, I told you.' He eased his foot off the accelerator and slowed down to 30 kph.

Anas sat alongside AM, Omran and Majdy were in the back. The three passengers carried their weapons, AM had his in the side pocket of the door and immediately available. Tonight there would be no stop and search by officious police as they made their way towards their destination. It was all or nothing. In, do the job and out. Then out of the country.

They would use the water pipe for their escape and had identified a connecting manhole about a kilometre from the target. That was where they parked the car. The street was silent, nobody walking about and no traffic moving. The air was muggy, a thunderstorm threatened.

No one had challenged them so far but this was Iran. Their luck ran out as AM zapped the doors locked and they turned to walk away.

Three policemen, all armed, were standing at the corner of the street watching as they approached. The four men didn't so much as glance at each other but continued walking steadily towards the officers. They were similarly dressed in jeans, open-necked shirts and loose jackets that hid their silenced automatics. Over their shoulders they carried small canvas bags with their gear. If they were stopped the officers would insist on looking inside the bags. At that time in the morning it wasn't a question of if and so there was no choice.

AM was at the edge of the sidewalk and Anas was next to him. Behind came the other two, hidden from the cops. They had their hands wrapped around the grips of their weapons though their guns were still nestled in their holsters. Unlikely though it was, if they weren't stopped then the officers would have a lucky escape, one that they would never know about. Unfortunately, the officers made a series of mistakes.

First they allowed the Israelis to get to within five metres, next one of them held up his hand and said, 'Papers now!' and thirdly all three left their weapons in their holsters. The Mossad agents had little choice.

AM and Anas stepped right and left, Omran and Majdy drew their guns and fired. Omran shot the man on the left twice in the torso, Majdy did the same to the man on the right. The man in the middle received four bullets, which was overkill. The silencers fixed to their weapons were proof that Italian engineering was excellent.

They quickly dragged the three corpses down an alleyway and hid them behind some trashcans. They would be found soon enough but with luck not before daybreak by which time they hoped to be far away.

They split up, two either side of the street, a further hundred metres distance between them. They weren't strolling but they weren't hurrying either. They kept their heads down ensuring the cameras didn't record their faces. They went down a dozen steps. AM slung his bag off his shoulder and held it out to Omran. He took a sachet the size of two fingers of what looked like black tar from his pocket, peeled off some backing paper and placed it securely on the smooth bottom of the thermal device. He cut it with his Ka Bar and as the black glue oozed out AM pressed the device firmly onto the upper hinge. They did the same to the lower hinge and turned away as the devices went off simultaneously. There was no bang only a faint flash followed by intense heat.

Majdy grabbed the door handle and pulled. The door fell open, Anas only just getting his hands to the top of it to prevent it landing with a thud. He tottered under the unexpected weight. It was steel lined. Standing on the other side with his mouth open was a man with an AK74, an updated version of the AK47.

The man's rifle was slung over his shoulder that meant he didn't stand a chance. He seemed to wake up and tried to swing the gun into his hands but had barely moved when Majdy shot him between the eyes from close range.

It appeared as though the man had been about to exit the building. From the packet of cigarettes and lighter lying next to him it was obvious he had been going outside for a smoke.

'Proof,' whispered Anas, 'that smoking is bad for your health.'

The others were too tensed up to manage even a smile..

The entrance hall was about three metres wide and four metres deep. It was in darkness. Facing them was a second door, slightly ajar. There was a small window at head height through which light was shining. To the left of the door was a second displaying a sign for a man, indicating a toilet. To the right was a third door showing it was for use by women.

AM took the gents, Omran the ladies. The other two stood ready to shoot anyone who came through the middle door. In seconds AM and Omran were through and both shook their heads.

They dragged the body of the dead man across the floor and dumped it in one of the ladies' cubicles.

AM looked through the window. The room was about 20 metres by 20 metres. Running left to right were solid looking workbenches with a walkway through the centre. He counted five rows. There were men stood behind some of the tables but AM thought two of the people were women dressed in Western clothes.

'AM,' said Majdy in a loud whisper, 'this is the electricity junction box.'

Each man reached into his bag and removed a pair of night vision goggles, putting them on their heads and across their foreheads.

'Take a look through the window,' said Omran. 'I counted twelve people.'

'I can't see any weapons,' whispered AM.

'They'll be there somewhere. Can you see what they're doing?' Anas asked softly.

'Four are handling red balls,' said Omran, 'four are doing something with them and four are packing them in boxes.'

Anas said, 'Majdy, you take the switch. Stay here and cover our backs. I'll take the four on the right, Omran left, AM those in the middle. Ready? Good. Hit the lights!'

Minutes earlier an excited Iranian police officer said, 'Sir, I am saying that it is unusual, that is all.'

'Pejman, you call me at this time of night?' An exasperated and irritated police lieutenant asked glaring bleary eyed at the alarm clock on his bedside table. It was too indistinct for him to read so he followed the question with a string of invective.

'Sir, I have been on duty overlooking the building for ten days. I have never seen anyone enter at this time of the night. There were four each carrying a bag. I thought you should know.'

The lieutenant stifled a groan. If only the idiot hadn't phoned. Now he would have to do something about it.

'Are you on your own?'

'No, sir. Officer Kazmi is here as well. What do you wish us to do sir?'

The lieutenant thought for a few seconds. Now that he knew something could be up he didn't dare ignore it. On the other hand he had been given explicit instructions not to enter the building nor allow any of his officers in either. Which, when he thought about it, was a stupid order to begin with. There was no way of contacting the people on the premises. So why were they standing guard watching the place? His mind went round and round until he came to the only conclusion possible. As had been proven many times in the past his superiors were mentally retarded fools.

'Both of you take a look. I don't suppose there's anything wrong but we can't be too careful. Call me back in ten minutes and report. Oh, and not a minute later.' He hung up the phone.

His wife stirred beside him and asked, 'Who was that?'

'Just some idiot. Go back to sleep.'

'Yes, sir,' said the officer but he was speaking to the dialing tone. He looked at his colleague. 'You heard?'

'Sure. It's a waste of time but it's better than sitting around here.'

Both men carried automatic pistols but both were inexperienced and both were nervous. Standing in a quiet and safe place watching what was going on was one thing, investigating something untoward was entirely different.

'Ready?' Kazmi croaked and then cleared his throat. He said again, 'Ready?' This time his voice was clearer, stronger, but still with a quiver of nervousness.

Pejman nodded. He was too scared to reply. They exited the building opposite their target and crossed the road. There was no moon and it was a cloudy night. There was little light and it was difficult to see down the steps to the basement. They waited a few seconds and then Kazmi spoke.

'Something is going on. Look,' he said excitedly, 'the door is on the ground.'

Pejman squinted his eyes and looked more closely. 'I think you're right. What shall we do?'

'Call the lieutenant. Let him deal with it.'

'What if something happens while we wait for him? They'll blame us for not acting. By the prophet, peace be upon him, we could get into serious trouble. You know what they are like.'

As quietly as possible they went down the steps. Pejman stood on the door and it rattled beneath his feet. He froze but nothing happened. They moved forward slowly and stopped in the doorway. They saw three men standing at the doors opposite and one man next to a junction box. The four men had weapons in their hands.

The two officers froze for a second and then fumbled for their weapons.

5

Majdy pulled the handle disconnecting the power to the distribution box. As the room plunged into darkness the four Israelis pulled down their NVGs. Majdy was the only one to hear the noise of the police officers and reacted quickly. He turned and aimed his silenced automatic. Unfortunately he aimed at the wrong man. Kazmi was pointing his at him while Pejman was still trying to grab his weapon from its holster.

Majdy fired a double tap into Pejman, knocking him off his feet and killing him in seconds. Kazmi couldn't see his target but fired three shots in Majdy's direction. The sound of the shots echoed around the room startling the other three men. They looked over their shoulders in time to see the second officer killed by Majdy.

Professionals to their fingertips they turned back to the job in hand. Majdy tottered a couple of paces before collapsing. A bullet had hit him in the thigh severing an artery. He was rapidly bleeding to death.

The three Mossad agents hadn't noticed their injured friend, they were too busy. They had pushed open the swing doors and stepped inside. Four targets each was asking a lot now that seconds of surprise had been wiped off their timetable. Luckily their targets were slow to react. They suffered from the same problems as every other civilian or untrained person. First, they couldn't believe they had heard gunshots. Second, they didn't want to look foolish in the eyes of their compatriots by either ducking down or dropping to the floor. Third the sudden darkness left them confused. What was going on? They had no logical answer and so they froze.

There was no time for double taps. The three Israelis began the turkey shoot. As their targets dropped two people at the back of the room finally had the presence of mind to duck down on all fours. The problem was there was nowhere for them to go. There was only one door and the gunmen were standing in front of it. Only they weren't. The three men were already moving further into the room. Quick glances showed their bullets had hit their targets.

Anas reached the back of the room first. He saw a pair of feet sticking out from under a table. Kneeling down he looked at the back of a man who was lying with his head cradled in his arms. He wasn't moving. Anas grabbed the man's ankle and the Iranian jerked. Anas shot him in the back of the head.

Silence reigned supreme while the Israelis took stock, still listening and looking. There was a scuffle coming from a corner of the room and AM and Omran rushed towards the noise.

They found someone pressing themselves against the corner of the wall and AM realised the person was female. He hesitated. He knew he should shoot her. He knew if the situation was the other way around the girl, for that's all she was, maybe 19 or 20, wouldn't hesitate. Shooting an Israeli was a terrorist's dream. Or so he told himself. It was still too dark for the girl to see anything more than a couple of silhouettes but she held her hands out in front of her as thought expecting a bullet and somehow preventing it from killing her.

Both men looked at each other, their faces distorted by the goggles. At that moment Anas called out, anguish and fear in his voice.

'Come quickly. It's Majdy, he's dead.'

'You go AM. See what is happening. I'll take care of things here.'

If AM knew what his friend meant he didn't show it but merely nodded. There was no pity in Omran's heart. He had seen some of the gear on the tables and recognised PE when he saw it. So they had been making bombs and a lot of them by the look of things. If the explosives had been distributed to the right people, many innocent men, women and children would have died. He hated these people so much that he had no qualms about putting two rounds into the girl's head. He aimed and fired quickly not feeling as good as he thought he would.

'Lights!' AM called out.

They closed their eyes as the lights came on while at the same time whipping off their goggles. Omran blinked as his eyesight quickly returned to normal. He didn't want to know what had happened to Majdy. Instead he began examining his surroundings and what was on the workbenches.

Plastic explosives were being packed into half a ball and some form of detonator was being inserted in the other half. It was obvious the two halves twisted together to form a red ball with a seam that looked exactly like a cricket ball. Omran was taking a closer look at the detonator when the other two re-entered the room. They both looked as grim as death.

AM spoke harshly. 'Majdy is dead. He was shot in the thigh and bled out.'

'Was there...'

'No, there was nothing we could have done. The artery was severed and he was gone in a couple of minutes at most. We have a problem. Two cops are at the door, both dead. One has a phone in his pocket and it's ringing. If nobody answers it then others will come to see what's wrong. So we haven't long. I've rigged a trap across the door. I've taken Majdy's ID and passport as well as the money he was carrying. We'll switch off the power before we leave in,' he looked at his watch, 'five minutes max.'

The other two nodded. They had work to do. They would mourn their friend at a later date.

'Anas, I figure the tunnel runs alongside that wall,' AM pointed. 'Blow a hole in the bottom corner about 50 centimetres round. Then find something to hide the hole behind. It should give us a few minutes extra and I have a feeling we'll need every second we can find.'

Anas used a small explosive device that he stuck on the wall, set the timer for 60 seconds and stepped aside.

Anas then began to video the room using his mobile 'phone while

AM placed explosive devices at different locations. They would be detonated remotely using a transmitter they each carried in their pockets.

In one corner was a cupboard. AM pulled open the door to reveal shelves of what looked like packets of pastry but which he knew to be plastic explosive. A closer examination showed it to be Semtex 10, manufactured in Czechoslovakia.'Four minutes gone,' yelled Omran who had been busy stuffing balls into one of the bags.

'This cupboard is full of Semtex,' AM said in a loud voice, 'it'll take the place down.'

'Tough,' was Omran's callous reply. 'The Iranians put this bomb making factory here so they can take responsibility. This stuff will kill a lot of innocent people, so let's not forget it.'

'You're right.' AM put two explosive devices behind the Semtex and closed the door. AM suddenly rushed for the door.

'Where are you going? Omran called after his friend.

By way of an answer AM reappeared dragging Majdy's body. He gently deposited it next to the cupboard of Semtex. He had to fight back his tears but there was little choice.

'DNA,' was all AM said.

The other two nodded in understanding. They couldn't take him with them and they didn't want the Iranians to get hold of his body. DNA testing could give an indication of his nationality, which was the last thing the Israelis wanted or needed right then.

'Fire in the hole,' Anas said loudly using the old fashioned warning first coined by coal miners in the 19th century. The explosive blew a ragged hole through the wall, creating a cloud of dust. The shaped charge ensured an effective, focused explosion but still made a loud noise.

Hurriedly Anas got down on his knees and scrabbled through the rubble. He looked into the hole, using a flashlight to examine what was on the other side.'It's the tunnel all right,' he said with relief.

He got to his feet and looked around. A brush and dustpan stood in one corner alongside a large bin. He dragged the bin over and began to clear up the mess. When it was done to his satisfaction he crossed to one of the benches and dragged stools to the corner. He lined them alongside the wall. Anyone glancing in that direction wouldn't see anything of interest. A closer look and it was all too obvious.

'How do these things detonate?' Omran asked AM.

'No idea. I've never seen anything like it before. We'd better get them back to the boffins and leave it for them to work out.'

In one of the bags they shoved a handful of switches.

'Let's hope,' said Omran, 'that these things are stable.'

'If they're not,' said AM, 'we won't know anything about it.'

'Okay, that's us. Let's go,' said Omran hefting his bag in his hand. They hurried across the room to the hole in the wall.

'Climb over the stools and wriggle through the hole,' said Anas.

They scrambled across four stools and then onto the floor next to the hole. AM and Omran quickly crawled through. Anas followed behind and reached back to lift down a stool and place it in front of the hole.

Suddenly there was an explosion from the entrance hall.

'That should have killed a few of the swine,' said AM.

They found themselves in a dry tunnel and not a pipe about two metres in diameter. From its state it appeared to be centuries old. AM rubbed a hand over the stone and some flaked off. 'Which direction?' Asked Anas.

'This way,' said AM hurrying away from the hole.

After about 50 metres they stopped and AM flicked a switch on his transmitter arming it. He pointed it back the way they had come and pressed a button. There was a huge roar as the explosive devices they had set detonated the PE in the cupboard. They felt the earth tremor and shake as the building began to collapse. A crack appeared in the roof of the tunnel and Omran pointed at it.

'The tunnel's collapsing!' he yelled.

As one they turned and ran. The surface was smooth underfoot and easy to navigate. The rumbling behind followed them down the tunnel and looking back AM aimed his flashlight at the ceiling. Fissures were appearing like a network of a spider's web. Dust and flakes of stone were fluttering down like confetti at a wedding.

'We'd better speed things up,' gasped AM. 'This lot could go at any time.'

They put a spurt on.

'This is it,' said Anas, shining his torch at the manhole cover.

'Are you sure?' asked Omran, his hands on his knees, gasping for breath.

'As sure as I can be. Look behind us. We've no choice other than to get out.'

All three aimed their torches back the way they had run. Some of the stone was now dropping from the roof of the tunnel.

There was no ladder but the manhole was less than two metres above them. Omran reached up and pushed on the iron cover. It didn't budge. AM joined him and together they managed to move it a fraction. After a couple of minutes they stopped, gasping for breath.

'Come on fellows,' said Omran, 'this tunnel is getting worse by the minute.'

He was stating the obvious. Whatever damage had been done to the hotel and apartment complex it was continuing to have reverberations. They could see the tunnel actually collapsing about 200 metres back.

AM took out a knife and ran it around the lip of the cover. 'We give it another go and if that doesn't work we run like hell.'

He and Anas stood back to back and pushed up as hard as they could. As the crumbling tunnel edged closer they pushed harder. Suddenly the manhole cover lifted and they shoved it open.

AM cupped his hands in front of him. 'You first Omran.'

Omran stepped into his friend's hands and reached upwards as AM suddenly jerked his arms upwards catapulting Omran through the hole. Omran got his elbows onto the road and wriggled free. He looked around him. They were precisely where they had hoped; in a small alleyway only a few metres from their car.

He leant into the hole. 'Pass up the bags!'

The two bags were handed up and then Anas repeated the same move as Omran. The two Israelis lay each side of the hole and reached down and grabbed AM's hands. They pulled him up far enough so that he could grab the edge of the hole and as he pulled himself out they grabbed an armpit each and helped him. They could feel the ground shaking beneath their feet as the tunnel continued to collapse.

'We'd better move or else we could get trapped,' said AM.

They piled into the car, AM driving. He hit the accelerator hard and the car sped out of the alleyway and across the road. They were just in time as a fissure opened up behind them as the tunnel collapsed.

'Hell,' exclaimed Anas, 'that was too close for comfort.'

They looked back along the road to see the fissure created by the collapsing tunnel widen and spread. Buildings were shaking, some collapsing. People were already pouring into the street most wearing nightclothes but a few fully dressed.

Omran had a map on his lap. 'Not too fast, we don't want to draw attention to ourselves.'

AM reduced their speed to 40 kph.

Omran guided them out of the city and onto the main highway, heading southwest. Baghdad was 700 kms away and would take them anything up to 15 hours to complete the journey. Maybe longer as the last 50 kms would involve back roads and dirt tracks.

Anas said, 'You guys want any water?'

'Yes,' said Omran reaching over his shoulder.

Anas unscrewed the tops and handed over the bottles. They drank eagerly, a combination of heat, dust and exertion having left them parched. Anas then handed them packets of chicken sandwiches but neither man was hungry. Adrenaline had taken the edge off their hunger.

'Better give me a pill,' said AM.

Anas opened a small bottle containing capsules of a Benzedrine based chemical, swallowed one and handed one to each of the other two. The pill was good for at least 24 hours of alert wakefulness after that it was anybody's guess. They'd never used them before.

They had also taken the precaution of changing all four tyres, which was just as well. Not only had the old set been badly worn but the wheel nuts had been rusted on and hard to remove. They also had four new wheels in the boot. Should it become necessary they could easily and quickly be changed. Getting the tyres and wheels had been an expensive job as both were in short supply in the country.

When they reached the highway they relaxed a little as they speeded up and settled at 80 kph. Now that stress and fear had subsided gloom enveloped them like a pall thinking about their friend.

'If only…' Anas began.

AM interrupted him, 'The two saddest words in any language.'

6

Hunter arrived in Scotland and collected his car.

It was a specially adapted Land Rover LR4S. Well known as the standard bearer for rugged SUVs, International Armouring Corporation had taken protection when in a vehicle to a whole new level. In spite of the bullet proofing, the interior had luxurious leather seats and the latest in dashboard technology including a parking aid as well as a rear view camera. Both enabled the car to be parked without opening a window and sticking your head out, a risky move when using a vehicle.

With a low centre of gravity and rigid body the car had excellent road holding capabilities. Its three litre supercharged engine gave the vehicle a top speed of 120 mph and 0-60 in 7.7 seconds. Its miles per gallon sent the supporters of green issues into a state of apoplexy. Urban driving meant 15 mpg while motorway use put that up to 19 mpg. A downside was the car's range of 320 miles on a full tank of petrol.

The car was equipped with run-flat tyres, reinforced suspension, ballistic glass, a reinforced ballistic steel body and an armoured battery, radiator and fuel tanks. The need for such a car grated on Hunter though he acknowledged it was better to be safe than sorry. The list of the organisation's enemies was growing daily.

The International Force Against Terrorism, acronym TIFAT, had started as a quasi-military organisation based at HMS Cochrane, the old Royal Navy base at Rosyth, Fife. It had evolved into an establishment run more on civilian lines with the only person now called sir being General Malcolm Macnair.

Hunter was just back from Cardiff and was contemplating the events in the pub. The ACC had confirmed there would be no mention of Hunter and that the police would take credit for preventing any civilian injuries. It was just the way he liked it.

His office was six metres square and was fitted out with a desk and leather swivel chair, a coffee table in the middle of the floor and two easy chairs either side. A sofa along one wall was comfortable as well as big enough to sleep on, a commodity that had proven useful from time to time. The filing cabinet in the corner held nothing more than coffee beans for the machine sitting on top of it, plus an unopened bottle of malt whisky. The small fridge held ice, milk and soda water. As usual the milk had gone off while the soda water was for use with the whisky he occasionally imbibed with a visitor. He acknowledged it was sacrilege to put soda water and ice in a malt but it was the way he liked it, so what the hell. In one corner was a sink with hot and cold water.

He topped up the water in the coffee maker and added more beans. He pressed the requisite buttons and watched as the coffee filtered out. As was often the case he wondered why coffee didn't taste as good as it smelled. He poured the coffee into a mug before sitting at his desk. He took a sip. He should have taken milk from the dining room.

Thanks to the fact that their mandate was to take the fight to the enemy TIFAT had enjoyed many successes in the never-ending war on terrorism. This was mainly because there was little or no chance of any case ending up in court. Certain powers-that-be were aware that to fight terrorists someone had to get down into the sewer amongst the rats and cockroaches. The problem, acknowledged by security services of the world, was the politically correct weren't prepared to countenance such action.

Kipling's poem *Tommy* came to mind.

O it's Tommy this an' Tommy that, an' "Tommy go away";
But it's "Thank you, Mister Atkins", when the band begins to play,

The poem summed up the attitude of many people in the Western world, screaming for help one minute castigating that help the next.

However, it was true to say that the majority of people were on the side of the military and were relieved when terrorists were killed. The problem was when one died another took over. One way of controlling any organisation by a government was to withhold funding while at the same time imposing restrictive obligations. The restrictions weren't necessarily written as laws or in tablets of stone but they could be highly intrusive and debilitating as far as TIFAT was concerned.

Funding was something else entirely. TIFAT had a budget that was insufficient for their needs. However, they had a first class technology department with some of the best computer brains on the planet. These people were highly paid as well as believing in the objectives of TIFAT. Where enemy assets were identified TIFAT appropriated them and put them to good use. This included state-of-the-art equipment, enhanced salaries and benefits as well as money to throw at any operation where needed.

In charge of the IT department of 30 personnel was Isobel Sweeney though she swore the real geniuses were Leo Kinski and Gareth Scarlatti whom she described as her right and left hands. To date they had purloined tens of millions of pounds, dollars, euros and just about every other hard currency of any value. After using the money within TIFAT they had given significant sums to various charities around the world. Their favourites were Help for Heroes and SSAFA, set up to support Britain's own military. SSAFA, - Soldiers, Sailors, Airmen and Families Association - had been established in 1885 and was an indictment to every government since then. The fact that it was still needed in the 21st century made Hunter's blood boil. Hence the reason TIFAT helped financially whenever they could.

He was sitting in his regular position with his feet on the corner of his desk perusing a file he held on his lap. It was the only one in his in-tray.

It was a report from the Israelis in regard to potential attacks in the West as well as a detailed report on a new explosive device dreamt up by their enemies. The West's enemies were Muslim fundamentalists who had been indoctrinated to embrace the ideals of jihadism. They were mainly men but also some women who found meaning to their very existence on earth by killing and injuring innocent men, women and children often in the foulest way possible. Like the majority of people, Hunter had read and heard stories but unlike the majority he had also seen some of it at first hand. Such knowledge reinforced the reasons why he did what he did. It inflamed him and others in the security services worldwide with the passion needed to kill the monsters they had to deal with while at the same time allowing the warriors to sleep peacefully at night. Hunter had killed more than his fair share of terrorists and slept soundly.

He read the details about the explosive device with interest. The Israelis had acquired twenty of them and had subjected them to a close examination. The outer layer was cork wrapped in leather and from the attached photographs looked like a cricket ball

The next part was more interesting. The explosive was a new formula. According to the report it had twice the blasting power of any known PE hence a relatively small amount was lethal. The firing mechanism was unique. A twist of the two halves of the ball around the seam to the first click meant the device was primed to explode on impact. By pressing down on the two halves of the ball a further twist to the next click set the timer for 5 minutes, while a third click set it for 30 minutes.

It was an impressive piece of kit. However, defusing it was simple. All it needed was to push the two halves together and twist anti-clockwise. The ball came apart leaving the explosive in one half and the firing mechanism, in the other. Simple yet highly effective, there was one drawback. You didn't know how long you had before it exploded. A problem faced by all men and women who defused IEDs.

The next paragraph had him sit forward and swing his feet to the floor. A fourth click described how a pressure switch could be set. A reduction in pressure armed the ball; an increase in pressure would then set it off. According to the report an example was the decrease in cabin pressure in an aircraft taking off followed by an increase as it came in to land. As a result any explosion was most likely to be over a populated area, which would considerably increase fatalities and injuries.

The enemy may be fanatics, he thought, but they were also, in many instances, intelligent and resourceful.

He finished his coffee and re-examined the explosive devices. The balls were a new development in the never-ending war on terrorists. They were easy to carry and could be deployed just about anywhere. An attacker could set the fuse for 30 minutes and wander around a city dropping a ball hidden in a paper bag in every rubbish bin. Nobody would be any the wiser until it was too late. The devastation would be enormous. Even worse, targets such as crowded trains or a football match would result in many casualties. The possibilities were endless as well as terrifying.

Then there was the big headline grabbing attack. Bring down a plane or two and the West would scream blue murder. A bomb in a crowd was a nine days wonder compared to the outrage and fear generated when a plane was blown up.

It was never ending. The terrorists came up with an idea, the security services countered it and the terrorists came up with something else.

The security services were hamstrung by the law and human rights legislation while the jihadists had no such constraint. Hence TIFAT. But, and it was a big but, as Hunter knew all too well they had to tread carefully. There were enough civil rights politicians and lawyers who wanted TIFAT wound up and its senior personnel arrested and tried for all sorts of crimes. These were the same people who wanted military snipers arrested and tried for murder.

Hunter, the eternal optimist, mentally shrugged; there was no point in worrying about it. *C'est la vie, c'est la guerre*. The French summed it up beautifully. He decided he could do with a drink but didn't want to drink alone.

There was no longer a dress code in the bar but no one abused the relaxation of the code. Hunter wore a white, open necked shirt, dark blue, single breasted blazer and grey trousers. He put on a yellow waterproof sailing jacket and headed for the bar. Outside, visibility was dropping and there was the feel of a storm in the air.

Lengthening his stride, he hurried across the parade ground. Entering the foyer he peeled off his jacket and hung it in a closet then went into the bar. The room was large and could easily seat 100 people. It was tastefully decorated with paintings of land, sea and air battles on the wall. They commemorated events from Agincourt to Waterloo and Trafalgar. Hunter grinned in spite of modern reality. The French had been Britain's enemy for centuries. The French had usually lost.

Further events were depicted such as the appalling Battle of the Somme, the destruction of HMS Hood as well as the Battle of Britain. That had become known as the RAF's finest hour although the actual period of time had been from 10th July to 31st October 1940.

Other paintings were more up to date. They included Afghanistan, Syria and Iraq. Since 1963 there had been 50 recognised battles/wars/uprisings in the region of the Middle East. There the majority of casualties were, as always, innocent civilians. They were the people who wanted merely to get on with their lives, bring up their families and live in peace.

There were only a few individuals in the room. Most of the Command was either on leave or on an operation somewhere around the globe. Although TIFAT's mandate was worldwide their main sphere of operations was Europe and the Middle East. Both were hotbeds of terrorist activity. In private, politicians the world over wished they had the courage to implement an Australian style immigration policy. The men and women at TIFAT were pragmatists and knew they would never defeat the terrorists in their lifetime. All they could do was their best to contain them and save as many lives as possible.

According to the analysis by the UK's security services, including TIFAT, now that the UK had left the EU, protecting the country's borders was proving a lot easier.

In one corner of the room, Hunter saw four of his team. Although he was responsible for operations and their planning, he also had a team he worked with regularly. He was angling with the General to recruit someone to take over as the Operations Director so he could spend more time at the coalface.

Jan Badonovitch had been born a Russian and had been a member of the Spetsnaz. Just days earlier he had been given British citizenship in recognition of the work he had done at TIFAT. Badonovitch was 5ft 6ins tall, with broad shoulders and was one of the strongest, toughest men Hunter had ever known. There was hardly anyone else he would want next to him when it came to a fight.

Then there was Don Masters, a Royal Electrical and Mechanical Engineer Sergeant who knew more about explosives than just about any man alive. Hunter was considered an expert but by comparison he was practically a novice. Masters was of average height and build and a legend in REME, when it came to handling all types and designs of IEDs – Improvised Explosive Devices.

Sgt David Hughes, SAS - Special Air Service, was one of the fittest men Hunter knew. He could run a marathon and keep going. His stamina was well known, as was his success with the ladies. He was also one of the finest shots with a rifle or handgun to be found in any of the armed forces.

Finally, there was Chris Bletchley, a former captain in the SBS – the Royal Marines Special Boats Service. A relative newcomer he had fitted in quickly with the rest. Bletchley was the same height as Hunter but with fair, wavy and unruly hair. He had brown eyes and a square, dimpled chin that gave him film star good looks. He also happened to be engaged to Hunter's much loved sister, Louise.

Hunter stood at the bar and ordered a pint of locally brewed real ale and gestured to the others if they wanted anything. They all raised empty pint glasses in his direction. He knew the four would be drinking lager.

Hunter carried a tray laden with five glasses across the room and placed it on the table. The men reached for the lagers while Hunter took a drink of his pint.

'Why the glum faces?'

The four men stared at him and frowned.

'Don't you know about the other attacks?' Hughes asked.

'What other attacks? What are you talking about?'

Bletchley said, 'The General told us what happened to you but there's been at least ten more attacks this evening.'

Hunter slowly put his glass on the table before shaking his head. 'Where?'

'All over England,' replied Badonovitch.

'So far,' said Bletchley, 'in pubs and bars. As far as we can tell they were all carried out in the same way. Two people, two automatics, a lot of people dead and many injured.'

'What time was this?'

'All the attacks happened around 8.30 this evening,' said Hughes, looking at his watch before adding, 'an hour and a half ago.'

'That was when I'd just landed.'

'Didn't the taxi driver say anything?' Hughes asked.

Shaking his head, Hunter replied, 'He was listening to a CD of rap music until I asked him to turn it off. Where's the General? Is he still onboard?'

'Over in ops,' said Bletchley.

'Any of our lads involved?'

'No,' Bletchley shook his head.

'I'd better go across and see what's going down.' Hunter looked regretfully at his pint and then pushed the glass away a few inches.

'Care to fill us in on the details about Cardiff?' asked Bletchley.

Hughes glanced towards the door and said, 'Here's the General.'

'Sir,' the five men said in chorus as Macnair arrived at the table.

The General nodded a greeting. He was 5ft 6ins tall, slim with a runner's physique. His hair was cut short, brown with grey sideburns, a square jaw and a nose slightly too big for his face. He had dark eyes that appeared to darken when he was angry. Right then they were pitch black. He was dressed in a dark blue, single-breasted suit with a white dress shirt and regimental tie. The dress code may have been relaxed but Macnair reckoned it didn't apply to Generals.

At that moment the barmaid came across. 'Can I get you anything, sir?'

Macnair looked at the woman and said, 'A large Laphroaig, a dash of soda plus an ice cube, please.'

'Coming right up, sir.'

'You okay?' The General greeted his Ops Director while at the same time grabbing a nearby chair and placing it at the table.

'Yes, sir. I just heard what's been happening and was about to come across to ops.'

'No point. There's nothing for us to do. You gave me the bare bones of what happened in Cardiff when you phoned, got anything to add?'

'I guess not. Like I said, they saw me, recognised me and kicked off.'

'I suppose,' said Macnair, 'they thought you were armed and that you knew what they were up to.'

'Which, if you think about it,' said Hunter, 'was ludicrous.'

'Thankfully many terrorists make stupid decisions under pressure.'

'They rely too much on Allah,' said Hughes, 'and not enough on themselves.'

The others nodded with wry looks but quickly came back to earth when Hunter asked, 'What about the rest of the country? How many attacks have there been? Do we know?'

'Counting Cardiff, a dozen,' said Macnair. He turned his head as the barmaid arrived and deposited a drink in front of him. 'Thanks, Gladys.' He took an appreciative sip.

'Sir, I've brought the mobile phones, wallets and passports of the two men. I was going to take them over to Isobel in the morning. Do you want me to take them now?'

Macnair shook his head. 'They have enough on their plate. They're working with GCHQ plus various police authorities examining what happened. They have hours of CCTV footage to go through as they try and ID the attackers.'

Hunter knew the Government Communications Headquarters in Cheltenham. It was the successor to the famous code breaking Bletchley Park that did so much during WWII to bring the fighting to an end.

Thanks to GCHQ dozens of terrorist attacks had been prevented. It was part of the Five Eyes network code name ECHELON. The FVEY were the USA, UK, Australia, Canada and New Zealand and they had been co-operating in the war on terrorism since the 1940s. In the beginning the targets had been countries plotting war. ECHELON was America's NSA code name for the computer system itself while the software programs were called SILKWORTH and SIRE.

GCHQ was a vast circular headquarters often called the ring of power. ECHELON exercised unparalleled levels of surveillance over the citizens of the world, collecting every e-mail, every telephone call, and social media message and every instance of internet access. Millions of times a minute the information was filtered through the ECHELON Dictionary as it searched for clues as to who was sending the message. The words and phrases became more refined until they ended up on the desk of an analyst. When that happened a much closer look was taken at the message and the sender. Massive systems in all five VEY countries undertook the work and if one of them discovered useful information it was shared with the other four.

'Didn't the perps have ID on them?' Masters asked.

Macnair shook his head.

'So why did the men Nick killed have some?' Bletchley enquired and then shook his head. 'Stupid question. It's obvious when you think about it. They were on a recon. They'd have ditched their ID before the actual attack.'

'I guess that makes sense,' Hunter sipped his ale before adding, 'but it's one heck of a coincidence.'

'They do happen,' said Bletchley.

'Where have the other attacks been?' Hunter enquired.

The General replied, 'Four in London, two in Manchester and one in each of Leeds, Birmingham, Portsmouth, Plymouth and Newcastle. Add in Cardiff and that's twelve in all.'

'Any more likely?' Hunter asked.

It wasn't such a stupid question. The security services would already be examining every scrap of information available in an effort to identify other potential attackers. What had happened was behind them. Now only the future mattered.

The General shrugged. 'There's nothing so far but I doubt it. At least for tonight. It's getting late and bars and restaurants will be emptying.'

'How about people being mowed down by fanatics driving vehicles at them?' Bletchley asked. 'People who have left the bars and restaurants are vulnerable.'

'Police forces across the country are on high alert,' said Macnair. 'There have never been so many officers on the street at any one time.'

'What about the army?' Hughes asked.

'Being deployed as we speak. 'The General lifted his glass and took a drink.

'How did we miss this?' Masters continued. 'The terrorists must have been operating to a level of security we haven't seen before.'

The statistics were well known by security forces the world over. The vast majority of attacks were foiled though some inevitably were successful. These were usually the loners, often using a vehicle or a knife, low tech at any rate. On occasion there may be two attackers but rarely, if ever, more than that.

If too many people were involved then the chances that an attack was being organised was more likely to be discovered. Most Muslims wanted a quiet and peaceful life and found the attacks by the jihadists as abhorrent as did every other ethnic community. Unfortunately, it wasn't nearly enough.

Macnair said, 'Either they were damned lucky or else they have upped their techniques and skills. Let's pray it's the former.'

'Now all we need to do is find the financiers and planners behind the attacks,' said Bletchley, 'before they do it again.'

The others nodded in agreement before taking long drinks of lager.

'The various organisations are working on it even as we speak,' said the General, looking at his empty glass as though surprised to find the whisky finished.

'Another, sir?' Hunter offered.

'No thanks, I'd better keep a clear head for the morning.'

The team exchanged cynical glances. When it came to alcohol the General had the hardest head.

'How bad was it?' Hunter asked.

'Dreadful. However, SCO19's response in London, was good if not exemplary.' He was referring to Specialist Crime & Operations, the firearms specialists. 'Birmingham and Newcastle's Armed Response Units also did well.'

'But in the other five cities it was abysmal?' Hunter suggested.

Macnair nodded and signalled the barmaid having changed his mind about a second whisky. 'You men?'

Gloom had settled over them and they nodded, opting for double whiskies.

Macnair called out. 'Bring the bottle please, plus the soda and a bucket of ice. Put it on my tab.'

'Abysmal is a polite way of putting it. In Newcastle it seems the bar they attacked had half a dozen marines from an RN ship that was on a goodwill visit. Two were killed but the other four managed to overcome the attackers but by then eighteen people had been shot, twelve fatally.'

'Empty mags?' Badonovitch suggested.

The General nodded. 'Apparently they fumbled the reload and the marines were able to deal with them. Both the attackers are in hospital having sustained serious injuries. The marines didn't hold back. Both have broken legs, broken arms and faces damaged beyond recognition. Oh, and I am assured the man will never father children.'

'You said the man,' said Hunter, 'are you saying the other attacker was a woman?'

'Yes. It seems the marines hadn't realised she was a female.'

'What about the use of excessive force? Will there be any comeback?' Hunter enquired.

Macnair shrugged. 'You know how it goes. Some lawyer somewhere will be putting together a case to have the marines arrested and put on trial.'

'That shouldn't happen,' said Badonovitch, 'they should get medals.'

'We know that but it's the world we live in,' said Masters.

'Don't worry,' said Macnair, 'the press will scream blue murder if the lads aren't treated like the heroes they undoubtedly are.'

The barmaid arrived with glasses, whisky, ice and soda. Dave Hughes began pouring the liquor and as he did so he asked, 'What about the other cities, sir?'

'That's all the detail we have so far, but I've been told it was pretty bad.'

Hughes finished pouring and they each helped themselves to ice and soda as it suited them. They raised their glasses in salutation and sipped.

The talk became more general but focused on the inequities of the law when it came to dealing with an unseen enemy. The big question facing Britain as well as the rest of Europe was what to do with the men and some women who had been in the Middle East supporting ISIS.

'What about the notion,' said Masters, 'put forward by that government minister that they should all lose their British nationality after serving a prison sentence and be deported to the Middle East or wherever they're from. With luck they'll be killed.'

'Huh,' snorted Hunter, 'fat chance. If they have dual nationality then there's a possibility it can be done but if they are British, as so many are, they cannot be stripped of their nationality and made stateless.'

'Why not?' Hughes asked.

Macnair said, 'It's against their human rights.'

'What about the human rights of the innocent victims who will be killed by these people,' Badonovitch asked reasonably, 'once they're released from prison?'

Macnair stared pensively at the glass sitting on the table in front of him. These were the very issues he had raised when he had proposed the formation of TIFAT.

The General stood up, drained his glass and said, 'I've had enough for the night. I'll see you all at morning prayers, 08.05 sharp. We'll possibly have more information by then.'

There was a chorus of goodnights as the General left the room. The others dispersed shortly afterwards.

Hunter had chosen to live on a boat, a modern motor cruiser named *The Busted Flush*. He had re-named her in honour of one of his favourite fictional characters, Travis McGee, who had won his boat of the same name in a poker game. She was 35 tons of luxury, steel hulled with a heavily reinforced fibreglass superstructure. The maroon hull measured 45ft bow to stern and was 18ft wide, while the topside was white. Twin-engined and luxuriously fitted out, Hunter had bought her only weeks earlier.

He grabbed his jacket and stood in the doorway for a few moments watching the rain bucketing down. He slipped the hood over his head and stepped outside. It was also blowing a hoolie and he bent his head as he hurried across the parade ground and down to the wooden pier that graced the edge of the Forth.

He stopped short of the berth and reached into a pocket for his mobile phone. To all intents and purposes it looked like a basic piece of kit but had been heavily modified by specialists working for TIFAT. He pressed the requisite buttons and aimed the camera lens at the boat. It stayed blank. If anyone had been hiding onboard the screen would have glowed a faint red. He hadn't expected any intruders but he knew he could never be too careful. His enemies were growing in number.

He stepped onboard, the deck rocking gently beneath his feet due to the choppy water lapping against the hull. She was berthed starboard side to, facing into the current, making it easier and safer to go alongside.

He unlocked the starboard bridge door and stepped inside. Internally she was solid teak with reverse-cycle air conditioners and diesel central heating driven by the engines. The wheelhouse was large and had leather bench seats big enough for two people on both the port and starboard sides. The control console was a mass of dials, switches and displays necessary to automatically drive the boat on the correct course and at the designated speed. With both engines running flat out she was capable of 9.2 knots. The sat-nav system was the latest on the market and could be programmed to take the vessel to any destination in the world. The controls were replicated on the fly bridge above, a place to enjoy sunshine and fair weather.

The bottom half of the wheelhouse was lined with teak while the top half was reinforced glass windows that could be raised and lowered as needed. The windows were in fact bullet proof and had been fitted shortly after Hunter had bought the boat. Ever cautious, Hunter checked a silent intruder alarm found under the console. Nobody had been onboard and nobody was onboard. It was confirmation of the information on his phone.

He went down the half dozen steps to the main saloon. It was also teak panelled and measured 20ft by 16ft wide. The galley was better equipped than a newly built house with a fridge/freezer, microwave, garbage compactor, gas cooker and oven, a filter hood as well as both fresh water and salt water taps. Not surprisingly, there was also a state-of-the-art coffee maker. Although there was a well stocked bar it was rarely used.

There was a table anchored to the deck capable of sitting six with leather dining chairs as well as a sitting area of a Chesterfield settee and two Chesterfield armchairs. A TV stood in one corner. In the bows was a useful store holding ropes and other paraphernalia necessary for keeping a boat such as this one in good sea going order. The store was accessed from the corridor as well as the deck. There were two forward guest cabins, each with two bunks. Next came the engine room and then a shower/toilet and a storeroom where Hunter kept his diving gear and other equipment. Aft of the saloon was the main bedroom with a large bed, a shower and a toilet.

Aft of that were the steering compartment, gas cylinders and fuel tanks. Fresh water was held in cleverly concealed collapsible tanks hidden behind the panelling. There was also a highly efficient desalination system for use when at sea. There were a number of secure but easily accessible cubbyholes where he had a collection of useful pieces of kit, including two automatic pistols and a taser gun.

The boat was easy to handle and suited Hunter in every respect. He switched on the pressure pad alarm system. The boat was connected to an electric power source ashore that kept the batteries topped up and as a result he had all the luxuries needed to make life comfortable. He zapped some milk in the microwave and pressed the requisite buttons to make a mug of coffee before calling it a day.

7

The following morning Hunter's alarm woke him at 06.30 and though there was time he skipped his usual run. He made a cup of tea which he drank while he shaved and then showered. While he did so he listened to Radio 4. The programme was dedicated to the appalling events of the night before. So far the death toll was stated as over 150 and the injured more than 220. Not all of the injured were expected to survive. Many who did would be maimed and disfigured for life

The Home Secretary was interviewed but as usual came out with the same old platitudes. Terrorism wouldn't change our way of life; we would not give in to the terrorists; we would fight them at every opportunity; we would continue to live our lives as we have always done. Except for the families of the dead and injured. Their lives would be changed forever.

Hunter knew that the government had a massive problem. So few people believed them. How could they when they saw derisory prison sentences being handed out by the courts to people who fomented fundamentalism and encouraged jihadism? And what about those who preached hatred of everything Western, treated their women as third class citizens and saw non-Muslim women as objects to be used as Muslim men wished? Ordinary people knew the obscenity that was Sharia law and its application through what were in reality courts outwith the law of the land. Yet nothing was being done about it. He shook his head as though to clear his thoughts. The same facts and arguments were swirling around his cranium like sewage. Like the previous night had proven, it was a subject they and other Special Forces organisations worldwide debated regularly.

The radio had become a background drone, its interviewers showing their usual bias and as far as Hunter was concerned a real turn-off. He would get more accurate data at morning prayers.

It had stopped raining. Wearing a white shirt, a cream safari jacket and black trousers he made his way to the base dining room. There was a buffet style breakfast laid out and he helped himself to scrambled eggs, bacon and mushrooms. The coffee, as usual, was pretty good and the orange juice freshly squeezed.

It was 07.45 when Badonovitch, Hughes and Masters strolled in. They had obviously been for a workout as they were wearing tracksuits and trainers. Bletchley followed them in five minutes later.

Hunter had a copy of the *Daily Telegraph* propped up on an 'A' frame in front of him. It was the military signal that he wanted to be left in peace to enjoy his breakfast and read his paper. It was a custom more honoured in the breach than the observance, as Shakespeare put it so eloquently. Except in this case. The others knew to leave Hunter in peace. Bletchley was of the same ilk, except his paper of choice was the *Daily Express*.

Hunter and Bletchley left at the same time and walked briskly across what had once been the parade ground. One military tradition still existed on the base and that was the raising of the Union Jack at 08.00, known as "Colours".

There was no fanfare as in the past, merely those on the parade ground standing to attention and watching the flag rise. For Hunter it signified what he stood for and what he fought for. He was the old fashioned type of patriot – a man who loved his country.

He often thought it was a pity the UK's politicians didn't think the same way.

This was shown to be a fact when it came to the British Army doing back-to-back tours in war torn Middle Eastern countries. Recruitment was now at its lowest for centuries. The politicians had fooled the people for long enough. "Options For Change" was shown to be what had been intended – a serious reduction in manpower and equipment. Frontline troops would give their eye teeth to put some of the country's politicians in army fatigues, in inadequate vehicles, poorly armed and send them into combat. It would never happen but they could dream.

Macnair not so much walked as marched across the parade ground to the Operations Centre. The way he moved with his upright posture was testimony to serving over 30 years in the Army. It had been his report on fighting terrorism that had resulted in the formation of TIFAT. Knowing he had gone as far as he had hoped within the military structure he had jumped at the chance to head the organisation. It had been his idea to hide TIFAT's real role behind a smokescreen of writing and publishing reports on international terrorism. Some of the reports were highly classified and for "eyes only" of the heads of security services worldwide. In spite of the documents being so classified some still trickled down to the lower echelons and then to the enemy. In reality TIFAT had a mandate to take the war to the terrorists rather than be reactive to atrocities.

Their mandate was the envy of many other security services who also wished they weren't hamstrung by the law. Macnair mentally shook his head. He was back at the conversation he'd been having in the mess the night before. What he hadn't said was there were moves afoot to curb their activities. He knew he had to tone down their operations, obfuscate their real activities even more effectively. That was far easier said than done. The war had been raging for nearly two decades and was hotting up even further. The terrorists were becoming more sophisticated and better organised by the month.

There were eight separate operations in progress each manned by teams of three or four and progressing in a satisfactory manner. On the base was the A team - Hunter, Masters, Badonovitch and Hughes. Bletchley was relatively new but was fitting in nicely. His military rank and experience meant he would have his own team once suitable operatives were recruited.

Most of his staff were ex-military. They had a lot in common. They were highly qualified, bored with military life, fed up being unappreciated and poorly paid. Macnair was an exacting boss who demanded and got high standards. Nobody applied to join TIFAT. Instead, there was an HR department of six, two whose job it was to identify and sound out potential recruits and four who dealt with administration.

His bleeper sounded and he pressed the acknowledged and cancel buttons. He picked up his pace. As a step towards civilianising the establishment he was wearing a dark suit and his regimental tie. His uniform had been relegated to the wardrobe in his house in Edinburgh.

Reaching the door to the ops centre he swiped his pass and pressed his left thumb on a print reader, the lock clicked and he pulled the door open. To one side was a reception desk manned by one of the women hired from the Royal Corps of Signals. Not only was she an expert in information technology and communications she was also highly adept with a pistol and rifle. A Glock 21 was clipped to the underside of the desk, exactly where she was standing. Macnair smiled. He knew her hand was clasped around the butt and there was a round up the spout and the safety catch was off. Although she had seen who it was on the monitor on her desk she was taking no chances. You can't be too careful was a mantra drummed into all the staff. It was overkill, he knew that, but the adage 'better safe than sorry' applied particularly to a frontline Special Forces organisation. There were too many deaths and injuries in Western armed forces due to a sloppy and inept attitude to basic precautions. The SAS at Hereford was a good example of how to behave.

'Morning, sir.'

'Morning, Sally.'

He went through to the main room where twenty-eight men and women were bustling about or at computer screens, monitoring information that was arriving continuously from the ECHELON network, comparing data on a worldwide scale. They were marrying up snippets of information to create a bigger picture. Hopefully, this would enable the security services to identify the jihadists before an attack took place. Macnair couldn't help sighing. This time they had missed it. But then so had MI5, MI6, GCHQ and the rest of the West's anti-terrorist organisations.

He crossed the room acknowledging the morning greetings of his staff. The words were said in subdued voices coupled with glum faces.

Morning prayers was sparsely attended because so many of the teams were on operations. Each op had been carefully analysed, assessed and decisions taken. So far, two of the operations had been cancelled and the teams were being recalled due to the lack of cooperation between local law enforcement and TIFAT. The main objectors to TIFAT being involved in any operation were the French and Swedish but that came as no surprise to Macnair.

'Morning, Isobel,' Macnair greeted his director of IT.

'Morning, Malcolm.'

Isobel Sweeney was the only person on the base to call Macnair by his Christian name. She was in her mid-fifties and divorced after a bad marriage. Now she put her energies into her work in spite of the fact at 5ft 6ins, with a nice figure, shoulder length fair hair and an attractive face she wasn't short of men asking her out. She accepted occasionally though her relationships didn't last long. It was a state of affairs she claimed suited her and as she appeared to be a contented individual nobody doubted it.

Today though, like the others, a pall of sadness hung over her.

'Any more news on the casualties?' Macnair asked.

Isobel nodded. 'Six of the wounded died during the night.'

'What's the total?'

'That makes a total of 192 dead and 256 injured in hospital.'

'Christ!' Macnair responded.

'Leo has been collating information and will update us,' said Isobel. 'First of all we'll run through the existing operations.'

Macnair pondered the dilemmas faced by them on a daily basis. Isobel dealt with on-going ops quickly and succinctly. They were all liaison jobs involving other national security organisations and as such meant that Macnair had little control over what was going down. It was more a question of supplying warriors who had done the business, including killing terrorists. The majority of anti-terrorist personnel had never actually been called upon to shoot a terrorist, though a few had yelled halt and surrender or else. The "or else" was rarely acted upon. The problem faced by many forces was lethal action could only be used as a last resort. With body cameras in wide use a police shooter could easily find himself or herself arrested for murder because the enemy wasn't given an opportunity to surrender. The notion that a hefty amount of compensation was available if an event was proven in a court of law to be a homicide was often too tempting for members of the attacker's family. Better still was payment without a court case. The authorities didn't want the publicity and truth be told, neither did the attacker's family. It meant too much publicity, which in turn made them targets for other groups.

One problem was that most family members, along with close friends, knew what attacks were being planned and supported them even if it meant martyrdom.

TIFAT volunteered to take down the terrorists, an offer sometimes accepted sometimes declined. As a result a database of personnel in various locations but especially Europe who could be relied on in an emergency had been created. These were the senior officers who didn't think of career and pensions but only of ridding the world of terrorists, however unlikely. They would never get rid of terrorism only contain it. Perhaps reduce some of its more vile acts but even that was a forlorn hope as was shown in the attacks the previous evening.

Macnair took a deep breath and got his emotions under control.

The briefing took 45 minutes when they broke for ten minutes. It gave them an opportunity to help themselves to coffee brought in by the catering staff.

Once they were seated again Leo Kinski took the floor. He went over the details of the attacks. He also went into some of the details regarding the huge manhunt that was underway across the country. No stone would be left unturned. Raids were taking place and arrests being made while the lawyers who were recognised apologists for the terrorists were having a field day.

As the presentation continued Hunter looked as glum as he felt. The writ of habeas corpus would be tested to breaking point in many of the country's courts. Police officers and the Crown Prosecution Service would be burning the midnight oil for weeks and probably months to come. He was grateful TIFAT didn't have to operate to the same rules otherwise stopping terrorists, difficult as it was, would become impossible.

'Before we go on has anyone anything to say?' Macnair asked.

'Sure, sir,' said Hunter. 'One thing is as clear as daylight and that is the attacks have been carefully planned, co-ordinated and carried out for maximum impact. A dozen attacks spread over twelve months or more is one thing, all twelve at the same time is something else entirely.'

Macnair nodded. 'We have to take into account not only the planning and manning of such an op but also the logistics. How did they get their hands on automatic weapons and so much ammunition?'

'Sir,' said Bletchley, 'with the effort needed to plan and execute the attacks surely we should also be asking how they were able to do so without being detected. If this is an indication of more to come then we have massive problems ahead.'

'Thank you, Chris,' said Macnair, 'I appreciate your observations. Any ideas?'

'Yes,' said Badonovitch, raising his right arm. All eyes turned towards him.

'It was planned well in advance, contact was person to person with no electronic devices involved and timing was exact. That way no amount of eavesdropping by ECHELON would amount to much.'

Masters said, 'It takes the sort of planning we don't associate with jihadists which means a whole new ball game when it comes to preventing attacks.'

'It's a sobering thought,' said Macnair. 'I suspect you're right Jan but even so we have the whole ECHELON system being minutely trawled in case we missed something. It means that the enemy is becoming more sophisticated, less reliant on God and more so on their own abilities.'

'It's possible,' said Bletchley, 'that they could be morphing into an army with a command structure otherwise such co-ordinated attacks couldn't happen.'

The others nodded.

Badonovitch said, 'Sir,' looking at Macnair, 'if that's the case and I agree with Chris, then presumably it won't be a case of suicide attackers but an enemy that wishes to live. In turn it will enable them to carry out more attacks. Kill a few people and keep going intermittently. The overall death and injury toll being that much higher per attacker.'

'Were all the attackers killed?' Macnair addressed Kinski.

'As of half an hour ago we're not certain. There's some ambiguity about the killers carrying out the attacks and escaping or being killed.' He shrugged. 'You know how it is. People look at the same events and see different things. Especially if there are guns going off at the time and you're a target. Oh, there's the two the Royals dealt with.'

'Can we talk to them?' Macnair enquired.

'No, sir, they're already advised by lawyers to say nothing. And apparently they're in a bad state of health so to speak.'

Macnair nodded. 'Let's hope they're in a great deal of pain.'

At that moment Gareth Scarlatti entered the room and said, 'Sir, there's an interesting development as regards the identities of the two men in Cardiff.'

'Which is?' the General asked.

'They're Iranians and not Saudis.'

'What about their passports?' asked Macnair.

'False. They're good but definitely fake.'

'Are you certain?' Hunter asked.

Scarlatti nodded. 'Yes, positive on both counts. False passports and Iranian nationalities.'

'How can you be so certain?' Bletchley enquired.

'We ID'd one of them from our database of suspected terrorists. We're also doing the same with the other attackers at some of the other sites and so far we've identified three as Iranian. If need be we can check their DNA but that means going to the lab in Edinburgh.'

They knew what he was talking about. From a person's DNA it was possible to identify their nationality and very often the region of the country they came from.

'Think it's necessary?' Macnair asked.

'No, sir, there's no doubt in our mind that they are Iranians.'

'That's a surprise,' said Hunter with a grimace. 'There's no love lost between the Saudis and the Iranians.'

The fact was relations between the two countries were so strained that diplomatic contact had been broken off three years earlier. Bilateral relations between the two countries had been bad for a number of years prior to the diplomatic rift. The fundamental problem was their different interpretation of Islam. Saudi Arabia was a right-wing conservative Sunni Islamic kingdom with close ties to the West and the USA and the UK in particular. Iran on the other hand was Shia dominated and in bed with Russia, Cuba and China. Furthermore, the rulers of both countries were jockeying to be the acknowledged leader of the Islamic world.

As far as stability in the region was concerned they were also at war with each other by proxy. In the Syrian civil war Saudi supported the rebel groups with arms and money while Iran supported the government militarily as well as with billions of dollars of aid. Ironically it was money it could not afford. From the regime's point of view it was lucky there was no such thing as a free press in Iran. The political elite, who were also the religious elite, presided over a more absolute dictatorship than existed when the Shah ruled the country.

'Okay,' said the General, 'we know that Iran would like nothing more than the relations between Saudi Arabia and the West to go toxic in a big way. Anymore details on the attacks?'

Scarlatti grimaced, cleared his throat and said, 'In one of the attacks in London, the shooters being killed but only after they had killed 36 and wounded 15.'

'Where in London?' Hunter asked.

'In a shopping mall in Maida Vale.'

'There's a mosque in Maida Vale also known as the Islamic Centre for England. It would be interesting to know how many Shia Muslims were killed.'

Macnair nodded slowly. 'I see where you're coming from.'

'Why should it matter?' Masters asked.

Hunter replied, 'The Iranians don't care if the victims are members of their own sect provided they can stoke up animosity against the Saudis on an international level. The Iranians can scream blue murder the Saudis were responsible, proof being the passports and the dead Shias.'

'Macnair looked at Isobel. 'Could you check how many Shias were killed, please?'

Isobel nodded acknowledgement.

Masters said, 'If the Iranians go public and claim the attackers were Saudis we can show the passports are fake and the DNA proves the attackers were Iranian.'

'And the Iranians will claim it's a stitch up by the West because of our pro-Saudi, anti-Iran, Russia and China stance we take on all things in the region,' said Macnair, tapping the fingers of his right hand on the table as though stroking the keys of a piano. 'There's already a heap of opprobrium being chucked at the Saudis due to Syria and the Yemen,' said Macnair. 'As well as their human rights record.'

The war in Yemen was another war by proxy. The US and Saudi Arabia supported the government while Iran supported the insurgents. Over 10 million Yemenis had been deprived of water, food and electricity as well as decent homes or even a roof over their heads. It was reckoned to be the biggest humanitarian disaster of modern times with starvation being faced by millions and far too little aid getting through. Both factions pointed fingers at the other while the world watched and screamed at Iran and Saudi Arabia in equal measure.

Hunter sighed. 'It's pretty sick, isn't it?'

'What is?' Isobel asked.

'We're supplying the Arabs with the means to wage war while the Russians and Chinese are feeding the other side.'

At that moment there was a knock on the door and an analyst appeared.

'Yes, Veronica?' Macnair looked inquisitively her way.

'Sir, we've identified more of the attackers. We accessed the Iranian army's personnel database and began running recognition software as soon as the photos from the attack sites came in.'

'Any problems running the program?' Isobel asked.

Veronica shook her head. 'None. Getting into their database was child's play. Their firewalls are totally inadequate, more for show than for anything serious.'

'I don't suppose,' said Hunter, 'that a data base identifying army personnel warrants close attention by anybody.'

'Actually we've done a lot more than that,' said Scarlatti.

'What do you mean?' Hunter asked.

'We've been working on various databases belonging to the Iranians from their banks to big businesses such as their petroleum industry. We've shared info on their oil exports with the cousins. Thanks to US sanctions their exports have declined significantly hence adding to their economic woes.' That was putting it mildly. Iran was in a full-blown recession spending a great deal of money fighting the Saudis in a war called The Middle East Cold War or The Iran-Saudi Arabia Cold War. As was often the case when it came to war, Iran, like most other countries couldn't afford it. Unfortunately, national pride often interfered with the decisions made but in this case it was religious fervour. Whichever, the end result was the same. In terms of what was happening across the Middle East, Iran was top of the West's crap list.

Scarlatti said enthusiastically, 'We can get in and out without a trace though that can change of course, but we've also installed our latest translation software. As soon as the Persian language appears, it's translated into English. It's pretty much perfect.'

'Well done. Have you shared this wonder tool with GCHQ?' Macnair asked.

'Not yet. We first wanted to make sure it did its job before asking for your permission.'

'You've got it. Also send it to the rest of 5VEY. Anymore in the pipeline?'

Isobel nodded. 'We're working on another three translations, Chinese, Farsi and Arabic. All three are nearly good enough to use.'

'Good, back to the issue in hand. The Iranian army being involved explains how they were able to organise and carry out the attacks so effectively.'

'It also means there could be more to come,' said Hunter, doodling on the pad in front of him.

'Inevitably,' said Macnair.

Scarlatti continued, 'We've also hacked into certain e-mail accounts and found a number of e-mails between the Iranian President and the Ayatollah.'

Although the President was the elected ruler of the country the man with the real power was Ayatollah Shahbazi, who had the authority to sack the President at any time. The current President was hanging on by a thread, as he was a comparatively moderate man wanting closer ties to the West and the rest of the world. The Ayatollah on the other hand, also known as the Supreme Leader, was a bigoted, misogynistic, xenophobe. And as his enemies said, that was on a good day when he was feeling generous to other races and other religions.

'What do they say?' Hunter asked.

'The President was advocating not to get involved with any action in the West and especially Europe but also the USA while Shahbazi was insisting on it.'

'It looks like Shahbazi won the debate,' said Bletchley.

'The threat of war between Iran and Saudi,' said Macnair, 'is real. And if it kicks off God alone knows where it could lead.'

'Is it likely?' Bletchley asked.

Macnair shrugged. 'Tension is running extremely high. Diplomatic efforts to stop it happening are best described as frenetic. However, if knowledge of these e-mails gets out then things could escalate.'

'I guess they could be leaked from the Ayatollah's office,' said Isobel.

'That's what we think,' said Leo Kinski. 'That's why, sir,' he addressed the General, 'I'd like permission to inform some of our allies starting with 5VEY and then the French, Germans, Danish and Dutch.'

'Why not EUROPOL?' Badonovitch asked.

Kinski shook his head. 'I have some bad news. As of about an hour ago we are certain that EUROPOL is leaking information to our enemies. In my opinion the organisation is leaking like a sieve and we can't trust them.'

Hunter knew that EUROPOL had been established in 1998 and its full title was the European Union Agency for Law Enforcement Cooperation. Its mandate was to act on behalf of the European Union, to handle criminal intelligence, and to combat organised crime and terrorism. This was usually attempted through liaison between competent organisations in EU member states.

Most people thought EUROPOL was a real police organisation with powers of arrest. This wasn't the case. The Agency, with no executive powers, was unable to arrest anyone. It couldn't even act without prior approval from the authorities in member states. Which beggared the question, what were more than 1,060 staff based in The Hague, doing with their time?

To date the organisation's success rate had been mediocre at best. The people at TIFAT knew why. There was far too much political interference from the bureaucrats who were the real rulers of the EU. Hunter dragged his thoughts back to the matter in hand.

Scarlatti continued. 'Just over a week ago we picked up messages sent by somebody in Eisenhowerlaan.' He was referring to the headquarters of EUROPOL. 'They were pretty innocuous and we ignored them. After all, we don't expect anyone at EUROPOL to be colluding with the enemy.' He paused and ran his tongue over his upper lip.

'So what's happened?' Hunter asked.

'Just before the attacks e-mails were being sent that were brought to our attention by the dictionary as well as the wording and nonsense of what was written. Whoever was sending them either doesn't know how ECHELON works or believes they will be ignored because of where the e-mails originate. There is a similarity in the way the e-mails are written. Like in the old days when a telegraphist transmitted a message his fist, as it was called, became known. It's similar in a way with what we read today. The system is pretty good at identifying the same sender based on sentence construction.'

'Surely,' said Macnair 'that's irrelevant. The e-mail address will tell you the sender's name.'

Scarlatti shook his head. 'The sender used different addresses from different computers all in EUROPOL. This morning we took a closer look. Julie, one of their analysts, spotted something and you know what she's like. Her instincts are pretty good.'

'What did she find?' Hunter asked.

'They were routed to different addresses but forwarded to an address in Greece.

'You're telling us,' said the General, 'that somebody in EUROPOL is helping the terrorists co-ordinate attacks in the UK using a conduit in Greece?'

'Yes sir, that's what we've learned.'

'Is there anything else out there?' Macnair asked.

'Yes, sir.'

'What?' Macnair asked irritably.

The computer genius looked even more distraught. 'We think there will be another series of attacks sometime soon.'

'Think or know?' Macnair scowled. He knew what the answer would be. Scarlatti wouldn't have said what he had unless he was pretty certain.

'Sir, we can't be sure but it looks probable.'

'Marks out of ten?' Hunter asked.

'At least a seven, possibly an eight.'

'That's good enough for me,' said Bletchley while the others nodded.

There was silence for a few seconds and then Hunter said, 'Two weeks to organise and co-ordinate eleven successful attacks, a twelfth if it hadn't been for a quirk of fate takes something the Jihadists don't normally display.'

'An ability to plan and follow through?' Bletchley suggested.

Hunter nodded. 'Correct. There have been instances but mainly it's been spur of the moment stuff. Careful planning was what was needed for 9/11 but that's twenty years ago. There hasn't been anything like it since.'

'Maybe this is the start of a planned campaign,' said Isobel.'

'That's all we need,' said Hughes, 'individuals carrying out unco-ordinated attacks using knives and vehicles. Also they scream *Allahu Akbar*, kill as many people as they can but expect to be killed or caught. In fact, they often want to be caught to give themselves a platform from which to spout their warped interpretation of Islam and to justify whatever they've done.'

'I agree. The recent attacks were planned and coordinated,' said Macnair, 'which suggests trained soldiers. Which in turn probably means government involvement.' Macnair looked thoughtful before adding, 'They could just be mercenaries. Trained in the army but now freelance. The world is full of such people on all sides.'

There was a knock on the door and a woman entered..

'Sorry to interrupt,' said the woman.

'That's okay Julie,' said Macnair, 'what have you got?'

She handed over a sheet of paper without saying a word.

'I wasn't expecting that,' said Macnair handing it to Hunter.

'What is it, Nick?' Bletchley asked.

'Nearly half the attackers were wearing a burka and full face veil.'

'Men dressed up as women?' Masters asked.

Hunter shook his head. 'Nope. The real thing.'

Hunter quoted, '*And she knows, because she warns him, and her instincts never fail, That the female of her species is more deadly than the male.*'

'On that note, expertly summed up by Kipling and quoted by the Commander,' said Macnair, 'is as good a time as any to end the meeting. By the way, Julie, good work on those intercepts.'

'Thank you, sir.'

'Before we go, sir,' said Hunter, 'are we getting involved with any ops?'

Macnair shook his head decisively. 'No. We'll pass any information we get to the appropriate authorities in whatever country is at risk. You are all standing down with a long weekend ahead. You've done enough and deserve some time off.'

Another analyst knocked on the door and entered. 'Sir, this just came in.' He handed a sheet of paper to the General.

'According to the police now they've done their checking it seems the attackers numbered twenty-eight.'

'How many were killed, captured or escaped?' Hunter asked.

'Six killed, four wounded, three captured unhurt.'

'So that leaves another fifteen unaccounted for,' said Hunter.

'We can only assume they got away,' said Macnair.

'Wearing a burka is a smart move,' said Hunter. 'They attack, leave the scene, remove the burka and step out in Western clothing.'

'Which means they are willing and able to attack another day. No more suicide ops but planned and co-ordinated attacks, hit and run, find other targets,' Macnair summarised. It was a sobering thought.

Wajeeh Soliman was 5ft 5ins tall and about the same round. He lived in what was now a one bedroomed apartment in Artemida, a town in Greece. Thanks to his work plus the near bankruptcy of the country due to European Union interference, he could have bought the whole street and still have had money in the bank. He did what he did for pure satisfaction and to show the rest of the world how clever he was.

Only the rest of the world had never heard of him and if he had it his way, never would. Only a handful of select clients knew of his existence. They each paid him a hefty retainer plus bonus on successful completion of a job. So far, he'd never failed but he was astute enough to know that one day he would encounter a system he couldn't beat.

The room he was in was large, the wall between the second and third bedrooms having been knocked down. Even so the space was jam-packed with electronic equipment, all of it was state-of-the-art computers plus associated gear.

He boasted to his clients that he was the best computer hacker in the world. Luckily his clients were so ignorant they were unable to contradict him. For all of his boasting there was no doubt he was good, very good. Probably one of the best though some distance away from being the best.

His latest commission was relatively simple. He was to break into the database of an airline in order to supply the duty roster of its pilots. He had asked if it was for anyone in particular but was told no.

He was contemptuous of the security systems operated by most big companies though it was true to say that financial institutions were improving. Whichever way he looked at it, it was becoming more difficult to hack into systems to extract information or send in bugs to destroy whatever was being held there. When he didn't have a job on he would randomly select a company or government department somewhere in the world and attack it just for fun. Sometimes he left whatever he found intact, other times he did maximum damage.

He had particularly enjoyed meddling with the 45th US President's campaign and having it blamed on the Russians. That had given him a degree of pleasure for months. However, as he knew, all good things must come to an end and he had pulled out of that one before anyone came looking for him. The good news was the President was still being harassed by the media as well as his own officials over the matter.

He enjoyed sowing gloom and despondency wherever he could. Reaching for a can of fizzy energy drink he drained the contents. He contemplated dragging himself out of his seat and waddling through to the small kitchen for another one but decided against it. He would reward himself with the drink after he had broken into the airline's computer system.

He set a timer and got to work. It was an easy way to make two hundred thousand US dollars.

It took him a mere 33 minutes to get into the airline's system and extract the information. He forwarded it to his client and grinned with satisfaction. His client's identity was known to him despite the client thinking otherwise. He had identified the man within minutes of taking his first commission three years earlier. Since then he had carried out six hacking raids on the client's behalf.

He would soon have to give serious consideration to getting out of the business and leaving Greece. He had always fancied living somewhere in the Caribbean. With his wealth he wouldn't be short of female company even though he knew it was his money they'd be after. On the other hand he had been toying with the notion of signing on for a fitness/fat reduction program and get back in shape. Not that he had been in such good shape at any time. It was why he had been known as Porky when he was a kid. He blamed his mother. She had over compensated for being a single parent and had fed him too much chocolate, too many sweets, fizzy drinks and junk food. He was fat at nine years of age and obese by the time he was 16.

In and out and nobody any the wiser, except this time he wasn't as careful as he should have been.

Hunter and his colleagues were sitting in the bar before dinner when the talk turned to the long weekend that was looming in front of them and what, if anything, they would be doing.

Badonovitch, Masters and Hughes would be staying at Rosyth and perhaps visiting Edinburgh a couple of times.

Bletchley said, 'It depends on Louise. She may be flying. She said something about us possibly going to Tenerife. I'll have to see.'

'Talking of Louise,' Badonovitch said, 'when are you tying the knot?'

They all knew and liked Hunter's sister. She was clever as well as beautiful and an airline pilot to boot. She was also witty, telling stories about what went on in the airline world.

'I am told it will be in November,' said Bletchley. 'The third Saturday was mooted.'

'Where?' asked Masters.

'Here. It'll be a humanist ceremony late in the afternoon followed by dinner. Then an open bar and live music.'

'Sounds like it's all planned,' said Hughes,

Hunter grinned. 'That's my mother and sister for you. E-mails and texts have been flying back and forth.'

'Don't you have any say?' Masters asked Bletchley.

The answer to that was an exchange of glances between Hunter and Bletchley before they burst into peels of laughter. The others grinned and then joined in.Shortly after that they went in for dinner. The dining room was set out cafeteria style and they helped themselves to the food. They all settled on steak au poivre, French fries and salad – the healthy part of the meal. However, as there was barely a pound of excess weight between them their diet was irrelevant. Any fat was quickly burnt off by the tough fitness regime to which they adhered.

After dinner Hunter left the others who went into the snooker room. Hunter wasn't a fan of the game and he was also pretty useless at it. The other four were better than average and he knew they would be playing for £20 a time. He returned to *The Busted Flush* and before going onboard he carried out his usual security checks. He often felt like an idiot for doing so but he also knew it was better to feel idiotic than to be seen dead.

8

Sitting at his laptop Hunter logged on. He didn't use Facebook or any of the other social media sites only e-mail. It was highly encrypted and would take a Fugaku computer to break the code. He'd installed a similar system on the computers and iPhones of those he cared about. There was a message from Louise.

Griffiths International Airlines was both a budget airline and long haul and was part of the Griffiths Group of companies. The conglomerate encompassed banking, insurance, shipping, tug boat operations mainly for the oil industry and a host of other smaller companies. It was quoted on the stock exchange with 22% of the shares being held in trust by members of the family. The value of the trust was around two billion pounds and though Hunter wasn't fully aware of the value of his share he knew it was enough to keep him in absolute luxury for at least half-a-dozen lifetimes. As it was, his dividends automatically bought more shares and dumped them in the trust. Some of the dividends he took when he needed serious funds. These included buying and modifying the boat.

He had been offered numerous jobs with the company in keeping with his skills and knowledge. However, he was honest with himself. He didn't like taking orders. His attitude hadn't squared with being a Royal Navy officer but it worked at TIFAT. Whenever an operation kicked-off he was let loose with his team. That was much more to his liking and suited his buccaneering temperament. He also accepted the fact that someone had to remove the terrorists from the face of the earth so why not him? It was a job that would never end and was needed more as the years went by.

He took a sip of coffee and logged on. The message read:

Did Chris mention this coming weekend? It's just been confirmed that my stop over on Tenerife is Fri, Sat and Sun. I can get seats for 3. Have you anyone to bring? No gooseberries allowed. L.

Hunter grinned. It was typical of Louise. Although more than competent with all forms of diving, dismantling bombs and other useful knowledge applicable to his job he also had an old-fashioned attitude. This included names, addresses and telephone numbers. For that he had the obligatory little black book, which he now extracted from a drawer. He flicked through it. Most of the names were women he had known.

A couple of years earlier he had nearly settled down. He had been in love with Ruth Golightly, a Mossad agent who had been seconded to TIFAT.

Although it was recognised as bad form, he and Ruth had grown close and Hunter had asked her to marry him. She had accepted. Then Ruth had been badly injured on an operation in Columbia. Her knee had been crushed by a falling rock. Wonderful work by surgeons on a British aircraft carrier, HMS *Ark Royal,* followed by further surgery in Israel saved her leg. Although that was the physical outcome the emotional one was different. She called off the engagement and remained in Israel. He had gone to Tel Aviv to see if he could change her mind but to no avail.

Although initially saddened, Hunter's natural character reasserted itself and he got over the disappointment, propped up by a series of relationships and by throwing himself into his work. He had made up his mind that he wouldn't get married until he had given up his chosen way of life. It wouldn't be fair to any woman to put up with irregular, unknown separations mixed with the knowledge that it was highly possible he wouldn't return. Actually, highly probable was a more accurate description.

He had plenty of names and all but two had a cross through them.

He decided he needed a new address book. He looked at the two. Caroline was as career/job focused as he was and he knew there was never enough room for two such driven people in a relationship. It hadn't lasted long. He found a pen and put a line through her name. That left Beth. He shook his head. No, she would drive Louise mad in hours. Beth was what Louise politely called an airhead whose conversation ranged from the soaps on TV to the latest fashions in clothes and hairstyles. Hunter hadn't seen her in six months and doubted she was still available. He threw the book into a wastepaper basket. So much for that, he thought.

He pecked at his computer.

Sorry Lems, address book of no use. I'd be a goosegog. You two go and enjoy yourselves. N.

Lems was a hangover from when they'd been kids together. He could no longer remember where it came from or why but he still used it when writing to her.

Seconds later he received a reply.

That's what I expected. Hence I have arranged for you to meet Cathy Albright. She is cabin crew manager, witty, adventurous (likes diving et al) and is right up your street in the looks department viz, blonde and curvaceous.

Hunter grinned. Trust Louise.

In that case count me in.

The two men actually tried to get some of the other baggage handlers interested in cricket. It would have helped but their efforts were to no avail. All the others cared about and talked about was football, the national team, Real Madrid, the next game and whether or not individual players were up to their usual high standard. When they discussed future games they all agreed that Madrid was bound to win. As always, when it came to loyal supporters, it was a case of hope over expectation.

Both the Saudis accepted the fact with equanimity. The other handlers weren't needed but would have added to the misdirection.

During their breaks one would throw a cricket ball to the other who blocked it using a bat. He didn't swipe at the ball for fear of hitting it too far and causing damage. There were a couple of aircraft parked close enough that a ball could strike the plane. That would be a disaster, as they would not have their jobs for long if something did happen.

On the fourth day they were in the queue for staff entering the airport. They were a few metres apart, standing to one side of the others throwing a ball to one another in a friendly fashion as though bored with the wait. There were a few people in between who watched with grins and comments about it being a stupid game. It was for cowards and sissies not like football. That was for real men.

Somehow they managed to keep their nerve. One of the men went through the scanner and his friend threw the ball around the machine. He caught it and threw it back. It was forwarded again to smiles and jokes. This time the catcher put the ball in his pocket. A few minutes later his friend joined him.

If anyone noticed how nervous the pair were they didn't comment on it. They were as ready as they could be to carry out their instructions.

Hunter et al flew Griffiths International Airlines (GIA) to Tenerife South Airport. Louise was in the cockpit, occupying the left-hand seat. She usually flew long haul but more and more she was flying the short haul routes in preparation for her nuptials. Long haul took it out on relationships and marriages. Although it was a short haul flight and a budget price airline the seats had a couple of inches more leg room than other airlines. The price of the seats was competitive enough to ensure the planes normally flew full and the airline made a satisfactory profit though margins were tight. This particular flight, departing in the evening, had a few seats left hence the reason Hunter, Bletchley and Cathy were onboard.

Cathy was just as Louise had described. A nice figure, naturally blonde hair and a sharp wit mainly aimed at politicians of all parties.

They landed at Tenerife, Louise completed the flight paperwork and they headed out to a taxi that deposited them at the luxurious hotel Bahia del Duque. Normally if the crews were staying over they stayed at far cheaper establishments near the airport. In this case Hunter was picking up the tab although they had told Cathy it was on the firm and hence free. She didn't question it. Bletchley had finally accepted and got used to Louise being wealthy although it sometimes wounded his pride. Louise had made it clear to him that she loved him, was used to spending money when she liked for whatever she wanted and wasn't about to change. Like her brother she was not overly extravagant and did not go in for designer clothes or accessories. She also pointed out that she held down a responsible job, was good at it and wanted Bletchley to share her life and good fortune. If he couldn't accept it then too bad, it would be over before their relationship went the final lap.

Following her ultimatum, Bletchley had a few drinks too many and confided in Hunter. He, in turn, told him to get used to it. It was what it was. Louise had inherited a great deal of money, there was no doubt Bletchley and Louise were good for one another, so make a life together and enjoy their good fortune. Oh, and Bletchley had better not hurt his sister. That was said only half jokingly. Bletchley had grinned and shrugged and acknowledged the warning, taking it with good heart, assuring Hunter he never would. At that they clinked glasses and ordered another couple of whiskies.

The approach to the hotel was magnificent. The façade was lit up like something out of a fairy tale. After booking in they sent their bags to their rooms while they headed to a bar for a drink. It was coming up to 20.00. Hunter had booked three rooms much to his sister's and Bletchley's amusement. He wanted to see how things panned out.

Hunter found himself in a quandary as the evening drew slowly to a close. They had eaten delicious snacks and drank an excellent white wine. Normally he wouldn't have any problem with the next stage of the night but this time he did. He thought about it. There was no spark but there could be a faint ember ready to burst into some sort of flame with the right coaxing. Yes, Cathy was attractive, intelligent and good company but he figured he'd reached that time of life when notches on the bedpost didn't cut it anymore. How was he going to circumvent the problem? What excuse could he make up? It wasn't so long ago he wouldn't have had the slightest compunction in bedding Cathy.

'We're off to bed,' said Louise. 'See you both in the morning. Have a busy night,' she said, with a sly smirk.

Then there was just the two of them. There was an awkward silence, and then Cathy spoke.

'It's okay, Nick. Really it is.'

'What is?' He looked slightly startled.

'I don't want to either.'

'Don't want to what?'

She leant forward and rested her hand on his and said, 'I don't want to sleep with you.'

'Oh! Right. Okay.'

Cathy laughed. 'The relief on your face is comical.'

Hunter smiled. 'In that case I'd better not play poker again.'

'Nick, I don't particularly fancy you. You're a nice guy. Good looking, good company and from what little I know about what you and Chris do then,' she shrugged, 'double-o-seven eat your heart out.'

'Trust Louise, she shouldn't have said anything.'

'Yeah, well, anyone seeing you and Chris wouldn't think for a second that you have desk jobs.'

Hunter was about to protest but changed his mind. Instead, he shrugged. 'You're right. It's my turn with the compliments. You're very attractive, clever and funny, but I don't know, there's no real, what should I call it, lust?'

Cathy smiled. 'Good word.' She took a sip of wine. 'I'm the same. I'm 31 next month. I've known enough men in my time, mostly airline captains. By that I don't mean biblically. Just men I have met for the occasional drink or dinner.'

'Heaven forbid that I thought your friendships with the opposite sex was anything more than that.' Somehow he managed to keep a straight face as he spoke.

103

Cathy chuckled. 'The objective of many of the female cabin crews is to meet and marry an airline captain and settle down to a comfortable life in some suburban town or village. A nice house, a couple of kids and an SUV all contribute to a perfect life. Only it doesn't often work that way. You've snared your captain and he goes on short and long haul flights. He stays over and you remember what it was like. Jealousy raises its ugly head and your ideal life becomes corroded.'

Hunter nodded then said, 'Can I get you a drink? I'm having a beer.'

Cathy nodded. 'That's fine by me.'

Hunter crossed to the bar and returned with two opened bottles of cold lager. He handed one to Cathy, they clinked bottles and smiled at one another.

'Here's looking at you, I won't say kid,' said Hunter.

'You'd better not. *Casablanca* had some great lines but the plot made no sense at all. Or at least it didn't stand up to close scrutiny.'

Hunter smiled. 'I couldn't agree with you more. But the one liners made up for it.' He changed the subject. 'Did you start out wanting to be an air stewardess?'

'No. I trained as a nurse. I did four years at Edinburgh Uni and qualified. After another four years mostly in A&E I quit. I wanted to travel and thought being an air hostess would fit the bill. So I applied. Being a trained nurse helped and I immediately got a job with GIA. Eighteen months later I was promoted to cabin manager, which doesn't mean that much except for a pay rise.'

'You said you had been thinking about leaving?'

'Sort of. Before we left Edinburgh I had a message that HO wanted to interview me.'

'To do what?' Hunter sipped his beer.

'As I understand it, I would be managing the cabin staff recruitment office.'

'Sounds good.'

'Yes, it does.' She spoke hesitatingly.

'You don't like the idea?'

Shrugging, Cathy said, 'It's not that. I do. It would mean I could settle in Edinburgh, do some travelling to interview applicants in various countries and maybe meet the right man.'

'And create the nice life you crave?' Hunter smiled.

'Perhaps, though I don't think I crave it that much. I need to think about it.'

'What's the alternative?'

Shrugging, Cathy raised her bottle to her lips and took a sip. 'No idea.'

'So?'

'So I don't want people to think I got the job because of my friendship with Louise and I don't want Louise to think I befriended her to get a better job.'

Hunter slowly replaced his bottle on the table in front of him and looked closely at Cathy. She stared right back.

Hunter leant forward on his elbows and shook his head. 'You really don't know Louise that well if you think for one moment she would use her influence, assuming she has any, to get you a job. But let's assume for a moment she does have some she would only recommend you if she thought you could do the job. Now, in my family we believe in nepotism used properly.'

'What's that supposed to mean?'

'Just that. Perhaps Louise knew about the job vacancy. Perhaps she contacted the right person and suggested you for it. Perhaps her opinion was acted on. Perhaps a host of things but one thing I can tell you.'

'What's that?'

'You'll never know.'

'What do you mean?'

'She isn't going to say anything. She obviously values your friendship. She knows and I know that friendships can be seriously damaged if not destroyed if one person is seriously indebted to the other. There's no balance in the relationship and pretty soon it fizzles out.'

'You sound as though you're speaking from personal experience.'

Hunter shook his head. 'No. It's never arisen with me. The military works on different values. You do a good job you get promoted. It's as simple as that. There's only one line to follow. In a large civilian organisation you can branch off in all sorts of directions.'

'I was thinking of asking her about it.'

'Want my advice?'

Cathy frowned. 'I guess so. Otherwise I wouldn't have said anything.'

Smiling, he nodded. 'Just accept it. Don't say a word. If you get the job enjoy it and do your best. If you don't,' he shrugged, 'resign and move on.'

Silence reigned for a few seconds while Hunter drank more beer.

'You're right. Though I was led to believe that the job is mine for the taking.'

'Good. Then I might get the opportunity to meet up with you in Edinburgh.'

'With no spark?'

'Sparks can be created.'

'Perhaps. I hope Louise isn't disappointed. She was trying to fix us up.'

'That's my dear sister for you. Has she said anything to you about what she intends doing after they're married?'

Cathy smiled. 'Not exactly, but reading between the lines I would say quit her job, settle down and have children. She has it all mapped out in her head.'

Nodding, he smiled. 'That sounds just like my baby sister.'

'You know she's popular with the staff, especially the cabin crew. She's also a superb pilot.'

Nodding, Hunter said, 'I've flown with her in small planes. We both took our pilot's licence' at the same time. Only she took it all the way while I became a diver.'

They chatted a lot longer until they realised it was nearly 01.00, the bar was closed and so they headed to their rooms. They said goodnight in the corridor, Cathy planting a peck on his cheek.

The following morning they all met in one of the restaurants for breakfast. It was a superb buffet with a range of hot and cold food. Louise and Chris were in the picture as to what had, or more precisely, hadn't happened and avoided the subject.

Their plans for the day were simple. They were to loll beside one of the swimming pools, use room service as required and generally take things easy. Hunter and Bletchley were bored before midday and went scuba diving while Louise and Cathy took a rain check announcing they wanted to work on their tans.

9

The palace was situated on the edge of Jeddah and sat in 60 acres of plush gardens. It belonged to a Saudi Prince named Abdul-Hameed Saud. The land had been sculptured to perfection and was an idyllic setting for the grand building. An army of 35 people, men and women kept the area immaculate. The majority were little more than slaves, brought into Saudi Arabia by people traffickers promising them a better life than the one they had in the country of their birth. Some were from South Sudan escaping war and famine; some were from Nigeria escaping the anti-Christian pogroms that were sweeping what should have been a wealthy and stable country. They had assumed they were being taken to Europe and had paid a significant amount to get there. Instead they had ended up in Jeddah where Christianity was not only banned but if worshipped often resulted in being stoned to death. They had been told that after two years they would be taken to Europe. Some had been there five years with no sign of an end to their plight.

Others were from Iraq and Libya escaping death and poverty caused by Daesh, one of the most violent and evil organisations the world had ever known. They had escaped one form of hell for another. They believed the lies told to them by the smugglers but their dreams of a better life had been shattered.

Once they had reached Saudi they were taken to the palace, arriving a few at a time. The newcomers replaced others who, they were told, had been transported to freedom in Europe. Once in Europe, those who made it were housed and fed, given cushy jobs and welfare payments that allowed them to live in a degree of luxury. None really believed that such a Utopia existed but they wanted to believe and so lived in their own dream world. It was those dreams that kept them going, kept them alive, enabling them to accept the most degrading treatment meted out to them.

They were in the middle of Saudi Arabia. It was one of the most inward looking, controlled and despotic countries on earth with possibly one exception - North Korea. Beneath the veneer that was the civilised face of the regime lurked the most repressive and despotic rulers, controlled and organised by a faction of Islam known as Wahhabism.

The palace boasted 60 bedrooms and 30 public rooms. Various parts of the complex were designated for the use of certain members of the household like the Prince's four wives, his remaining three sons and three daughters. All of his surviving offspring were married and had children. The Prince wasn't sure how many grandchildren he had, what sex they were and certainly was unable to name them. The reality was he rarely saw them. That state of affairs was his decision and his alone. He was fully aware of his relationship with his family and knew that they were relieved. In public they were dutiful and affectionate but the affection was false and the Prince knew it.

Spying on one's nearest and dearest was second nature in the kingdom. Survival in the royal family at any level meant knowing what was really going on. The only person who was safe was the king and even his position was precarious at times. It was not how things were presented to the Prince by the hypocritical back stabbing members of his family. The Prince's paranoia was inflamed from time to time when certain facts were brought to his attention. Whatever the cause, anyone showing the slightest disloyalty was swiftly dealt with. It didn't mean the death of the culprit. Threats were usually enough to quell any rebellion, coupled with the loss of financial support and privileges.

Without the continual vigilance he doubted that he would have reached 72 years of age. During his lifetime he had found it necessary to do away with two family members, a number of sycophantic hangers-on as well as a few acquaintances. The two family members had been a younger brother and a first cousin. Their demise had been arranged by Ahmed, his previous head of security, through a third party in such a way as to ensure no suspicion fell on him. A car crash on a winding road in rural France had ensured the job was done discreetly. Ahmed had been one of the few men the Prince had really trusted and he had been genuinely sorry when Ahmed had died of a massive heart attack. However, his replacement was proving equally adept at his job.

The Prince had pushed eight men and their families into penury. Two of the men had killed their wives and children before committing suicide. He knew that he was often referred to as being utterly ruthless. It was a description he not only promoted but actually relished. Fear was a powerful weapon when it came to personal safety.

There had been one son who had taken after him, who was now dead. He had been tough and passionate in his beliefs and support for the one true religion. On a table nearby were a number of photographs of his son from the age of five up to his 24th birthday, which was celebrated just a few weeks before his death. The Prince thought murdered was a more accurate word and he shook with rage and hatred as memories came back. It had taken over $1,000,000 in bribes and fees to discover who had been responsible for killing him.

He ignored the fact that his son and others had been planning an attack on innocent people in Berlin. That the death toll would, in all likelihood, have been appalling with many innocent men, women and children killed and injured. He had helped to plan the attack, reining in some of his son's more extreme ideas. It had taken all his persuasive powers to convince his son that just because they were doing God's work, God would not be watching over them and protecting them. God looked after those who looked after themselves. It was why, within certain bounds, man had been given free will and the ability to think for himself. But mankind still needed to be reminded about God's requirements, which had been spelt out by the prophet Mohammed, peace be upon him.

Bile erupted in his stomach and he began gasping for breath. Grabbing the oxygen mask next to him he placed it over his nose and mouth. He gasped, gradually bringing his breathing back under control as tears welled in his eyes. Were they for his dead son or for the fate that awaited him? He wasn't sure. All his life he had adhered to the five pillars of Islam. He recited them to himself.

Shahadah: sincerely reciting the Muslim profession of faith.

Salat: performing ritual prayers in the proper way five times a day.

Zakat: paying an arms tax to benefit the poor and the needy.

Sawm: fasting during the month of Ramadan.

Hajj: taking a pilgrimage to Mecca, something he had done many times.

He liked to think of himself as a true believer, an adherent of the one true faith, a warrior in the name of Islam. Only his contribution to the fight against non-believers was financial not physical. His life was far too valuable to be wasted killing infidels. But his had become a life wasting away with the disease that was eating him alive. His journey to Jannah was set and he would arrive at his destination soon. Trepidation coupled with excitement surged momentarily through him.

Again bile erupted in his stomach when his thoughts turned to the new king of Saudi Arabia. He was being lionised by the West as a modern monarch; a man who would bring the kingdom into the 21st century. They spoke of reform, modernisation, and education, along with more open government coupled with greater and better rights for women.

His stomach erupted again and he reached for a packet of antacid pills that he carried with him at all times. He took two and chewed them slowly. He put the mask back on and inhaled steadily, avoiding the gasps he was prone to suffer as he struggled to breathe. His pulse steadied along with his breathing, and he allowed his thoughts to return to matters of the kingdom.

He was sitting at his desk in his office. The room measured 20 metres by 15 metres and was opulent beyond imagination. It was also packed with tables, chairs and sofas. His desk was so big that even if he leant over it he could barely touch the other side. Its width was also more than double the span of his outstretched arms. The only thing to be found there was a laptop. Its only use was to watch pornography but he had lost interest months earlier. Now all that mattered was getting his revenge before he died. The nature of his revenge would also help him on his journey to Jannah, a journey he would undertake in the not too distant future. One thing he was sure of, he would not be journeying to Jahannam. He shuddered at the thought. No, he had lived a just and good life, and had followed the word of the Qur'an to the letter.

He dismissed the idea that his version of what was good had been instilled in him by mullahs who still lived in the 6th century.

He coughed harshly, dragging himself back into the here and now. He spat into a white linen handkerchief before wiping his mouth. Dropping the handkerchief into a wastepaper basket, he didn't look at the red mess. The irony was, he had always enjoyed good health until the previous year. That was when the doctors hit him with the devastating news. He had one of the most dreaded and frightening diseases known to man - lung cancer. It wasn't fair. It was unjust after all the precautions he had taken with his health.

In his late forties he had realised that overeating had caused other members of his family to have strokes, heart attacks and diabetes. He had been determined it wouldn't happen to him. He had regulated his food intake, like a good Muslim he had never drunk alcohol but was fond of cold sweet tea and strong sweet coffee. He had learnt to take both drinks without sugar or any other type of sweetener. He had lost 50lbs within six months and felt better for it. He knew he wouldn't live forever, but he had been determined to try and outlast many of his relatives. So far he had outlived numerous cousins, uncles and aunts. Although he had thought of it as an achievement of sorts the law of averages had been on his side. After all there were over 20,000 people in the extended royal family, although its wealth was in the hands of less than 2,000. More importantly power was in the hands of only a few dozen, rapidly oozing to the peak as represented by the king.

According to Forbes, the family's wealth was estimated at $1.5 trillion. He knew that estimate was much too low. His own fortune was $20 billion plus change but with his investments spread so far and wide it was virtually impossible to have an accurate figure. The change was anything from $20 million to $100 million.

He was six feet tall, now with a stoop, taking an inch or so off his height. He was slim, albeit with a slightly protruding stomach, and had a shock of silver hair. His face was long and narrow, with thin lips, a hooked nose and a scar across his right cheek. If asked, which was rare nowadays, he told people it was an old duelling scar. In fact he had received it whilst at school in Eton, England, when playing rugby. It was a game he detested but had no choice when it came to whether or not he played. The alternative had been cricket and he described that as worse than watching a corpse decompose. He had been tackled, knocked to the ground and one of the other boys trod on his cheek accidentally. There had been a huge fuss afterwards and he never played the game again. He had also left the school within three months. He had then received private tuition at his home in Jeddah, the house he now occupied.

There was a knock on the door.

'Enter!' His voice was low and hoarse, the result of smoking far too many cigarettes, his one vice and the cause of his illness.

A servant entered the room and bowed. 'Your Excellency it is time for the Dhuhr.'

The Prince waved his hand at the man who immediately left. The servant had only one task and that was to remind his master when it was time for prayers. There were five to be recited each day. The Fajr pre-dawn, the Dhuhr at or just after noon, the Asr late afternoon indicating an end to work, the Maghrib in the evening just after the sun has set and the Isha just before bedtime.

The Prince did his utmost to ensure he performed all five each and every day. This was now even more important as he faced his own mortality. He stood up and crossed the room to where his prayer mat was laid out. He faced Mecca and praised the greatness of God and then recited the obligatory prayer standing holding his left wrist in his right hand with both above the navel. Not only did he recite the prayer but he followed the obligatory movements, bowing, going down on his knees, sitting back with his hands on his knees careful not to make a mistake in accordance with the Holy Qur'an.

When he had finished, his thoughts turned once again to his dead son.

His son had been as ruthless as he was and as dedicated to the Islamic cause. That cause was to spread Islam throughout the world until it dominated everyone, everywhere. If it took a thousand years then so be it, but it would happen one day. The non-believers were worse than dogs. Most had stopped believing even in their own perverted idea of God such as Christians, the enemy of Islam. For that there could only be one answer. Worship God through Islam or perish. He didn't care which.

His eldest son had been named after him - Abdul-Hameed Saud. The son who was to inherit his mantle and continue making their family great and a real power in the kingdom. He clenched his fists. His son was dead and he now knew who had killed him.

There was a further knock on the door. When he called out two men entered. One was his head of security the other was a European, a German who had come highly recommended. He specialised in assassination.

10

On the second evening in Tenerife, Hunter and the others were sitting at a table on the balcony overlooking the immaculate grounds with the sea in the distance. The sun had set, the temperature was about 25°C with a gentle breeze blowing in from the Atlantic. Soft music was playing and taken together gave the hotel an idyllic charm.

In the morning all four had spent a few hours windsurfing. Much to Hunter's surprise Cathy had proven to be particularly adept at the sport. After a light lunch they had spent most of the afternoon under sun-shades reading and dozing. Occasionally the women had ventured into the sun requiring the men to massage sunblock onto their bodies. They had also cooled off in the pool and drank cold, non-alcoholic drinks.

At 18.00, having showered and changed, they had played a game of Scrabble, which Louise won. Now they were perusing menus, deciding what to have for dinner.

Louise wore a pale green, short sleeved dress, while Cathy's was light brown. Hunter and Bletchley had on white, short sleeved shirts and dark trousers. Hunter couldn't help noticing that Cathy wasn't wearing a bra and he was beginning to wonder if he had made the correct decision. Maybe it wasn't too late. She was sitting opposite him and he looked into her eyes. His mouth was suddenly dry as she smiled at him as though she knew what he was thinking. What would her response be if he made a move? He doubted a slapped face, more likely a polite "No thank you".

However, there was a more important issue to deal with than whether or not he was rejected by Cathy. There was no doubt that the two men sitting across the terrace under a palm tree were taking an undue interest in them. Maybe it was the girls. They were both beautiful and eye-catching. Hunter hoped that was the case.

'I need the loo before we eat,' announced Louise.

'Good idea,' said Cathy. 'I'll come with you.'

The two women stood up ready to leave when Hunter said, 'Chris and I have something to do. We'll be back soon.' As he spoke he topped up their glasses.

'You noticed them as well, Nick.'

'Yeah. Let's take a stroll in their direction and then go around the back to the small gate to the tennis courts. It's nice and quiet. We'll see what happens. We're probably being paranoid and they're only interested in the girls.'

'A healthy dose of paranoia helps us stay alive. And if they come after us?'

Hunter's smile wasn't nice. 'They'll wish they hadn't.'

They walked in the direction of the table where the two men were seated, not looking at them. As they approached the men looked at each other, one said something, then they stood up and rushed down the steps.

'Should we follow?' Bletchley asked.

'They're running and have a head start. What do you think?'

'I think it's a waste of time. They're already in the street, there's a horde of people around, we don't know who they are and all they did is look and run away.'

'Precisely.'

They turned and began to stroll back to their table.

'By the way, I have a message for you from your sister.'

'Oh?'

'Yes.' He grinned. 'Cathy's changed her mind.'

'About what?'

This time Bletchley chuckled. 'That was all she said. So I leave it to you as to what it means. But it doesn't take Sherlock Holmes to work it out.'

Hunter grinned in return. The evening had taken on a tantalising promise. 'Any thoughts about the two men.'

'Lots of questions but no answers. One thing, if I had to guess, I would say they looked Middle Eastern.' A few seconds later he added, 'Possibly Saudi.'

Nodding, Hunter said, 'Saudi is as good a guess as any. Whoever they are they seemed to recognise us.'

'There's no beating about the bush,' Bletchley shook his head. 'It's you. In certain quarters you're becoming rather well known and not in good places either.'

'Ever heard of Charles Mackay?'

'No.'

'Google his name. He summed it up perfectly.'

'How?'

Hunter quoted.

'You have no enemies, you say
Alas, my friend, the boast is poor;
He who has mingled in the fray
Of duty, that the brave endure,
Must have made foes! If you have none,
Small is the work that you have done.
You've hit no traitor on the hip,
You've dashed no cup from perjured lip,
You've never turned the wrong to right,
You've been a coward in the fight.'

'On one level it sums things up. Charles Mackay got it right but I think there was an attack going down and I happened to be there. For the terrorists wrong place, wrong time. For us, luck and the right place at the right time.'

'Agreed. But the point I am making is they recognised you. And that's at foot soldier level.'

'Chris, that was one maybe two people. Nothing to get bothered about.'

Bletchley shook his head. 'You need to be ultra careful Nick, that's all.'

'If I was any more careful I'd lock myself in a room and not come out for a year or two until everyone who is anyone has forgotten all about me.'

They arrived back at their table only moments before Louise and Cathy.

'Are we ready to order?' Louise asked. 'I'm famished.'

All four ordered starters of mussels in a tomato sauce followed by fish and potato pie for the women and steaks with fries for the men. As a side dish they had bowls of salad with a local dressing. With the mussels and the fish white wine was served while the men switched to red with their steaks. They drank little and ate well.

Finally, around 23.00 Louise said, 'Time to go. I need to be fresh and sober in the morning for the flight home.' Standing up she looked Hunter in the eyes, smiled and winked.

To him the gesture was as subtle as a gunshot. Cathy may have changed her mind but the question was, had he? The thought had barely entered his head when he dismissed it. He knew he had.

Bletchley also stood up and, with a smile said 'See you at breakfast. Goodnight.'

Then there was just the two of them. Hunter suggested a nightcap. Cathy nodded and they settled on a rather fine brandy. It was smooth and tasty but as far as the waiters were concerned utterly ruined when they both asked for a cube of ice with the drink.

Hunter could feel an electricity building up between them and smiled at Cathy who smiled back. They both knew where they were going to end up and so took their time. Anticipation was the food of lust as far as Hunter was concerned.

'Tell me about your job,' said Cathy, sipping her brandy, watching him over the rim of her glass.

Hunter shrugged. 'There's not a lot to tell.'

'Yes there is. I made the comment about you two not having desk jobs and you changed the subject. So what do you do? If you kill bad men it's okay with me. I am not a bleeding heart liberal. There are a lot of people in the world who need to die and that goes for women as well as men. Don't get me wrong, I'm not bloodthirsty, just pragmatic.'

'Pragmatic is a good word.' Hunter raised his glass and took a sip, wondering how much he could or should say. His natural instinct was to say nothing but to lie with the ease acquired by practice.

'I'm waiting,' said Cathy.

'What for?'

'For you to tell me what you do. I do know you work in Rosyth for TIFAT.'

'I told you, we acquire, collate and report terrorist activity worldwide.'

'No, you don't,' Cathy smiled. 'The International Force Against Terrorism is precisely that. You use force against terrorists. Her tone changed to one of anger, possibly hatred. 'I hope you kill them and kill many of them and I hope they die bad deaths. Better still, I hope they are crippled and spend their lives in some stinking hole in sub-Saharan Africa or the Middle East.'

If Hunter was surprised by Cathy's outburst he didn't show it. He watched as she took a gulp of her brandy, emptying the glass. He gestured to a waiter and waved at the table and held up two fingers. The man nodded and headed to the bar.

'What brought that on?'

Looking sheepish, Cathy replied. 'My niece was at Manchester Arena when the bomb went off. She was about 30 feet from the blast. Her left leg was so badly damaged that it had to be amputated, luckily below the knee. She's only twelve.'

She paused as the waiter appeared and exchanged their glasses. Cathy lifted hers and took a sip. Hunter did likewise.

'You said luckily,' he prompted gently.

'Yes. The girl standing next to her was killed. Three others in close proximity were badly injured. Even so it is difficult for a twelve year old to accept the fact that, under such appalling circumstances, she was deemed one of the lucky ones.'

Hunter nodded. A pall of gloom had settled over them.

'Did you know that apart from 22 individuals being killed, 250 were injured? The dead were mainly teenagers with the youngest victim being just eight years old.'

'I know. I read the reports and watched events on the television.'

Sighing, Cathy said, 'My niece was a vivacious, outgoing and happy child who now needs a lot of attention. She's coming to grips with her prosthetic lower limb for which there is a great deal of help. However, she has mental problems, sleepless nights, nightmares. The sorts of things now recognised as PTSD. So believe me when I tell you how much I hate these people. They are cowards and need putting down.' She sipped her drink and looked Hunter in the eyes. 'Do I shock you?'

Hunter shook his head. 'I not only agree with your sentiments but I endorse them.' He swallowed more brandy. 'Look, what I will say about my job is that I help to eliminate the bad guys. How that's done varies a lot but I do it as best I can.'

'Does it give you sleepless nights?'

'What?'

'I won't beat about the bush. Killing these people.'

Hunter shook his head. 'Not for a second, I sleep well and I sleep easily. I confess I have to work at not becoming bitter and twisted. It's easy to hate but that's a highly corrosive emotion. I detest the people who commit the atrocities. That goes double for the men behind the terrorist attacks. Maybe I do hate them,' he shrugged, 'I don't know. I do know I feel a boiling rage whenever there is an atrocity and I use that rage to channel my efforts into tracking down those responsible and ensuring they don't survive for long.'

Cathy nodded, her mouth turned down. 'You're right about the hate thing. It can take over your life. My niece's mother is my sister. As you can imagine she is bitter beyond belief to a degree that I think is spoiling her life.'

'How? But first, another brandy?'

Cathy looked at Hunter for a few seconds before replying. 'Yes to the brandy, thank you.'

Hunter gestured the waiter again.

'How?' Cathy repeated. 'By hating everyone and all things Muslim. I know how she feels and I have a great deal of sympathy but she takes it too far. When I said I hated the terrorists that's as far as it goes. I don't hate Muslims and I don't hate Islam. I don't like Islam. As a religion it has a great deal to answer for in the 21st century. But the majority of people who worship Muhammad on the whole are decent, law-abiding individuals.' She paused and then added, 'But, and it's a big but, it is so easy to lump all Muslims together and condemn them. I don't know,' she broke off and looked at the waiter. 'Thank you.' She summoned up a smile.

'It's a huge problem. One that's talked about endlessly by Western security services, armed forces and politicians the world over. I sometimes feel we're like children with our fingers in the dyke trying to hold back the deluge that is building up and will burst over us.'

'Sadly our reaction to the terrorists is what they want.'

'You mean to drive a wedge between Muslims and non-Muslims.'

'Yes, but we mustn't let it happen.'

'Cathy, I agree entirely. It's the fundamentalists I have problems with.' Hunter paused, took a sip of his drink and added, 'That goes for right wing Christians as well as other faiths.'

'So when can we expect this deluge?' Cathy asked.

Hunter shrugged. 'Soon, later, sometime, there's no way of knowing. But one thing must be acknowledged. We in the West think in terms of weeks, months, a few years. As far as the fundamentalists are concerned if it takes a thousand years they will work for an Islamic world based on the teachings of Mohammed.'

'Meaning mud huts, no sanitation, male dominance and praying half the day?'

'Yep. That about sums it up. Only prayers are five times a day and can be cut down to a couple of hours.'

Cathy smiled. 'That long?'

'Maybe I'm exaggerating. In fact, I'm sure I am. To be honest I don't know how long they take but I do know it's a lot longer than reciting "Our Father".'

'Are you religious?'

'No. Though a few times when things have been a bit hairy I've called on help from above. Is he listening? I doubt it. There must be at least a million prayers a day to the Almighty, if he's there.'

Cathy smiled again and said, 'Why shouldn't God be a woman?'

'I hope that is the case and when the Jihadists get to where they are going that's what they find.'

'They're all going to hell.'

'You're right. The biggest laugh of all would be to find the Devil is female.'

They both chuckled and their mood lifted. They finished their drinks, stood and headed for the lift. Once in the lift Cathy stood shoulder to shoulder with Hunter. He took her in his arms and they kissed until the lift stopped and the door opened.

When they stepped into the corridor Hunter asked, 'Your room or mine?'

'Mine, if that's okay with you.'

'Just as the lady desires.'

'The lady knows what she desires.'

The two men stood until invited to sit by the Prince. The German had been briefed in some detail by the other man as to the etiquette when in the presence of the Prince. He found it degrading and farcical but he was more than willing to go along with it. The fee hinted at was too high for him not to comply. The Prince waved an imperious hand and the two men sat facing him.

'I have read your dossier, Herr Gunther,' said the Prince, managing to stifle a cough, 'it is impressive.'

'Thank you.' The German was in his mid-forties, 5ft 11ins tall with narrow shoulders. He had been a marathon runner in his younger days, but the sport was now behind him. Too much road running had begun to affect his knees. Although fit for his age his main activity was as a practitioner in Taekwon-Do. He had a long, narrow face and a nose slightly too big. His ears had stuck out as a child but he had now had them pinned back though he was still self-conscious. His blond hair was thinning and swept back reaching down to his collar. His eyes were brown, he was clean shaven and had thick tufts of eyebrows. He was wearing a white shirt and red tie, a fawn coloured suit and light brown shoes.

'If it's true.'

The German narrowed his eyes and stared at the Prince. His instinct was to verbally lash out but his greed kept his response in check.

The Prince waited for a reply but received none. He nodded and Wajeeh picked up a file from the Prince's desk and opened it. Soliman was the head of the Prince's bodyguard.

Looking down, Soliman said, 'You are Michael Gunther, late of the KSK, the Kommando Spezialkräfte where you were a Sergeant.' The head of security looked up from his reading and glanced at the other man.

Gunther nodded, crossed his right leg over his left knee and did his best to look nonchalant. He wasn't finding it difficult. He hated Arabs, but they were good payers and this job would allow him to retire in style.

'According to this file you have been involved in a total of twelve assassinations, two of which failed.'

Gunther's eyes narrowed. How in hell did they know? 'If you say so.' He wasn't going to admit to anything. Besides which, they had their facts wrong. He had carried out eighteen successful assassinations and three botched jobs. None of which, he had convinced himself, were his fault. He made no attempt either to correct the numbers or justify what had gone wrong.

The Prince waited a few seconds, cleared his throat with a deceptively gentle cough and then asked, 'What happened?'

Gunther understood the question and shrugged. 'Circumstances interfered with two of the operations. There was also a degree of luck on the other party's side. These things happen. No operation can be foolproof. However, my success rate is exemplary. This is why you have come to me. We have a number of details to agree but they are precisely that, details.' Like his fee though he didn't say as much. 'I have accepted in principle despite the fact that I don't know who the target is.'

'Have you any idea?' The Prince's voice was a croak.

Gunther licked his lips, waited a few seconds and then nodded. 'According to the rumours your son was killed by a British naval officer. I can only surmise you want him dead.'

'That is correct. My son died before his time. It should not have happened.' This time the Prince coughed harshly, using his handkerchief to wipe his mouth. He flicked his hand towards Soliman, inviting him to carry on.

'His Royal Highness wants the man dead but also wants him to suffer.'

There was a knock on the door and two servants entered carrying trays of small cakes and a pot of coffee and one of tea. The items were placed on the desk and the servants left.

Soliman said, 'Please help yourself to the delicacies, they are exceptionally good. Tea is in the round pot, coffee in the tall one. Sugar and milk you can see.'

Gunther helped himself to coffee, black, no sugar. It was done in silence. Neither of the other two took anything. After a few seconds that stretched into half a minute he realised that they were waiting for him to expand on his statement.

'The man I believe you want me to kill is well known in certain quarters. His reputation goes before him. I cannot guarantee he will suffer, only that he will die.'

The Prince sighed, frowned and looked down at his hands resting on the desk. The Prince inclined his head towards Soliman.

'The Prince is offering a fee of 20 million dollars to ensure the man suffers.'

Gunther took a sip of his coffee. It left his mouth as dry as sawdust. Seconds passed in silence. Gunther licked his lips, thinking hard. So it was out in the open. No haggling, no pleading how difficult the job would be. Just like that. The highest paid assassination ever. It was a huge sum. Unprecedented in the world he inhabited. If the target was whom he thought it was then he figured there were only three other people in the world capable of carrying out the job, all of whom would give their eye teeth for the chance. However, if he was right about the target then he was without doubt one of the most dangerous men on the planet. The man's reputation was growing as was that of the organisation he worked for. On the other hand, if he succeeded, his name would go down in the history of assassins. That was assuming he was correct about the target's identity. It was still to be confirmed. Gunther nodded slowly.

'Does that mean you are willing to take the job?' The Prince spoke slowly before reaching for his oxygen mask and sucking deeply. His breathing became less laboured.

Gunther nodded again and croaked, 'Yes.' He cleared his throat and said again. 'Yes,' in a clear and loud voice.

The Prince used a finger to slide a second file across the desk. Soliman took it and opened the cover. He slid a series of coloured photographs towards Gunther who reached for them. They showed a man in various poses. One sitting at a restaurant table, another face on, shot from a hidden camera and a third, side on while he was driving a car. They weren't particularly good but they were adequate.

The face was slightly angular, the nose straight and narrow, the eyes blue. His hair and brows were black, while his mouth showed a sardonic smile as though he found life one big joke.

'This is the man,' said Soliman.

It was whom he had been expecting. He narrowed his eyes and asked, 'How many assets do you have in the West?'

'Hundreds,' was the stark reply croaked by the Prince.

The German stifled a sigh. Arabs were all the same, lying, exaggerating, duplicitous swine.

'I'm talking about people you can trust.'

Anger flashed in the Prince's eyes but before he could reply

Soliman spoke. 'We can trust them all. They are true believers and wish death to the infidels.'

Gunther felt like admitting that he was an infidel but thought better of it. He was honest with himself. He detested Arabs but he'd do business with the devil if it was lucrative enough.

'I appreciate that hundreds of jihadists have entered Europe and many into America, in spite of the avowed intention of the US president to stop Muslims from travelling to his country. Most are fanatics without any skills and without discipline. I wish to know if you have real assets who can move freely around the West and go where I tell them.'

The Prince looked at his head of security.

Nodding, Soliman addressed the Prince. 'Yes, your Royal Highness, we have 40 maybe 50 men we can count on.'

Gunther figured the man was still lying. He was boasting to him as well as the Prince who nodded in satisfaction.

'But,' the Prince lifted the facemask away from his face to croak, 'there are many more we can call on if we need to.'

It occurred to him that Arabs and other ethnic minorities from the Middle East and sub-Saharan Africa stood out like sore thumbs. If he was going to succeed he would have to pick his own crew. However, he would cross that bridge later. One or two names had already come to mind. Meanwhile he would keep the Prince happy.

'If I cannot do the job using the numbers mentioned then I shouldn't be in the business.' And I won't be after this one, he promised himself.

'I wish it done as quickly as possible,' said the Prince. He coughed harshly, unable to speak further. The need to hurry was all too obvious.

In reality it was the sort of job that couldn't or shouldn't be rushed. Gunther knew that wasn't to be. Hence the very high fee.

Taking a sip of coffee, he said, 'I wish for a list of names and contact details of your men. They must have European passports and be able to travel where and when they want. Or, more precisely, where I tell them to go.'

'It shall be done,' said the bodyguard.

Now came the difficult part. 'I want half payment now and the balance when I complete the job.'

'A quarter now,' rasped the Prince.

Hesitating, the permutations ran through Gunther's mind. Five million with the promise of another fifteen he couldn't be sure of collecting. But it was still a large sum. Slowly he nodded and said, 'All expenses will be taken care of?'

The Prince nodded, the oxygen mask back in position on his face

Soliman said, 'I will credit you an operational account to be used as and when you need the money. The account currently has one million dollars in it with access using a credit card. You can withdraw up to twenty thousand dollars at any one time at any bank in most countries in the world. Civilised countries that is.'

'I prefer payment by bank transfer. I can give you my account details.'

Soliman opened his jacket and extracted a number of cheques. He fanned them open. 'I have your money here. Fifteen, ten, seven and a half, ah, here it is. Five million.' He was about to hand over the cheque when he shrugged and put it back with the others. 'However, you prefer a bank transfer. It will be done.'

The little charade was not lost on the German. Cheques were never used. Apart from anything else they left a paper trail a blind man could follow. The fact was the Arab had been prepared to go to fifteen million. Ah well, too late now. He managed to cloak his annoyance with a smile.

'If you will follow me,' said Soliman standing up.

The German stood, then both men faced the Prince and bowed their heads. The ritual annoyed Gunther. Being subservient went against the grain.

Lifting the mask clear of his mouth the Prince said, 'Incidentally, Mr. Gunther, I won't tolerate failure.'

'I won't fail. But if I do I will be dead.'

'That's what I want you to understand. I also want a realistic time scale.'

The Prince coughed and used his handkerchief once more, crunching it in his hand, not looking at the mess it contained. Gunther let his eyes flicker to the hand before looking directly at the Prince.

'I cannot be precise. Normal targets have promulgated itineraries, most with known bodyguards with set procedures. This man has none of those. He is also an expert in his, let us call it, tradecraft.'

'I have been led to understand that you are also an expert.'

Waving his hand in the air as though flicking away a pesky fly, Gunther said, 'With all due respect your Royal Highness, you are missing the point. I need to learn more about him before I can launch an attack.'

'Do not take too long.'

Gunther was about to say that he would take as long as necessary but then he restricted his reply to 'I won't.'

'Keep me informed of your progress. You will have full access to Mr. Soliman,' he nodded in the direction of his head of security before breaking into a paroxysm of coughing, 'night or day, every day, either by phone, or e-mail.'

Gunther nodded in acknowledgement. 'Your Royal Highness, I shall expedite matters as much as possible but it will still take weeks to plan, but perhaps only a short time to implement.'

'It is often the way with these matters. This is not the first such order I have given.' The Prince stared at the German until the latter looked away.

The message was clear. He wouldn't hesitate to do so again.

Nothing further was said and the German and the Arab walked out of the room.

'What details do you have of the target?'

'Some. Let us go to my office and we can discuss it.'

'How do you want him to suffer?'

'By killing the ones he loves most.'

11

Gunther followed Soliman through a maze of corridors until they stopped outside a door with a sign in Arabic.

'What does that mean?' Gunther enquired.

'Head of Security, a job I take very seriously, Mr. Gunther.'

The room was large but unlike the rest of the palace was starkly furnished. There was a desk next to a window that overlooked the courtyard with a chair on either side. There was a coffee table with two leather chairs each side and walls covered with paintings of desert scenes. On the desk sat a computer and telephone.

Soliman sat at his desk and waved Gunther to the chair opposite.

'I believe the Prince made it very clear that we will not tolerate failure. Do you understand?'

Gunther stared into the eyes of the other man before nodding. 'Perfectly. What did the Prince mean when he said his son died before his time? He would have died during the attack anyway.'

'When he was killed he was wearing a suicide vest, only it was a dummy.'

'Why?'

'A number of reasons.'

'I'd like to know.'

Soliman drummed the fingers of his left hand on his desk while he considered whether to answer. Then he shrugged. 'The Prince's son has always given the impression of being devout. He followed all the correct rituals and acted within the letter of the Qur'an. He took part in a number of attacks but of course never blew himself up. Those with him died and thought he went with them. The son of a Prince? What could be more encouraging than that? However, there is a passage in the Qur'an that is never referred to. It says that whoever kills themselves will be punished in the same manner of death on the day of judgement. To be precise, suicide is forbidden however it is achieved.'

'I didn't know that.'

'Few people do. Particularly Muslims who consider they are partaking of a holy Jihad against the infidels.'

'People of other faiths don't go around killing indiscriminately.'

'I will have that philosophical debate with you some other time.'

Both men knew that would never happen but it was as good a way as any to change the subject.

Gunther said, 'I should explain that I work to my timetable and with my own people. I asked about help being available in Europe but to be used only as backup.'

Soliman seemed to think about it before nodding reluctantly. 'There is one thing you need to know.'

'What's that?'

'We have a number of operations running in Europe even as we speak. His Royal Highness made it clear that he wants the target to suffer. His Royal Highness has decided that the way to maximise his suffering will be to kill members of his family. One such operation is nearing fruition and should complete imminently.'

'I see. And if it succeeds what happens then?'

'It will be of little consequence. You will still take over. The members of his family are his sister and parents. All three must be killed before the target dies.'

Gunther nodded. It amounted to $5 million per corpse plus the expense account. Whichever way it went he would have sufficient to live a life of luxury. The big question was would he live long enough to collect it?

'But the target will be on the alert.'

'Possibly, possibly not.'

'When is the attack on the sister due?'

There was a few seconds silence. 'Tomorrow.'

Gunther nodded. 'Good. That will leave only three people to kill, elderly parents and the target.'

Soliman nodded acknowledgement. 'I assume you recognised the man.'

'Yes, his name is Hunter and he works for TIFAT based in Scotland.' Curiously enough when shown the photos by the Prince the operation felt unreal. Now it was coming home to him what he was taking on. It was too late to change his mind, he had already accepted the commission. He gripped the arms of the chair and stared at the man opposite. A bead of perspiration dampened his forehead and upper lip. He hoped Soliman didn't notice. Then he realised the man was looking at his forehead. He wanted to wipe it and then thought what the hell. He took out a handkerchief and dabbed his face.

'It's warm in here.'

'Yes.'

The Arab had a smirk that made Gunther want to punch him.

'Is the job too difficult for you?'

'This man has become well known in certain places as someone to stay clear of and that applies to the organisation he works for. Their successes are known worldwide. He won't be an easy man to kill.'

'There is no question of killing him until his family have been exterminated. Preferably dying, shall we say, from bad deaths? The more pain they suffer the happier the Prince will be.'

Gunther shook his head. 'Look, Mr. Soliman killing him is one thing, killing members of his family is something else entirely. He would come after us with all the power of his organisation and when, and I do mean when, not if, he catches us we would suffer very bad deaths indeed.'

Smiling, the Arab said, 'I thought they were an information gathering and report writing organisation.'

Gunther snorted. 'If you believe that then you believe in fairies.'

'I don't believe in either. Do you want the job or not?'

Gunther knew it was too late to back out. He nodded. 'Can I have some more time to think about it?'

'I am afraid not, Mr Gunther. The Prince wants this dealt with sooner rather than later. As you must realise he has not long to live. Killing this man has become an obsession with him. Ever since he found out he was responsible for his son's death.'

'How long ago did the son die?'

'Seven months, it has taken most of that time to find out what happened. It leaves us little time to find someone else. You have accepted the job. You will carry it out. I will give you a fortnight from tomorrow to complete your tasks. With the sister dead that should be time enough. If you fail, either the target will kill you or I will. Please don't make the mistake of thinking we are all incompetent buffoons. We choose not to get our hands dirty. We have enough money to pay for someone else to do our dirty work.' Soliman smiled. 'Can I get you tea or coffee?'

'A coffee, please.'

Soliman pressed a bell; a servant appeared and took the order.

'Would you care for a cigarette?'

'No, thank you, I don't smoke.'

'Very wise, it's a filthy habit, but so very addictive.'

The coffee arrived and was poured into delicate espresso cups by a young, subservient girl. She came and went without a word.

Gunther sipped his drink. As usual it was excellent. In the kingdom they made up for lack of alcohol with excellent teas, coffees and soft drinks. Outside the kingdom their hypocrisy shone through and many drank alcohol.

Soliman stood up, crossed to a cupboard, opened it and said, 'Here, catch.'

'What is this? It looks and feels like a cricket ball.'

'It looks like one but it's about fifteen percent heavier. It is a ball of specially modified PE with a barometric pressure switch. There are a number of settings.'

'I don't have any use for it.'

'I have decided to tell you about the operation currently taking place. One of the targets will be flying a plane out of Tenerife tomorrow.' He then explained what was to happen to Hunter's sister. If Gunther was horrified he didn't show it.

'If they succeed in killing the woman...'

'Then it is over to you. His parents are alive and live in a small Scottish village called Crosshall, near Edinburgh. They will be an easy target. Originally the intention was to delay three or four weeks to build on the pain of the sister's death. He would then lose his parents and suffer more pain. Then he would die. However, the Prince wishes to live long enough to see the target dead. I will emphasis the Prince wants him killed but only after he has lost those he cares about the most.'

Soliman had no idea who or what they were taking on. TIFAT had earned the reputation of being the most ruthless organisation in the West. They didn't kill or injure indiscriminately but with precision. If innocent people were likely to be hurt any operation was abandoned until an attack was safe. To date, as far as Gunther was aware, their success rate had been extraordinarily high, both in taking out their targets as well as protecting the lives of the innocent. The man in the photograph was recognised as not only ruthless but highly competent.

'Once his family members are dead then Commander Hunter is to suffer a long and painful death if it can be arranged.'

Gunther shook his head.

'You don't agree?'

'If anything happens to a member of Hunter's family he will come after us with all the force at his command. Given the resources and reputation of TIFAT that is considerable on both counts. Any delay in killing Hunter would be disastrous.'

'Then what do you advocate?'

'If the sister dies tomorrow then there is no trace back to us.' He meant himself but thought it best to associate himself with the Saudi. 'I will plan and implement an operation to kill the parents and Hunter at the same time. That's the best I can offer. If you would like to convey that to the Prince...'

Soliman shook his head. 'No. It would be better not to tell him. I will let him think that Hunter died at least a few days after his parents. He won't know any better and he can die a contented man.'

Silence reined for a few seconds.

'Do you want the job or not? You know the conditions and requirements.' He looked icily at the German, 'I can always arrange to cancel the contract.'

Gunther knew what he meant. He had long passed the point of no return when it came to the job. He was boxed in and both men knew it. He summoned up a smile.

'Of course I will take the job.'

Wajeeh Soliman watched the German depart. He couldn't help thinking about the road he had travelled to end up as the head of security to the Prince.

He and Abdul-Hameed, the Prince's son, had been close friends as children. They had been born on the same day, Soliman being a couple of hours older. While Abdul-Hameed was the son of a Prince he was the son of a couple who worked for the Prince. His mother was a first class chef and his father a talented carpenter whose job was to keep the palace in pristine condition. To help him he had a squad of 22 tradesmen, from plumbers, electricians and bricklayers to wood turners and painters.

By the time the boys were two they were virtually inseparable. Abdul-Hameed had even taken to eating in the kitchen with him. Although that wasn't so surprising as the alternative was the nursery. The nursery had been stuffed with toys, three nursemaids and an elder sister who liked to make the future Prince cry. The boy rarely saw his father unless he was sent for and displayed like a trophy. The Saudi royal family's attitude to their children pervaded their households. It was a case of children should be seen occasionally and not heard ever.

At the age of 13 Abdul-Hameed was sent to Eton. After six months he ran away. He went to the Saudi Embassy and demanded to be sent home. Instead of returning to Saudi Arabia he was taken back to the college and told not to leave again. So he wrote a letter to his father explaining that he was being bullied and that was why he had absconded and begged to return home. Instead of taking his son out of school, he sent Soliman to stop the bullying and protect Abdul-Hameed.

During the six months his friend had been in England, Soliman had taken up boxing, a sport he found he was good at. So far his prowess had been confined to the ring, the three-minute bell and the Marquess of Queensberry Rules.

Their reunion was a joyous occasion and it quickly became obvious who were the bullies. Two boys, older by two years and taller than Abdul-Hameed went out of their way to name call as well as bump into him whenever there were no masters around to intervene. The bullies had also nicknamed Abdul-Hameed 'Ham', a name that he found particularly offensive in view of his religion.

Soliman was often present when the bullies picked on Abdul-Hameed but they ignored him.

A few weeks after he had arrived at the school he found one of the boys alone in a side corridor. Soliman walked straight to the other boy who stopped in surprise. The boy began to abuse Soliman for his parentage as well as his nationality. Soliman stood with his hands on his hips and stared at him. The boy suddenly stopped talking and looked around nervously. They were alone.

As the boy took a step to walk around him Soliman hit him in the sternum with as much force as he could muster. The boy went flying backwards, hitting his head on the wooden floor. He was gasping for breath and for a second or two Soliman thought he was going to suffocate. Instead his breathing eased and he groaned. Soliman nudged the groaning body in the side using his foot.

'If you touch or abuse Abdul-Hameed again I shall put you in hospital.'

With that he turned and walked away.

He now needed to find the other one and teach him a similar lesson. A few minutes later he saw him but he wasn't alone.

He never had to lay a finger on the second boy. Both stayed clear of Abdul-Hameed as well as himself. It was about then that his friend declared his hatred of all things Western and non-Islamic and the longer he was at Eton, the deeper Abdul-Hameed's hatred became. In order that they remained friends Soliman needed to mirror Abdul-Hameed's attitude though it took some effort. Looking at the West with an open mind it was obvious that the people of non-Islamic cultures had a more free and better life. He had tried to persuade Abdul-Hameed to agree with him.

Instead, his friend saw only debauchery and non-believers who hated the one true faith. Soliman had tried to explain that the majority of people could not have cared less for Islam, the prophet and God but that seemed to inflame Abdul-Hameed even more. Finally, Soliman gave up. He would stay with his friend until they finished university and then they could go their own ways.

Abdul-Hameed learnt about the dark web and began using it. It didn't take long before he was fully radicalised and convinced that he needed to do something in the name of Islam. For a number of years all Abdul-Hameed did was talk about jihadism. However, he was slowly but surely being dragged further into its murky world. He had tried to persuade Soliman that it was his duty to God to go on what he called the spiritual journey with him but Soliman resisted. He had no intention of becoming a martyr.

Soliman enjoyed the fruits of the Western world. He liked the women he met and relished the social life. While he embraced the lifestyle his friend denigrated it but at the same time indulged himself. He called the women whores, alcohol was the drink of Satan and Jesus Christ was neither a prophet nor the son of God. There was only one true prophet and that was Mohammed. The bible was a work of fiction and only the Qur'an contained the true word of God.

Soliman had learnt to his cost not to contradict Abdul-Hameed. If questioned he would fly into a towering rage. He would quote certain passages from the holy book, usually out of context and often incorrectly. But that was typical of Abdul-Hameed. He never let the facts interfere with his prejudices.

While Abdul-Hameed stayed in Europe, Soliman had returned to Saudi Arabia and joined the Prince's protection squad. He had quickly risen to second-in-command and then taken over when the commander died in a car accident.

Abdul-Hameed was killed, along with the others, prior to a planned attack on a football match in Berlin. Their security had been poor but they believed that God was on their side and so they couldn't fail.

They never reached the venue. They never even left their staging post before they were killed.

The death of his son had festered in the Prince's mind and he had sworn he would have his revenge. It had taken some time and a great deal of money to identify those responsible. It had turned out to be the UN appointed organisation, The International Force Against Terrorism, also known as TIFAT.

Although the Prince had sworn to revenge the death of his son, he had done nothing about it. Now that he was dying of cancer he had become obsessed with achieving his objective.

Knowing TIFAT was responsible, the Prince had wanted an attack on the organisation and as many killed as possible. He had ordered Soliman to make the necessary arrangements and had made it clear that he expected Soliman to lead the attack. Martyrdom still held no appeal and so Soliman had tried to persuade the Prince that it was not possible to carry out his wishes. However, the Prince had insisted. Finally, in desperation, Soliman drew up a plan while at the same time exaggerating the organisation's defences. He had then suggested that an easier target would be to kill the man who had led the attack in Germany. At first the Prince had demurred but eventually came to the same conclusion as his head of security.

Soliman was sure that if he had not hired the German the Prince would have insisted on his direct involvement and that could easily have led to his death. He had no intention of dying for a cause he didn't believe in; he enjoyed life too much. He wasn't ready to meet God and doubted he ever would be. He wasn't a believer in any sense of the word.

The problem he faced was what to do once the Prince died. The majority of the family hated him and for understandable reasons. They knew he spent a large part of his time spying on them. The fact it was ordered by the Prince would not count in his favour in any way whatsoever. When the Prince died he knew he had only one choice and that was to abscond. He liked the word. It sounded better than run away. He was no coward but the thought of what could happen to him sent shivers down his spine. He was planning to escape as soon as possible after the Prince's death.

12

Nick and the others had arrived at the airport in good time. Louise went through the door marked 'Aircrew' while the other three went through to departures.

'Do you two never relax?' Cathy asked as they sat at a table with coffees in front of them. Both men had angled their chairs to watch the concourse, their backs to a wall their eyes moving continuously.

'Sure,' said Hunter, 'we are relaxed. You should see us when we're hyper.'

She looked from one to the other, smiled and said, 'I'd rather not, thanks.'

They made their way to the gate. They had been offered priority boarding courtesy of Hunter's sister but had declined choosing to be last instead. They had front row seats which gave more room for their legs and greater comfort.

Aiza Shaker checked her baggage. She had just turned 22 years of age and knew she would never see 23. By any description she was beautiful. She had long, shiny black hair, wide and large brown eyes, full lips and a slightly dimpled chin. She was slim, tall and a jihadist to her fingertips. Today she was dressed in loose fitting black trousers, a white blouse and a black hip length flared jacket. She had no headscarf and felt naked without it. It was bad enough not wearing her burqa but to go without her hijab made her feel as though she was being violated; unclean like the women non-believers. However, it was a great day in her life. She was going to achieve her objective. She was going to martyr herself in the name of Allah.

She hadn't been radicalised. She had grown up hating all things Western, a believer in Sharia law. Her parents had ensured her devout lifestyle from the day she was born and had indoctrinated her in the glory of martyrdom. It had only been a question of when and how she martyred herself. The when was now, the how was a bomb on an airplane full of non-believers. Any Muslims on board would also die for the greater good. *Inshallah.*

In the second ladies booth of the airport toilets next to the coffee shop she found the cricket balls hidden behind the cistern where she had been told they would be. She sat on the toilet and turned one of the balls in her hand. It was precisely as it had been described. Finally she gripped the ball either side of the seam and twisted it about 10 or 15 degrees. The fuse was ready for setting. A decrease in atmospheric pressure would open the tiny, sensitive plunger and an increase caused by the plane descending would complete the circuit. A timer would run for 30 seconds and the PE would explode. She had been told there would be a complete loss of control causing the aircraft to crash rather than blow it out of the sky. It would give the passengers time to fear the horror of their impending doom. She had questioned the ability of such a small amount of PE to do the job but had been assured that the new form of accelerant would make all the difference.

She completed setting the other two balls, placed them in a plastic container and wrapped it in decorated paper announcing it was a birthday present. The tag said it was for her dear cousin Abdul. She returned to the concourse just as her flight was called.

Boarding was just beginning and she joined the queue. The passengers shuffled along, showing passports and boarding passes. To her surprise, now that the time had come, she was unsure about what she was going to do. She looked at the happy faces around her.

She was suddenly overwhelmed with her desire to live. She wanted to turn and run. Looking at the children queuing politely she knew she wanted children of her own. She wanted to be loved, to live a normal life, to have a family and to enjoy the world as she had seen it away from the fighting and desolation that infested the whole of the Middle East. It hit her like a hammer blow. She wanted a life like the one experienced and enjoyed by the people of the Western world. At that thought she gasped in horror.

'Are you all right, dear?' An elderly woman standing in front looked over her shoulder.

'Yes, thank you.'

'If you're worried about flying don't forget it's the safest form of transport in the world. I tell myself that every time I take a flight. That and a large gin and tonic or two makes all the difference.' She smiled encouragement.

'Thank you, I'm all right.' Aiza summoned up a smile and added, 'But thank you anyway.'

That was something else about the West she had discovered. People were often nice to her. Polite and kind summed up many of those she had met over the years. In Saudi few if any women asked after a stranger. It wasn't done in their culture. The burka was a signpost saying don't come near me. And as for the men! She shuddered at the thought of their attitude towards the opposite sex.

She fought against feelings and thoughts that were totally alien to her. Feelings she had never experienced before. She realised that her own death in the abstract was one thing, imminent death was something entirely different.

She prayed like she had never prayed in her life, begging Allah for the will, the strength, to carry out her mission. She breathed deeply, her hands stopped shaking and she removed a tissue from her handbag to dab her forehead.

'Are you sure you're all right?' The same elderly lady asked again, looking at her, concern written on her face.

Aiza nodded. 'Yes. Yes, thank you.' She managed to smile again. She wished the woman would leave her alone.

'Where are you from? I'm from Edinburgh. Such a beautiful city.'

'Yes, isn't it. I'm from Syria.'

'That must have been awful. You're so lucky to have escaped the death and destruction. Is it as bad as they show on television?'

'Worse.' Now go away and leave me alone you old crone, she thought. They took a few more short steps forward. Some people were having their bags checked for size, and one or two bags were being taken to be stowed in the hold. Nobody objected. They knew the rules; they had just been trying it on. Her bag was a small backpack holding the gift-wrapped balls and a sweater. It was slung over her left shoulder and seemed to weigh heavily on her. She approached the desk and held out her passport and boarding pass.

The attendant looked at her with some concern. 'Are you all right, madam? You don't look too well. Is there anything you need?'

Aiza managed a smile and said, 'No, I'm fine thank you. I'm a nervous flyer but I assure you I'm okay.'

'Very good, madam.' Her passport and boarding pass were handed back and the automatic statement, 'Have a good flight,' ended the brief meeting.

Aiza continued her way towards the plane. She was using the front entrance, as her seat was 13A, which meant the port side next to the emergency exit.

She inched her way up the steps, was greeted with a phony smile and found her seat. She shoved her bag under the seat in front of her.

The Airbus A320 had 30 rows of seats, three each side of the cabin. Of the 180 seats available 97 were being used. There was also a cabin crew of four and a pilot and co-pilot. The total number of people onboard was 103. Aiza didn't know the exact number, only that it would be a mighty blow for Allah.

Her arrival in Jannah would be guaranteed. It was expounded regularly that men were greeted by 72 dutiful virgins to attend their every need. For women it was to spend eternity in a beautiful garden surrounded by vineyards and women made virgins again. For her 'again' did not apply. She would die a virgin. However, it was a great honour to serve God in the manner chosen by the Imam of her mosque. A great man, one who made it clear that he wished he too could carry out such an act. But his talents lay in planning the attacks. Now he was needed more than ever. With ISIS on the run in the Middle East, their attention was now focused on Europe.

Before being told to put any electrical devices to flight mode she switched off her mobile phone. There were no last minute calls to make. Her parents knew where she was and she had received their blessings and been told it was a great honour for the family. They had parted with guarantees that they would meet in Paradise.

'Morning, Isobel,' Macnair greeted his head of IT. Seeing her look he added, 'What's going on? You look as though you found ten pence and lost a tenner.'

'We had a heads-up from Mossad.' Isobel Sweeney was in her early fifties, attractive, fair hair with streaks of grey, dedicated to her work but known to have an occasional liaison when it suited her. She acknowledged to herself that her desires in that direction were waning. She put it down to age.

Mossad was the Israeli secret service and acknowledged as being the most effective organisation of its type in the world. That accolade didn't bother Macnair but it did rankle with the CIA. They thought of themselves as the pre-eminent anti-terrorist organisation. Macnair left them the delusion.

'I'll cut to the chase. They believe there's a bomb on the plane that Nick and Chris are on.'

Macnair kept his usual poker face and nodded. 'May I?' He indicated the coffee machine, crossed the room and poured himself a mug. He took it black, no sugar. He waved the pot at Isobel who shook her head.

'No, thanks.'

'When did you find this out?'

'About ten minutes ago. We're checking the story right now. Leo and Gareth are cross-referencing information that came in overnight.'

The General sat down opposite Isobel and stretched out his legs. The casual pose was in sharp contrast to his thoughts.

'How sure are we?'

Isobel shrugged but looked bleak. 'Pretty sure. Remember the report a couple of weeks back about the cricket ball explosive device?'

'Of course.'

'The Israelis have done some more digging. The explosive is an enhanced form of RDX.'

'How enhanced?'

'As you know, RDX is about one and a half times more powerful than TNT. If its compressed to a gravity reading of 1.7 in a confined space it will explode at a rate of 27,000 feet per second. The gravity reading is 2.1 and so the actual force will be significantly improved.'

'I didn't know that.'

'The gravity reading refers to the actual compression of the molecules of the explosive. The closer together the molecules the more powerful it becomes. The Israelis also told us that they are using an improved accelerant.'

'The jihadists are all the time becoming more sophisticated, more violent and more deadly.'

Isobel shrugged and replied, 'We know.'

'Sorry, Isobel. I'm thinking aloud. The jihadists are like the hydra.'

'You mean cut off one head and two grow back.'

'Precisely.'

'If they are able to manufacture this explosive on a large scale then we are in serious trouble. Its production must be stopped.' Then she shrugged. 'I apologise for stating the obvious.

'How did Mossad find all this out?'

'They knew about the balls but had no way of knowing where they were being made. Then they had a piece of good luck. Do you know anything about the medical side effects connected to prolonged exposure to RDX?'

'Not a thing. I didn't know there were any.'

'Prolonged exposure has neurological effects when inhaled or ingested and can result in seizures.'

'How does it become ingested?'

'Believe it or not from chewing C4 as an intoxicant.'

'You have to be kidding.'

Isobel shook her head. 'There's no reason for doing so but people do it. When making the RDX they inhale the dust which, in excess, can lead to a kind of seizure..'

'Good, I hope it's fatal.'

'Rarely. The body returns to normal if there is no exposure for a few weeks.'

'That's all very interesting but where's this leading?'

'A consultant at a hospital in Riyadh did some tests on a patient who'd had a seizure. Just routine blood and urine samples. To cut a long story short he was able to identify the problem as exposure to RDX. He passed the information to a contact who passed it to the Israelis.'

'That's a bit unusual, isn't it? Someone in Saudi passing info to the Israelis?'

'Malcolm, you know all too well that not all Muslims are jihadists, not even fundamentalists.'

'Yes I do know.'

'Because he recognised the symptoms he understood what it meant.'

'Indiscriminate bombings resulting in death and injury.'

'Precisely, not just men, women and children but people of all religions, nationalities and colour.'

'A brave man,' said Macnair. 'He helps to restore one's faith in humanity.' Macnair sipped his coffee before asking, 'Anything else?'

Macnair was managing to keep his cool though he wanted to rant and rave. Not only were two of his best men in imminent danger but so were over a hundred innocent people.

'Yes. Mossad are sending someone to brief us on what's happening.'

'Did they say why they were coming?'

'No but I suspect they want to dump the lot in our lap.'

Nodding, Macnair said, 'I suppose they have no choice.'

He didn't need to spell it out. To get any of the other government agencies involved, such as the CIA or MI6 and the SAS would take too long. Asking one or other of them to operate in a foreign country would involve cutting through a lot of red tape. It would be worse for a country considered to be a friend of the West, and would mean jumping through many hoops before a decision was taken. The Saudis were recognised as one of the top three countries financing and supporting terrorism worldwide. The other two were Pakistan and Iran.

The inability of the West to act against terrorism had been one of the reasons used to support the formation of TIFAT with its wide ranging mandate. Macnair had stated that if the sewers where the terrorists lived were to be cleaned, someone had to crawl down there and do the cleaning. It took a number of horrific attacks on the West before agreement was reached for TIFAT to be established.

It was Macnair who had argued for it and as a result was given command. He knew it was a poisoned chalice. Already the politically correct, left wing, anal retentives as he liked to describe them, were trying to close them down. It was only due to the support of the US President and numerous other leaders that they still existed. The Prime Minister of the UK was proving to be weak and useless when it came to the fight against terrorism. TIFAT's successes were legendary but even so siren voices were baying in the background. Human rights lawyers were continually raising their sanctimonious heads. It was a highly lucrative business for them, who claimed they were not doing it for the money. Few people believed them. The money was paid mainly by the Saudis and Pakistanis, through front organisations dedicated to the destruction of Western intelligence agencies and other specialist services.

The most recent situation made Macnair's blood boil. Three Iraqis had taken the British government to court where it was argued that they had been held in stressful situations for a month. They were awarded £30,000 each in compensation. At the same time the same government was offering a £10,000 bounty to any senior non-commissioned officer who rejoined the army. Both these incidents occurred in the same week and were virtually ignored by the press.

What made matters worse was the fact that Macnair knew about the three Iraqis. They were jihadists to the depth of their souls.

'How effective is the stuff?' Macnair asked Isobel.

'They tested another ball earlier today. It's powerful.'

'Do they have any idea what could happen to the aircraft if one goes off?'

Shaking her head slowly Isobel answered, 'No, it's possible the aircraft would be blown out of the sky or lose control and crash.'

'Have they any suggestions what to do about the ruddy things?'

'One thing is for sure. Under no circumstances try and open the ball and defuse it. Once set it can't be made safe. The increase in pressure as the plane descends sets a special fulminate fuse that eventually sets off the main explosive. It's very clever and, worse still, highly sophisticated.'

13

Hunter settled on a sausage roll and coffee. When he'd finished eating he leant back and closed his eyes. Flight time was 4hrs 50mins or so depending on headwinds. Like most servicemen he had the knack of dozing at any time.

Bletchley followed suit.

Hunter was in 1D, starboard side, aisle seat. Cathy was next to him and poked him in the ribs. He opened his right eye enquiringly and smiled.

'Thanks for a lovely weekend,' she whispered.

'Think nothing of it. Thank Louise. Besides, I want to thank you. Maybe we can do it again sometime?'

Smiling, she replied, 'Yes, maybe.'

This time he opened his other eye and looked at her more closely. 'I'd like to do that. Take a cruise along the north east of Scotland.'

'A cruise?'

'Yes. Didn't Louise tell you I live on a boat?'

'No. She forgot that small detail. She was too busy telling me all about your other, shall we call them foibles?'

Hunter chuckled. 'Foibles is a good word. But that's my sister being polite.'

'She's important to you, isn't she?'

'Aren't all sisters when it comes to their brothers?'

'Nooo,' she drew out the word, 'I can assure you of that.'

'Oh?'

'Long story. It'll keep for another time.'

'So there's to be another time?'

'I guess so. A cruise sounds like it might be fun. Though there's a condition.'

'And that is?'

'The wine doesn't spill when we reach the open sea.'

'I can assure you of that.'

'Oh? How can you be so certain?'

'I have a set of non-spill wine glasses.'

'Seriously?'

'Seriously. Made of glass with a lid like a child's cup to drink through.'

'I've never heard of them.'

'I'm not surprised. I know the glass blower who made them for me.' He chuckled. 'I promise you it's true.'

'Okay, I'm being tempted. I suppose the side benefits are adequate but I guess I can get them improved.'

Hunter raised his left eyebrow and asked, 'Are you complaining?'

Cathy laughed. 'No, it's my applied sense of humour.'

'Applied?'

'Yes, Louise told me you and the rest of your team like puerile and infantile jokes so I'm merely obliging.'

Hunter smiled. 'I knew I could rely on my sister to put in a good word.'

'She did. Oh, she did. I thought too many at first.'

'And now?'

'And now I'm not so sure. Jackie,' she spoke to one of the stewardesses standing next to the drinks cart, 'can I get a coffee please with just milk?'

'Sure, Cathy,' the stewardess replied, pouring fresh brewed coffee into a cardboard mug and handing over a little milk. 'Had a pleasant stay?' She looked at Hunter who deigned not to notice.

Cathy shrugged. 'It was okay, I guess. You know how these things are.'

'I sure do.' She raised her left hand and jiggled the single diamond ring with her thumb.

'Who?'

'James Cavanagh.'

Cathy laughed again. 'Good luck.'

'Thanks. Sir, can I get you anything?'

'Please. Another coffee, thanks.'

The stewardess was joined by a steward who went to the front of the trolley. They began to push it along the aisle, their faces plastered with matching smiles.

'I hope she knows what she's doing,' said Cathy.

'What do you mean?'

'I told you, a stewardess dreams of marrying an airline pilot. Good salary, comfortable life style, raise a couple of kids and join the local women's groups.'

'And reality?'

'Apart from boredom and separation there's the nagging thought that on the overnighters they're not being faithful. After all, some of the pilots are on their second and third marriages. Yet we never learn.'

'We?'

'I was engaged to a captain a couple of years ago. All was idyllic, lovey-dovey, and a complete bust.'

'What happened?'

'Do you really want to know?'

Hunter shrugged. 'Only if you want to tell me. You started down the conversational track we're on.'

'So I did. Let's just say he made Casanova appear saintly and chaste.'

'I'm sorry to hear it. But his loss is my gain.'

'Louise also said to be wary of you, that you're a charmer. I guess she's right.'

'That's the result of naval training and the pursuit of the finer things in life.'

'Is that how you see me? One of the finer things in life?'

'The finest.' He leant closer to her and kissed her cheek.

'I'm not sure if that's a compliment but I'll accept it as such.'

They finished their drinks in companionable silence, Hunter leaned back, closed his eyes and thought about Cathy. Plenty of plus points but not long term was his reluctant conclusion.

He was dozing when there was a light tap on his shoulder and he opened his left eye to look up at Jackie's face hovering close to his.

'Commander, you're wanted in the cockpit,' she whispered.

Nodding, he looked at Cathy who shrugged. Bletchley had also opened his eyes. Hunter undid his seatbelt, stood, stretched, stepped the few paces to the cockpit door and went in. His sister and the co-pilot were looking over their shoulders as he did so. Both looked bleak.

'It's General Macnair for you, Nick.' She indicated the jump seat next to the rear bulkhead.

As he picked up the headphones he asked, 'What is it?'

'No idea, he just said it was important.'

Hunter sat down and placed the headphones over his ears. 'Sir?'

'Ah, Commander.'

Hunter knew that whatever it was, it was bad. Being called Commander as well as the tone was evidence enough.

'What's up, sir?'

'There's no easy way to tell you but we're pretty certain there's a bomb onboard the plane.'

Hunter didn't so much as twitch as he looked from his sister in the left-hand seat to the co-pilot in the right. They were both staring at him.

'I see. Have you any details?'

'Some. The Israelis discovered that the Iranians got their hands on some modified plastic.'

'How modified?'

'Enough to make it twice as powerful as it would be normally.'

Hunter swore under his breath. 'How do we know?'

'Mossad gave us the heads up about your aircraft. We had ECHELON look at any and everything connected to the airline and we found that its crew roster has been penetrated. One name was of particular interest.'

'Louise?'

'Correct. The information was downloaded to a computer in Greece. We have the location and we'll follow it up later. In the meantime we need to deal with this little problem.'

'Do we know what to look for?'

'Believe it or not, a cricket ball.'

'Did you say cricket ball?'

'Yes. The explosive is pressure controlled.' Macnair went on to explain what they knew.

When he'd finished Hunter was silent for a few seconds and then said, 'Okay, it's a problem but we should be able to deal with it. Surely such a relatively small amount of explosive can't bring an aircraft like this down.'

He heard his sister gasp and looked at the two pilots. She was staring at him, horror struck, as was the co-pilot.

'Nick, how sure are we there is a bomb? Are we a hundred per cent sure?'

'No.'

'More than eighty?'

'Yes.'

'Is it in the hold?'

Louise was firing questions at him.

'Not likely, it's probably in the cabin. If it was in the hold the power of the explosion could be dissipated enough so that the plane lands safely. If it's in the cabin the plane may not crash but people would die.'

Hunter was about to add that Louise wouldn't be hurt but changed his mind. He didn't want to spook her further by telling her she was the target.

'Do we know anything else? Anything that can help us?' he asked Macnair.

'Not really. Once set there's no way of accessing the inside. The Israelis said it's one of the cleverest detonation devices they've ever seen.'

'Is Don with you?'

'He's talking to some engineers at Airbus,' the General replied.

'We're sure it's a pressure mounted switch?' Hunter asked.

'Positive. It has the attributes of being robust while at the same time sensitive to any pressure difference.'

'Any?'

'According to the Israelis, the difference between sea level and cruising altitude.' Macnair tried not to sound alarmist but failed.

'Any other good news?' asked Hunter, dryly.

'Now that the plane is at cruising altitude the detonator is probably set.'

'Probably?'

'Almost inevitably. So if you descend at some point it will explode.'

'I appreciate that, sir. So why don't we keep the cabin pressure low, at the same level all the way down?'

'It doesn't work that way,' said Macnair. 'It helps to keep the cabin pressurised at height but automatically allows the pressure to increase as the plane descends. In theory, one less thing to go wrong.'

The cockpit door opened and Chris Bletchley entered. He looked from one face to the next and asked, 'What's up?'

'There's a bomb onboard,' replied Hunter, his hand covering the microphone.

Bletchley nodded and smiled at his fiancée who managed a wan smile back.

Louise lifted her hand and turned to face out the cockpit. She acknowledged the call. 'Changing now.'

The plane began a slow and gradual change of course to starboard.

'Has Louise received the new flight plan?' Macnair asked.

'She's altered course to starboard about fifteen degrees.'

'Eight,' said his sister over her shoulder.

'Where are we going?' Hunter asked.

Macnair was quick to reply. 'To Samedan airport.'

'St. Moritz?'

'Correct. It's the highest airport in Europe at 5,600 metres.'

153

'Nice call, sir.'

'It's not mine. It's Don's.'

'Tell him I'll buy him a pint when we get back. Will it help?'

'We don't know but hope so. Don's got a few ideas he'll share with you. Where are you now?' Macnair was beginning to sound more positive.

'Where are we Louise?'

'Hang on.' She flicked a couple of switches. 'Malcolm can you hear me?'

'Loud and clear.'

'We're just past Gib. That's a thousand miles to go. So ETA St. Moritz is 14.53 in just about three hours time.'

Louise looked as cool as a cucumber but Hunter could see the slight tremor in her right index finger as she fiddled with the satnav. At that moment he could not have been more proud of her. Which was more than he could say for the young co-pilot who appeared to be on the verge of bursting into tears. Louise looked over her shoulder at Hunter who managed a grimace of a smile and nodded at the co-pilot.

'Matthew,' said Louise. There was no response. 'Matthew,' she said with more vigour, prodding him in the arm, 'check course and distance to go as well as ETA at St. Moritz.'

Matthew seemed to come out of a trance and looked at Louise. Tears started to trickle down his cheeks. 'I don't want to die,' he whispered.

Louise looked at the young man intently. If she felt any pity for him she didn't show it. 'Man up, Matthew, or by God I'll slap you. The passengers, crew and plane, in that order, are our responsibility. Once this is over if you want to keep your job you'd better get control of yourself.' She appeared to relent slightly and jerked her thumb over her shoulder at the two TIFAT officers, 'These two thugs are amongst the best professionals in the world for dealing with this problem. We're just lucky to have them onboard.'

The co-pilot nodded, wiped his face on the back of his shirt sleeve and started pushing buttons and turning knobs.

'Nick?'

'Yes, Don.'

'I've been speaking to a couple of structural engineers in Toulouse with regards the strength of the plane.'

'Any good news?'

'Maybe, I'm not sure. The plane you're on is only a couple of years old. Its structural integrity is like nothing that has come before. There are no guarantees but certain struts and crosspieces and a host of other technical connections have been strengthened to withstand a possible explosion.'

'That sounds good.'

'Yes, but that's only passing a test on the ground. The real problem is the effect of the air pressure difference. The internal forces on the hull are huge due to the difference between the pressure at cruising altitude and the ambient pressure in the cabin. The slightest rupture could result in damage to the hull then it's all over.'

'Thanks for sugaring the pill, Don, it's much appreciated.'

'You'd have it no other way.'

'True enough. What you say makes sense.'

There was a low moan. Hunter leant forward and ripped the headset of the co-pilot. 'Shut up! Sorry Don. The co-pilot is having a meltdown. Carry on.'

'If the explosive isn't touching the hull then the blast is dissipated in all directions. That could be enough to prevent a catastrophe. The Israelis have sent schematics and photos of the firing mechanism and I must say it's pretty cute.'

'Don, save your admiration for later.' Hunter sounded slightly critical.

'Sorry, Nick, but we've plenty of time. Trouble will begin on landing.'

'Thanks for that. It's a comfort to be reminded.'

'The point is, the change doesn't have to be that great in actual pressure but the gauge is highly sensitive and has a distance of just 1.5 centimetres to travel.'

'How will that help?'

'It's the reason you're being diverted. That slight change in height above sea level could make all the difference.'

'Between detonation or not?'

'Yes. But there is another plus.'

'Yeah, I've got it. We'll be closer to the ground, less distance to go, less height to travel, less pressure on the hull.'

'Right. It's not much but it's all we have right now.'

'Thanks, Don.'

'There's one other thing. Don't try to defuse the bomb. The Israelis have tried and the ball has exploded each time.'

'Okay, thanks. I'll buy you a beer or two when we get back.' He broke the connection.

Louise stared at her brother and said, 'When, not if? Always the optimist Nick, and I love you for it.'

14

Aiza could feel her hands sweating. Beads were also appearing across her forehead and she wiped them away with a paper handkerchief. She felt sick. She wanted to take out the sick bag and empty her stomach. She also wanted to empty her bowels. Oh God, what had she agreed to do? What had she done? In the abstract it was simple. Blow up a plane and kill many non-believers. But here she was sitting next to a young girl about seven or eight years old who was being nice to her. She prayed like she had never prayed in her life. What could she do? How could she stop it? How could she save the people? The fact was, she couldn't. That had been made clear to her right from the beginning. There was no turning back. It was a one way ticket to Jannah.

For most of her life she had been indoctrinated with the notion of martyrdom and becoming a good wife. She had never managed to reconcile the two ideas and so had never married. This was in spite of being pressured by her parents to marry a distant, older cousin. Then on her 18th birthday she announced she would never marry and that she was preparing herself for holy jihad. Her parents had been ecstatic.

She had been responsible for at least a dozen deaths in two years after intensive training with ISIS. Now she was going to kill over a hundred men, women and children, possibly more when wreckage from the plane hit the ground. How would she be remembered? Honoured by the believers, vilified by the non-believers?

It was of no matter. Being vilified by non-believers was of no consequence. Being revered by those of the one true faith was everything.

'Are you all right?' asked the little girl.

Summoning up a smile, Aiza replied, 'Yes, thank you. She reached for the sick bag, put it to her mouth and dry heaved. She hadn't eaten or drank for the best part of a day.

'Are you okay, miss?' asked the steward.

She wanted to scream at him, to go away. To leave her alone. That they were all going to die and she would be responsible. Her hands began to shake and she put them between her legs and squeezed. After a few seconds the tremors lessened and she had control of her breathing and her stomach.

'I am sorry, but I'm fine now. I think I ate something that disagreed with me.'

'If you need anything just ring the bell.'

She nodded, turned her head and stared out of the window. What if she told the crew what was happening? Could they do something? But what? The design had been explained in detail in order to make sure she didn't try and stop the explosion. Once jihad was implemented nothing was to stop it. She reached under the seat in front of her and lifted out the bag, clutching it on her lap.

Macnair looked worried, which was inevitable in the circumstances. It wasn't just the situation but how were they to stop the bomb exploding? Reducing the actual impact of the explosion was all well and good in theory, but in reality? There wasn't a lot they could do but he knew that anything, however seemingly inconsequential, could make all the difference. From what Don Masters had told him the fractional change in air pressure could mean the difference between the bomb exploding or not.

'Are you okay, Malcolm?' Isobel broke the silence.

'Yes, thanks, Isobel. I just hope Nick can identify the bomber and find the ball in the cabin. It may give them a chance. Speaking of which, how are your guys getting on?'

'I have twelve people combing the CCTV as well as Leo and Gareth.'

The vast majority of passengers are not aware that as they follow

158

the roped passages through security at an airport, they are being photographed. The black, glass domes in the ceiling hold the cameras. The images are flashed through a face recognition system that can single out a passenger identified as "a person of special interest". Any person so identified would be taken from the queue for questioning. It is why people must follow the roped lines even if there is no queue to ensure the system has time to do its job.

'Anything to report yet?' asked the General anxiously.

'Nothing yet,' Isobel replied then, looking behind the General said 'Yes, Leo? Have you something for us?'

'It looks like it.'

He sat in front of a large screen mounted on one of the office walls and tapped a few keys. The screen came to life showing a video of Tenerife South Airport. People were milling around the concourse, some hurrying, most ambling, many looking lost and anxious as they scrutinised the departure display boards.

'What are we looking at?'

Leo pointed. 'See this woman?'

'Attractive young lady,' said Macnair.

'Watch.'

They watched as the woman went into the ladies toilet and returned soon after.

'So?' Macnair said.

'Now look at her as she queues up to show her boarding pass.'

After a few minutes Isobel said, 'She doesn't look too good.'

'She's showing all the classic signs of stress, anxiety...'

'And fear,' said Macnair, finishing Leo's sentence.

'Precisely.'

'Maybe she's afraid of flying,' said Isobel.

Both men looked dubious. 'Just being devil's advocate. But it is possible.'

'Do we know who she is?' Macnair asked.

Leo turned and faced the other two. 'Yes, her name is Aiza Shaker.'

'What do we know about her?, enquired the General.

'According to her passport she's a Syrian. We're checking that but so far it seems to be true. We've asked the cousins but they've nothing on her. In their vernacular she's a clean skin. However, we've done some deep digging. Her father has the reputation of being a real hardliner. A fundamentalist to his finger tips. The National Security Agency has had him in their sights for years. He's made a lot of noise but not been directly active. His eldest son left Syria two years ago and vanished probably somewhere in Europe.'

'Is he a threat?' Macnair asked.

'I asked the Yanks the same question and they were honest enough to say they couldn't be sure. However,' he emphasised the point by raising a finger, 'they don't think he is.'

That meant nothing. There were thousands of fundamentalists who were hiding in plain sight across the Western world. They weren't jihadists ready to die for the cause but they were supporters who helped by giving money and aid if asked.

'What's your analysis?'

'Sir, I think she's involved.'

'So do I. Are there any other likely suspects?'

Leo shrugged. 'You know how it is, sir. There are no obvious accomplices. She could be innocent and there could be a fair haired, white convert fanatic amongst that lot who is the actual bomber.'

Macnair nodded and said, 'Possible but unlikely.'

Leo looked at the General and said 'I'll stake all I own that she's the one.'

'What about luggage?'

'She checked a bag into the hold.'

'So the ball could be in the hold?'

'Yes, but that's to our advantage,' said Isobel.

Macnair nodded. 'The explosion could be absorbed by the bags and suitcases surrounding it. If the plane is low enough there's a good chance of there being no injuries.' Macnair was always honest with himself. It was wishful thinking but he was ever the optimist, hence he hoped for the best but planned for the worst.

'Sir, if you look at the bag she's taking on board it hardly seems big enough for more than a few basic items. But more than enough for a cricket ball or two.'

'If the ball explodes in the cabin people will die even if the plane doesn't crash. There is less likelihood of death and injury if it explodes in the hold.'

Isobel said, 'Unless there is serious damage to the hull.'

'That goes without saying,' Macnair said with some irritation. 'We're in uncharted waters,' he continued. 'There have been plenty of computer simulations showing the effects of an explosion of varying magnitudes in a plane. Along with different locations and altitudes. But it's all best guesswork. Now we have to add a different explosive and a relatively small amount. There's no telling the outcome.'

Gloom settled over them then Leo coughed diffidently.

'Yes, Leo?' Macnair asked.

'Just an idea, sir. Supposing her suitcase in the hold has more explosive and that's meant to bring the plane down?'

'Then why have a ball in the cabin?' Isobel enquired.

'To ensure the girl dies. If the plane lands and there is no explosion for some reason then all it means is that they will try again and in theory, nobody would be any the wiser. But suppose it goes off and there are survivors including her? It wouldn't take long to identify the source of the explosion and find out who's behind the attack and so it's imperative she is dead. The ball in the cabin would also kill quite a few passengers so in their minds it's a win win situation.'

There was a short silence before Macnair and Isobel both nodded agreement.

Macnair pondered all he had heard and said, 'If the plane is blown out of the sky everyone dies and probably some people on the ground also. Or if the bomb goes off and the plane doesn't crash a lot of people die anyway. The latter figure in the tens as opposed to a hundred plus.'

'There may be more than one ball,' Isobel suggested.

Just then Masters said, 'Sir, a message from Mossad about the firing system.'

'Tell me it's good news.'

'I wouldn't go that far sir. As we now know, the actual connection is electronic. The power comes from the small flat batteries like those used in a hearing aid. An increase in pressure slowly lowers the upper terminal onto the lower and that's it. So the difference in pressure is only marginal to allow the terminal to travel.

'Go on,' said the General.

'Yes, sir. The point is, the difference in atmospheric pressure at sea level compared to the airport, even if a tiny fraction, could be a game changer.'

Macnair nodded. 'So it's possible the bomb won't explode?'

Masters replied, 'Sir, you know how it is with the more sophisticated explosive device, anything can go wrong.'

'Any idea how stable it is?'

'The Israelis say very stable. It's been kicked and thrown without exploding.'

'Maybe they just don't work,' Macnair said hopefully.

'They carried out a pressure test in an atmospheric box. It worked perfectly three times. We've checked the atmospheric pressure at Samedan and if the readings we have are accurate then it's touch and go.'

'So what you're saying is it could go either way,' said Isobel.

'By the merest fraction,' Masters replied.

'I'll speak to Nick,' said the General picking up the headset.

Hunter glanced at the display that had just flashed up when Louise pressed the requisite button.

'Wheels down in 48m 37s and ticking.' She glanced at Hunter and then looked further around at Bletchley. 'There's never a dull moment with you two.' She paused, 'Nick, I've got the General for you.'

'Yes, sir?'

'There's a young woman in seat 13A. We're pretty sure she's the bomber.'

'How sure?'

'Better than ninety percent.'

'Thanks sir. That's good enough.'

'Something else.' The General went on to explain their theory about bombs in the hold and the bomb in the cabin.

'Any good news?' Hunter said with a hint of desperation.

'I've got Don here. He has a few things to tell you about the mechanism.'

'Nick, we had some more info from the Israelis.' Masters explained about the firing mechanism.

'I guess that's something. But still very much in the lap of the gods.'

'Yes. They've also run some live tests. The new formula RDX and accelerant makes a significant difference.'

'So we were told. Anything else?'

'Possibly. Nick, if the bomb explodes when you're near the ground and the hull is ruptured, there's still a good chance you can make the landing.'

'That's what we're banking on.'

'We know the damage will be caused by the pressure wave but there's no shrapnel to inflict any physical injury though flying debris could be a problem.'

They had seen it before. People killed without a mark on them, internal organ failure caused by the pressure wave.

Hunter said, 'We can do something about that.'

'According to the computer the first few rows of seats next to the bomb will either be ripped out of the deck or their backs will bend. But by the time the blast has travelled ten to fifteen rows the pressure will have reduced to such an extent the seats should hold.'

'I guess that's something.' Hunter sounded a bit more hopeful.

Masters continued with his remarks. 'The seats can take a reasonable pounding and each one that's hit reduces the force of the explosion.'

'You don't say.'

'Sorry, Nick. I didn't mean to preach.'

'Okay then we'll get as many people as we can to lay down on

163

their stomachs, put their hands over their ears, and point crossed feet towards the ball,' said Hunter.

'That's what I'd suggest,' said Masters.

'What does the computer say about the blast along the aisle?' Louise asked after listening in.

'Those people lying in the aisle will feel the blast. How bad we can't be sure but in theory they should survive.'

'That's some comfort. What happens when it hits the cockpit door?' Louise was looking at her brother.

Masters answered. 'We ran a computer program three times.'

'And?'

'It's hard to say. We used slightly different parameters and each time of course we had different results.'

'Which were?'

'The first time the door flew open, the second time it held and the third time the door ended up hanging on its hinges.'

'And the pilots?'

'Their seats held. No injuries just burst eardrums.'

Hunter said, 'It's a pity the cockpit windows don't open. The blast could dissipate that much more easily. But Louise, once in landing mode, you can ignore piloting the plane, just lean forward and keep down below the top of your seats.'

They all knew that modern aircraft can land and take off without human help. Everything, including wheel brakes and air brakes worked automatically as did keeping on a straight line to the landing point. That was assuming everything did work and there had been no interference with the process, such as an explosion.

'Okay, Don, thanks for all that. I'll speak to you later.' He didn't add 'hopefully' but thought it. 'Actually, hang on a sec. How does the pressure change work? Surely there needs to be some sort of access to the mechanism for the change in pressure to register.'

'The terrorists thought of that. The ball has a small star embossed in it. The Israelis first thought a hole could be hidden in its centre but they were wrong. What they've discovered is once the two halves of the ball are twisted and the switch set, the two halves act as a pressure pad. That's the best way I can explain it.'

'I get it. It was just an idea. A piece of sticky tape over the hole could have solved the problem. Thanks Don. Speak to you later.'

'What's going on?' Cathy asked.

'Just a problem at HQ, nothing of importance.' Hunter didn't like lying but he couldn't be sure how Cathy would react. They needed to keep the passengers as quiet as possible for as long as possible. There was going to be enough distress as it was. He just hoped the phlegmatic British kept their collective nerve. He had what his family referred to as a misplaced faith in the bulldog spirit of the British. Today he'd find out how right or wrong he was.

He stood up and walked the length of the plane, heading for the toilets in the rear, looking along the port row of seats. Everyone appeared to be in high spirits. A few were taking advantage of drinks and snacks though quite a number were entertaining their kids to keep them quiet.

There was one anomaly in the pack. The young woman in 13A. She wasn't looking too well but that didn't mean anything. In spite of what he had been told it was possible she was an innocent who was frightened of flying. Besides, statistically the bomber was more likely to be a man. Usually relatively young, ill at ease and mumbling to himself as he prayed to Allah. Hunter was double-checking as best he could. He saw nobody who fitted the profile.

When he returned to his seat Bletchley looked at him and shook his head. He then leaned back and closed his eyes playing one scenario after the other through his mind. Finally, he settled on the best thing to do. He just hoped it was enough.

Hunter checked the time, leaned forward and spoke softly. 'Twenty minutes and then we move,' he said to Bletchley while Cathy stared intently at him.

'Okay you two, what's going on?'

'Keep calm and I'll tell you.' Hunter explained the situation. Apart from a shocked "Oh" and putting her hand to her mouth she had listened in silence. Hunter admired her for it.

She whispered, 'So what are we going to do?'

'We?' Hunter

'You. You two are the super heroes.'

'Hardly.'

'Commander Hunter?' The stewardess had stopped next to them. 'You're wanted in the cockpit, sir.'

Unfastening his seatbelt Hunter returned to the cockpit and, not waiting to be told, picked up the headset.'

'Hunter.'

'Nick,' said Macnair, 'we've identified a man dressed as a cleaner entering the ladies toilets in the airport. However, he came back out just a few minutes later. He wouldn't have had time to wipe a bowl never mind clean several cubicles. What's more I think it unusual to have a male cleaner entering the ladies toilets.'

'Ethnicity?'

'Probably Middle Eastern, but that doesn't mean much nowadays. We're running him through the face recognition software to see if we can ID him. Also, a few minutes later the girl Aiza Shaker went in but took her time. She was holding a cloth shoulder bag. Leo has run the video of her exiting the room a few times and is convinced she has something in her bag that wasn't there when she went in.'

'I guess that makes sense. Easy access, stands in the middle of the cabin or sits with the bag at her side and pushed against the bulkhead. It's safe to assume there's a ball of explosive in the cabin but we still have no way of knowing about the hold.'

'We assume there's explosives,' said the General. 'If there isn't all well and good, if there is there's little we can do about it.'

'Thanks sir. We'd better get moving.'

'Good luck.' The General broke the connection.

Hunter shrugged at his sister and then looked at the co-pilot. He was pasty white and looked as though he was going to vomit at any second. However, he was managing to do his job.

'You know what to do?'

'Sure Nick, piece of cake. Fly around the sky until we're flying on fumes and land on a tarmac runway that is 5,600ft long with a plane that needs close to 4,500ft to stop. It's just as well it's tarmac.'

'Why?'

'If it's wet then tarmac is better than concrete. Tarmac also sheds snow more quickly than concrete, which explains why it has been used at Samedan. That's the sort of thing the Swiss would consider when building an airport to service one of the premier ski resorts in the world. All those private jets, you know how it is.'

'Sure, I know how it is. Especially for the environmentalist brigade using their private jets.' Hunter's sarcasm was loud and clear.

'Let's leave that hobby horse for a later date,' said his sister. Then she added softly, 'Provided there is one. Okay, dear Nicholas, you and Chris had better get going. You've a few things to do starting with finding the damned bomb.'

Cathy had moved to the window seat so the two men sat next to each other. Hunter ran over his ideas for their next and subsequent moves.

Bletchley nodded before adding, 'Okay and we use the cabin staff to collect everyone's mobiles, cameras and I-pads and all the rest of the gubbins.'

'Good thinking. The last thing we want is to appear on social media. We tell the passengers that there's a possibility of the bomb exploding if they use any of their devices and that we are collecting them for safety. That they'll get them back after we land and the plane is evacuated.'

'Time to go?'

'Yes, once more unto the breach,' said Hunter.

15

Aiza looked up suddenly. A tall, black haired man, standing a few paces down the aisle, was staring at her. It seemed to her that his eyes were as cold as ice. She shivered. They looked like the eyes of a man without pity.

As she was sitting in the emergency exit row the man stepped forward and stood in front of her. He bent down, undid her seat belt and pulled her to her feet grabbing the bag off her lap.

'Hey,' said the woman sitting in the aisle seat. 'You can't do that. Be careful of my daughter.

'Sorry.'

The man checked inside her bag and then looked her in the eyes. She felt herself shrink. It seemed to her she had never seen such hatred.

'It's in the parcel, isn't it?'

Aiza nodded.

A few people were looking as he marched Aiza towards the cockpit, one hand on the back of her neck the other in the middle of her back. It was so unexpected that the passengers who noticed something was amiss sat in stupefied silence.

He opened the door, placed a hand on her shoulder and pushed her in. He grabbed her by the shoulders and steered her to what was once the engineer's seat but was now a third seat available for visitors to the cockpit or instructors.

The man opened the bag, removed the package and ripped it apart.

When he saw the three balls his stomach clenched. He took one out.

It was exactly as described by Don Masters, right down to the star. Aiza didn't say a word.

'Are all three armed?'

She didn't answer so Hunter put his face close to hers and asked again.

Aiza nodded and began to shake, tears trickling down her cheeks. If she thought she could move Hunter in any way she was seriously mistaken. Hunter was the old school royal naval officer – a gentleman at all times when it came to the fairer sex. When it came to terrorists and criminals he knew that the female of the species was as deadly, if not more so, than the male.

'Why do you want to kill all these innocent people?' he asked her.

She stared at him, like a snake staring into the eyes of a mongoose.

'Why?' This time his tone was harsher.

He became aware that his sister had climbed out of her seat. Louise leaned past him and slapped Aiza very hard across the face. Hunter didn't intervene. He knew Louise was under the greatest strain possible. She was responsible for the lives of everyone onboard and like every airline captain the world over, she took her responsibilities very seriously. But that applied to technical factors, safety of the plane, flying through, around or over bad weather. Safety and comfort drilled into them during their training. This was out of her control. This was a scenario possibly talked about over coffee but never confronted. There was something to be done, in reality a bomb on a plane meant it was all over. Another factor was that nobody knew there was a bomb until it was too late.

'Christ, I want to kill you,' Louise said, her face close to Aiza's.

The girl stared back. She had stopped shaking and her tears had dried. 'Inshallah,' she said softly.

'God willing? God willing?' This time Louise took a handful of the girl's hair either side of her face and shook it back and forth as hard as she could. After a few seconds her brother placed his hand on her arm.

'Okay, Lems, take it easy.'

Louise looked at him and then at her own hands. They were

shaking. She took a deep breath and said, 'Sorry. I had to get it out. I've been sitting there wondering how I would react if we found who was responsible. Now I know.'

'You reacted as I would have done but I'm more able to control my anger.'

Louise sat back in her seat. 'In that box are some zip-ties. We have them just in case any of the passengers become too unruly.'

Hunter opened the box, took out four zip-ties and fixed Aiza's arms and ankles to the seat. Hunter looked at the ball in his hand and at the girl's face.

'I asked you why?'

'You are enemies of the one true faith and the one true God.'

'The children on board are enemies of your faith?' Hunter asked her.

'Yes, they are all the spawn of the devil.' Her face was contorted. Her fear was gone, replaced by hatred.

'Do you really believe such rubbish?', Louise asked her scornfully.

'Yes! There is only one true prophet of God and that is Mohammed, *peace be upon him*.'

'What has that to do with the innocent people on this plane?' Louise asked.

'There is only room for one religion in this world and that is Islam. All non-believers must either convert or die. That is the only way. The death of a non-believer means a peaceful journey to Jannah for those who have fought holy Jihad.'

'She's brainwashed,' said Louise in disgust.

'Many are,' said Hunter softly. 'Okay, Lems, ETA?'

Louise looked at her screen and replied, 'Twenty-eight minutes give or take.'

While she was speaking Hunter called the General and told him of events.

'Nick,' Louise said, 'air traffic control are getting a bit antsy. The original change of course wasn't unreasonable but now I need to come to port and aim for the UK. The French have us and you know what they're like. They're becoming excited.' She had transmitted the message and Macnair had also heard what she had to say.

'Louise, leave it to me,' he said. 'I was about to alert the powers-that-be.'

Their original turn to starboard on a heading for Switzerland hadn't been unreasonable though no explanation had been given. Now it was time to turn to port and head for the UK. The French air traffic control people were being perfectly reasonable in ordering Louise to turn only she didn't dare.

Macnair pressed the speed dial for the Chief of MI6, a title first used in the 1920s and still in use. It was a direct line that diverted to the Chief wherever he happened to be. That particular number was held by only a handful of people.

'Marcus?'

'Yes, Malcolm, as it's you it can't be good news.'

Sir Marcus Cunningham had been in post for a little over six months. So far he had proven to be an adept hand at his job, keeping an eye on what was happening on a worldwide basis and most importantly keeping interfering politicians off the backs of the rest of the Secret Intelligence Community. Although MI6 answered to the Secretary of State for Foreign and Commonwealth Affairs in the same way that MI5 was under the auspices of the Home Office, the Home Secretary tried too often to interfere in foreign affairs under the guise of international security issues.

There was a certain irony that the Chief had the name Marcus Cunningham. The first Chief of SIS, the Secret Intelligence Service, was Captain Sir Mansfield Smith-Cumming, Royal Navy, who signed documents with a capital C in green ink. The tradition still lived on and all Chiefs had been known as "C", the letter written in green ink when used.

'Where are you, Marcus?'

'With the PM. We're reviewing the live ops we have here and elsewhere.'

'Is Colin with you?'

'Yes. Malcolm it's a COBRA meeting. Seeing as it was you I answered but please get to the point.'

COBRA made it sound like a special operations team ready and able to take the fight to the enemy. The media often spoke of it as though it was of some relevance. It wasn't. All it stood for was Cabinet Office Briefing Room A.

'Right. Put me on loudspeaker.'

'You're on.'

'Thanks. Prime Minister we have a situation.'

Macnair explained the state of affairs in detail including what they planned to do. He was heard out in silence after the Home Secretary tried to interrupt twice and was told to be quiet by the Prime Minister.

'Let's get this straight, Malcolm. The bombs have been found, they cannot be defused, they could bring down the plane killing everybody onboard but Commander Hunter and another of your people are there in control of the situation.' The speaker was "C".

'I wouldn't go that far.'

'What do you mean?' This time it was the Prime Minister who spoke. Her icy tone was as cold as an Arctic winter. It was jokingly said of her that she could curdle milk at five paces with a glance. Macnair respected her and on the dozen or so occasions they had met he had liked her. A no-nonsense, highly intelligent and focused woman she commanded respect just as her famous and redoubtable predecessor, Margaret Thatcher.

'Hunter doesn't have control as such. He has the situation contained but that can easily change once they start their descent. He is about to tell the passengers what's happening. We don't know if anyone will panic but just hope he manages to get them to do as he says.'

'Is there anything we can do?'

'Yes, ma'am. Now we know the situation get hold of the Swiss authorities. We need hospitals put on standby, ambulances and medics on site, and any fire engines and rescue staff deployed as soon as possible.'

'Why weren't we warned before now?' asked the Home Secretary.

'Because we weren't sure what was happening,' Macnair replied with some annoyance. He hated idiots in powerful jobs.

Cunningham said, 'We understand. If we sent out an alert every time we think something is amiss we'd never stop.'

Macnair knew the words were meant for the others in the room, not him.

'Malcolm,' said the Prime Minister, 'we'll get on to it right away. Is there anything else we can do?'

'Ma'am, there's nothing we can do. It's in the lap of the Gods and Commander Hunter. And I know which one I put most of my faith in.'

'Amen to that, General,' said the Prime Minister. 'If you do speak to Commander Hunter before things kick-off, give him our best wishes.'

'I will, ma'am, I'm sure he'll appreciate it.'

Macnair broke the connection. He had never known a man to disdain recognition of his achievements as much as Hunter. His Ops Director was a rarity. Put simply Hunter was a patriot, through and through. He believed in his country, its people and its ideals. There weren't many people who did, particularly amongst the political elite.

He'd let the politicians do what they did best - talk, squabble, point the finger of blame and get nothing done.'

He needed to speak to Heinz Mettler of the Swiss Federal Intelligence Service.

He speed dialled the Swiss boss. He may have asked the politicians for help but he knew he needed it more urgently than they were capable of delivering.

'Hello, Malcolm. I take it this is not a social call.'

'I'm afraid not, Heinz. We have a problem.'

Macnair briefly explained the situation and Mettler listened in silence.

'Okay, I'll get things moving. You say Nick is onboard?'

'Yes. He has a few ideas that might help but to be frank we'll just have to wait and see. Presumably your local military can help with ambulances and fire trucks.'

'Yes. We Swiss are good at fire fighting.'

Hunter was in the cockpit going over a few last minute details. Finally, he said, 'I'd better get out there. The passengers and the cabin staff will be wondering what's going on.'

He slung the bag with the balls in it over his shoulder, stepped out of the cockpit and looked at the four young faces of the cabin staff. Cathy stood next to them. All five had strained looks on their faces, which was hardly surprising.

'Have you been told what's happening?' Hunter asked.

They shook their heads. Hunter guessed that a fear of the unknown was adding to their anxiety. They may have been young but they were bright enough to realise something serious was going on.

Hunter continued. 'You are to do what Cathy tells you. I take it you all know who she is?'

They nodded and glanced nervously at her.

'We need you to remain calm,' said Hunter. 'We have a problem we need to deal with.'

'It's a bomb, isn't it?' asked Ellie, one of the stewardesses.

There was no point in denying it so Hunter replied. 'Yes.'

'Oh, my God,' said Sally, another stewardess. Her eyes teared up and she said, 'I don't want to die.'

'Pull yourself together, Sally,' said Cathy, 'no one is talking about dying. Nick, this is Rob and this is Jack.'

Hunter shook their hands. Rob's was damp while Jack's was dry but both looked at him steadily enough.

'We have things to do so pay attention.'

The four exchanged glances and nodded nervously. 'Cathy, over to you.' Hunter hoped her calm assurance would help to instill the same in them.

'The most important thing is to ensure there's no panic,' said Cathy. 'You've been drilled on this and now it's time to put what we've been taught into practice. Sally, are you okay?'

She had gone white and was swaying slightly. Rob was standing next to her and clutched her arm to steady her.

'She's pregnant,' said Ellie. 'This was to be her last flight before a desk job in Edinburgh.'

'How many months?' Cathy asked.

'Four months.'

'You'd better sit down,' Cathy pointed at the front row of seats. Sally did as she was asked. Cathy issued more instructions and the three walked up the aisle.

By now some of the passengers in the front few rows were looking at them and Hunter knew it was time to impart the bad news. He opened the cockpit door and looked in. 'ETA?'

'Eighteen minutes and counting.'

'Make the announcement.'

'Ladies and gentlemen, this is the captain speaking. Please pay attention to what I have to say.'

Some people went quiet, others continued to talk.

After a few seconds Hunter shouted, 'Silence please!'

Most of the cabin fell quiet in surprise. One man just a few paces away continued talking to the woman sitting next to him. She was shushing him up.

'It's just the usual load of crap. Take no notice,' said the man.

Hunter's patience was wearing thin. 'Chris,' he said and inclined his head towards the passenger.

Bletchley stepped forward, leant down until his face was only inches away from the man's and said, 'Shut your mouth or I'll shut it for you.'

The man was shocked for a second or two and then began to bluster. 'You can't talk to me like…'

He didn't get any further. Bletchley grabbed the man's throat and squeezed. The man gargled and tried to pull Bletchley's hand away but to no avail.

'Now shut up and listen.' He dropped his voice and added, 'That is if you want to live.'

Silence reigned in the cabin. It was as though a frisson of fear had swept through the passengers.

'Ladies and gentlemen,' Louise started again, 'please listen to the two senior military officers who are standing at the front of the cabin. You must do as they say.'

All eyes were on Hunter and Bletchley. The cabin staff had positioned themselves along the aisle with one explicit instruction. Nobody was to use a mobile phone or any other device that could take photographs or video. If they tried it was to be confiscated immediately.

Neither Hunter nor Bletchley wanted their picture spread across any social media, newspaper or news programme.

Hunter picked up the bulkhead receiver. 'Ladies and gentlemen, we have definite proof that there is a bomb onboard the plane.'

As expected there were screams and yells while panic was beginning to spread amongst the passengers. Hunter called for silence but was ignored.

'Quiet! Quiet!' Bletchley called out walking through the plane. 'We are diverting to Switzerland where there is specialist equipment to deal with our problems, should we need it.'

Hunter continued speaking into the receiver. 'We have a few things we need to do as well as a few things we need to explain. Will you all please come down to the front and fill the forward seats.' Then he added, 'Do not, under any circumstances, use a mobile, an I-Pad or any other device that takes photographs or video. It could detonate the bomb.'

He waited patiently as the passengers moved forward. They filled the first 16 rows. A few had tears on their cheeks, a few were moaning and a few were hugging their children.

One man sat down and, in spite of what Hunter had just said, reached for his mobile. He took it out and started pressing buttons. Hunter knew he needed to make sure nobody else did the same. He grabbed the man's hand and snatched his phone.

'You can't do that!' The man yelled in Hunter's face.

16

'Which bit of what I said about setting the bomb off with an electronic device such as a phone didn't you understand?' Hunter had ripped the phone from the man's hand, dropped it on the deck and stamped hard on it.

The man glowered at Hunter but said nothing.

Now that the passengers were closer Hunter had dispensed with the phone. 'Look, ladies and gentlemen, please believe me when I say we can't be too careful. Anything from photographing to transmitting can set off this type of device. Right now it's stable and will remain so.'

'Until when?' A woman asked, raising her hand to attract his attention.

'Until we land. This man,' he nodded at Bletchley, 'is an explosives expert. So am I. We know what we're doing. If you do as we ask then we'll probably come out of this okay.'

'You said probably,' a silver haired elderly man said.

Shrugging, Hunter replied, 'There are no guarantees.'

'Except death and taxes,' chipped in the woman sitting next to the man. They were holding hands and were obviously husband and wife of long standing.

Hunter smiled. 'As you said, except death and taxes. And right now I know which I prefer to pay even if the government does waste our money.'

That raised just a few smiles.

Another hand went up. 'So what are we to do? Just sit here until the bomb goes off and do what? Pray?' The young man sat in the aisle seat with his arms crossed. 'It doesn't sound like much of an option.'

'No,' said Hunter. 'There are a few things we can do.' He'd made up his mind. If they were going to die they had the right to know how. 'This particular type of bomb won't explode until we are close to landing. Even then, it might not go off. The firing mechanism is controlled by atmospheric pressure. That's why we're landing at St. Moritz.'

'Why St. Moritz?' one of the passengers queried.

'It is the highest airport above sea level, which means the device may not actually explode. I wasn't sure how much to tell you. I can sugar the pill or tell you the way it is. We know exactly how it works and what to do to help mitigate the blast should it explode.'

'Where is it?' The silver haired gentleman asked. If he was at all nervous he wasn't showing it.

Hunter was grateful for that. The man was helping to calm the fears pervading the cabin.

Hunter felt like taking a ball out of the bag and showing it to them but decided that was a step too far. A bomb in the abstract somehow didn't seem as bad as one in reality. 'It's at the back of the plane.'

A tannoy announcement interrupted him. 'This is the captain speaking. We will be making our approach in fourteen minutes, possibly a little later.'

The announcement was for Hunter's benefit. Louise was basically telling him to get a move on.

They needed the cooperation of the passengers and nothing more enraged people than being told what to do without explanation. Hence Hunter explained about the pressure wave and how they were to sit as far forward as possible with some people lying on the deck, outstretched with their feet pointing at the rear of the cabin. He explained about covering their ears, not because of the noise but because the pressure wave would easily burst eardrums.

There was a bright looking teenager who raised his hand. 'Sir, the biggest problem if a bomb goes off is failure of the airframe. That's correct, isn't it?'

Hunter nodded.

'Being at a high altitude makes it all the worse.'

'Correct.'

'At low altitude the big problem is often the aviation fuel. An explosion is one thing, the resultant fire something else entirely. It's a fire that does most damage.'

Smart kid, thought Hunter. 'You're quite right.'

'So what are you going to do about it?'

'We'll be landing on fumes. It's the safest way.'

'You mean we'll have run out of fuel?' asked someone.

'Pretty much.'

'So then we fall out of the sky,' a voice said.

'Believe it or not but these aircraft glide,' said Bletchley. 'I have it on good authority.'

'What authority?' A man asked in a fearful tone.

'The pilot's.'

The man whose mobile Hunter had taken yelled out, 'The captain's a woman!'

Bletchley stared at the man, probably in his twenties, until he squirmed.

'And your point is?'

'Everyone knows that women are not as good as men when it comes to certain things like flying.'

'You idiot,' said Bletchley, angrily. 'While you lot have been on the verge of panic she has been dealing with a very difficult situation with a professionalism we expect of British-trained pilots.'

Hunter wanted to say that Louise was one of the finest pilots he had ever known, was Bletchley's fiancée and his sister. The problem was it wouldn't take a journalist long to track down who they were and that was the last thing the officers from TIFAT wanted.

Some of the passengers exchanged looks, others looked down at their laps while others were mumbling to themselves and at the same time making the sign of the cross. It was obvious that panic was just a few degrees beneath the surface. In some respects Hunter couldn't blame them. They had no control over the situation. As far as they knew, they could be blown out of the sky.

179

'Please believe me,' said Hunter, 'there is no danger until we are approaching touchdown and even then there is a better than even chance that the bomb will not go off.' He knew he was gilding the lily but he needed to give them the facts while not creating panic. 'If it does explode then we'll be in a good position not only to survive but to get out without any injuries.'

Just then Louise announced, 'Cockpit.'

'I'll see what she wants,' Hunter said, stepping into the cockpit. 'What's up?'

'We're nine minutes or so out. The airport has been cleared of departing aircraft while those due to arrive have been diverted to other airports.'

'Good.'

'However, we still have too much fuel onboard. We need to circle for a while.'

'How long?'

'Looking at the gauge I'd guess twenty minutes. Nick, I've done this a few times in theory on a computer simulator. I know what I need to do but sitting in front of a computer screen playing at it is one thing, doing it for real is something else.'

'I understand. Why don't you just dump the fuel?'

'Where?'

'Where? Into the atmosphere.'

'There are people living down there. We are over the middle of Europe. I am not spraying people with a highly flammable liquid such as avgas. It's far too dangerous. The damn stuff can explode from an electrostatic charge generated during pumping or tank cleaning. Then there's the danger of someone looking up at a low flying aircraft being showered with the avgas. If we were over the sea then no problem, here it could be. I admit it's unlikely but I'm not going to risk it.'

'Fair enough. I mean it when I say you know best.'

'Oh God, Nick. All those people in there are relying on me.' Louise's hands began to shake and she held them up to show her brother.

He put his hand on her shoulder. 'Lems, if I had the choice of picking anyone in the world to pilot this thing now it would be you.'

'Yeah, sure.' She pulled her mouth back in a rictus of a grin and said, 'See, I believe you and I'm smiling.' She held her hands up again. 'And look, I've stopped shaking.' She licked dry lips. 'I'm going to circle the field at 10,000ft. We need to hit the runway at the edge as we've only 1,000ft spare to play with and hopefully no fuel for reverse thrust. I don't know if that's enough. If we land too far along the runway we'll end up on the grass perimeter.'

'That's a good thing, surely.'

'The nose carriage won't like it and will probably dig into the ground and we'll plough in. That will probably happen because I've been checking the weather around here for the last fortnight.'

'Why?'

'If there had been no rain or very little then the ground would be hard. But it's been raining cats and dogs for weeks so the ground is saturated and soft.'

'Surely that's to our advantage.'

'I'll have no control whatsoever. If the forward wheels dig in the back will slew around. It could be enough to send us spinning.'

'Does that matter?'

'It does if we start slewing to starboard. The terminal building isn't that far away. We could hit it.'

'Have you told the airport authorities?'

'Yes. They said they're evacuating the building even as we speak.'

'So what's the problem?'

'Oh, nothing. Unless we hit the building nose first and we hit it hard and it collapses down on top of us oh, and we get crushed.'

'Won't the plane take that sort of impact?'

'I've no idea. I don't think they've run a computer program titled "What is the effect of a three story building landing on an airplane."'

'I guess they did. Lems, if it looks like we're going into the building abandon ship and throw yourself onto the deck next to the seat.'

'You think that will help?'

He looked into his sister's eyes and shrugged. 'Possibly, possibly not. But at least you'll have done your best.' He looked at the co-pilot who had sat there mute, staring at Hunter. 'You got that?'

The man nodded but said nothing. It appeared to Hunter that he was suffering from extreme fear.

'I'd better go and help Chris.'

'Okay. Nick,' she managed a smile, 'good luck.'

Leaning forward he kissed her on the cheek. As he turned to leave he looked down at Aiza who stared defiantly back at him. He resisted the temptation to hit her though it took a great deal of willpower.

In the main cabin Bletchley had arranged for the first eleven rows to be occupied. The children were all on the floor, under the seats with their feet facing aft. The only sound apart from the air-conditioning and engines was the occasional whimper or a child talking to its mother or father.

Half a dozen men had been detailed to help.

'Everyone,' Hunter called out, 'please listen. We are going to circle for fifteen minutes to reduce the fuel onboard. When we begin to land the captain will tell us.'

There were a few curses from some passengers but now the moment of truth was imminent people accepted it. There was nothing else for them to do.

'One other thing,' Hunter yelled, 'once we land and the emergency slides have deployed move as quickly as you can. Do not attempt to use the rear doors.' He lowered his voice. 'Okay, Chris, let's get to work.'

'Nick, cockpit.'

He hurried along the aisle.

'We're shortly going to turn on to finals. Whatever you're going to do you've got about five minutes.' His sister stared at him and said, 'I have faith, brother dear.'

Hunter managed a weak smile before exiting the cockpit. He hurried along the aisle to the toilet. Passengers' bags were stacked up outside the door.

'How's it going?'

'The balls are down the toilet,' said Bletchley. 'Now we pack the bags.'

Hunter handed the bags to Bletchley who stuffed them into the cubicle. It only took a few minutes for the cubicle to be full. Bletchley rammed the door closed.

'This is the Captain. I have some important information, which I wish to impart. Any second now the engines will cut out due to lack of fuel.'

There were gasps from a number of women and curses from some of the men.

'Do not panic. We decided it was better to use up the avgas, this is the fuel planes use and is highly combustible. So much so it could cause an explosion when we land. There is nothing to be worried about. All planes are designed to glide so if we lose the engines at a height of 6,000ft we will glide to touch down. During that time I still have control to turn left or right and head down more steeply if we need to. So please do not be alarmed.'

At that moment the engines spluttered, picked up, spluttered again and stopped. The silence was eerie. The whimpering, wailing and cursing stopped. Instead there was some mumbling as the passengers began to pray.

Louise gave a final message on the address system.

'We are now landing and should be on the ground in just over two minutes thirty seconds. Good luck everyone.'

May God have mercy, she said under her breath. Now that it was all about to kick off she wasn't feeling so nervous. She she took stock of herself. Heart rate a little above normal, breathing steady, hands steady, eyes scanning the instruments without a flicker and brain absorbing the info. Yep. All good.

More facts and figures flashed through her mind. The runway was 1,707 metres above sea level. She was going to aim for the end of the runway from a height of 2,438 metres above sea level, a difference of 731 metres. All the information was displayed on the screen in front of her. The angle of dive from five miles out would be shallow and gentle enough. With full flaps and taking into account the number of passengers then stalling speed was around 95 knots. That was through the air. There was a head wind of 15 knots hence in theory the landing speed was 80 knots. Fat chance. The wind was unpredictable, the speed/weight ratio a guess and there were too many other unknowns. She had decided to make their approach at 110 knots. At low altitude if the plane stalled they'd all be in serious trouble.

She told herself to concentrate. She ran through again the many possibilities. If the bomb did go off and they were low enough and the controls weren't destroyed and the drop in pressure wasn't catastrophic – which it shouldn't be at a low height, and they hit the runway just right and the wheels gripped, the brakes worked and they stayed in a straight line and didn't slew into the terminal building and… she gave up.

It was a good idea to shove the balls down the toilet. The strength of a plane was in its hull. The internal fittings were as light as possible without being flimsy, giving an image of strength. Thus the plane had a longer range for the same amount of fuel. If the bomb expended its force downwards then much of that force could be dissipated through the hull. That was the theory. The ball down the rubbish shute was a different problem.

She bit her lower lip as she came to another decision. She couldn't leave it to the computers. If the explosion did enough damage the chances were the computers wouldn't react fast enough. But she could. So she had to watch what was happening all the way down.

She narrowed her eyes as she stared at the instrument panel and made a few slight alterations. Speed through the air 99 knots and edging slower so she put the nose down a couple of degrees and watched the needle steady at 97 knots. She glanced at the speed over the ground indicator. It read 91 knots. Good.

She glanced at her co-pilot. The man looked back at her. His hands were shaking and he looked as though he was about to vomit.

'Take a grip, Nigel!'

'You know we are all going to die.' He moaned and then began to cry.

'When, and I say when, not if, we get out of this mess you will never pilot another plane as long as you live.'

'We're not going to live, you stupid cow!'

She looked over her shoulder at Aiza who glared back with hatred etched in her face. 'He is right.'

'No, he isn't,' Louise snapped back.

She glanced at the gauges. Angle of dive about right, speed stable, height sufficient to ensure they reached the runway. She altered course three degrees to port. Line up perfect. Another two degrees angle of attack to keep up their speed and to hit the runway as close to the edge as possible.

She licked dry lips. So far so good. Just over three miles to go, which meant touchdown in three minutes.

The control tower confirmed her observations.

They were still just above the cloud, which she saw was thick and black. The CT informed them that it was bucketing with rain. The plane dropped through the cloud and into open air. Visibility was poor but Louise was able to see enough. The windscreen had a chemical sprayed on it, which stopped water droplets accumulating. A wiper was used at slow speeds, particularly after landing. She switched them on. Visibility improved further. Then they were out of the storm and in clear weather.

So far, so good she repeated. The mantra went through her head another 15 times and then the wheels were over the runway. Height 50ft, landing speed reducing, 88 knots, 75, 50 and then the wheels touched down, the air brakes came on and the wheel brakes began having their effect. She had just convinced herself that they had landed safely when the explosion occurred.

17

The co-pilot jerked upright and the girl behind them screamed. The tail of the plane sagged and then dragged across the tarmac. Sparks flew everywhere.

Louise pressed down on the foot brake as hard as she could, adding to the automatic force already deployed. The plane began to slew to starboard and it took her a second or two to realise that the manual control of the plane, had been blown.

The airbrakes should have worked automatically but due to the catastrophic damage to the plane's underbelly they hadn't deployed. With a prayer she used the hand control and saw through the port window that the airbrakes were working. She could feel the plane slowing but the display was no longer lit up and so she had no idea how fast they were travelling. However, she did know that the reduction in speed was taking too long. They were going to reach the end of the runway within a minute and plough into the soft ground beyond.

Hunter had been ready for the explosion right up until a second or two before it occurred. The wheels had touched down, the relief of a safe landing washed over him and then the explosion had shattered his illusion of safety.

In the rear the deck buckled, like a malignant boil erupting and the tail collapsed to the ground. Hunter was shocked to his core. The explosion had been far greater than he'd expected. If it had happened at height then the plane would have been blown out of the sky with the resultant deaths of everyone onboard. Luckily he and Bletchley had taken their own advice and laid down on the deck, feet aft, hands over their ears. They exchanged glances. The noise of the plane scraping along the tarmac was loud and frightening but the passengers stayed silent and didn't move. Hunter realised the ball dropped down the rubbish shute hadn't exploded just those in the toilet bin.

The forward wheel slipped off the runway, dug into the ground and the plane slewed violently to starboard. In seconds it had turned 180 degrees and was continuing to turn and slide. The lights from the airport building loomed closer. Speed was bleeding off now as the centrifugal force of the turn helped to slow it down. The airport lights were only metres away. The tail hit the edge of the wall, smashing through the brick, shattering windows, slowing the plane even further. However, the combination of speed and weight gave the plane enough momentum that it continued to turn and slide, smashing down more of the wall, causing the first floor to collapse under its own weight.

The nose hit, bricks dislodged and showered down onto the plane. That was the last thing Louise knew.

The plane came to a stop. The cabin staff opened the front doors and the central emergency exits and deployed the shutes.

There was no jostling and shoving. The passengers did as they were directed, removed their shoes, kept them in hand and slid out into the cold and wet night. Emergency crews were at the foot of each slide to help people to ambulances and then to the local hospital if required. It seemed nobody was injured.

As the plane emptied Bletchley entered the cockpit to check on Louise.

'Nick! Nick! Louise is hurt. Cathy, get the first aid box!' Bletchley called out.

Hunter pushed his way past the few people still standing in the aisle and went through to the cockpit. Louise was sitting with her head drooping forward, kept upright by the straps over her shoulders. Blood was seeping from a wound on the side of her head.

The co-pilot was staring at her, making no attempt to help. Concrete and bricks lay about him, some in his lap. He turned to look at Bletchley. 'Is she dead?'

Bletchley said, 'No.'

Hunter looked at Aiza. She was slumped to one side, half-a-dozen chunks of concrete and stone around her. One look was enough to show she was dead.

Cathy appeared with the first aid box and pushed the two men aside as she tenderly lifted Louise's head to take a closer look.

'It looks worse than it is,' she said. 'Scalp wounds bleed a lot but as long as her cranium isn't damaged then she should be okay.'

'Can you tell?' asked Hunter, his calm exterior hiding the turmoil going on within him.

'No. She needs an x-ray. I'll wrap a bandage around the wound and then we'd better get her to an ambulance.'

'I'll call for help,' said Bletchley.

He went to the open doorway and yelled out. A woman wearing a hat depicting her as a member of an ambulance crew looked up at him. In German Bletchley explained what had happened and she replied in English that they would have a stretcher ready.

Hunter appeared with Louise wrapped in his arms and slid down the shute carefully holding her. Bletchley and Cathy followed. By now the plane was empty and the passengers were thinning out as airport buses took people away. As far as Hunter could tell the only person needing hospital treatment was Louise.

'Chris, you go with Louise. Phone and let me know what the doctors say. I need to stay here.'

'Right, Nick.'

'What about you, Cathy?' Hunter asked.

'I'll go with Chris and Louise if that's okay with you.'

'Sure it is.'

They had been standing under the starboard wing out of the rain. Two paramedics with a stretcher appeared and Hunter tenderly placed his sister on it. They hurried away, leaving Hunter alone. After a few seconds he speed dialled the General.

'Sir?'

'Nick! Are you okay?'

'Yes. The bombs in the septic tank went off but the one in the rubbish container didn't for some reason. We had just touched down when they exploded.'

Anyone hurt?'

He explained what had happened.

'Damn! Let me know as soon as you can how Louise is doing.'

'I will.' From where he was standing he could see the forward starboard chute and just then the co-pilot emerged and slid down it. The man hit the ground, stood up and walked away.

Hunter continued, 'I have the bomber's mobile. It appears to have been used once, maybe twice. There's a text message in Arabic. It arrived after we'd taken off.'

'Okay. Can you forward it?'

'Yes sir. I'll do it right away.' He paused and then said, 'Sir, the explosion was far greater than I expected.'

'How so?'

'Sir, if I didn't know better I'd say the explosion...' he trailed off.

'You were saying?'

'Sir, I've got to go.' He broke the connection and quickly forwarded the Arabic message to Scotland. He stood with his hands on his hips as a group of five people approached. He recognised one of them. Heinz Mettler was the boss of the Swiss Federal Intelligence Service. They had met in Switzerland when Hunter had been successful in preventing two plutonium based devices from exploding.

For their efforts the team had received a thank you from the Swiss government. They had been amused to discover that since 1848 there was no national honours system for recognition of outstanding bravery or achievement. The Swiss military awarded medals for length of service, training, sports and involvement with foreign missions, but not for actually doing anything of any significance.

Mettler smiled and held out his hand. 'Commander Hunter. Malcolm told me I would find you here.'

'Hello, sir. It's good to meet you again. I wish the circumstances were not so serious.

Mettler was about 5ft 8ins tall and sported an expanding waistline, testament to rich Swiss food. He was known to be very sharp, utterly ruthless and ideal for the job. He was also a Swiss nationalist to his fingertips though he understood that co-operation with other countries was not only good for his country but necessary.

He was also married to a Scottish woman and very pro-British.

'How did you get here so soon?'

'Malcolm gave me a heads up so I came by helicopter from Bern. I've been waiting half an hour. Care to give me the details?'

'How about the people in the terminal?'

'Luckily we evacuated them just in time.'

'That's for sure. What did the General tell you?'

'Only that there was a bomb onboard, pressure operated and hence the reason why you had diverted to Samedan.'

'There were three bombs made to look like cricket balls.' He briefly explained what they had done with them.

'So you think two exploded and one didn't?'

'Yes. Why the third ball didn't explode God alone knows. The woman who carried the bombs was killed when the masonry landed on the cockpit.'

'That's a pity,' said the Swiss thoughtfully, 'I would have liked to have spoken to her.'

A mechanised set of steps was brought into play and pushed against the hull.

'Shall we take a look?' Mettler led the way and Hunter followed.

They entered the cockpit and looked dispassionately at the girl's body. In death she looked even younger than she had done in life.

'What a waste,' Mettler shook his head. 'Why do they do it?' The rhetorical question hung in the air.

Mettler looked along the aisle to the rear of the plane. 'You say there is another ball that hasn't exploded?'

'Yes, in the rubbish collection bin. Did Malcolm tell you they couldn't be defused?'

Yes. It means the thing is primed to explode and could go off at any second. A slight movement, a minor change in atmospheric pressure and it could explode.'

'So we had better get off the plane and get everyone to move away.'

Why?'

'Hear that?' Hunter pointed upwards.

'Yes, heavy rain.' The meaning suddenly dawned on the Swiss and he said, 'We'd better hurry.'

Mettler stood at the top of the steps as the rain lashed down and yelled, 'Everyone back! Stop what you're doing and move clear away.'

The men and women looked up at Mettler and quit what they were doing.

'It may be enough to set off the bomb in the rubbish bin,' said Hunter.

'Let's hope so.'

Both men had realised that the approaching storm was bringing a spike in barometric pressure associated with heavy weather. If the ball hadn't exploded then the probability was it was on a knife edge and ready to go.

The wind and rain increased to a fully fledged storm, the two men had reached the corner of the building when there were two explosions. They exchanged looks. There was no need to say how close things had been.

'Two?' Mettler queried.

Hunter nodded. 'It probably means the first explosion was one ball alone exploding. Why the second wasn't sympathetically set off I don't know but it means they are frighteningly powerful.'

Both men stood in the open and gazed at the wreckage.

Mettler spoke. 'The pressure change must have been miniscule. Nick, you were all lucky. All three balls exploding and who knows what would have happened.

Do you know anything about the girl?'

'Her passport says she's Syrian, although we know the balls are being made in Tehran.'

'I suppose that makes some sort of sense. The Syrians and Iranians have been strategic allies since the Iran-Iraq war when Syria declared for Iran. They hated Saddam Hussein and all he stood for.'

Hunter said, 'Syria also sends armaments to Hezbollah in Lebanon as well as other Palestinian groups. They have also made it clear that they hate America as well as Israel and have vowed to sweep all Jews into the sea and retake the land for Islam.'

'Sadly you are absolutely right. So what have we in the Middle East? If peace were to break out across the region what would the armies do? What would the leaders do? Hold open and fair elections?' He snorted. 'Shaking his head Mettler added, 'If you hadn't been onboard then this would have been a catastrophe. Landing here was an inspiration.'

'It was suggested by HQ.'

Mettler, Hunter and an officer known as Hans climbed the steps and entered the cabin. Hunter led the way to the cockpit. Aiza looked a pathetic sight, lying crumpled up with masonry and dust all over her. Hans quickly searched her.

'Nothing,' he said in German.

Hunter could have told him there was nothing to find but instead picked her bag up off the floor and handed it to him. 'I have her passport.'

Hans withdrew a bulging purse. He opened it and flicked through a handful of plastic cards. 'Credit cards in the name of Aiza Shaker. She has a German driving licence with an address in Dusseldorf.'

'I'll pass it on to the Bundesnachrichtendienst,' said Mettler, 'that is as long as TIFAT has no objection?'

' No, of course not,' Hunter replied in feigned surprise. 'We all know how efficient the BND are.'

Mettler chuckled. 'Point taken. As soon as we get back to the office I'll have everything scanned and forwarded to Germany.'

'Thanks, sir. I think that's for the best. Where can I collect the originals?'

'I'll be in the local police station. Come around in the morning. Being Switzerland I can promise good coffee and better pastries.'

Hunter smiled and said, 'I look forward to it.'

'You may like to know that the crash people told me to expect the worst because of the fuel. But I understand from air traffic control that the pilot landed on fumes. That he deliberately used up the fuel before attempting the landing.'

Hunter nodded. 'He's a she and is my sister, Louise.'

'I didn't know. Is she okay?'

'She sustained a head injury. I'm waiting for Chris Bletchley to phone.'

'Who's that?'

'One of the officers at TIFAT and Louise's fiancée. He was also on the plane. What are you doing with the passengers?'

Mettler shrugged. 'Although shook up and upset nobody is hurt. I made a few arrangements while you were still in the air. If there were any survivors then the uninjured would be put up in a local school and the injured of course, taken to hospital. The army will be arriving shortly with enough camp beds.'

'Not a hotel?'

'Sorry, Commander, the hotels are pretty full. We could scatter them around different hotels but that would take time. The airline has already contacted us and said a plane would be here first thing in the morning.' He chuckled and then added, 'It's also good practice for the military. An exercise in disaster management. It gives them something to do.'

'Will a plane be allowed to land with this mess?' Hunter asked.

'No. I meant in Switzerland. This airport is closed for now. The passengers will be taken to Zurich where the plane will be waiting for them. What will you do?'

'Go and find my sister.'

'She'll be at the local hospital. You can use one of the police cars.'

'Thanks, sir. I appreciate it.'

Mettler walked Hunter to a car and ordered the policeman to take him to the hospital. They shook hands.

At the hospital he was directed along a corridor to the Accident and Emergency Department.

Bletchley was sitting in a chair at reception, his feet outstretched, his head on his chest, his arms crossed.

'How is she?'

'They're not saying much. They've done a brain scan and taken a few x-rays. They seemed most concerned as to who was going to pay for it all.'

'What did you tell them?'

'I gave them my TIFAT credit card and told them to help themselves.'

Hunter nodded. 'We'll move Louise to Scotland asap. You okay, Cathy?'

Managing a wan smile she said, 'Sure. Why wouldn't I be? Bomb explodes, plane crashes, we all survive but good friend possibly badly injured.' She shrugged. 'What's not to be okay about?'

'Sorry,' said Hunter. 'Perhaps a better question would've been are you hurt?

She nodded. 'Yes. Don't worry about me. I'm tougher than I look. It's Louise we need to worry about. I'll go and see if she's awake yet.'

Before Cathy could leave a doctor approached them. 'I believe you are with the pilot with the head injury?' She spoke accented but idiomatic English.

'Yes,' replied Hunter. 'She's my sister. How is she?'

'She's going to be fine. She suffered a concussion but we are certain there has been no damage to the skull. The wound looks worse than it is because of all the blood. She'll have a headache for a few hours, maybe a day or so but she'll get over it. We'll double check in the morning after a good night's sleep.'

'Thank you, Doctor,' Hunter glanced at his name badge, 'Wyssbrod. Can she be moved?'

'She can but I would leave her here until the morning. Then she will be ready to travel.'

Is it okay if one of us stays with her?' Bletchley asked.

'Of course. There is a visitor's chair next to her bed. Though I cannot guarantee its comfort. She is sleeping at the moment. I have given her something to ease her headache and help her sleep.'

'I'll stay,' said Bletchley. 'I was about to say as long as you have no objections, Nick, but even if you do, tough. I'm staying.'

Hunter grinned. 'You get my vote.' He changed the subject and told them what had happened. 'Now let's find a hotel, have a few drinks and a decent meal.' His remarks were aimed at Cathy.

'I thought we were to stay at the school,' she said.

'That's for the passengers to be ferried by bus to Zurich where they'll be flown to Scotland. We'll make our own arrangements.'

'Okay,' said Bletchley. 'In that case I'll see you in the morning. If there's any change, I'll phone.'

'Right. Now I had better phone my parents and tell them what's going on. The story will soon be hitting the headlines. Fortunately, they don't look at social media.'

18

Wajeeh Soliman watched the report unfold on CNN. He was in a dilemma. What was he going to tell the Prince? It had been made absolutely clear by the Prince that he wanted Hunter to suffer and that would be best achieved by killing the man's family first. The Prince had wanted their deaths to be slow and painful but Soliman had managed to persuade him that would be too difficult to arrange. He advocated killing the family first, let Hunter know why they had died and then ensure Hunter died a slow and painful death. Trying to do the same to a sister and two parents separately was too dangerous. There was too much room for error.

In spite of Soliman's arguments, his employer still insisted that Hunter was not to be killed before his family. The Prince was heavily medicated all the time and, while he appeared normal he was barely so. He spent most of his time gazing at a photograph of his dead son, Abdul-Hameed Saud, named after him, his future. The only one of his brood capable of leading the family to greatness.

When Soliman had escorted Gunther from the Prince's presence he had recognised the signs of fatigue and his periods of lucidity were dwindling. Time was vital if the Prince was to enjoy watching Hunter die. If he couldn't be there in person then a video would be made and sent to him. For the Prince to be present it would require Hunter to be brought to the kingdom. That was the Prince's preference, but Soliman doubted it was achievable.

He hadn't liked the idea of bringing in the German. However, he acknowledged the fact that the German and the men he would hire were more likely to blend in with the local population in most areas of the UK.

Walking across the room to an antique credenza he opened the left-hand door and removed a bottle of rum. Abstention in the kingdom was for the masses, not the rulers and their close staff. In private, the Prince treated him like the son he had lost, while in public Soliman accepted his role as head of security. However, he acknowledged to himself that he had a looming problem. The death of the Prince would leave him in a very difficult position.

He poured a generous slug of the rum into a crystal glass, added twice as much cola, a slice of lime and ice and took a drink. He sighed with pleasure as he often needed a drink after being in the Prince's presence.

There was no way on earth that he could take over the mantle of the family. There had been talk a few years previously of the Prince adopting him but that was all it had been, talk. The Prince was given to procrastination, as he had shown time and again and now it was too late. Although in truth Soliman had never believed it would happen. There were too many opposing factions in the family to have allowed it. Eventually, the Prince had dropped the subject and it was never mentioned again.

Unfortunately, the Prince's other sons and daughters knew about it. That had created a deep-seated enmity that was impossible for him to ignore. In reality, it meant they could and probably would have him killed. He knew that only too well. He'd made similar arrangements on a number of occasions in the past.

He took another sip of his drink. For several years he had diverted funds to his overseas account at the Royal Bahamas Bank. He opened his laptop to check the balance. It stood at US$ 15,678,345 and a few cents.

In spite of existing in a bubble of unparalleled luxury he had never been particularly comfortable with the lifestyle. He didn't need luxury yachts, private jets and hotel rooms costing more for a night than the average worker earned in Saudi Arabia in six months.

Over $15 million was more than sufficient for his needs. He sipped his drink, the alcohol was helping to oil his thoughts.

He had realised some time ago that the family would never let him leave. There was no other country on the planet, with the possible exception of North Korea, that had as many paranoid people as Saudi Arabia, virtually all of whom were members of the ruling family. Jockeying for the King's ear was nonstop as one Prince after another squabbled for a bigger slice of the huge cake that was the family's fortune. Like many people with massive wealth enough was never sufficient. They always wanted more.

Agitated by his thoughts he took a long drink of his rum. The questions he faced were when and where. Frowning, he sat back and put his feet up on the desk. It was easy to decide when, that was as soon as the Prince had died. But he suddenly had second thoughts and decided he wouldn't be killed. The family knew how sick their father was. If he was planning to have someone killed he would already have it arranged. All that would be necessary was to press the button. Were the Prince's sons intelligent enough to think ahead? The answer was a resounding no but his eldest daughter was. The woman was not only intelligent but he knew her to be ruthless.

Soliman's eyes narrowed as he thought through his position. She was aware that he knew all there was to know about the family. He knew where the bodies were buried. He had come to realise how perilous his situation was but as the death of the Prince drew nearer he needed to take action.

He observed his empty glass and crossed to the credenza to replenish his drink. This time he used more rum and less cola.

He could feel his anger growing as he drank. He wanted to throw the glass against a wall, kill the Prince and get the hell out of the country.

He would need to vanish so that he was never found. He pondered the problem and then half smiled. An idea had been swirling around the back of his mind for some time. He just needed to make a few preparations so that he could get away quickly.

Since the Americans had shackled Iran's wealth with sanctions, the Iranians had become desperate to get their hands on foreign currency. The Prince had learnt about the cricket balls and insisted Soliman acquired a batch. They were on sale to all comers at $10,000 each. He had thought them expensive, while the Prince couldn't have cared less. The Prince had instructed him to buy twenty. The idea was for the devices to prove their effectiveness before a substantial order was placed.

The prospect of more sales was irresistible to the Iranians and a deal had quickly been agreed. The irony wasn't lost on Soliman. The Iranians and the Saudis hated each other with a passion. However, the Prince would sit and sup with the devil in his quest for revenge.

He had become sickened by all he saw around him. The lavish lifestyle of the few at the expense of the many had finally got to him. There was also the issue of slavery and the treatment of foreigners who came to do menial tasks considered beneath the Saudis. The immigrants found themselves treated as slaves. Their passports were taken from them, they were paid very little money and the majority were kept out of sight. They were a hidden army molested and abused at the whim of the Saudi hierarchy.

Soliman felt his hand squeezing the glass, acid burning his stomach. A few years earlier he had tried to explain it to his friend but it had been of no use. As far as Abdul-Hameed had been concerned the Saudis had the unalienable right to treat non-believers in any way they wished.

He brought his own problems back to his thoughts. He had been playing a dangerous game trying to keep Mossad and TIFAT happy on one side and the Prince on the other.

Hunter and Cathy spent a restless night in the Hotel Bernina. In the morning Hunter kept his appointment with Mettler.

'You know you were lucky,' Mettler observed.

Hunter nodded. 'If the bombs had gone off at a greater height it would have been a different story. On a more mundane matter what are you doing with the passengers' luggage?'

'Already taken care of. The army has taken it to the school. Yours is in the corner,' he nodded in the direction of four suitcases.

'Thanks.'

'How's your sister?'

'Okay, I think. I'm on my way to the hospital now to pick her up. We'll fly out this afternoon. I'd better go. You were right about the coffee and pastries.'

The two men shook hands and Hunter took his leave, a secretary helping him with the suitcases. Cathy was outside sitting in a taxi, the meter running. When they returned to the hospital they found Louise dressed, champing at the bit to leave while Bletchley was insisting she wait for the all clear from a doctor.

Shortly afterwards a doctor arrived. She tried to usher the others out but Louise told her not to bother.

'In that case, how's your head?'

Louise shrugged. 'It's okay I guess. It's sore but not like a headache. Just a localised niggle really.'

'Good. That's what I'd hoped you'd say. I'll send a nurse with the necessary discharge papers for you to sign. She'll also bring you a bottle of painkillers. Take one as required but don't overdo it. You were extremely lucky and you shouldn't forget it.'

'Thank you, doctor. I assure you I won't. Please thank the nurses for their kindness.'

The doctor nodded, wished them a good day and left the room.

'Can you do anything with my hair?' Louise looked at Cathy.

'I can try. Why don't you guys get a coffee at the coffee shop by the main door? I'll wait with Louise for the nurse. Hopefully it shouldn't take too long.'

The two men left.

Louise was not best pleased when the nurse insisted she be taken to the entrance in a wheelchair. However, she acquiesced with good grace and a smile.

Hunter and Bletchley met them at the main door. Louise stood up quickly from the chair and staggered half a step. Bletchley caught her arm.

'Careful. You heard the doctor. You're to take it easy for a few days.'

'I'm all right.' She didn't look too bad. The small bald patch created around the cut on the side of her head was hidden by the artful manner Cathy had styled Louise's hair.

'Don't be so pig headed,' said her brother. 'We know about head trauma. It can be worse than it looks but in your case I doubt it.'

'And why is that, Mr Know-it-all?'

'Your skull is too thick.' Hunter grinned and Louise half smiled back.

A taxi pulled up and a passenger alighted. They commandeered it to take them to Engadin train station.

'I thought we were in Samedan,' said Bletchley.

'That's the name of the airport,' Cathy replied, 'this is the town.'

'Mystery solved,' Bletchley said, waving a hand.

Hunter said, 'There's a plane from Zurich this afternoon that we should catch easily enough. Someone from the embassy will be there to meet us with our tickets.'

Exactly on time the huge beast of a train crawled majestically into the station. They climbed aboard and settled at a table in the first class section. An attendant was strolling the aisle pushing a trolley and so they ordered coffee and pastries. As expected, both were excellent.

'Did you tell mum and dad what's happened?'

'Yes, they want to know when we'll arrive in Edinburgh and they'll meet us.'

'Didn't you tell them your car was there?'

'Yes, but you know what they're like. I'm afraid you'll have to put up with being mollycoddled in Crosshall for a couple of days at least.'

'You're lucky,' said Cathy, 'to have a mum like that.'

Hunter and Louise looked at each other and laughed.

'What's so funny?' Bletchley asked.

'Mum won't be doing any mollycoddling,' said Louise.

'Then who will?' Cathy asked, perplexed.

'Dad,' Hunter and Louise spoke in unison.

201

Paul Henke

At the KLM information desk they found a young lady from the embassy who gave them their tickets. Hunter sent a text to his parents with the plane's arrival time.

Security and boarding was the usual hassle though no one complained. For the four, what had just happened was a reminder of the need for continual vigilance. They landed on time at 17.40.

Once through arrivals they saw Tim and Sian Hunter. Sian was slim with black hair touched with grey, which she refused to colour. She had an oval face, blue eyes and a wide smile. She was wearing the smile when she saw Louise and Nick come through the arrivals door. When seen together, Sian and Louise could almost be mistaken for sisters, almost but not quite. Sian was the first to admit she had too many lines on her face to hide her age. As ever she was elegantly dressed in a blue skirt and matching waist length jacket and white blouse.

Their wealth came from Sian's side of the family. It had taken Tim Hunter a while to accept the fact but Sian had made it clear the money was there to be used. It was the same situation Louise found herself in with Bletchley who finally, with a degree of reluctance, accepted their financial situation. He hated the idea of being considered a gold digger.

Tim Hunter was of average height and build. His hair was brown and his sideburns grey. He had a square jaw and brown eyes. His nose was slightly hooked as a result of it being broken when he'd been a young reporter in Shanghai. He'd had the misfortune to be in the wrong nightclub when a fight had broken out between rival criminal gangs. He always figured he'd been lucky to escape with only a broken nose. Knives had been wielded and people killed. He had smashed an empty beer bottle on the head of the man who had broken his nose and then escaped through the backdoor. It had taught him a lesson. From then on, when on an assignment, especially in foreign countries, he made sure he had an exit route.

He acknowledged the fact that he was becoming fatter in the waist, but otherwise, he was in pretty good shape for his age.

202

While his wife kept herself fit Nordic walking and gardening he liked to use the swimming club in Edinburgh. After years of covering all types of international stories as a reporter, they had first settled down in Balfron, a village in Western Stirlingshire. However, a couple of years ago, they had moved to Crosshall, a few miles south of Edinburgh.

The property they had bought had over an acre of garden allowing them to build a house to their liking.

Tim Hunter joked that his next move would be in a wooden over-coat, though he hoped it would be many years before he put one on.

Their reunion was joyful, beaming smiles, kisses, hugs and handshakes all round. Hunter introduced Cathy.

'I'd better grab a taxi,' said Cathy. 'Home beckons.'

'You'll do no such thing,' said Hunter, 'I'll take you home. I'll see you all in Crosshall.' At that moment his phone rang. A glance told him it was General Macnair. 'I'd better answer it.'

He pressed the requisite button and said, 'Sir?'

'Where are you?'

'Edinburgh airport. My parents are here to take Louise home. I'm taking Cathy home.'

'Good. I just wanted to make sure everything is all right.'

'It is.'

'Take a couple of days. Things have quietened down for now though I daresay it's more than likely the calm before the storm. We know a handful of those balls are out there somewhere though where we start looking God alone knows. A NOTAM has gone out so we may get lucky.'

A Notice to Airmen was issued concerning any changes to any aeronautical facility, procedure or warning of a potential hazard. NOTAMs were becoming more common when the content was dealing with hazards connected to acts of terrorism.

'We'll be back Wednesday in that case.'

'Enjoy yourselves,' said the General breaking the connection.

'What about you, Chris? You coming with us or going to Crosshall with Louise?' Hunter asked.

Bletchley looked at Louise. 'I'll come with you, if that's okay.'

'Of course,' she said. 'I want to see the new house now it's finished.'

It had recently been completed and Sian and Tim Hunter had finally moved in. The new house was an imposing building with a large upstairs lounge with balcony, a bedroom, bathroom and office. Downstairs was a kitchen/dining room, significant entrance hall, TV lounge and bedroom with an en-suite shower room. The underfloor heating kept the house warm while the air-source pump was environmentally friendly. They had now joined the bowls club just across the road from the house and both found they liked the game as well as enjoying the social aspects of the club.

Hunter had joked with them that they had finally admitted their ages and joined the wrinkly club!

19

Louise and her mother sat in the back, her father drove while Bletchley sat next to him. The car was a Jaguar I-Pace, a luxury electric car with a range of over 200 miles on a full charge.

As usual it was the accepted Edinburgh Airport kerfuffle getting out of the place after paying an exorbitant fee for the privilege of doing so. Louise's head was aching and she could have used one of the pills given to her at the hospital. However, she had been putting it off due to her in-built aversion to taking pills of any sort.

'Are you all right, dear?'

'Just a headache, mum.'

'You should have said something.' Reaching for her bag, Sian opened it, rummaged around inside and extracted a small plastic bottle. 'Aspirin. The oldest and still the best.'

'It's okay, thanks. The hospital gave me these. I've just been putting off taking one.' She opened the bottle and popped one into her mouth.' She leant back and closed her eyes.

'Try and rest, even doze if you can,' said her mother.

'I will.' It didn't take long before she felt the throbbing in her head easing.

The car gave the smoothest ride imaginable as well as the quietest and Louise gradually drifted off to sleep.

'Care to tell us what happened?' Tim Hunter glanced at Bletchley.

Sian leant forward. 'Shush. Louise is asleep. We can hear the details after we get home.' Then she realised Louise was awake. 'How are you feeling?' she asked.

'Not bad, mum, thanks. I'm looking forward to a cup of tea.'

Leaning back and closing her eyes again Louise felt a tide of thankfulness wash over her. It could have been so much worse if it hadn't been for Chris and her brother. She opened her eyes, glanced at her mother and smiled. Her mother returned the smile before turning her head to look out the window. She didn't turn it fast enough. Louise saw the tears forming and reached across to grip her mother's hand, giving it a squeeze. Her mother squeezed back before reaching for a tissue and blowing her nose. She summoned up a smile and looked at her daughter, keeping hold of her hand. Louise was content to leave it in her mother's grip.

Fifteen minutes later they turned into the village of Crosshall.

'Where did you put my stuff?' Louise asked.

'In the granny flat,' said Sian. 'I haven't put anything away. I thought you might like to declutter before you filled the cupboards and drawers. Chris, some of your clothes are there too.'

'Thanks, Sian.'

'And Nick's?'

'In the garage,' said her father. 'There's not much. He can shift his gear into the spare room if he wants to but I doubt he will. He usually brings a bag whenever he stays with us.'

They zigzagged around the bends, passed the library on the left and the Co-op on the right. They headed down Fitzwilliam Street, passed the police station, the surgery and the filling station then they turned right into a short drive.

'Do you like the new place?' Louise asked.

'Her father answered. 'We've had a few snags but nothing major. The underfloor heating needs attention but nothing serious.'

'It is ideal,' said Sian, 'easy to maintain with plenty of room for visitors especially if there are young children amongst them.'

Louise smiled well aware what her mother was more than hinting at. 'I'll get married first. Chris and I have finally decided and thought a September wedding.'

They pulled into the carport. As they climbed out of the car her mother gave a radiant smile, 'I'm so happy for you. Aren't we darling?'

'What? Oh, yes. Delighted, absolutely delighted.'

'Okay, dad, what's wrong?' Louise asked as she lifted her case out of the car.'

'What? Nothing. Really, nothing.' He walked around the car and held out his hand to the Royal Marine. 'Look after her and welcome to the family.'

They shook hands. 'Thank you, sir. I will.' Bletchley smiled.

'I hope you'll be very happy together.' Tim Hunter smiled in return. His smile was contrived and both the women knew it. Sian pursed her lips and gave a slight shake of her head. Louise knew it meant she'd get to the bottom of what was wrong.

Tim Hunter unlocked the door and allowed the other three to enter before him. 'I'll put on the kettle,' said Sian.

Louise followed on her heels. 'Wow, mum, I like this.'

The kitchen was large and well kitted out with appliances.

'I see you kept the old dining table and chairs.'

Tim Hunter said, 'Yep. It and they have lasted nearly thirty years and will last another thirty. No point in wasting money.' It made him sound like a skinflint but he was a very generous individual.

'Come on I'll show you both the rest of the house and then the granny flat,' said Sian.

The front of the lounge situated upstairs had a balcony just big enough for a small garden table and four chairs. The view of the Moorfoot Hills across the valley was invigorating.

'It's lovely, mum. You've done a great job.'

'Thank you, Louise. I enjoyed selecting everything we needed from wall colours to blinds. Your father,' she cast a baleful glance at her husband, 'was as useful as a chocolate teapot.'

Tim Hunter had the good grace to look put upon before he grinned and said, 'But you secretly enjoyed it.'

'Huh. Let's go into the granny flat.'

'I'll stay here while you three carry on.'

Paul Henke

'Easy on the whisky,' his wife said as they left the room.

'If you don't mind Tim, I'll stay as well. I can see the flat later.'

'Good man. Malt do you?'

The query was greeted with a nod. Tim Hunter smiled and opened the drinks cupboard in the dining room. He checked the time. 18.05.

Bletchley said, 'The sun is well and truly over the yardarm.'

His future father-in-law poured a couple of generous measures of the amber liquid and offered ice, soda or water.

Both took ice and a dash of soda.

'Cheers,' said Tim Hunter, raising his glass in salute. 'Remember Chris, happiness when married is to agree to everything your wife says and then do your own thing. It's the only way.'

Bletchley smiled. 'Thanks for the tip,' he said, sipping his drink.

The two women returned. Sian said, 'We've changed our minds about tea. We'll settle for a glass of Prosecco.'

'What about the painkillers?' Bletchley asked.

'One glass won't hurt,' said Louise.

'Be it on your head, if you'll excuse the pun. I'll get it,' said Bletchley, opening the fridge door. He extracted a bottle, removed the foil and popped the cork.

Meantime Tim Hunter took out a couple of flute glasses and placed them on the kitchen island.

'The granny flat,' said Louise, 'is ideal. There's a kitchen/diner/living room downstairs and an en-suite bedroom upstairs. The sofa opens into a double bed so it could sleep four if required. We'll claim it for ourselves. If that's okay,' she added hastily.

Her mother smiled. 'Of course it is. That's what your dad and I thought.'

Louise said, 'Thank you, darling,' as Bletchley handed her and her mother their glasses.

Over their drinks Louise and Bletchley recounted what had happened. The result was that dinner was later than usual.

'Chris, I don't know how you and Nick do it,' Louise said in a soft voice. 'Nor the others come to that. I was terrified. She looked at her hands holding her knife and fork. They had a slight tremor and she felt tears welling up.

Her mother put her hand over her daughter's. 'It's OK, let it out. But remember, your skill helped to save lives and that's something to be proud of and also to remind yourself what you did.'

'I know, mum, I keep telling myself that but even so, I keep thinking there was so much that could have gone wrong.'

Tim Hunter said, 'It could have but you had Nick and Chris with you. If anyone was going to find a solution it would be those two.' He grinned. 'Like Batman and Robin though I'm not sure which is which.'

Louise summoned up a chuckle while Bletchley grinned.

'Don't tell Nick but I know who is who,' said Louise.

They all smiled at the comment which eased the tension.

'What's for dinner anyway?' Bletchley asked.

'We're having pizza,' said Sian, 'with extra cold meat, cheese and olives on the side.'

The Royal Marine smiled. 'Excellent. Just what the doctor ordered. Along with a glass of red wine,' he added.

Tim Hunter stood and walked across to the wine rack in the utility room. He returned with a bottle of red. 'Australian Merlot. Full bodied and not French.'

The comment elicited a chuckle from Bletchley, a wan smile from Louise and a suffering sigh from his wife. Her husband's antipathy to all things French was well known. Whenever Sian challenged him about it he would say let's not forget Agincourt, Trafalgar and Waterloo. Not to mention two world wars when Europe's future was saved from tyranny. Though he had the good grace to admit, with help from the Yanks and the Commonwealth. The latter in his opinion was where the real friends of Britain were to be found. Without any doubt in his mind they weren't to be found in Europe with a few exceptions such as the Polish and Dutch.

Bletchley and Louise exchanged smiles.

'We know, dad. The French have the unique ability to be arrogant with nothing to be arrogant about.'

'Precisely,' her father said, pouring wine into a glass.

Bletchley picked up the glass. 'Cheers, here's to a long and happy life.'

They clinked glasses and uttered, 'Cheers.'

'What's that naval toast?' Tim Hunter asked. 'About a sickly season?'

Bletchley smiled. 'We have the same in the RM. The toast is to a bloody war or a sickly season. Hence accelerating promotion for those who are left.'

Louise grimaced. 'Charming.'

'It's all in good fun. That's the Thursday toast, the Saturday toast is to our families.'

'And what pray, is the catch?' Louise asked.

Bletchley grinned. 'We add 'to wives and sweethearts, may they never meet.'

Louise punched him on the arm. 'You're a bunch of male chauvinists.'

'Of course we are,' Bletchley said in mock surprise, 'but it is said we are also gentlemen.'

'Huh, prove it!'

'That's easy,' he looked at Louise. 'We open doors for ladies, pay for the drinks and most importantly,' he paused.

'Most importantly what?'

'Take our socks off in bed.' He chuckled and his future in-laws smiled.

Louise said, 'Huh,' and crossed her arms. But then spoilt her display of pique by smiling.

The mood lifted and they spoke of pleasanter matters. The subject of the wedding came up but was quickly dropped when the two men adroitly turned the conversation to worldwide political matters. It wasn't long until the question of terrorism and the involvement of both Saudi Arabia and Pakistan were being discussed. The latter had become particularly prevalent because the American President had brought up the subject in his "State of the Union" speech earlier that year. In it he had threatened to withhold American aid to Pakistan if they didn't desist in their activities. So far the threat seemed to have had little effect.

'Why should it have any effect,' said Bletchley, 'it's not as though they need the money.'

'Still, 'said Tim Hunter, 'a billion dollars is a lot of money.'

'Which,' said his wife with scorn, 'goes into the pockets of the politicians and not to help the poor and destitute.'

'That's true,' said Louise, 'and I think most of our aid goes the same way.'

There the four of them were in agreement. It was a sentiment shared by the majority of the people not only in the UK and America but the rest of the Western world as well. However, they did acknowledge some aid did get through to the right people and lives were saved.

Sian said, 'Wasn't it Confucius who said, give a man a fish and you'll feed him for a day. Teach a man to fish and you've fed him for a lifetime?'

Tim Hunter nodded. 'And he was born in 551 BC, twenty-five centuries ago. Yet still we haven't learnt.'

On that philosophical note they said goodnight, Bletchley and Louise exiting the front door for the granny flat.

20

Michael Gunther couldn't help thinking about the $20 million. It was a vast sum but he didn't kid himself. It would be hard earned. However, if he played his cards right he would be able to disappear forever. Maybe even have a face-lift. Not too much, just enough to change a few things.

First he needed a crew. A greedy, hungry and ruthless hit squad. There were two people he knew who fitted the bill. He also had a shrewd idea where to find them.

Edith and Jacob Bodenheimer would be a good start. They sounded as though they were married but in fact were brother and sister. Despite their family relationship Gunther knew them to have a more intimate one as well. Something he found abhorrent. He had been on two jobs with them and they had proved they had all the characteristics he was looking for. Added to which they were also innovative and efficient. Bearing in mind the target and objective both attributes were necessary. His quandary was how much to pay them.

They wouldn't come cheap. Two million as a start but allow them to haggle three or even three and a half. He'd get as much as possible out of the expenses fund. In fact if he made it clear to Soliman that he needed them it was possible the whole amount would be paid by the Prince.

They were Jews, a fact he had to keep from the Arabs even if the pair no longer practiced their faith. As far as the Arab nations were concerned once a Jew always a Jew.

Soliman's idea of using Iranians or Arabs to do the job was not to be countenanced. If Gunther was to succeed he would need his own people on whom he could depend.

Edith was the businesswoman, the negotiator and keeper of their finances. She did it for the money while Jacob did it for the pleasure. So who should be the third member of the team? It would have to be someone the other two trusted and who could be relied upon. Someone equally without a conscience who was prepared to kill to order. A name came to him. Stefan Gashi - half Albanian and half Hungarian. He was sure the Bodenheimers had worked with him in the past. He frowned, dredging his memory. A hit job in Paris when the target had been the husband but the wife and two teenage children had died as well. A bomb in the car. Collateral damage but effective. A few pedestrians had been injured also.

Like many in their profession they knew each other either personally or by reputation. The majority were loners, distrusting others and wanting to keep the fee for themselves. But some jobs called for cooperation and when it did they tended to use the same people. Those who had earned their trust although that was only up to a point. Their world floated on paranoia, greed and ruthlessness.

He didn't try and contact the Bodenheimers. They, like him, didn't trust electronic communications or phones but he knew how to get in touch.

He disliked Paris in the summer. It was hot, humid and packed with people. Travelling in the city was a nightmare. What made it worse was the fact he didn't speak French apart from the usual pleasantries and to order a coffee or beer. The Parisian waiters and waitresses pretended not to understand him, which made his blood boil.

The Café de la Rue was used as a drop zone. It was owned by an ex-mercenary by the name of Pierre Marcel who had managed to get out of Africa more or less intact. He had lost his right leg from the knee down. Marcel had made the loss of his leg a positive. He used an old fashioned pegleg and told all and sundry that he had lost his leg when he had been serving with the French Foreign Legion in Sudan. He even had the medals to prove it. They were displayed in a box behind the counter, noticeable but too far away to be properly identified. He had bought them in an antique shop in Marseille.

The café did well but he liked to supplement his income by passing messages to those still in the business. Gunther had been using him for the past ten years and had no reason to doubt the man's discretion.

Gunther walked into the coffee shop to be assailed by the tantalising smell of fresh ground coffee and home baking. The room held a couple of dozen tables each with four chairs. They were far enough apart to enable customers to have a private conversation as long as they leant forward and lowered their voices. Along the window were smaller tables each with two chairs. Gunther took one at the corner of the window and back wall. He was next to the counter and was immediately noticed by the proprietor.

'Sylvie,' Marcel called to one of the waitresses, 'take over the till.'

No please or thank you but that was typical of the man.

'Coffee?' He leant on the bar and spoke to Gunther.

'Double espresso.'

They spoke German rather than English. Too many people spoke English while Germans rarely visited Paris in the summer, preferring the sand, sea and sun of the south.

A couple of minutes later Marcel joined him with a coffee as black as tar and almost strong enough to hold a spoon upright.

Gunther sipped his coffee and nodded approval. 'As excellent as I remember.'

The other man nodded in acceptance of the compliment but said nothing.

'Are you able to contact the Bodenheimers?'

'Yes.'

'Quickly?'

'Today.'

'Are they here in Paris?'

'Yes.'

'I'd hoped so, 500 euros to meet me at 17.00 beneath the Eiffel Tower.'

'Certainly. The coffee is four euros.'

Gunther handed over two notes in settlement and left without finishing his coffee. He then spent most of the day as a sightseer around the city, never still for long, careful of those around him. By the time he arrived at the Eiffel Tower he was certain nobody was following him.

Gunther walked slowly around the tower, its splendour lost on him. He ignored the man in the electric wheelchair with the woman alongside him walking at an angle to pass in front of him. He glanced at the man. From the look of his face and the way he was sitting it was obvious he had suffered a stroke and a bad one at that. The man was staring at the ground, the woman was staring at him. With a jarring shock he realised they were the Bodenheimers.

The wheelchair stopped a few feet away, the man half raised his hand in salutation while the woman nodded her greeting. Gunther nodded back, unable to speak for a few seconds. They were like a frozen tableau captured on a French canvas, the tower in the background.

Edith was petite at 5ft 3ins with a slim figure, a round face and wide smile. Her hair was shoulder length blonde but streaked with grey. She looked as gentle as a lamb. It was an attribute that had stood her in good stead on many occasions when she needed to get close to her target. That day she was wearing a green and white patterned dress with a wide leather belt around her waist.

Jacob was equally small. His hair was short, grey and he sported a beard that he hadn't had the last time the three had met. Jacob was wearing black trousers and a blue open collared shirt with an incongruous bib around his neck. It was rumoured they were twins but no one knew for certain. Their passports gave their ages as a couple of years apart but a passport could be made to show whatever was required.

Gunther cleared his throat. 'Hello, Edith, hello, Jacob.'

'Hello, Michael,' Edith replied. 'Jacob cannot speak.'

Again they were speaking German rather than English the only other language they had in common.

The man in the wheelchair made a grunting noise. Gunther could see the drool seeping out of the corner of Bodenheimer's mouth, his right eye watering.

'We got your message,' said Edith.'

'Why did you bother coming? You must have known it was for a job.'

'Of course we did. However, meeting you was an excuse to get out of the apartment.' She scowled. 'An opportunity to meet another living being apart from the man who runs the patisserie on the corner of our avenue.'

Gunther nodded as though he understood when, in reality, he didn't. He asked, 'What happened?'

'A massive stroke six months ago. On the eve of his fifty-ninth birthday, funnily enough. According to the hospital it could have happened at any time.'

'I am sorry to hear that.' He was sorry but not for them, for himself.

'So what's the job?'

Shaking his head he replied, 'Never mind. Can you put me in contact with Stefan Gashi?'

'If you want Stefan then it must be an important job. No, wrong word. A difficult job more like.'

He shrugged. 'Let's just say it's a demanding job and leave it at that.'

'What is it?'

'I can't say.'

'Can't or won't?'

'Won't.'

'Then you don't get to speak to Stefan.'

'Why not?' There was real anger in Gunther's tone.

Edith raised her hand, palm outwards and said, 'Take it easy, Michael. It is not our decision. He will only take a job after he knows the target.'

'Is there a reason?'

'Yes, a few years ago he took a job he thought was going to be easy. It turned out the target was a Mafia boss with strong political connections on Malta.'

'In other words protected by the system.'

'And how. He tried to cancel the deal but he had taken the money and as far as the client was concerned a deal was a deal.'

'The client being?'

'The boss of another Mafia organisation in Sicily wanting to take over Malta.'

'Let me guess. If he didn't do the job as agreed, he'd become the target.'

'Precisely, so now he insists on knowing what he's up against.'

'Will you help?'

She thought about it for a few seconds, glanced at the head of her brother and then nodded. 'Maybe, who's the target?'

Gunther licked his suddenly dry lips. 'There are multiple targets to be precise.'

'A bomb usually does the trick.' She spoke as casually as if she was talking about the weather.'

Gunther smiled. 'The target is the family of a man by the name of Hunter. Commander Hunter.'

She gasped. 'TIFAT?'

He nodded.

'His family?' There was no disguising the concern in her voice.

'His family and him.' Now that he had given Hunter's name he found he could talk about it more easily.

Her brother was suddenly agitated. The other two looked down at him. It was obvious he was telling his sister no.

'He's right,' she said in a voice barely above a whisper. 'Are you mad? You know who he is?'

'Of course I do. He's just a man. A target and as vulnerable as anyone else.'

Edith leant forward. 'No, he isn't,' she hissed. 'His reputation goes before him. If I was asked to name the five most dangerous men on the planet he'd be on the list. Maybe even number one. You know

217

his history. You know what he's been involved in and what he's capable of.'

'I know but the fee reflects what you're saying.'

'Michael, you've heard the saying there are no pockets in a shroud, well it happens to be a fundamental truth.

'Come on, Edith, think of your reputation. In the right quarters you and Stefan would be legends.'

'We'd be dead. What would they put on our gravestone? Here lies a dead legend, too stupid to know when to say no to a job.'

'He's no superman.'

'Suppose we succeeded and killed him and his family? Do you know what would happen then?'

Gunther shrugged but it was obvious he knew all too well.

'I'll tell you. TIFAT would hunt us to the end of our days. And that's an organisation I wouldn't tangle with for all the tea in China. My God,' she gasped, 'supposing we killed the family but not Hunter?' She shuddered as though someone had just walked over her grave.

'I'm sorry, Michael but I won't get involved.'

'Then how about contacting Stefan for me?'

'You'll be wasting your time. There's no point.'

'How do you contact him?'

'Through a dead drop.' She didn't tell him it was the same one he had used.

'All right, tell him I'll pay ten thousand euros to meet me and I'll tell him who the target is.'

'What's in it for us?'

'Five thousand.'

Reluctantly, Edith nodded.

Gunther reached into a pocket and extracted an envelope. 'Here's the money,' he said, and handed it over without counting it.

'You were expecting us to say no?'

'No. I had it with me in case I needed a retainer.' Also for immediate expenses but he didn't say so.

'Michael, I urge you to drop this job. It's not worth it.'

'You may be right, Edith, but it's too late.'

She nodded in understanding. People in their profession had to fulfil their end of the bargain once it had been agreed. A reliable reputation was vital.

'I'll contact Stefan. When and where do you want to meet?'

'Can he be here tomorrow, say midday?'

'Possibly. I'll phone you later tonight.'

Gunther gave her his mobile number.

'Even if Stefan agrees to the job you'll need one maybe two others.'

Gunther frowned. 'I know. I intended to ask if you could recommend anyone.'

'Surely you know enough contractors.'

'I do. I wanted to compare who I think would be suitable to those you thought could do the job.'

'Leave it with me. One or two names come to mind but I'm telling you Michael, no one will take the job.'

'Even if Stefan agrees?'

'He won't,' she said with certainty.

From Gunther's point of view the meeting the following morning at midday beneath the Eiffel Tower was a disaster. Gashi was of medium height and weight, and somewhere in his mid thirties. He was narrow shouldered with a long face, a beak of a nose and brown eyes set too close together. He was an unprepossessing individual with a look that reeked of insincerity. However, in the world of international terrorists he was acknowledged as a master when it came to using explosives. As the day was warm, he was wearing black trousers, a white, open necked shirt and a lightweight jacket. The jacket hung slightly lower on his right side due to the brass knuckle-duster he habitually carried. He had many enemies and twice had come close to being killed. His attackers had both died, blown to pieces in their respective cars. The second explosion had also resulted in the deaths of the man's wife and baby son. Gashi didn't lose any sleep over it.

The only language they had in common was English. When Stefan Gashi was told the target as well as the conditions, he laughed.

'What are you laughing about?' Gunther spoke angrily having just parted with 10,000 euros.

'Mr. Gunther, you must be out of your mind. Even if I succeeded in killing him and his family his organisation would not only move heaven and earth to get to me, they would hunt down everyone concerned. You must be mad.'

In spite of his efforts to appear unconcerned Gunther felt serious misgivings crawling through his stomach. His mouth was parched and he could feel a sheen of sweat on his forehead.

'I take it you don't want the job?'

'That is correct.'

'Then give me my money back.'

Gashi shook his head. 'That was to pay for this meeting but I will be generous. It also pays for my silence.'

Gunther took half a pace forward, 'Why you…'

Gashi's hand was in his pocket and he partially withdrew it showing the knuckle-duster. 'Please be careful. If you think I won't use this then think again. I have broken the jaw of more than one man.'

Gunther stopped and forced himself to relax. 'I am not threatening you. If I gave that impression then I apologise.'

'Apology accepted. Mr. Gunther. Let me say something. I understand you accepted the job. Give the money back and walk away. If you fulfilled your end of the contract by killing his family first and not getting him at the same time, then no matter how far and fast you run he'll find you. Like I told you, the word on the street is if any operative at TIFAT is killed then they will not rest until the death is avenged.'

'What do you mean the word on the street?'

'Exactly what I said. One last piece of advice. If you want somebody to do the job then use the fanatics from the Middle East. There's any number to choose from.' He offered a piece of paper to the German. 'Here are two names. One of them might be able to help.'

220

With that Gashi turned and walked away. Gunther stood watching him depart. He was in a quandary. He had made it clear when speaking to Soliman that he would use his own contacts. He had been disparaging when Soliman had offered reliable people to do the job. People who would carry out the operation regardless of their own safety. He glanced at the piece of paper and smiled. Amin Shirvani, he should have thought of him before. One of the caveats to the job had been there should be no way of tracing it back to the Prince. One way was to use Iranians. The world and its mother knew how much the Iranians hated the Saudis and vice-versa. Shirvani was a fanatic and psychopath who had killed many people in the name of Islam.

Gunther returned to his hotel and dialled the number Gashi had given him.

'Amin? A mutual friend gave me your name.'

'I have been expecting your call.'

Hiding his surprise he said, 'You were?'

'Yes, our mutual friend told me about a job and for the right price I will do it.'

'What did he tell you?'

'Not over the phone. I will be available tomorrow morning. Let us meet.' He gave a time and place and abruptly disconnected.

Like most people in their trade, surveillance by ECHELON was never far from their minds.

21

The jungle drums were beating loud and clear, thought Hunter, his feet up on the corner of his desk. Something was up. The attack on the synagogue in Paris was the fourth in as many days. Each had been carried out by different groups from different countries. So far the Western powers had identified Iranians, Saudis, Afghanis and Sudanese. Some reports identified the attackers as home-grown jihadists and they were the stuff of nightmares as far as the West was concerned.

Standing up Hunter crossed to the coffee machine and busied himself making a jug of Arabic No 6. The West was on the highest state of alert. It meant very little operationally. Every security service worldwide was on high alert for terrorist activity but then they had been for months. The politicians were talking sanctimonious crap, as usual, appeasing the politically correct instead of unleashing the special ops teams. Shakespeare had it right when he had written "Cry Havoc and let slip the dogs of war". It was a phrase Hunter had used more than once.

Coffee mug in hand he sat back at his desk and read the e-mail that had just arrived. It was from Macnair.

Mossad officer arriving tonight with special info. Please meet same in bar around 20.00.

He wrote back, '*Yes sir.*'

He checked the time, 19.40. After a day analysing the data being accumulated by the security services he decided to leave the coffee and have a whisky instead. He thought that there were two attacks in the offing, both in London. He had forwarded his observations to the General to do with as he saw fit.

A few minutes later he was standing at the bar with a large malt diluted with a splash of soda and an ice cube. He pondered on what he had learnt. He was looking in the mirror at an angle that showed him the door. If he was surprised when he saw who was entering he didn't show it. Instead, he turned and smiled at the woman walking towards him.

'Of all the bars in all the military establishments in all the world you had to walk into this one.'

'Hello, Nick, still paraphrasing Casablanca I see.'

Hunter shrugged. 'Great lines, ludicrous story. How are you, Ruth?'

'Is that the best you can do?' She leant forward and offered her cheeks for three pecks in the European fashion.

Smiling, he said, 'You look ravishing.'

'Liar. But I'll accept the compliment.'

She did look ravishing. She was dressed in dark blue trousers and matching waist length jacket with a white blouse. Over her shoulder was a bag that Hunter knew had been chosen to hold a purse and Glock automatic. The former no doubt she had, the latter not a chance.

'Drink?'

'Please. A gin and tonic would go down a treat.

Hunter ordered a double. They stood in awkward silence waiting for the drink. When it arrived Hunter said, 'Shall we take a seat?' He gestured towards a corner table. Ruth nodded and he escorted her across the room.

They sat opposite each other and Hunter raised his glass in salute, taking a sip. Ruth did likewise.

'I take it you're the Mossad officer we've been waiting to hear from?'

'A last minute substitute.'

'So how have you been keeping?'

'Fine,' she conjured up a smile. 'The knee hurts on wet and cold

223

days though luckily, we don't have many of those in Israel. Apart from that I can't complain.'

Hunter examined his feelings. Maybe there was a twinge of regret but nothing to write home about. He realised he was well and truly over her. Maybe his love for her and been more ephemeral than real. He dismissed the thought. No, it had been real enough. It was just that life had moved on, each taking separate paths.

'How's what's his name?'

'My ex-husband you mean?'

'Yeah, I guess your answer tells the tale.'

'It lasted all of six months until I discovered he was screwing as many young students in the university as he could.'

'Charming.'

Nodding, Ruth said, 'He was. Very charming.'

'That's not what I meant.'

'I know.' She took a deep breath and exhaled slowly. She looked into Hunter's eyes. 'I made a mistake.' She spoke in a soft voice. 'Sinatra almost got it right. Regrets, I have a few, I guess you're one.'

'The past is the past and best left there.'

'I know.' She looked in some surprise at her empty glass. Hunter had barely touched his.

'Another?'

'No thanks. I could do with something to eat.'

'I know an Indian in Dunfermline.'

'Sounds good to me.'

They took a taxi. They stayed off the subject of why Ruth was in Scotland and talked about inconsequential matters such as politicians, the war against terrorism and the bias of the media.

The food was okay while the Indian beer was cold and refreshing. They were back on base by 22.30 where they said an awkward goodnight. Hunter kissed her cheek, Ruth kissed his. He wasn't sure how he felt about seeing her only he knew there was not a scintilla of lust behind his feelings for her.

He returned to his boat, carried out his usual security checks and went onboard. He thought about a nightcap and then dismissed the idea. He neither wanted nor needed one.

The following morning he awoke at 06.00 and put on his running gear. He did a few toning up exercises followed by fifty sit-ups and fifty press-ups. He headed for the running track that surrounded the base and started to trot. He quickly built up his speed until he was running as though in a sprint but after 800 yards he slowed back to a fast pace that wouldn't disgrace a marathon runner. He couldn't help it but Ruth kept intruding into his thoughts. He thought about Cathy. More voluptuous, prettier and more of a laugh; good for a few entertaining weeks but not a lifelong partner.

Ruth had been the opposite. However, they were from different worlds. He wasn't prepared to give up his way of life and neither was she. She was an Israeli to the core and would always put her country first. On one level he couldn't blame her, on another he wasn't so understanding. Taking land occupied by another nation, people who had been there for generations, was unforgivable. He knew himself to be pro-Jewish but anti-Israel.

In reality, their relationship would never have survived. He had come to realise the fact a few weeks after they had parted. He had always assumed that Ruth had already arrived at the same conclusion. He suddenly realised he was running at a flat out sprint and slowed down to a reasonable pace.

He returned to the boat at 07.00, shaved and showered He thought about going to the dining hall for breakfast but changed his mind. He would have felt obliged to sit with Ruth, which for some reason he didn't wish to do. Instead he boiled a couple of eggs, toasted some bread and washed it all down with coffee.

He was at morning prayers early, checking with Isobel if there had been any terrorist activity the previous night. It seemed there hadn't. He went into the meeting room where, as he'd expected, he found fresh coffee.

The others trickled in and exchanged greetings while also heading for the coffee. Finally Macnair and Ruth arrived together. They all sat round the table and waited to hear what was going down.

Macnair looked at the faces and said, 'You all know Ruth apart from Chris.

'We met at breakfast,' said Bletchley. 'No introductions are necessary.'

'Good. Ruth is here to brief us rather than risk any message interception, something we are all cognisant of nowadays.'

The chances of an interception of messages between TIFAT and Mossad or any other agency were remote. Macnair figured she had wanted an excuse to visit Hunter. However, he would keep his thoughts to himself. Looking at his second-in-command he was pretty sure Hunter considered the relationship dead and buried.

'Ruth, the floor is yours.'

'Thank you, Malcolm.' She was dressed casually in blue jeans, a white blouse and lightweight black jacket. Like the others her jacket reached below her waist in order to hide any weapon she might have been carrying.

Ruth looked at the tough faces staring back at her. She knew Masters, Hughes and Badonovitch. They had been with her when her knee had been crushed. She had been introduced to Bletchley over breakfast and learnt he was engaged to Louise. She knew what had happened to the plane and was relieved that Mossad had played such an important part in saving the people onboard. Not, she acknowledged to herself, for the sake of the passengers although she was gratified nobody had died except the terrorist. No, what was of greater significance was the fact that the West now owed Israel a huge debt and one day they would need to collect. It was inevitable and after today they would owe even more.

The smile on her face was more a grimace. 'I guess I would like to start by saying it's not so much message interception we're concerned with but the importance of what we've learnt. First, let me brief you about our attack on premises in Tehran.'

Ruth went on to give a succinct account of what had happened during the attack, finishing with, 'Losing one of our men was a blow. However, when you callously weigh up the cost against the benefit I guess his death was, I'm not sure how to put this, but let's say on the right side of the ledger.'

The others understood all too well and nodded. The cost/benefit ratio was important. Dying was one thing, dying in vain something entirely different.

'We thought the place we hit was where the balls were manufactured as well as the explosive. Not so. It was a sales centre for supplying the balls to the customers. The explosive and balls are made elsewhere. Furthermore the balls come with different triggering mechanisms. The ones on the plane were pressure operated as we know but there are others with timers. As far as we can gather they come in three settings, fifteen seconds, one minute and fifteen minutes.'

'Presumably,' said Hunter, 'two are for throwing while the third is for placement and to give the terrorists time to escape.'

'That's the way we figure it,' said Ruth. 'And a cricket ball being thrown, even in a crowd won't frighten people apart from calling the thrower an idiot by which time it'll be far too late.'

The General said, 'Israel can't go it alone with another attack on Iran. They've already taken a huge risk. The Middle Eastern countries would have a field day if they found out. Iran would deny what they were up to and castigate Israel for an unprovoked attack. Islamic countries will scream blue murder while Iran will claim that many innocent people have been killed. All lies but unprovable. Even if proven nobody in the Islamic world would accept it.'

Ruth nodded. 'You're right. The finger of blame will be pointed firmly in our direction. That's why I'm here.'

Hunter said, 'While the world is yelling at Israel you'll be able to say the UN is involved through us thanks to our charter.'

'Correct. But also you can supply the truth as to what's happened and why. People will listen and we may be able to keep social media comments to a minimum.'

Macnair shook his head. 'I doubt that. Those not wanting to believe us won't.'

'Are you saying you won't help?' Ruth spoke sharply.

'No, of course not,' said the General. 'It's as much in our interests we stop production of the explosives and balls as it is yours. Rest assured we will do all in our power to help. Do you have the location for the manufacturers?'

'Not yet. We're expecting that information any day now. We know something else is in the offing though we don't know when or where.'

Badonovitch raised his hand to his shoulder. 'How do you know?'

Ruth shrugged. 'Jan, you know what it's like. A word here, a rumour there. Some people have dropped out of sight which is a sure sign they're up to something. We've shared everything we've got with Isobel and though it adds up to an attack somewhere, we can't be sure where and when.' Ruth paused and then added, 'Plus we have a source in Saudi who has proven to be reliable in the past. He also said something was going down though he wasn't sure what.'

'In Europe?' Masters enquired.

'No. The UK.'

'Using the balls?' Hunter asked.

Shrugging, Ruth said, 'We're not sure. However, we need to stop the manufacture of the balls and the explosives before they can be used again.'

'So what do you suggest we do?' Bletchley asked.

Ruth replied, 'The actual attack will be on the hoof but we need to plan getting to the target as well as a means of extraction.'

'We have two choices,' said Hunter, 'a high/low or vehicles. It will depend on where the plant is.'

A high/low was jumping out of an aircraft from as high an altitude as was reasonably safe, wearing oxygen and thermal suits and opening a specially designed aerofoil close to the ground. They had practiced it often enough though a refresher jump was in order provided they had the time.

'I opt for the jump,' said Bletchley. 'It will be quicker than crossing lousy terrain in a vehicle.'

The others nodded.

228

'And how do we get out?' Hunter asked. 'The only way is by vehicle.'

'Either pinch what we need,' said Masters, 'or have cars delivered somewhere accessible and we make a dash for it.'

'I think,' said Macnair, 'that we plan different strategies and pick what we need closer to the time and after we get more intelligence. I need to leave you to it as I have other operations that need my attention. Not least trying to find out where the attack on the UK is going to take place and when.' With that he left the room.

'More coffee before we start?' Hunter asked.

Amin Shirvani was a small man with a bushy moustache but otherwise clean shaven. Gunther guessed he was in his early thirties. He was dressed in a smart brown suit, white shirt and red tie. He looked the epitome of a successful businessman. By contrast, Gunther was wearing blue jeans, a plaid, open-necked shirt and a fawn jacket. Neither man was armed. In France like many other countries in the West it was safer not to carry a gun. If the police came for them it would be with overwhelming odds. Better to argue their case in court than be shot down in the street like a dog.

They were sitting outside a small bar on the outskirts of Paris. They were the only two people there. Sitting at a round table they watched the busy street and pavement. As far as they could tell nobody was taking any notice of them. They leant a little towards each other, speaking quietly. Both were smoking and had double espressos which had barely been touched.

'Did Stefan tell you anything?'

'Only that you wanted a family killed. He told me the time scale was too tight and so he couldn't do the job himself.'

'Does it bother you to kill a family?'

The Iranian shrugged. 'I prefer them not to be of my faith but it does not bother me even if they are. For the right price a job is a job.'

'The target is elderly parents and a daughter.'

'Where?'

'Scotland.'

'That makes it more difficult.'

'Why?'

'I have never operated in Britain. I have no contacts and no way of getting the supplies I will need.'

Gunther nodded knowing the man was lying. Shirvani had once detonated a van outside a house that had killed five people, the parents and three children. The house had been situated in private grounds in the county of Surrey, the target had been the defence minister for Saudi Arabia. The ploy of telling Gunther he had no contacts was to give him a bargaining chip.

They started to haggle but in reality it was all one-way. Finally Gunther accepted the terms as he had no choice.

A four man squad, $500,000 dollars for three of them, two million for Shirvani. Most importantly, weapons supplied in Britain. Payment was to be 50% up front and the balance when the job was done.

They picked up their coffees and sipped in celebration. Gunther suddenly had a thought. If he procrastinated paying Shirvani but told Hunter who had killed his family he could save $1,750,000. Or Shirvani could get lucky and kill Hunter, which was the outcome he most desired. Whichever way he looked at it he couldn't lose. If Hunter killed Shirvani and his crew that would leave Gunther with the money to hire someone to kill Hunter. Or if Gunther delayed long enough for the old Prince to die he would walk away with the money. The permutations swirled around his head.

Amin Shirvani didn't believe in suicide bombers. At least not for him and his close team. Dying for the cause was not on his agenda. He liked soft targets and a route out. He liked to plan and take his time. Neither was possible in this case. Speed was required. Even so he refused to act too quickly for two reasons. First he already had a job to do and second, he wanted the best chance to get away with his team. His consideration for the others had nothing to do with sentiment. Shirvani was utterly ruthless and cared nothing for human life, not even the lives of his own men. No, his consideration was due solely to the fact that he had trained them and created a disciplined and effective team. The other three were as equally ruthless as Shirvani.

Gunther reached down to a briefcase at his feet and withdrew a laptop. He flashed it up and brought up Google maps.

He pointed at the photograph. 'You see the old white house? The family used to live there. Now they occupy a new house, which they've just built. I downloaded the plans of the house from Stirling council and printed them.' He reached down again and handed over some A3 paper folded in half. 'Examine them at your leisure.'

Without comment Shirvani folded them again and shoved the papers into an inside pocket.

' There's a downside and an upside to hitting them there. Firstly, it's a quiet rural area and you could arrive and leave without being noticed. Secondly, Glasgow is only half an hour away. You can lose yourself in a city that size. You can lay low and after the heat has died down get out. Or head straight for the motorway and drive to London. That would be up to you.'

'What is the downside?'

'There's a police station just a couple of hundred metres along the road. Police cars come and go.'

Shirvani sneered. 'Huh, British police are not armed. If they tried to stop us they would die very quickly.'

Gunther nodded. The man's attitude was only to be expected. Nowadays the deployment of a Rapid Response Team was honed to a fine art. Any police patrol noting the Iranians would first of all call it in. Secondly only one of the two cops would approach and thirdly if the first man was shot, the second would take off like a bat out of hell. It wouldn't be from cowardice but pragmatic good sense. The Iranians would be lucky to escape which in the final analysis would suit him.

'If the police catch you then you will spend most of the rest of your lives in prison.'

'If they try to stop us a gun battle will follow. We will not surrender.'

Gunther nodded, suppressing a smile. That was precisely what he

231

wanted to hear. Furthermore, he knew it wasn't bravado. Shirvani meant it.

'As soon as you've carried out the attack let me know. I will immediately transfer the balance of the funds to your account. In that way you will know that I have kept my side of the bargain.'

Fat chance, he thought. A call to the police would be the order of the day.

22

It was early evening and Macnair was in his office. He had dealt with myriad matters that crossed his desk every day but had spent the last two hours reading up-to-date intelligence reports. The bottom line was they did not make for agreeable reading. The Jihadists had stepped up their attacks and the right leaning fascists of Europe were responding in kind. Innocent men, woman and children on both sides were being killed or maimed. His phone rang interrupting his gloomy thoughts.

'Macnair.'

'Malcolm,' said Isobel, her tone was without inflection, which was a bad sign, 'put on your TV. The news channel.'

Macnair picked up the remote, aimed it and pressed the on button. The picture sprang to life showing a BBC reporter holding a microphone.

Still with the receiver to his ear Macnair said, 'Where is this?'

'Paris. According to reports bombs have been blown up in a shopping mall. The attackers were seen to be throwing them from the first floor to the ground. There were also bombs left in rubbish bins. People said the bombs looked like tennis balls. The police broadcast that there were four attackers of Middle Eastern appearance. If members of the public suspect anybody, they are to call the police immediately and not approach them as they may be armed and dangerous.'

'How long ago did this all happen?'

'Over an hour.'

'They are long gone.'

'I agree.'

Paul Henke

Amin Shirvani was in a good mood. Ecstatic would be a better description. The attack had gone well and according to the news on his car radio over 200 people were dead or injured. He couldn't keep the smile off his face. It had been an attack for the prophet, peace be upon him, and a blow against those who did not believe in the one true faith.

Shirvani was a highly educated man who had a doctorate in religion and politics from Tehran University. His intention was to become a politician and to do so he needed a deep knowledge of Islam as well as a deep war chest. His university degree was ideal for his purposes. His plan was to work his way up the ladder of government and once he had the power he intended to wage war on the West. It might take 20 years but he was in no hurry. By then Iran would have access to nuclear weapons. He would use them, whereas the cautious West wouldn't dare. He felt a surge of excitement at the prospect. It might be decades away but it would happen. He was as sure of that as he was sure that the one true faith was Islam. And it was beginning. He had learnt that morning that he had been selected to stand in a rigged election for deputy governor of a province in the southeast of the country.

Following the successful attack on Paris he would say an extra prayer when he had the opportunity.

He was an hour away from Calais where he would return the car to Hertz. Dressed in a smart light brown suit, a light blue shirt and dark blue tie he looked like a successful businessman. His French passport and e-mail confirming a meeting in London would ensure he had no trouble with immigration.

The meeting was above board and on the face of it, so was the company. It was in fact a front for an Iranian cell. The company was a genuine developer of software used in the control of surveillance equipment. Two members of the company were the developers, four were salesmen and one was the CEO. The business was self-financing thanks to their customer base being amongst the Muslim communities of the UK. There were other companies just like it, spread across Europe.

234

They were able to supply a number of things - cash, weapons and explosives. The balls they had used had come from one such company established in Marseille, the London company was still to receive theirs. For the next job they didn't need explosives, only weapons. After studying the Google maps and photographs he had decided how they would carry out the attack.

The other three who made up his team were travelling by different routes. They all had a number of things in common. They were smartly dressed, carried French passports, European identity cards, credit cards plus cash.

Contentedly he drummed his fingers on the steering wheel of the Citroen while listening to rap music on a CD threatening death to non-believers. It was the sentiment plus the beat he enjoyed.

He returned the car after filling up with petrol. A check was made for any scratches. There was one. They tried to charge him for it. He had expected them to do so and had been meticulous in checking the car in Paris. He showed the customer services manager a photograph of the scratch using his iphone. The manager couldn't hide his disappointment much to the Iranian's delight as evidenced by his wide grin.

Shirvani strolled to the ferry terminal, stopped at the office to buy a return ticket and then headed for the restaurant. It was lunchtime and he was in need of sustenance. Fish soup and a bread roll did the job.

In the course of the next hour he received three messages. They all said the same thing. One word – arrived. It was written in English. If the word had been written in Farsi or some other Middle Eastern language it might have been picked up by ECHELON. Unlikely, but possible. He never took a chance unless he had to. It meant the others had arrived in the UK, one in Harwich, another in Hull and a third in Dover. All three were on trains heading for London.

Onboard the ferry he leant on the guard rail smoking a cigarette watching the wake. He was enjoying imagining the destruction of Calais with a single bomb. He stood up, mentally shaking himself.

He needed to concentrate on the job in hand. He flicked the cigarette butt into the water and headed for the bar for a cup of tea. He grimaced. Westerners had no idea how to make a decent cup of tea.

The bar was self-service and he stood patiently in line waiting to be served. He looked around and what he saw made him boil with anger. Western women were sluts, parading in front of the men showing their bodies. As far as he was concerned they should be whipped! Some, he thought, looking at a young woman wearing a low cut blouse, should be stoned as a lesson to others. He realised he was staring at her when she stared back and gestured at him with the middle finger of her right hand at the same time saying something to the young man with her. The man looked over his shoulder at him while Shirvani turned away.

The urge to kill them both was overwhelming and it took willpower not to cross the deck and do just that.

'What can I get you?' The voice was female and pleasant. The smile was false but practiced.

'Nothing,' he croaked and walked away. He realised his tight grip on the small case he was carrying was painful. He changed hands and flexed his fingers before stepping on to the deck outside, walking around the ferry to calm down.

After crossing the Channel he disembarked without any problems and quickly found himself on the train to London. During the journey he received text messages from the others confirming their arrival in England's capital and in the safe house.

The safe house was a four-bedroomed, detached house with a large garden in Putney. A hire car was already waiting for them. It was a Ford Fiesta. Probably the most inconspicuous vehicle to be found anywhere in the world. The owner of the house was in Iran on business while his family was taking an extended break in Torquay with his wife's sister. He was the CEO of the software company and in spite of his superior lifestyle compared to anything he could expect in Iran, he hated the West. He interpreted just about any comment as a slight against Islam in general and Iran in particular. His wife had tried to persuade him to change his attitude but after being slapped often enough she gave up. To get away from her husband was one of the reasons she was in Torquay.

The owner of the house had left weapons hidden in the basement along with instructions on how to access them.

Early on Monday morning they left London. Dana Ahmadi was driving and Shirvani was sitting contentedly behind him. Ahmadi was the one he trusted the most to get the job done. Not only was Ahmadi fearless, he was also very intelligent and hated the West as much as he did. It was clear Ahmadi was ready to die for his faith.

Alongside Ahmadi was Hooman Salan, as fanatical as the others and who shared Shirvani's political ambitions. Those ambitions were the reason he wasn't prepared to die for the cause. Like Shirvani he wanted to annihilate the West once and for all. That would take real political power in Iran and access to nuclear weapons. Dreaming of both allowed him to sleep contentedly while justifying to himself the murders he had committed and torture he had inflicted on non-believers.

Shirvani glanced at the man seated next to him. Ghazi Hosseini was a good soldier and had proven himself on numerous occasions. He wasn't the brightest but the most obedient. He did as he was told without question, prepared to kill or hurt as ordered. Shirvani knew he enjoyed doing both, which often caused him concern.

The three were of average height and weight, clean-shaven and dressed like businessmen. They were so inconspicuous, they would be lost in a crowd of two.

They had left London at 06.00 before the rush hour was really biting even though the traffic was already busy. The distance to their destination was approximately 400 miles. Sticking to the speed limit it was 7 hours. Add on delays for various reasons then they should be in Crosshall by 3.00pm at the latest.

They hit their first delay at the M40/M42 junction. They had travelled all of 95 miles and the time was just coming up to 07.55 when the traffic ground to a halt. There was no reason in evidence just a solid mass of traffic. They inched forward, Shirvani fuming at the delay.

It took 55 minutes to travel less than three miles as the motorway lanes were reduced from three to one. When they got closer they saw there had been a bad accident. A lorry and three cars had collided. There were police cars and ambulances on the scene still with their lights flashing.

Hosseini said, 'I hope they were all killed.'

'As do I, brother, as do I,' said Ahmadi.

'Better yet,' said Salan, 'let us hope they are dying in agony.'

The comment brought chuckles from the other two while Shirvani kept silent. He was busy thinking how the delay affected their journey time. According to the car's satnav, Glasgow was 310 miles away and would take five hours. The only problem was the motorway was packed with vehicles barely travelling above 50mph. It still wasn't too bad. If there were no further holdups once they hit open road and wound up to 70mph they should still make it by 4.00pm.

The next delay was caused by roadworks at the Hilton Park Services. It took 30 minutes to get through. Shirvani began to curse Britain in general and British motorways in particular. He would not have been gratified to learn that everybody who lived on the British Isles echoed their contempt for British roads.

They stopped once for fuel, and to use the toilets. Salan took over the driving and they continued their journey bolstered by large coffees.

They reached the motorway turnoff just before 5.00pm. They then followed the satnav instructions displayed on the dashboard. It was just after 6.00pm when they were approaching Crosshall.

'It's too early,' said Hosseini. 'It won't be dark for another four hours at least.'

The car crossed the River Heriot, rounded the bend at the bottom of the village and started up the hill. As they went around a second bend they could see Crosshall Bowling Club on the right, a blank wall on their left. They were driving slowly but luckily there were no cars behind them.

They were opposite the filling station when Hosseini nodded to his left and said, 'There's the house.'

'What now?' Ahmadi asked.

'Stop on the other side of the road. I just saw something,'

There were no cars coming in either direction and Salan pulled over. Shirvani looked back in time to see three people exit the driveway. Two were in their sixties, the woman with them he guessed was in her thirties.

'That's them,' said Shirvani.

'How can you be certain?' Hosseini asked.

'I was given a description. Where are they going?'

A couple walked past, one carrying a heavy looking small canvas bag over his shoulder. They glanced into the car. A minute or two later, another couple did the same thing.

As they passed the man looked behind him and stared into Shirvani's eyes. The man then looked to the front and said something to the woman next to him. She also looked back. Shirvani was still looking out of the back window. He faced the front and cursed.

'Drive on. Let's get out of here.' Yet again he couldn't resist looking over his shoulder. This time he saw the man holding something to his face and then putting whatever it was in a pocket. Shirvani was sure the man had just taken a photograph of the car.

If they killed the three targets in the house it would be hours before their bodies were found. With luck possibly as late as tomorrow at the earliest. Whatever he said about British police he knew them to be highly capable and tenacious. It was inevitable they would see the photograph. They would track down the car and discover it was hired using false ID and an untraceable credit card. The photograph would easily be enhanced to show his face. In spite of his usual bravado, he felt his mouth suddenly go dry.

'Did you see where the three people went?'

'Yes,' said Salan, 'to that green building. Next to the lawn.'

'The bowling club?' Shirvani asked.

'Yes, that's it.'

'That is where these other people are going,' said Shirvani. 'I think we shall do something different to what we planned. Go straight out of the village. We'll find somewhere to stop and come back later.'

'What are we going to do?' Ahmadi asked.

'Kill them all,' was the stark reply.

Hunter had just ordered a beer for himself and Jan Badonovitch. The bar was empty and looked like staying that way. It was typical of a Monday. Hughes and Masters were on the firing range while Bletchley had the weight. In other words, he was on duty should anything happen that required a response.

Hunter raised his glass to take a sip when the door was flung open and Bletchley appeared.

'Nick! Nick!'

'What is it Chris?'

Ruth appeared just then. She was slightly breathless having run from the Ops Room. Her face was ashen.

'Ruth will tell you.'

'I've just received a message from Tel Aviv. It's from our informant in Saudi. It's not good news. Nick, you and your family are targets. The explosion on the plane was an attempt to kill Louise. As far as the man who wants you and the family dead is concerned, the more collateral damage, that is to say dead and injured, the better. We have also been told it is imminent.'

Hunter's blood ran cold. 'Who is it?'

Ruth replied, 'Prince Abdul-Hameed Saud.'

'Never heard of him.'

'The operation in Germany,' Bletchley recalled.

'What about it?'

'His eldest son was killed and now he wants revenge.'

'They attempted to kill Louise and now intend to kill my parents?'

Ruth nodded. 'Nick, we've tried phoning your mother, father and Louise but there is no answer on any of their mobiles.'

Hunter looked at his watch. 'It's 18.45. They'll be at the bowling club. They usually turn their phones off to avoid distractions. They all take bowls very seriously.'

'What do you want to do?' Bletchley asked. 'I'm going there now.'

'Right. Forget about being duty officer.'

'Are you going to contact the police?' Ruth asked.

'No, by the time we reached an officer senior enough to sanction the deployment of a Rapid Response Unit my family would be dead.'

'We'd better draw weapons from the armoury. Ruth, please contact the General and tell him what's happening. He's probably at home in Edinburgh.'

'Can't I come with you?'

'There's not enough room. Dave and Don are on the firing range. They'll be coming. That's five in the car. Do we know who the attackers are?'

Ruth shook her head. 'We're rattling cages but nothing so far. We do know there could be as many as six but probably not less than four.'

Hunter knew he had to dismiss the notion that it was his family in danger. He needed to focus, concentrate and plan. The three men ran out of the building and down to the armoury and shooting range. A few brief words with Hughes and Masters while the others drew weapons and in minutes they were on their way.

All five were armed with Glocks carried under their left armpits, butt down. They also had silencers ready for use when they reached their destination. It gave them a small advantage. After a head is blown off, for a second or two everybody is in shock which gives the team long enough to switch targets.

Hunter switched on the blues and twos and slammed his foot down when they reached the road. Thankfully the traffic was light and what vehicles there were moved over quickly when the Land Rover appeared behind them. They had just over 48 miles to go, which would take one hour if they obeyed the speed limit. Hunter had no intention of doing that and had already wound the car up to 80mph.

The car phone rang and Bletchley pressed the receive button and put the phone on loudspeaker. 'Yes General.'

'Is there anything I can do?' Typically, he wasn't wasting his breath asking what they were doing.

'No, sir.' Hunter answered. 'We'll be there in about thirty minutes. We'll need to tell the police at some point,' he added.

'After the event is always best Nick, as you know only too well,' said Macnair. 'The procedures they have to go through could mean innocent people will die. We've seen it often enough. Ruth explained about the bowling club. I hope you're right.'

He didn't need to say that if his parents and sister weren't at the club then it was likely they were at home and dead.

23

There were twenty players. The eleven men would never see 60 again, the seven women ranged in age from 55 to 75 while the two youngsters had yet to reach 15.

They were in teams of four, playing on five rinks. They were also playing 12 ends, six one way and six back. The lawn was immaculate and the regulatory 40 metres square, surrounded by a ditch 300 millimetres wide and 150 millimetres deep.

The bowling green had one of the most spectacular views of any club in the UK across the valley to the Moorfoot Hills.

The sky was overcast with a hint of thunder in the air. The heat was oppressive and the type of weather favoured by the midges. Anti-midge cream had been liberally smeared on and those who were euphemistically described as folically challenged all wore lightweight hats.

The four Iranians drove back into the village. They parked opposite the doctor's surgery. A couple walked past with a black Labrador on a lead ignoring both the car and the men.

'Wait until they have gone around the bend. That is when we will make our move. We need to be quick. It is a shame we don't have silencers.' There were no silencers as they hadn't been expecting to carry out the attack in the open.

Moments later Shirvani said, 'Hooman drive down to the entrance to the ambulance station. We will stop just before it. Remember the family is to die a painful death. That means a bullet in their knees, elbows and stomach. The others we will be more merciful with and put a bullet in their heads. Remember to search the men for their phones. We must find the phone used by the man I am sure took a photograph of the car.'

'Amin, we know all this,' said Ahmadi. 'We have already been over it.'

'I am just reminding you.'

If any of them were nervous they didn't show it. In fact, they appeared as though they were looking forward to the carnage they were about to commit.

'The sooner we do this the sooner we can get away.'

The car stopped and three climbed out. Salan stayed behind the wheel.

Coins had been tossed and bowling had begun more than an hour ago. Louise had decided to play along with her parents who were on the verge of becoming as addicted to the game as the other players. After a few days at home she was feeling as good as new.

She lined up, swung her arm back and delivered the bowl. It rolled rapidly along the lawn losing momentum. It veered to the right and stopped about a yard short and a yard to the right of the white jack. How it had ended up there she didn't know. But that was the thing with bowls. The skill required was considerable. She shrugged her shoulders at her partner, Jacqui who smiled in return. Jacqui was in her late sixties, a slim elegant woman who was adamant she wasn't a good player. Louise knew all too well it was false modesty. She consoled herself with the fact she had played so rarely and hence was well below the standard of the other players. The two players they were playing against, Neil and Steven were excellent even if Steven was fast approaching his 90th birthday.

Louise stopped and stared at the three men walking down the short path to the gate. Her premonition of something being wrong quickly turned to fear when she saw they were carrying automatics. Before she could shout a warning a shot was fired into the lawn.

'Stay where you are or you will be shot,' one of them yelled.

The other players stopped what they were doing and looked at the three men. If they were frightened they didn't show it.

'Who amongst you are the Hunter family?'

Heads turned to look at Tim and Sian confirming Shirvani's original ID. They were at the far end of the lawn, in different teams a good 40 metres away.

'Come here.'

Shirvani needed them much closer to ensure the Iranians hit their targets.

Louise was playing at the other end of the lawn from her parents and not too far from the attackers. She sidled closer to the edge of the lawn and nearer to the attackers. She held her bowl down by her side. Of one thing she was damned sure, she would go down fighting.

One of the young lads, Jamie, showed great presence of mind. He was standing on the pathway at the far side of the lawn and jumped over the wall and onto the field. He scrambled to his feet and ran like hell. Only he ran in a straight line.

The three terrorists were lined up along the path with the clubhouse on their right. Hosseini was at the farthest end and he turned to aim his automatic at Jamie's back. The other players looked on in horror when Hosseini fired. He missed. He didn't get the chance to fire again. A man named Archie was standing near the terrorist with a heavy bowl in his hand. He threw it as hard as he could at Hosseini's hand and more by luck than judgement, hit his wrist. Because Hosseini was standing with his arm rigid and outstretched the bowl knocked his arm away and he dropped the weapon. Hosseini screamed, dropped to his knees and scrabbled around for the automatic. He couldn't clench his right hand and so used his left.

Gunther looked at his watch. According to his calculations the attack was either over or taking place. Only a few minutes earlier he had received a text informing him that the Iranians were moving into position.

He smiled. Already he was thinking what he would do with the money. He had to lose himself but the more he thought about it, the more he was sure he could do so safely. He gestured to a waiter and ordered another Courvoisier, a double like the first two he had imbibed. He had a hard head and the liquor was having no effect on him.

With the sister and parents dead that would leave Hunter. If the Iranians escaped then he would use them again. They were cannon fodder and expendable. Four against one grieving man was a foregone conclusion no matter who that man was. Even the infamous TIFAT wouldn't be able to prevent the outcome against four fanatics willing to die.

He finished his drink and decided it was time to eat. He placed sufficient euros under the empty glass to leave a gratuity and exited the bar. There was a restaurant on the corner he would try. One thing about the French in general and Parisians in particular - they were culinary experts.

Hunter had killed the flashing blue lights and siren as soon as they entered the village. He also dropped his speed to under 30mph. As desperate as he was to get to the bottom of the village, the last thing he wanted was an accident.

Three cars passed them going up the hill. A number of pedestrians were ambling along the pavement but took no notice.

The team knew precisely what to expect when they arrived at their destination. They had spent part of the journey examining Google Earth photographs of the area.

He slowed further and watched what was going on. The three terrorists were walking along the path on the left of the lawn while the players stood in a frozen tableau, watching them.

'Jan, Dave, Don go along the wall and fire as soon as you have a target. Chris, we go through the gate yelling.'

He didn't need to explain. The three men were the ones who would take out the targets, Hunter and Bletchley would be the distracters.

They watched Jamie running across the field and saw the shooter miss as the heavy bowl knocked his arm and with a scream he dropped his gun.

'In the car,' said Badonovitch.

'I see him,' said Hunter. He rammed the reinforced and heavy Land Rover into the back of the other car, shoving it a couple of metres down the hill and across the entrance to the club and ambulance station. The Fiesta's rear was buckled in against the wheels. The terrorist had smacked his head on the steering wheel and was dazed. 'Jan, I want him alive.'

Badonovitch already had the Land Rover's door open and leapt out grabbing his K-Bar. 'Okay, boss.' He reached the Fiesta and pulled open the driver's door. He rammed his knife into the deployed airbag before grabbing hold of the terrorist by the collar and dragging him out. The man wasn't wearing a seatbelt and collapsed to the ground. Badonovitch smashed the heel of the K-Bar's handle on to the man's temple. He went out cold. Badonovitch was glad to see he was still breathing.

It couldn't be helped. It was human nature. At the noise of the crash the players had looked up to see what was happening as did the terrorists.

Hunter yelled, 'Everybody hit the ground.'

Some responded others stood looking at the two men running their way. For Hunter it was as if time had stood still. He saw the scene playing out in absolute clarity.

Masters and Hughes were bent over and partially hidden behind a high stone wall, running as hard as they could. It would take a few seconds to get into position.

Hunter knew Bletchley was the better shot and said, 'Chris, shoot the nearest.'

They were outside the gate made of tall iron railings giving Bletchley a clear shot. Even so his target was at least 60 yards away. It was a tricky shot and they couldn't be sure the terrorists weren't wearing explosive vests.

Bletchley stopped at the gate, took up a firing stance with his gun hand supported by his left hand and pulled the trigger. The terrorist fired at the same time. Bletchley felt the wind from the bullet pass close to his left ear. His shot hit the man in the left shoulder causing

247

him to twist away so that the attacker's second shot went into the pristine lawn. Bletchley's second shot hit the man in the throat knocking him to the ground where he quickly bled to death in gasping agony. The other terrorists stood frozen, shocked into immobility. This was all new to them. They were used to killing unarmed and defenceless civilians, men, women and children.

Hunter fired at Shirvani and missed.

Shirvani screamed, '*Allahu Akbar*!' He pointed his automatic at Tim Hunter and fired. The bullet hit its target and sent Hunter Snr. flying to one side, knocking over a couple of the other men standing next to him. Unfortunately, one of the players, an ex-cop named Neil, had been standing behind him and the bullet hit Neil along the right side of his head.

Masters and Hughes were in position behind the wall. They took aim and fired. It was like a silent movie. Ahmadi and Shirvani had their heads blown apart.

Louise was kneeling by her father checking how badly he was hurt. The bullet had struck him in the front of his left shoulder and exited the back. Her mother was kneeling alongside, her face ashen and her hands trembling.

Hunter joined them. He could see his father was still breathing and that he wasn't bleeding too heavily.

He checked on Neil who was groaning and trying to sit up, his hand on the side of his head.

'Get an ambulance,' Hunter ordered.

Charlie said, 'Craig's gone for one.'

Dave Hughes had already run to the Land Rover, grabbed the first aid box and was back. He thrust the box at Hunter.

'Don, move the car so the ambulance can get out!'

Masters hurried away just as the doors to the ambulance station opened.

Hunter had ripped open his father's sleeve and was examining the wound. The bullet had left a small hole front and back. His father had been lucky. The bullet had passed just under his shoulder joint. Hunter

248

took a ready to use syringe, pulled off the needle guard and carefully injected the clear liquid into his father's upper arm. It was a powerful painkiller and would save his father from further pain as Hunter dressed the wound.

He placed a cotton pad on the entrance and exit and said to his sister, 'Louise, wrap a bandage around his shoulder over the pads and then take it around his torso to hold it in place.'

'Will he be all right?' Hunter's mother asked. She was still kneeling by her husband, his right hand clasped tightly in hers.

'Sure, mum, he's tough,' said Hunter.

'How can you be so sure?' she said, anguish etched on her face.

'Because I've seen wounds like this before. If we needed it, we have plasma in the car. Here's the ambulance.'

'Are you okay?' Bletchley asked Louise, putting his arm around her and pulling her to him.

'I...I guess so.' Her eyes welled up with tears. 'My God, what the hell is going on? First the plane and now this.'

Bletchley didn't know what to say apart from sharing a few platitudes with her and he knew she wouldn't appreciate them and so he kept quiet.

Two men ran over carrying a stretcher. Both were paramedics and checked Hunter's work.

'An adequate job,' said one of them. 'After we get him into the ambulance we'll connect him to a plasma drip.'

The straw-yellow plasma was a clotting factor and would help to stop the bleeding.

'Where will you take him?' Hunter enquired as they carefully lifted his father onto the stretcher.

'The Edinburgh Royal Infirmary.'

'Mum, are you going in the ambulance?'

'Of course.'

Meanwhile Dave Hughes had been checking on Neil. He had used a surgical wipe and cleaned the wound. Blood had trickled down the side of the ex-cop's face and he looked shaken.

Hunter asked, 'Are you okay?'

Helped to his feet, Neil looked at Hughes and said, 'Thanks.'

'No problem. You should go in the ambulance and get your head examined.'

'We've been telling him that for years,' said Steven, always the joker.

There were a few chuckles. It was like the waking of automatons as a frisson of awareness that brought the others back to life. One by one they stood up. One of the ladies began to cry while a few of the men let rip cursing the gunmen.

'I'm glad the swine are dead,' said Rory. 'I'll call the cops.'

'What about the cop shop up the road?' Bletchley asked.

Neil shook his head and winced. 'Good guys who do a good job in a rural community. The odd speeding and drunk and disorderly, maybe a burglary but not this. We need the heavy mob. *Allahu Akbar* and all that 'God is Great' crap makes my blood boil.'

'You seem to know a lot about it,' said Hunter.

'A few years ago I left the force as a Detective Chief Inspector. I worked for the British Police Anti-Terror Unit. Luckily I retired before the bloody Scottish government screwed it all up. Best thing I ever did.' Taking his mobile out of his pocket he switched it on. 'I know the right number to call.'

Hunter nodded. 'Tell whoever you speak to that TIFAT was here.'

Neil narrowed his eyes and examined each of the team. 'Yep, I see that now.'

Hunter nodded. If the man had been a senior officer in the ATU he'd know all about it. 'Tell them to phone General Macnair in Rosyth. He can do the explaining. Chris, why don't you drive Louise and take Don with you? Mum, give Chris the keys to the car.'

He didn't need to explain. They were bodyguards for the family.

Sian handed over her house and car keys. Bletchley hurried away.

Hunter realised the safest place for his family was at Rosyth.

One of the paramedics returned and said to Neil, 'Are you coming?'

'I'm okay. A & E have more to do than check me out. A whisky or

250

two will see me fixed.' He took a couple of paces towards the club-house and tottered.

Jean said, 'Neil, you're going to the hospital and that's the end of it.' She grabbed hold of his arm, one of the other ladies took the other and they led him away still protesting that all he needed was a large whisky.

'Let's go,' Hunter said to Badonovitch and Hughes.

'What about the bodies?' Harry pointed at the three dead men.

All the players looked where he was pointing, one of the women moaned and fainted while one of the men was sick all over the lawn. The remainder held their nerve though most had gone a chalky white.

'The police will deal with them.' Hunter speed dialled Macnair.

'Sir? We got here just in time. Three terrorists down. My father took a bullet in the shoulder but he should be okay.'

'No live one?'

'Not that you need to know.'

It wasn't spoken rudely. The General realised people were probably listening and that Hunter didn't want them to know he had captured one of the terrorists.

'One?'

'Yes, sir. We're leaving. One of the men here is ex-ATU and has phoned the unit. In the meantime, can you speak to the CC?'

'Right away. You'd better get a move on. The last thing we need is you being questioned by the police and your guest being taken into custody.

While they were speaking Hunter had been approaching the dead men. He and Macnair said their goodbyes. Hunter knelt by each body in turn to quickly check their pockets only to find them empty. There was no ID, not even a credit card.

He turned to the players. 'Don't touch anything and that includes the guns. Leave everything as it is for the police.' He smiled. 'May I suggest you all head for the bar? A few whiskies won't go amiss.'

'Huh,' said a lady by the name of Freda, 'I shall have a cup of tea thank you very much.'

'Good for you,' Hunter smiled. 'That would be my choice as well. Tea is just about right for every occasion.'

'At times like this I like mine with a large shot of brandy.'

Hunter watched her walk away trying hard not to smile. Tea with brandy was a new one on him.

One of the ladies called out, 'I'll come as well Freda, only I'll have a black coffee with my brandy.'

Turning to Archie he said, 'Well done. I don't mean to sound patronising but that was quick thinking as well as requiring guts.'

Archie shrugged. 'I was too angry to think about it. We'd been winning and now the game is cancelled. I suppose there's always next week. Now I need a large whisky and I think on this occasion I won't bother with soda or ice.'

There were a few chuckles as they all streamed towards the clubhouse.

Someone had gone inside and returned with a couple of towels and thrown them over the heads of the dead terrorists. 'That's better. It's a ghastly sight.'

Hunter headed for the car. Badonovitch had already transferred Salan into the backseat of the Land Rover while Hughes had checked the terrorists' car.

'Four bags, boss. I've put them in the back of the Rover. The car's okay. Just a few scratches and a slight dent.'

'Good. In that case we had better foxtrot oscar. The local cops might be told what's going on and be here any second.'

Hunter climbed into the passenger's seat; Hughes was driving while Badonovitch sat behind him.

'Is he going to live?'

'Yes, boss. He's awake. I used a few tie-wraps. He isn't going anywhere.'

'Good.'

'Where are we going?' Hughes asked starting the engine.

'Go straight. I'll drop the pair of you at the next village. There's a hotel there. You can order a taxi to take you back to Rosyth.'

He knew he was wasting his breath but he thought he ought to make the offer. What he was planning went way beyond illegal.

'Jan, did you see that?'

'The pigs you mean?'

'Yeah. They flew pretty close.'

'Okay, you pair of clowns.'

All three knew that what was to follow wasn't going to be pretty but they had no choice. Information was vital and there was only one way to get it.

'So where are we going?' Hughes asked.

'Base.'

'So why the rigmarole about a taxi?' Badonovitch asked.

Hughes answered. 'To give us an alibi.'

Just then a fleet of police cars, lights flashing and sirens sounding screamed past heading for Crosshall. It didn't matter what Macnair said to the Chief Constable, the system had been prompted into action and they followed a strict procedural path.

The CC would keep TIFAT out of things as far as possible although there may be a few questions asked as to why the team hadn't stayed around to answer questions. The stock answer was they had things to do. They were following up information received and couldn't waste any time. The stock reply suited everyone. The police could let TIFAT do its thing while they returned to more mundane affairs such as robberies, rapes and murders. The contribution made by the police was never denigrated by the teams, they just had different problems to deal with. The police hated the idea of "halt or I fire" as much as the general public did. Shoot the terrorists first and question them after, was a notion favoured by many law-abiding citizens.

'We daren't take a risk,' said Hunter. 'No matter where we go there is always a danger of being seen. The only thing to do is go to sea.'

The journey was uneventful and an hour later they were back at base. They then drove straight to the pier where Hunter's boat was berthed. Hughes parked the car as near to the boat as possible. Hunter carried out his usual checks to make sure the boat was as he had left her. Satisfied, they left the car locked with the terrorist securely trussed up. While Hunter carried out pre-departure checks Badonovitch made them a mug of coffee. By the time they had finished drinking it, night had fallen and brought with it a cloudy, moonless sky.

Hunter stepped ashore and unlocked the car. He opened the back and looked down into the eyes of the terrorist who glared back. The gag he had around his mouth was crushing his lips into his teeth and was soaked in blood.

Hunter leant down, grabbed the man by his ears and dragged him out of the car, on to the ground. He was about to pick him up when Badonovitch took over, threw the man over his shoulder, and dropped him on to the boat deck.

'Thanks, Jan.'

Hunter flashed up the engines, Hughes let go the berthing ropes and they eased gently away from the wall and headed down river.

Hunter's phone rang. A glance showed it was his sister. His heart was in his mouth when he asked, 'Hi, how's Dad?'

He could hear the relief in her voice when she said, 'He's going to be okay. He just needs plenty of rest. Nick, do you know what's going on? First the plane and now this. It can't be a coincidence.'

'It's not. Someone wants me dead but only after you've been killed.'

Louise gasped before she replied, 'Thanks for sugaring the pill.'

'There's no time for that. Tell Chris and Don that as soon as Dad is able to travel, to take him, you and mum to Rosyth. The General will arrange for a doctor to visit every day to change dad's bandages and whatever else might be needed.'

'Do you think that's really necessary?'

'Louise, think about it. We've been incredibly lucky so far. Rosyth is about the safest place on earth and I want you where I don't have to worry about you.'

'What will you be doing?'

Hunter's voice was as bleak as an Antarctic storm, 'Making sure nobody comes after my family ever again.'

24

Two hours later they were abreast of Fidra Island near North Berwick. It was just after midnight and Hunter was sitting at the console in the chair looking out of the windows. The other two were below sleeping.

He looked at the Isle of May and counted two white flashes every 15 seconds. Another 45 minutes at 12 knots and they would be near the island. He swept the horizon using binoculars, checked the radar for ships and went below to make coffee.

He had spent the previous couple of hours checking the bags and documents of the four terrorists. The documents he had scanned in and sent to HQ. Although it was the middle of the night, duty personnel would already have started examining the paperwork. One thing was clear to Hunter. For the four men to get to Crosshall they must have had help. He wanted to know who had helped them.

He knew from the passports he had found that the man lying on the deck was named Hooman Salan. Whether that was his real name or not Hunter would know soon enough.

He reduced speed so that the boat merely had headway to enable her to steer a straight course then, with a coffee in a travel mug he went out on deck. Salan was hog-tied with his wrists and ankles secured to the anchor chain with tie-wraps. He was asleep. Hunter woke him up by the simple expedient of kicking him in the ribs. He kicked hard. The man would have yelled but the gag did its job.

'I'll be back in a few minutes,' Hunter said pleasantly, taking a sip of coffee. 'Then I'll ask a few questions which you will answer.'

The man struggled against the tie-wraps, making angry noises through the gag.

Sipping more coffee, Hunter smiled and said in Farsi, 'You may think you're tough but you will talk, I can promise you that. Whether it is after I have cut off one or all of your fingers, and your toes, I promise you, you will answer my questions.'

The man looked at Hunter in utter astonishment. The last thing he had expected was to hear Farsi being spoken. He squirmed further, pulling hard against his restraints but to no avail. Instead, the tie-wraps tightened a notch or two making them even more painful. He glared up at Hunter, who removed the gag.

The man let loose another round of invective followed by a demand that he was handed over to the authorities.

Shaking his head, Hunter said, 'You don't seem to understand Hooman, you will die. It will be later today. You can die after hours of agony or enjoy, if that's the right word, a quick and painless death. It's entirely up to you.'

Hunter stared at the inert figure who glared back defiantly. Then Hunter placed a piece of canvas across the deck and tied it down at the corners. Next he stepped up to Salan and kicked him hard in the mouth. The man went limp and Hunter cut the restraints holding him to the anchor cable. He picked up the inert body and dumped it on the canvas. Again he used tie-wraps to secure the terrorist spread-eagled across the deck.

It was then that Badonovitch and Hughes appeared on deck.

'It's okay you guys, I can manage.'

Neither spoke but stared down at Salan for a few seconds.

Badonovitch spoke. 'We want to help, Nick. I want to see this scum suffer.'

'So do I,' said Hughes.

Hunter took a towel and wrapped it around Salan's head. Badonovitch had filled a bucket with water and poured it slowly over the towel. The man bucked and struggled, coming back to consciousness. He had the sensation of drowning, a technique devised by the CIA when questioning terrorists held at Guantanamo Bay, an American base on the south coast of Cuba. It was known as water boarding.

Hunter took no pleasure in torture. He knew it wasn't totally effective, which meant there were no guarantees the information would be genuine, but he'd do whatever it took to protect his family from the vendetta paid for by a Saudi prince.

Hunter lifted the towel. Salan coughed, spitting blood along with a tooth. He worked phlegm into his mouth and was about to spit at Hunter who dropped the towel back over the man's face. Badonovitch immediately poured more water over the towel, causing Salan to begin squirming and coughing. The man was panicking in absolute terror, the tie-wraps tightening even further, cutting off his circulation.

Hunter lifted the towel and let Salan breath.

'Who sent you to kill my family?'

By way of answer, Salan screamed abuse at Hunter and his family. Hughes kicked the man in the ribs. He kicked hard, causing Salan to scream.

None of the warriors from TIFAT enjoyed what they were doing but if they were to stop any further attacks, they had to roll up the organisation responsible, all the way back to the Prince.

'Do you speak English?' Hunter asked.

There was no reply and so Hunter kicked him again only harder this time.

'I asked you a question.'

'Yes.'

'Good. In that case we will speak English.'

In reply, Salan let loose with a barrage of invective in Farsi. Much of it had to do with Hunter's parentage and ancestors. Hunter let him rave for a few minutes before placing the towel over his head again. Salan shook his head back and forth trying to dislodge the cloth but to no avail. Badonovitch poured seawater over the cloth. This time he kept pouring far longer than previously.

When the bucket was empty Hunter flicked away the cloth. Salan was gasping for breath and took a few minutes to get his breathing under control. He glared at the three men staring down at him.

'The bacon?' Badonovitch suggested.

Hunter nodded. It had been effective in the past. Muslims who believed literally in the word of the Qur'an did not eat pork. They wouldn't even touch it.

Badonovitch went below and a few moments later returned with a packet of sliced bacon. He held it up in front of Salan and then peeled it open.

Salan looked on with disdain. It was not the reaction that Hunter had been hoping for.

'Do you know what this meat is?'

'Bacon,' was the sullen reply.

'Yes, and I will wrap it in your body when I drop you over the side.'

Salan made a noise that was a parody of a laugh. He then said, 'Forbidden to you are dead meat, blood, the flesh of swine, and that on which hath been invoked the name of other than Allah.'

'So you know your Qur'an,' said Hunter. 'That doesn't alter the situation. You will die with the bacon wrapped around your body.'

'Go ahead. I do not care for the pathetic ramblings to be found in a book that is fifteen hundred years old. I may be a Muslim but I do not believe as others do.'

'Then why do you do what you do?' Hunter asked.

This time Salan's forced laugh carried a little more conviction. 'The money, the lifestyle, the fun of killing Westerners. The alternative is a life of poverty in Iran ruled over by a bunch of psychopaths.'

'You speak very good English,' said Hughes.

'I had a good education. I trained to be a lawyer but didn't have the right connections to succeed in Iran. However, that all changed when I joined Shirvani.'

Now that he had got Salan to talk Hunter was determined to keep him going.

'You consider it fun to kill Westerners?'

'Yes, I'm not a believer in the true sense of the word but I hate all of you.'

'Why?'

'Because you killed my sister.'

'When and how?' Hunter asked.

'Two years ago. It was a drone attack in Syria.'

'What was she doing in Syria?'

Salan clamped his mouth shut.

It took a few seconds but Dave Hughes understood. 'She was ISIS.'

'She saw it as fighting in the name of the one true prophet, Mohammed,' then he added, 'peace be upon him.' Which, considering his denial of Islam was surreal.

'She was a part of the most evil, psychopathic group ever to come into existence since the Nazis,' retorted Hunter.

The terrorist said nothing, merely glowered his hatred.

Hunter put the cloth back over the man's head and Badonovitch poured more water over it. Salan bucked and struggled but to no avail.

They left Salan with the cloth over his head and went below where Hunter made some fresh coffee.

'What do you think? Is he going to talk?'

'Nick, he's a tough son of a bitch but you know as well as I do that everyone talks in the end,' Badonovitch replied.

'You're right. But I don't want to waste time.'

As he spoke, he poured three coffees, added milk and handed them round.

'Maybe he was lying about his fear of bacon,' suggested Hughes.

'I don't know. He seemed to think the idea funny,' said Badonovitch.

'Yes, I think you're right, Jan.' Frowning, Hunter added, 'I have to find out who's behind the attack and that means rolling up their whole network. These people committed a cardinal sin attacking my family.'

'I thought we knew who was responsible, some Prince or other,' Jan offered.

259

'Prince Abdul-Hameed Saud,' said Hunter. 'I need to make sure it really is him. I don't want my parents having to live in fear or Louise having to give up flying in case they might try again. No, they are going to learn a lesson they won't forget.'

Hunter looked at his watch. 'That's twenty minutes of uncertainty. No more pussy footing around. You two stay here.' He looked at both men. 'I mean it.'

Hunter went forward to the workshop and storeroom and picked up a pair of bolt cutters. He returned to the deck via the forward hatch. Salan was lying still, the cloth over his face, but breathing. Hunter didn't delay. He stepped across the deck, knelt at the man's left side put the small finger of Salan's hand in the bolt cutters and clamped them closed. The finger dropped off, Salan screamed and arched his body while Hunter lifted the cloth from the terrorist's face.

'I want to know who helped you in this country.'

'What…What do you mean?'

'You know what I mean. Somebody helped you with the weapons and I suspect the car.'

Before Salan could answer Hunter's phone rang. He saw it was from HQ.

'Yeah?'

'Nick? It's Leo. First of all, the passports and driving licences they were using are fake. They are part of a batch stolen in France about a year ago and pop up from time to time. Europe is awash with fake EU licences and passports that can be picked up for peanuts if you know where to go. We had no joy with the car. It's hired but the hirer used fake ID and a credit card registered with a bank in the Bahamas. Payment went through okay but when we tried to trace the payer we came to a dead end. The card was honoured with enough in the account to pay the invoice in a week or two. I guess you can say money is no object.'

'There's a surprise. Okay, thanks, Leo.' Hunter broke the connection. It showed the enemy operated a professional set-up.

He looked down at the inert body. Salan curled his mouth into a sneer but before he could say anything, Hunter kicked him hard in the mouth, breaking teeth and crushing lips. He didn't speak but knelt down, took hold of Salan's index finger and tried to put the jaws of the cutters around it. The man curled his hand into a tight fist.

'I'm finished with being Mr Nice.' Letting the hand go Hunter stood up and then brought the heel of his foot down on to the fist. He could hear bones breaking. The terrorist screamed. Hunter knelt again, took hold of the hand, straightened the index finger and cut it off.

The man thrashed about, whimpering.

'Who helped you when you arrived in the country? There was no way you brought guns through customs.'

He took the middle finger of the crushed hand, pulled it straight and placed the cutters around it. The man screamed again in agony as the broken bones in his knuckle grated together.

Hunter said, 'You can have all the agony you can take or you can have a painless death. What's it to be?'

Salan was gasping for breath and tears were streaming down his face. 'All right,' he gasped. 'All right.'

'What's all right?'

'I don't know the man's name but we went to a house in London. An area called Putney. The road was Royal Crescent, number twenty-five.'

Hunter now had a dilemma. Was the man telling the truth and if not how was he to confirm it one way or another?

He phoned Leo. 'Can you check on a house in Putney?' He relayed the address. 'Find out who owns it as well as their nationality. Thanks.' He broke the connection.

'You'd better be telling the truth. Otherwise I'll take the rest of your fingers.'

It didn't take long.

'Nick? The house belongs to an Iranian businessman who has leave to stay indefinitely. His name is Akram Javid. He owns a software company and according to his tax returns is doing well for himself.'

'Where is he now?'

'In Iran.'

'Has he family?'

'Yes. A wife and three teenage kids. The kids were born in the UK and go to private schools. A girl and two boys.'

'Are they also in Iran?'

'No. A far as we can tell they didn't leave the country. There's something else. He's due back tomorrow.'

'When did he fly out?'

'Six days ago. We've looked at a Google photograph of his house. It's in the multi-million pounds bracket.'

'Okay, Leo thanks. That fits.'

'It looks as though you were telling the truth.'

Night was fading and dawn wasn't far away. Hunter went down through the forward hatch and returned with a couple of leaded diving belts and some thin wire. He slipped the weights off the belts and threaded them with the wire. He wrapped the weights around Salan's waist. He undid the rope holding the canvas in position and tied it around his ankles and neck, leaving his head free.

'I curse you and your family. You will go to Jahannam for all eternity as will your family.'

'If I do, I will no doubt see you there.'

'Wait. I recognise you. You will be dead soon.'

'How do you figure that out?'

'The contract has been issued and cannot be stopped. You and your family will die.'

Shaking his head Hunter said, 'It won't happen.'

In spite of the pain he must have been in and what was about to happen, Salan gave a half laugh. 'You are a fool. The contract won't be revoked. You are a dead man walking.'

Hunter shoved Salan over the side and watched as the body floated for a few seconds before vanishing beneath the undulating sea. Hughes and Badonovitch appeared on deck.

'Back to Rosyth. We've got work to do.'

25

It was just after 08.00 when they berthed alongside at Rosyth. They made their way to the Operations Centre. The General was talking with Isobel and Leo.

'Any fallout from Crosshall?' Hunter asked.

Macnair shook his head. 'Not as such.'

'What do you mean, not as such?'

'It was inevitable but one of the bowlers spoke to the press. They in turn have already interviewed a number of the players. Your name along with ours obviously came up.'

Hunter shrugged. 'It was inevitable. That's why I would like my parents and Louise billeted here for a while. Provided you have no objection, sir.'

'Of course not.'

'I need to phone the hospital and find out how the old man is doing.'

'I already checked,' said Macnair. 'Your father will be okay. He's a tough guy. The bullet did no serious damage. It nicked the bone but he should be released in a couple of days. I've sent Beta squad. Two on and two off. The CC offered police protection but I pointed out he needed his officers for routine policing which he agreed. I think he was relieved we were taking care of it.'

'Good. Thanks for that. I'll phone anyway if you don't mind.'

'Of course not. When you've finished come into the briefing room.'

Hunter confirmed what he'd been told. 'Louise, have the other team arrived?'

'About ten minutes ago.'

'Then why are you still at the hospital?'

'But dad…'

'No buts. It'll be easier and safer for the guys to protect just one person.'

'Nick…'

'Bloody hell Louise, just do as I say. I've had a long night and can't be bothered to argue.' He softened his tone. 'By the way, how's the guy who had the bullet to the side of his head?'

'Neil? He's okay. He's been sent home.'

'Good. Now put Chris on.'

Hunter could hear his sister. 'It's Nick, he wants you.'

'Yes, Nick?'

'Chris, drag Louise and my mother out of the hospital if you have to. Take them home to pack enough clothes for a fortnight. They need to collect Winston. The poor dog must be crossing his legs by now. Oh, and don't forget to tell them to take bathing costumes and gym gear. They may as well get fit while they're here. Dad can join them later. We've got something on and I want you and Don back here asap.'

'Connected with what's happened?'

'Yes, I'm going to roll up their organisation no matter what it takes. I want anyone who's planning to attack my family to know that I'll track them down and ensure they have a bad death.'

'We're on our way.'

Hunter hung up and went into the briefing room and poured himself a cup of coffee. He waved the pot at the others but they already had full mugs.

Present were Macnair, Isobel, Leo, Gareth, Badonovitch, Hughes and Ruth. Hunter sat down and sipped his coffee.

'What have we got?' Hunter asked, placing the mug on the table.

'Quite a bit, thanks to Ruth,' said Macnair. 'From her info and what Leo and Gareth put together we've identified what we believe are most of the players.'

264

'Most?'

Isobel said, 'Nick, you know all too well that we can never be sure if it's every player. We'll keep digging. If we learn any more, we'll let you know.'

'Okay. So what have you got?'

'Ruth, tell Nick what you know and I'll explain what we did with the info.'

Ruth nodded. 'Fair enough. We now know there are two overriding operations. One is attacks on Europe using those balls. There are a fair number of attacks planned, however we don't know how many or where. We do know the attackers are Iranian and that many are embedded into European society. Isobel has all the details and may be able to identify some of them. We're eavesdropping like crazy on the names we have and have had some success.'

'Are we dealing with them?' Hunter asked.

'No,' said the General. 'We're passing the info to MI5 as well as GCHQ. They can take the credit. I'm told the first op is tonight. As I understand it, they are going in mob handed as well as hard. We'll wait and see.'

'What about warrants?' Hunter asked.

Macnair shook his head. 'All done under the anti-terrorist emergency act.'

Badonovitch said, 'That'll give their solicitors plenty to scream about.'

'They can scream all they want,' said Macnair. 'People are completely fed up with hearing about the rights of terrorists rather than the safety of innocent people.'

'So what are we doing?' Hunter asked.

'Nick, we have eleven ops on-going. Nine in Europe and two in Pakistan.'

'In Pakistan? Since when?'

'Yesterday. We are lucky we have Beta team to help otherwise your operation would have to be delayed. As it is we can continue.'

'Thanks, sir.' Hunter didn't say he would have gone anyway. But by the look on the General's face Hunter was sure he understood that.

Macnair was also aware that his team would have gone with him. Their loyalty to Hunter was total.

'Isobel,' Macnair looked at the head of IT department, 'what have you got?'

'Thanks to Ruth,' Isobel nodded in her direction, 'we've learnt a great deal. Some of it is conjecture some of it is verifiable.'

'Conjecture?' Macnair echoed.

Ruth spoke. 'It's information we received from our Saudi mole. Whoever he is he must be high up on the Prince's staff. His intelligence has been accurate since he first contacted us over four months ago.'

'Any ideas?' Hunter asked.

'None. We were dubious about him at first, but you know how it is. We trust nobody until we can prove they can do what they claim.'

'And has he?' Macnair asked.

'Yes, we were able to intercept arms deliveries to Daesh in Syria and to Iraq.'

They all knew that Ruth was referring to the terrorist organisation that consisted of the Islamic State of Iraq and the Levant also known as ISIS. Daesh was the Arabic language name of the organisation. It was a militant terrorist group of Jihadists who followed the Sunni doctrine of Islam. It was the same doctrine as the Saudis. Daesh claimed to rule a proto-state or quasi-state, which was a political entity but did not rule an autonomous sovereign state. It was also steeped in hatred of all things modern and Western. It killed indiscriminately, with no regrets for their victims. They made videos of beheadings and the shooting of innocent civilians and posted them on the Internet. They were loathed and feared in equal measure.

'Are you saying the Saudis have taken to supplying weapons or explosives directly to Daesh?' Macnair asked.

'No,' Ruth shook her head. 'As usual they want to deny any involvement with any of the Middle Eastern terrorist groups and pretend to be friends of the West. They supply the cash and third party intermediaries. We know what's going on, the Saudis know we know but politically, we turn a blind eye to it all.'

'For the arms sales and oil purchase,' said Hunter.

'You've got it in one,' said Ruth, 'or maybe I should say two. However, this is different.' She stared at Hunter. 'Nick, this is personal. Prince Abdul-Hameed Saud wants you dead after you feel the pain of the death of your family. This is in retaliation for the death of his son in Germany.'

Hunter nodded. 'That was because the suicide attack wasn't meant to include the son. His explosive waistcoat was a dummy.'

It was Ruth's turn to nod. 'It's something he'd done at least three times, possibly four. He didn't expect to be at risk. He planned to inherit his father's vast fortune and turn it into a weapon against Israel in particular and the West in general.'

'How do you know this? Your mole?' Macnair asked.

'Correct, but here's the thing. The Prince has lung cancer. He's in the final stages and probably won't last the month. That's why when he found out Nick's involvement in the death of his son, he moved very quickly and put one hell of a price on your head, Nick.' Ruth stared at her former fiancé.

'How much?' Hunter was intrigued.

'Twenty million, US dollars that is.'

'How satisfying to be valued so much,' Hunter quipped. If he was perturbed by the amount, he didn't show it.

'I want the whole network rolled up,' Macnair echoed Hunter's words from earlier. 'And by that I mean all the way to the Prince. Everybody who has had a hand in this attack must be eliminated. Once that's done, I'll ensure the word gets out. If that scum think they can attack my people or their families with impunity, they've another think coming.'

The meeting lasted another two hours, then one of Isobel's analysts appeared.

'Sorry for interrupting.'

'That's all right, Julie,' said Isobel, 'what have you found out?'

'As we thought, if Louise was the target then someone had to discover her schedule. They did.'

267

'Who,' Hunter asked, 'and how did you find out?'

'If someone manages to get into the database of a company or organisation and root around then they leave a trail. It's a bit like someone breaking in through a window and not closing it behind them. And then leave muddy footprints as they search the place. I think the person who broke in was very good but also careless.'

'How could he be both?' Macnair asked.

'Well, sir, he's either very good or very lucky. I was able to trace his attack from beginning to end. He took thirty-three minutes and a few seconds to get the info he wanted and quit the system. That's pretty good going even if the target is an unimportant commercial site like a personnel roster. I think that was when he became careless. To wipe out your tracks after breaking in takes some effort. Probably another twenty minutes or so. He obviously couldn't be bothered. I suspect because he reckoned nobody would be looking.'

'I suppose,' said Hunter thoughtfully, 'if the plane had been brought down nobody would have thought of looking. Just another terrorist attack.'

'Very likely,' said Julie, 'but we've managed to follow the trail to Greece.'

'Good work,' said Macnair warmly, 'it's something we can use. Somebody must have given this person the commission.'

'We'll know soon enough,' Bletchley said grimly.

'Do we have the actual address?' Hunter asked.

'Yes,' Julie replied. 'It's in a town called Artemida.'

'Near the airport,' suggested Badonovitch.

Julie nodded.

'You know it?' Hunter asked, looking at Jan.

Shrugging, he replied, 'I went there a couple of times on leave.'

'Okay, we can start there,' Hunter said.

'What about London?' Bletchley asked.

'Ah, yes. You're right. Thanks Chris. We'll pay a visit to London just to wrap things up. I'd like the Gulfstream please, sir.'

Macnair waved a hand in front of him. 'I figured you would. Whatever you need, just help yourselves.'

Use of the jet meant they could fly to Greece with all the gear they needed.

They could have their equipment delivered by diplomatic pouch, a euphemism for something the size of a briefcase ranging to a shipping container. As important, nobody at the British embassy would know they were even in the country, never mind carrying out an operation.

Macnair asked Bletchley, 'Are Louise and Sian comfortable?'

'I think so. They are in the VIP suite. One of the stewards is showing them around and looking after them. Tim should be here in two days. Sian was kicking up a fuss until he pointed out that they would be risking lives if she were to visit him in the hospital and that a couple of days was neither here nor there.'

'Good. Nick, when are you heading south?'

Hunter glanced at the wall clock. 'Wheels up at 14.00 or thereabouts. That gives us time to get our gear together. I'll let Burg know we need him.'

Burghard Schwarzkopf was an ex-German air force pilot and was licensed to fly various planes as well as helicopters. He had proved his value many times.

'Right,' said Macnair, standing up, 'we're finished. Carry on everybody.'

'I'm coming with you,' said Ruth, glaring at the men sitting opposite her, as though willing them to argue against it.

They in turn exchanged glances, shrugged and Badonovitch said, 'Why not?'

Ruth said, 'Thank you. I want to see the Prince die. His son was responsible for a number of attacks on Israel. Shortly after the third, my informant surfaced.'

'Okay. We'd better go.' Hunter, Bletchley, Masters, Badonovitch, Hughes and Ruth headed for the armoury. There were numerous pieces of hardware they wanted.

On the way out, Hunter phoned Schwarzkopf and told him what

they were doing and to prepare flight plans. The pilot was based at Prestwick and had spent the previous week flying teams to various destinations.

In the armoury they each chose a Glock automatic.

Dave Hughes also chose a new rifle, the Remington Modular Sniper Rifle. It was accurate to 1,500 metres and had a magazine of 10 rounds. Its suppressor was highly efficient and as a plus it weighed only 18lbs, an advantage when yomping across harsh terrain. Not that they planned to do so on this operation but they followed the Boy Scout motto of "Be prepared".

They took 10 minutes to pack their bags before piling into a couple of cars and headed for Edinburgh airport. They located the Gulfstream in the area set aside for private aircraft, parked the cars and hurried into the plane. Schwarzkopf already had the coffee brewing.

Hunter joined the pilot in the cockpit.

'So what's up, Nick?'

Hunter briefed him while Schwarzkopf called the tower and finished preparing for departure. Twenty minutes later they were in the air and headed for Gatwick. Flying time was 1hr 30mins. After takeoff Hunter went back into the cabin to discuss tactics with the others. Masters, a qualified pilot and capable of flying the Gulfstream, took his place.

'You've all seen the photos of the house as well as the plans courtesy of Putney Council. Any ideas?'

Gareth had accessed the computer at the Land Registry and downloaded descriptive details as well as drawings of the house. The information had then been forwarded to the plane and printed out on A4 paper. They each had a copy.

'It seems straightforward enough,' said Hughes. 'Wait for what's his name...'

'Akram Javid.'

'Thanks, Ruth. Akram Javid to arrive and put a bullet in his head as a warning to others not to help terrorists in this country.'

The others nodded. It was simple enough.

'What about an alarm or camera coverage?' Bletchley asked.

'The house has the new electric meter that transmits the reading to the electricity supplier. Leo broke into the system and has been monitoring the readings. He reckons there is no alarm otherwise the house would be using a little more electricity than is showing. That goes for cameras as well.'

'How sure is he?' Ruth asked.

'Pretty sure, though not one hundred percent.'

Hughes asked, 'Who's going in?'

'Just me,' said Hunter. 'Ruth, you and Jan come with me to Putney. The rest of you stay in the hotel and relax. We daren't go in mob handed otherwise we could be spotted. According to Isobel, the target is landing at Heathrow at 21.00. Give him time to get through customs and immigration and it will probably be closer to 23.00 before he arrives home.'

'Are we sure he's on the flight?' Ruth asked.

'Yes, according to Leo. He hacked into the airline's passenger list.'

The irony of Leo doing what the man in Greece had done wasn't lost on them. Except Leo wouldn't have left a visiting card behind.

When they arrived at the airport they walked to the hotel. They checked in before Hunter, Badonovitch and Ruth met at the front desk, where Hunter signed for a Lexus UX, pre-ordered and pre-delivered.

Traffic to London was heavy and they didn't arrive in Putney until after 19.00.

Badonovitch dropped Hunter and Ruth off at the corner of Royal Crescent. They walked arm in arm along the road. On both sides were detached, imposing villas many with four or five bedrooms and all with basements. They paused at numbers 19, 23 and 25. They openly pointed at the structures and commented on the gardens. Most were well manicured lawns with flower borders, but some had paving stones for car parking. Number 25 was one of them, so lacked shrubs, flowers and grass.

Satisfied with what they saw, they walked to the end of the road and waited a few minutes until the car arrived to pick them up.

'Okay, boss?'

'Yes Jan. I don't see any problems.'

Akram Javid's plane arrived at 22.00, delayed by strong head winds. By the time he passed through customs and immigration, he was in a foul mood. His passport declared him to be Iranian, while the stamp in it identified him as having leave to remain indefinitely. God how he hated the English. They were supercilious swine who thought they still ruled the world.

The only light on the horizon was the text from his wife announcing she and the kids were staying in Torquay for at least another week. Good. That meant he would be able to send for one of the young Western sluts he liked to abuse. They were so willing. He liked them voluptuous, blonde and experienced. So far, the women supplied by the Russian had been better than all right. He was getting excited just thinking about it.

Another thought intruded. Should he divorce his wife? The problem was she owned 50% of the company. That was the deal agreed with her father when he backed the company venture. The fact that her father was being paid handsome dividends appeared lost on both of them. To make matters worse, she was now involved in the routine running of the business and had suggested changes that had improved the business considerably.

Their software for use by architects was superior to anything currently available. They were now selling in Germany, France and China with another two countries lined up. And the best part was that it was all done on-line and so costs were kept to a minimum.

Divorce was out of the question but another idea returned to tease him. The Russian could arrange it. An accident or a body lost and never found? Which was easier and more effective? It was a pleasant conundrum to contemplate as he stood in the queue for a taxi.

He had been delaying the decision for months and now it was time to act. He took out his phone. Which should he ask for first? Although it was late, he knew the Russian didn't mind being disturbed if it was for business and a chance to make money. In this case a considerable amount of money.

He smiled to himself. Ever since the business launched seven years earlier, he had been skimming off the top. He had nearly £3 million hidden in a Barbados bank account. He had acquired the money knowing that the day would possibly come when he would want to make drastic changes in his life. Getting rid of his wife was one of the changes.

He settled into a taxi before using the phone. It rang and seconds later a voice growled, 'Akram this had better be good.'

'It is. I have decided to proceed with that business we discussed a week ago. One million I think we agreed.'

'That was then. The price is now one point five and increasing.'

The greedy pig had him over a barrel and they both knew it. He hated Russians almost as much as he hated the English.

'How soon can you complete your end of the transaction?' He was all too aware that the driver was listening and so he was careful what he said.

'How quickly do you want it done?'

'This week if you can manage it in Torquay. I can e-mail you the address.'

'Do it tomorrow.'

'Okay.' He broke the connection and daydreamed a little more. The business was turning over £11 million and making a profit of £4 million plus change. Most of the change was what fed his nest egg. Ironically, he was a fair-minded and some would say good employer. Bonuses were paid quarterly and salaries reflected the industry average, which was high.

He thought about calling the Russian again and ordering some company for the night but decided against it. Tomorrow would be soon enough.

He alighted at his house at half-past midnight, angry at the delay, happy about his decision. Now he was at home he couldn't help thinking about the terrorist cell that had been in his house. He was happy to help the brotherhood and lending his house out for a day or two was no big deal. This had been the seventh time he had done so and he was well aware that he was accumulating good will from the regime in Iran. There was always the possibility that one day, he would be found out and have to return to the country of his birth. He shuddered at the thought. Although he was an Iranian and loved his country, in reality, he loathed the place along with its petty restrictions and punitive laws.

He'd had no choice other than to store the weapons, but it frightened him in case they were discovered. It was one of the reasons he kept in with the Iranian hierarchy.

He opened the door and switched on the lights. He walked through to his study where he kept his liquor cabinet. He might be a Muslim but like thousands of others, he was a hypocrite.

He stopped dead when he saw the man sitting in the armchair opposite the doorway with a long-barrelled automatic pointed at him. Then he realised it wasn't a long barrel but a silencer. Suddenly his mouth was dry and his bowels loose. He had to concentrate to avoid an unpleasant accident.

'What…what do you want?' he croaked. He cleared his throat and asked again, this time in a voice he barely recognised as his own.

'You,' answered Hunter.

26

'What do you mean, me?'

Javid was over his initial shock and was moving slowly towards the cabinet. Hunter watched him while hiding his amusement. He wanted to shoot him there and then but thought he'd allow things to play out a bit more. To help Javid he placed his automatic on the floor next to his chair and sat back, steeping his fingers together.

'May I?' Javid gestured at the cabinet.

'Please do,' Hunter replied courteously.

Javid opened the door, reached in and removed a bottle of malt whisky. He waved it at Hunter.

'No, thanks.'

Opening a drawer, Javid reached in then turned, pointing an automatic at him.

'Now tell me who you are before I shoot.'

'That's very melodramatic. My name is Hunter. I work for TIFAT. Have you heard of us?'

'Yes, in Scotland somewhere. You have been responsible for the deaths of many of my compatriots.'

I am pleased to tell you that not only the organisation but personally, I have killed quite a number of Jihadists. Some had easy deaths others didn't. Yours won't be easy unless you tell me what I want to know.'

Javid lifted the automatic and extended his arm. The gun was about five yards away and looked like a formidable weapon.

Hunter leant forward to pick up his own Glock when Javid pulled the trigger. It clicked on an empty chamber. He kept pulling the trigger with the same result while Hunter picked up the Glock and said, 'I found the weapons and explosives in the hidden ground safe along with a few bundles of cash. As you see, I removed the bullets from the gun you're holding and left it there for my amusement. I wanted to see your face when you realised you were about to die.'

Javid then displayed a modicum of courage and raised his arm to throw the gun at Hunter. Hunter shot him in the left knee. Javid screamed and collapsed. Hunter stood up and crossed to the man. Javid was gripping his knee and rolling back and forth, gasping in agony. Tears were rolling down his cheeks.

'I want my solicitor. I demand to see my solicitor. You cannot do this.'

'We do not arrest people.' Hunter's tone was conversational, even friendly. 'We destroy them. Especially scum like you.'

'Wait. I have money. I can pay you. A million pounds! Two! Two and a half. That's all I have. I swear.'

Hunter bent down, grabbed hold of Javid by the lapels, lifted him up and dragged him behind his desk before dropping him into a comfortable leather chair. 'You don't have any money,' said Hunter.

'I do. I swear.' Javid gasped as a bolt of pain shot through his body.

Hunter tapped the enter button on the keyboard of Javid's desktop computer and watched as the man understood the display on the screen.

Javid gasped. 'What is this? Where's my money?' His tears had stopped.

'Gone. Right now some of my favourite charities are becoming richer while you become poorer. So you see Akram, you have nothing to bribe me with. You run a safe house for visiting Jihadists. You supply them with arms and explosives and if necessary, given enough time and notice, you also supply documents from driving licences to passports. Usually from one of the other EU countries particularly the Balkans.'

Hunter walked back around the desk and stood facing Javid. 'You arranged things for four men sent to kill my family. I want to know who sent them.'

'I swear I don't know. I swear…'

He didn't get any further. Hunter shot him in the elbow. Javid screamed and looked at the wound. His lower arm was hanging off. The wound felt numb for a few seconds and then the pain hit him. He opened his mouth to scream and Hunter leant across the desk and hit him in the mouth with the end of his silencer. Javid moaned and spat out blood and a tooth.

Gasping, Javid said, 'I only dealt with Amin Shirvani. I swear.' Tears were again rolling down his cheeks. He repeated, 'I swear.'

Hunter believed him. He turned away and looked over his shoulder at the man hunched over his desk gripping what was left of his elbow. Javid's involvement in the international terrorist movements that targeted the West had resulted in the deaths of many innocent people. It had been his intention of putting a bullet between his eyes and giving him a merciful death. But then he thought of his father and changed his mind. Instead he shot Javid through his other elbow with the same result. As the blood spurted from the new wound Javid looked at Hunter and opened his mouth to speak. Instead of saying anything he fell forward and died. Hunter picked up the three spent bullet cases and left through the front door, closing it behind him. He dialled Badonovitch's mobile and broke the connection before it was answered. He walked along the street and minutes later, the car drew up alongside him and he climbed in.

'How did it go?' Ruth asked from the front passenger seat.

'I found weapons and explosives. I'll text the General and tell him. Apart from that it was a dead end. I believed him when he said he had dealt directly with Shirvani. So now we head for Greece and have a chat with our computer hacker. It should be an interesting conversation.'

While he had been speaking, he had speed dialled the General. In spite of the late hour, Macnair answered after only one ring.

'Nick?'

Hunter explained what had happened.

'Okay. Good work. I'll phone the Counter Terrorism Command.

277

Sandy Sheffield is one of the good guys. He can take over and assume all the kudos for cracking the case.'

'I know Sheffield. When did he get the top job?'

'A week ago. He's already had some success using info we've fed him.'

'Anonymously supplied I take it.'

'Yes, he's the only one who knows it came from us.'

Hunter sighed. The problem faced by the authorities was the need for a warrant for just about any action taken against terrorists or criminals. A phone tap? Warrant. A car search? Warrant, unless a crime was being committed. Search a known safe house used by Jihadists? Warrant. Didn't read the culprit his full legal rights? Wrongful arrest. And so it went on.

The Jihadists had solicitors on their payrolls who were adept at playing the system causing the Police, Special Branch, MI5 and MI6 to squander personnel and financial resources.

'I've left everything there including his laptop and any records CTC might find. Javid may have had contact with other safe houses. A chain of houses being shut down would be very satisfying.'

'You never know, it could happen. By the way, Leo is pretty sure he has identified the EUROPOL agent who has been coordinating the attacks.'

'How did he manage that?'

'Working back from the Greek. He's an immigrant from Iraq, but now a Dutch national, and a Muslim, of course.'

'I'm surprised he got a job at EUROPOL.'

'He has full command of seven languages and has already shown his worth.'

'You mean a few sacrifices for the good of the cause?'

'Something like that.'

They arrived at the hotel and managed a few hours sleep before departing.

Flying time to Athens was four hours. They took off at 11.15 and arrived at 15.10. They adjusted their watches to 17.10 local time.

They were booked into the Sofitel Athens Airport Hotel for three nights. They figured that was more than enough time to acquire the information they needed. The hotel was a five star and reeked of luxury.

They ordered a Lexus SUV to be delivered with all of them as named drivers.

After settling in, they met a couple of hours later in the bar. The team sat together and should they be overheard talking, it would be about diving, wind surfing and para sailing; also bars, nightclubs and women.

Meantime, Hunter and Ruth sat apart. She looked very attractive in white slacks and a blue blouse over which she wore a lightweight jacket that reached the top of her thighs. In her purse she carried a Glock 42, the smallest handgun manufactured by the company. The weapon was just short of six inches in length and weighed only 17 ounces when loaded with six 0.38 calibre bullets. It was the ideal weapon for close-up work.

Hunter's weapon of choice was a Glock 18. It was similar to the 17 with one important difference. When a turret-shaped selector switch on the right rear side of the slide was turned clockwise up the Glock became semi-automatic and each pull of the trigger fired a single round. When the selector switch was turned counter-clockwise the gun became fully automatic and fired 1,200 rounds per minute. The magazine emptied in a second. To compensate, a magazine holding 33 rounds was available but it made the gun too bulky, so Hunter didn't use it. The weapon was hidden in a specially designed holster carried on the left side of his back, prohibiting a fast draw.

Their silence was awkward for a few minutes after they ordered bottles of alcohol-free beer. Their conversation was desultory and the elephant in the room was their now defunct relationship. Hunter knew he didn't want to renew it but wondered what Ruth thought.

'Ruth, I...'

'Nick, I...'

They both started together.

'You first,' said Hunter.

'No, you say what you need to say and we can clear the air.'

'Life has moved on. I came after you in Israel but since then my feelings have changed into, let's call it friendship.'

Ruth sighed. 'Thank God for that. I wondered how I would feel when I saw you but truth be told, I felt nothing more than that. No spark and no lust.' She smiled.

Hunter smiled in return. 'Good. I'm glad. Anything further about those damned cricket balls?'

'I received a text this morning. We've confirmed the location of the factory where they're made. It's somewhere south of Tehran. I'm waiting for the details. On a different note, there are two operations going down. The attack on the West in general and the one on you in particular. The former is being orchestrated by the Iranians the other by the Saudis.' Ruth raised her bottle to her lips before realising it was empty.'

Hunter indicated to a waitress that they wanted two more plus menus. They waited for the beers and menus to appear, had a quick perusal and decided to eat out.

'We can drive to Artemida and check out Meteoron Street. There may be a suitable restaurant.'

They took the A64 Attiki Odas for a dozen kilometres before turning off on to the street where their quarry lived.

The left side of the street consisted of a series of bars and small restaurants. The pavement was wider than usual to accommodate a roped-off seating area for use by those who wanted fresh air and those who wanted to smoke. The smokers outnumbered the others. They couldn't find a parking spot and ended up a couple of streets away.

Hunter and Ruth strolled arm in arm back to Meteoron Street, stopping from time to time to look at menus and to be hassled by youngsters trying to coerce them into eating in their hostelry. The area was busy, the restaurants full of happy diners, enjoying warm sunshine, cold drinks and what appeared to be tasty dishes of food.

They paused opposite the building they were looking for. It was four stories high and looked as though it had once been an office block.

The road wasn't very busy but they had to wait for a couple of vehicles to pass before crossing to the other side. They paused outside a glass door and looked at the list of names. There were two lines of four. Top right was Otis Angelos, their target.

'Let's cross back and have something to eat in the restaurant. There are a couple of empty tables outside.' Hunter smiled at Ruth. 'Do you fancy a glass or two of retsina?'

'God no. I'd rather drink cough syrup.'

'Do you realise the Greeks have been making retsina for over 2,000 years? The taste originally comes from sealing the wine vessels with Aleppo Pine resin.'

'And now?'

'No idea. That's as much as I know.'

'Do you like the stuff?'

'Like is too strong a word. When in Rome and all that.'

'Only this is Greece.'

'Ah, you noticed my mistake. Still, there are some good Greek wines.'

'I'll have a Chianti.'

They grabbed a table. A waiter appeared and Hunter handed him an ashtray that was in danger of overflowing with butt ends. He pulled a grimace in disgust. At the same time, he ordered a large white retsina and a large red Chianti. With the wine came the menus. They were written in nine languages including Arabic.

They both started with a salad followed by mussels in a white wine sauce. The food was first class. They restricted themselves to the one glass of wine and so drank fizzy water with the meal. The coffee was excellent.

'The lock looked easy enough.' Hunter spoke quietly, as he leaned forward.

'When?'

'Later tonight.'

'Alone?'

'Yeah. May as well. On second thoughts I'll take Jan with me. He's more intimidating than the others.'

Ruth smiled. 'Maybe. The reality is you're all intimidating.'

'Even me?'

'Especially you. Nick you have a presence that reminds me of a stalking leopard. You have an alertness and a predatory aura about you that, yes, at times can be quite scary.'

'That's news to me.'

'I've had time to think about it. A couple of years at least.' Ruth smiled. 'However, *Non. Je ne regrette rien.*'

Smiling, Hunter quipped, 'Edith was spot on. *J'aussi.*'

By now it was dark. There were streetlights on both sides of the road but the lights thrown out by the bars and restaurants, made the pavement opposite murkier.

They finished their meal, paid the bill and departed. Arm in arm they again strolled along, not a care in the world, heading for the car. A short while later they were back in the hotel.

Hunter called the others to his room. He described what they had seen.

'We can't go in mob-handed just in case we're seen even if it will be the middle of the night.'

'On that point,' said Ruth, 'it makes far more sense that I go with you.' Before Hunter could object, she raised her hand and said, 'I know, I know. But you and Jan could attract attention. If it's you and me, nobody will give us a second thought.'

The men exchanged looks and then Masters said, 'She's right, Nick. And we all know that Ruth is no wilting orchid. She can give as good as the rest of us.'

'I'm sure you meant that as a compliment. Either way I accept it as such.'

'Good. It was meant to be.'

Hunter nodded. 'I guess you're right. We'll move out at 02.00.'

27

Michael Gunther watched the TV with knots in his stomach, a dry throat and a tremor in his hands. The knots suddenly unravelled and he jumped from his armchair and made it to the bathroom before being sick. After emptying his gut, he dry heaved a dozen times. He staggered to his feet, turned on a cold water tap and using his hand, gulped water. He felt refreshed for a few seconds before his mouth turned dry again.

He could hear his mobile phone ringing in the lounge. He had a shrewd idea who it was and was reluctant to answer but he knew he had no choice. He needed to delay the inevitable to give himself time to find a hiding place. He had a few ideas.

'Yes?'

'Herr Gunther, I wish for an explanation.'

The voice was unmistakably that of Wajeeh Soliman.

'About...' his voice croaked and he cleared his throat. 'Sorry, I seem to be going down with something.'

'You know what. I want an explanation as to what happened in Scotland.'

'I don't know what you're talking about.'

'It's in the news. An attack on a bowling club in some village near Glasgow.'

'Sorry. Like I said I think I'm going down with something. I've not heard the news for a couple of days.'

'Are you telling me you had nothing to do with what happened?'

Gunther knew he couldn't say that. He had no choice but to admit it. He could pretend ignorance that it had gone wrong.

'I have a team carrying out the attack on Hunter's parents and then they have instructions to kill Hunter. I presume they have killed the parents.'

'You presume wrong. Not only are the parents still alive but the men you sent are dead. Hunter's father was wounded but according to the news, he will survive.'

Gunther cursed aloud.

'You said that the people who would carry out the attack would be Caucasian not Middle Eastern. That was why I contacted you. I was assured that you were the right man for the job.'

'I need to find out what went wrong and start again with a new team.

'How many men did you send?'

'Four.'

'In that case I have bad news. Only three were killed, the fourth is missing.'

'He may have escaped.' Even to his ears his words sounded hollow.

'Maybe, but I doubt it very much. You have proved to be incapable of carrying out our agreement and so I wish the money to be returned immediately, including the money you have used for expenses. That is $5 million, plus the money used on the credit card.'

Somehow Gunther held it together and spoke in a steady voice. 'Failure was not my fault. I hired four men reputed to be the best there is. They failed, I did not.'

'Herr Gunther, that is not how it works as you know. You were responsible, you took the commission, you have been paid a great deal of money with a further massive sum to follow. I know from the credit card account that you have taken in excess of $300,000 though what you have spent it on, I do not know. Every cent is to be repaid by this time tomorrow.'

The voice was patronising and the fact the speaker was an Arab put Gunther's teeth on edge.

'That's impossible.'

'Herr Gunther, the money we paid you is not all you possess. You have been in the business long enough to amass a significant amount.

I want our payment returned in order to make alternative arrangements. If I do not receive the money, every cent of it, then the Prince will issue a fatwa against you. With a reward of, let us say $1 million. A nice round sum which every two-bit assassin will want to claim. You understand I am not using the word fatwa in its true and historic meaning. I use it in the modern sense. I hope I make myself clear.'

'Yes.' This time his voice was a croak. He broke the connection and climbed to his feet. He crossed the room to a handmade drinks credenza made from seasoned oak. Opening the central cupboard, he took out a bottle of cognac, while from the right hand glass cabinet he removed a brandy glass. He poured a good measure of the Courvoisier into the glass and took a mouthful. He was unused to hard liquor and gagged as it burnt its way down his throat. Somehow he managed not to cough it up again. He went into the kitchen, added the same again in soda and topped the drink up with a handful of crushed ice. This time he took a sip without the burning sensation.

He sat at his desk for some minutes collecting his thoughts. Fatwas had at one time meant judgements on which Sharia law was based. The word had been corrupted in the late 20th century to mean punishment of various sorts from amputation of arms and legs to heads being cut off. If you were lucky, it meant a bullet you didn't see coming. For a million dollars there were many people who would gladly track him down and carry out the deed.

He needed to escape. Five million plus the expenses money plus what he already possessed should see him find somewhere to hide and live out his life, if not in luxury certainly in comfort. As the thought took hold he convinced himself that he could do it. First, he needed to liquidate his investments, which as of yesterday had been valued at more than $11 million.

He sent an e-mail to his stockbroker telling him to sell his shares, and gave details of the bank account where he wanted the money sent. Next, he opened a new account in the Bahamas using passwords and no signature, and transferred the money from three different accounts into it. The bulk of the cash was the $5 million paid by the

Prince. However it had totalled a healthy $7 million plus change. He thought about taking the expenses money but decided against it. He would buy some time by returning it to the Prince and explaining that he had to liquidate assets to repay the bulk of the money. He convinced himself it would work.

Thoughts of Hunter and TIFAT intruded. It wouldn't take the man long to discover his involvement and he'd be after him! The more he thought about the situation, the more he became convinced that he should never have taken the job. Why had he? But he knew the answer. Money!

He had three passports, legacies from previous jobs. They were German, Albanian and Rumanian. He used all three from time to time. Which one should he use now? Whichever he used, he would have to get rid of it so as not to be tempted to use it again. But why not keep it in case he needed it again? He stood up, crossed the room and replenished his glass.

He had never owned property, only rented. He looked around the room he was in. Comfortable but with few personal items cluttering up the place. He had never been one to accumulate things, not even a large wardrobe of clothes. He had spent his money on luxury holidays, superb wines and eating in some of the finest restaurants.

Hunter and Ruth went arm in arm to the door. He was about to remove the lock-gun from his pocket when he realised the door wasn't closed properly. He pushed it open and they both went in. The lights in the hallway were on a motion sensor and came on as they moved. There was a lift to the right but neither considered using it for fear of being trapped.

The hallway was a couple of yards wide with bare walls of plaster painted white. There was a door on each side of the stairs leading to apartments 1A and 1B. Under the stairs they found a cupboard with an electricity junction box. A few seconds perusing it and Hunter found the right switch. He flicked it up and plunged the hall and stairs into darkness. They both switched on their Night Vision Goggles and immediately the dark became light with a green hue.

He led the way up the stairs. Halfway up they heard loud voices behind them. In spite of the fact it was 02.45, people were entering the building. They sounded the worse for wear.

Hunter and Ruth picked up the pace. At the top of the stairs Hunter used the lock-gun on a simple tongue and groove lock and opened the door. The noise of the drunks was getting closer and Ruth stepped through the door just as the first one reached the landing.

The room was filled with electronic equipment. They could see four desktop computers as well as two laptops. The desktops were connected to high quality printers and, much to their surprise, there was also an old-fashioned fax machine.

A settee faced a large screen TV. It was obvious that the room had once been two and that a wall had been removed. At the far end was an alcove leading to a small kitchen with a dining table and one chair. On the other side were two adjacent doors. A glance into one revealed a toilet and shower.

Hunter pointed at the other. 'Must be the bedroom,' he whispered.

Although they both wore holstered Glocks, Ruth also held a taser in her right hand. She was down on her knees when she opened the door slowly. They both recognised the sound of a silenced automatic being fired and saw the chip of wood fly off the edge of the door. If Ruth hadn't been kneeling the bullet would have hit her. Hunter had been standing next to her and was equally lucky. However, he now faced a dilemma. Shoot the man, try and overpower him and risk being shot or try and taser him. He chose the latter. However, before he could grab the weapon from Ruth she aimed and fired.

The man was standing beside the bed a silenced automatic in his hands pointing it at the door. His hands were shaking but he managed to pull the trigger again even as Ruth fired 50,000 volts in his direction. The bullet missed Ruth but the two barbs from the taser hit the man in the chest. He shuddered and collapsed.

'That was too close for comfort,' said Hunter.

'Indeed,' said Ruth, relief in her voice.

'How did he know we were here?'

'We can ask him.'

'Let's hope he hasn't had a heart attack.'

They crossed the room and checked on the inert form.

'At least he's still breathing,' said Ruth, as she removed the two barbs and the wires from the man's body.

Hunter took a kit bag from his back and removed a handful of tie-wraps. He quickly trussed the man's feet together as well as his hands behind his back. He slipped one of the tie-wraps around the man's neck and left it loose.

'How's he doing? Ruth asked.

'He'll be out for a while yet.'

They removed their goggles and switched on the lights. The bedroom was large with a king-sized bed and two double wardrobes. The wall opposite the bed had the biggest TV screen they'd ever seen.

Ruth and Hunter returned to the lounge and began searching the drawers and cupboards. There wasn't a piece of paper anywhere.

'Presumably every piece of equipment is turned on to allow 24/7 contact with the outside world,' said Ruth.

'Knowing what he does, I guess there are no set office hours.'

Hunter phoned TIFAT and was surprised to find Leo on duty in the ops centre. Hunter brought him up to date and Leo gave some instructions, which he followed.

'Thanks, Nick. I'm in. Leave things as they are and we'll have his systems raped in no time.'

'Don't forget his bank accounts.'

'Don't worry. Have I ever?'

'I guess not.' He broke the connection. 'How long has he been out?'

'Half an hour at least.'

'Okay, he's had long enough.'

'You know it can take up to an hour before the effects wear off.'

'Not if you're as fat as he is.'

They returned to the bedroom. Hunter leant down and slapped the man's face. He groaned and so Hunter hit him again only harder this time. The man's eyes opened. He was pasty white and gasping for breath.

'Inhaler,' he managed to say pointing at the bedside cupboard.

Ruth opened the drawer and removed a blue inhaler while Hunter cut the tie-wraps from their prisoner's hands. She handed the inhaler to the man. Eagerly, he sucked in the light spray of Salbutamol Sulfate, which quickly eased his breathing.

'Asthma,' he gasped.

Hunter and Ruth exchanged looks. The man was lucky to be alive, 50,000 volts and asthma didn't sit well together.

As his breathing improved, the man asked. 'Who are you?'

'My name is Hunter. You don't need to know this lady's name. In case you're wondering, I'm from TIFAT.'

'So? What's that to do with me and what is whatever you called it.'

'TIFAT is The International Force Against Terrorism. You are Otis Angelos and you specialise in hacking into computer systems to sell information to various people or organisations. Out of interest, have you ever tried to breach the systems say of the Pentagon or MI5?'

'No, it's possible I could do it but I'd be inviting trouble to even try. I know a couple of hackers who've tried and are no longer around. Whether in Gitmo or under the ground in some deep hole I don't know, but I suspect the latter.'

Angelos suddenly realised he was talking too much. Gibbering more like, so he clamped his mouth shut.

'Otis, I want to know a few things. First of all you hacked into the pilots' roster for Griffiths Airlines and passed the info on to someone. I want to know who. '

'I don't know.'

Hunter bent over the man, gripped the end of the tie-wrap and pulled it tighter. It wasn't enough to cut off his air supply completely but enough to leave him gasping. Angelos managed to get his fingers into the loop and pulled hard easing his breathing. He began to cough and Hunter slid the tip of his K-Bar into the gap and cut the tie-wrap. Angelos had a coughing fit and used his inhaler a few times before getting his breathing under control.

'I have three options for you. A slow death, a quick and easy death or no death. I'm assuming you'd prefer the third option?'

Angelos nodded vigorously. He was staring at Hunter and didn't notice the puzzled look Ruth gave Hunter.

'Let me describe what I am prepared to do. First, the slow death. You've already sampled what I can and will do. You'll last probably as long as half an hour but you will die as though you were locked in a small box. Second, I can put a bullet in your head and spare you the terror of your impending doom and your slow suffocation. Third, and it's what I'd advise, you work for us.'

The Greek stared at Hunter. 'What do you mean?'

'It's simple enough. Any contact from anyone is to be passed to us at TIFAT HQ. You will be supplied with highly secure encrypted systems to enable you to do so with complete safety.'

'Huh, there is no such thing,' retorted Angelos.

'Believe me, there is. Otis you have 30 seconds to tell me what it's to be.'

Hunter dropped another tie-wrap over the Greek's head and pulled it tight. Not enough to choke him but sufficient to show what would happen if he didn't cooperate.

'All right. All right. I'll tell you what you want to know and I will work for you. I don't have much choice.'

'Otis let me make things crystal clear. If you renege in any way on our deal there will be no second chance. Try to run away and we will find you, believe me.'

Angelos nodded. 'I believe you,' the words came out in a croak.

28

'I would like a cup of tea,' said Otis Angelos, free of the tie-wraps and now standing in his lounge.

'The three of us would, I'm sure,' said Hunter. 'Please make some. Milk no sugar for me, no milk or sugar for Ruth.'

The Greek nodded and busied himself in the kitchenette.

Ruth asked, 'Do you have any queries from the power supplier about the amount of electricity you use? It's one of the ways the authorities check to see if illegal drugs are being grown. Usually cannabis.'

Cannabis plants needed heat producing lamps coupled with a suitable irrigation system to grow quickly. The police had long become adept at identifying excessive use of electricity and raiding those premises looking for the plants.

Angelos snorted. 'I have ensured that my electricity costs are modest.'

'You have an amazing amount of computer power,' said Ruth, looking around the room. She took the proffered mug of tea, thanked him and sipped it appreciatively.

'Do you have regular customers?' Hunter asked.

Angelos shrugged. 'I wouldn't call them regular but I've done more than one job for a few people.'

'Anyone in particular?'

'No. Whoever will pay me. I have no ideological convictions. I am a businessman in the computer industry.'

'You're a sleaze bag,' said Hunter, somehow managing to hold his temper in check, 'who profits from other people's tragedies.' Folding his arms, he looked down at the fat man sitting at one of the computers and said, 'Otis, I am finding it very hard not to kill you in the manner I described. You put the lives of my sister and over one hundred people at risk.'

'But I didn't know, I swear it. I supply the information, collect a fee and move on to the next job. I do not try to discover what connection, if any there is, between what I do and something that happens in the world. I am not interested.'

Hunter stared at the man and slowly nodded in disgust. 'God help me but I believe you.' His phone warbled.

'Hunter.'

'Nick.'

'Hi, Leo. What have you got for us?'

'We've been going through the files marrying up what's on the computers to events around the world. There are all sorts of connections, from manipulating the value of company shares to terrorist attacks on specified days.'

'Are the attacks mainly in the name of Islam against the West?'

'Predominantly, but there are others. You name the religion and it's probably involved somewhere.'

'Even Buddhism? I thought it was the religion of peace.'

'Think again, Nick. There were attacks by Buddhists recently in Myanmar, Sri Lanka plus a dozen other countries. American Christians are amongst the biggest hypocrites on the planet although they are more involved with killing Muslims on a small scale. More guns than bombs let us say.'

'Thanks, Leo. What about the accounts?'

'Relatively easy. Nearly two million euros but that's all. From what we can see he spends his money on state-of-the-art computer equipment and associated gear.'

'Okay. Stay on the line for a few minutes.'

'Okay.'

'Otis, open up whichever computer you use for contacting your bank.'

'Why?'

'Just do it Otis, before I get seriously annoyed.'

With trembling fingers Angelos opened his account and looked at the screen.

'How much is showing?'

'1,954,000 euros.'

'Leo? Empty it.'

As they watched, the figures vanished to show zero.

'What just happened?'

'We just emptied your bank account. It can stay empty or we can gradually put it all back. It's up to you.'

'What do you mean it's up to me? I told you I'll work for you. And what does gradually mean?'

'This is a demonstration of what we can do. Your account will have a trace on it. If you try and move the money, we will know about it immediately and we will automatically empty it. I will then come and find you. You will only use the computers in this room. You will not buy any more without contacting us first. If you do, the person you will need to speak to is Leo. He will be your liaison. Do you understand? Gradually means over the next five years. You ought to be able to live comfortably on that.'

Angelos stared back at Hunter and then dropped his eyes. 'I understand.'

'Good. Otis, you will continue to receive payment from your clients and you can keep that money. You just ensure your information is both timely and accurate.'

'Who did you get the pilots' roster for?'

Licking his dry lips he replied, 'I am pretty sure it was a Saudi by the name of Abdul-Hameed Saud.'

'Pretty sure? Don't you know?'

'Most of my clients don't tell me who they really are. However, when I take a commission, I like to track down who I am working for. It's easy. I just follow the money from the bank to the sender. Sometimes I have to travel through a number of banks but I always get there in the end. The clients are invariably lazy.'

'Do you ever have face-to-face meetings?' Ruth asked.

'No. I did when I first started but not now.' He paused then added, 'I realised I was vulnerable. What if a client didn't like whatever it was I'd done for them? What if they thought it would be safer for them if I disappeared?' He shook his head. 'I decided not to risk it. So I moved here from Cyprus.'

'How long ago?'

'Eighteen months.'

'How many commissions, as you call them, have you had in that time?'

'Eight.'

'That's not many.' Hunter commented.

'It's enough. I'm careful what jobs I take.'

Hunter said, 'One more time. You won't be able to hide from us. If you doublecross me I will find you.'

'I don't doubt it,' Angelos said in a croaked voice as he cleared his throat.

'I want you to talk to Leo. He will create a firewall that surrounds all your equipment but with a pipeline to our HQ in Rosyth.'

Hunter speed dialled TIFAT Ops Centre. 'Leo, I'm putting you on speaker so that you can talk to the man who operates the systems. I'll leave you two to sort out the details. His name is Otis Angelos.'

Hunter listened to them exchanging facts for a couple of minutes and then tuned out. 'Ruth why don't you go back to the hotel and get some sleep? I'll stay here and keep an eye on things.'

They were the other side of the room and far enough away so that the Greek couldn't hear them.

'I'm staying. We'll take it in turns to sleep. I don't want you waking up with a knife through your heart. I don't trust the man. Okay, you've put the fear of God into him but he's the type who thinks he's clever enough to escape after killing you.'

'He won't.'

'Of course he won't. Only he may not understand that. Look Nick, he inhabits a world where he feels superior to ordinary mortals.

294

He has a sense of being better than us. As a result his judgement is warped.'

'How do you know?'

'He has an air of superiority about him. He took very little time to get himself on an even keel and speak normally. Right now he can't be trusted.'

'So what do you think we should do?'

'Nothing. He'll come to terms with his situation and settle down to doing the job we want. His ego needs massaging not threatening.'

'Okay if you say so.'

'I do.' She stared at him. 'One thing. I want all information passed to Mossad whether it is relative to Israel or not. I want us to be the judge of the relevance of the information so that we can act accordingly.'

'I'll have to get the General to okay it.'

'Do that. You owe us big time Nick and I mean to collect.'

'Haven't we always done our best by you?'

'Yes, but we don't always see eye to eye on some things.'

Hunter pursed his lips and nodded. 'Fair enough. I'm sure we can work it out.'

He didn't need to explain. Every anti-terrorist organisation in the world jealously guarded information for fear of its source being exposed. In their world there was a saying – paranoia helped you to stay alive. It was true, as Hunter knew all too well.

'Okay,' Hunter looked at his watch, 'it's 06.00, you take the first couple of hours sleep and I'll take the next.'

There was a sofa in the room and Ruth settled down on it. She quickly fell into a light doze and then sank into a deep sleep. Meanwhile Hunter made a pot of tea, gave a mug to the Greek as well as one for himself.

Hunter used his phone. 'Don? Ruth and I are staying here for a few more hours. Angelos is co-operating and right now is working with Leo doing whatever it is computer geeks do.'

'You're not going to exterminate him with extreme prejudice?'

Looking across the room at the Greek, Hunter replied, 'No, he may deserve it but he's more valuable alive.'

'Okay, Nick. In the meantime what do you want us to do?'

'Chill out. There's a fitness room and pool, so relax. If I learn anything useful I'll give you a call.'

'Okay.'

Hunter had left Ruth to sleep then around 11.00 she woke up.

'I thought we agreed you would relieve me after a couple of hours,' she admonished him.

'Couldn't sleep so I left you to it. Tea or coffee?'

'Tea, thanks.'

They were silent while Hunter made a mug of tea and handed it to her.

She took a sip. 'Just what I needed. Is there anything to eat?' She put the question to Angelos who was so engrossed with what he was talking to Leo about that she had to repeat the question.

'Only what's in the tall cupboard in the kitchen. Which isn't much,' he added for good measure. 'There's a bakers down the street. I can recommend the paximadi bread, both sweet and savoury versions. Throw in some cold meat, olives and cheese and you'll have breakfast.'

'Sounds good,' said Hunter. 'Fancy a walk?'

'Just let me use the restroom. I won't be long.'

Five minutes later they were walking down the stairs. Outside the sun was high in the sky and the temperature was already in the low 30s.

'What do you think of your new recruit?'

'I haven't made up my mind. If he steps out of line he'll regret it.'

He didn't need to elucidate. Ruth understood what he meant.

'Which comes first, stopping the explosive balls or you getting revenge? Sorry wrong word. I should say protecting your family.'

Hunter didn't reply for a few seconds. 'Stopping the balls. We need to get in to the factory in Iran and wipe it and its operatives off the face of the earth. Sounds melodramatic and I suppose at one level it is, but my family are a few people. The balls could kill hundreds possibly thousands.'

'I received a text this morning forwarded from Aviv-Yafo,' she was referring to Mossad HQ.

'What did it say?'

'They are certain the factory is near Kavir National Park.'

'Never heard of it. Here's the baker's.'

They entered the shop to a tantalising and mouthwatering smell of freshly baked bread and the type of food found primarily in the European countries on the edge of the Mediterranean.

Hunter said, 'I reckon good food is spoilt in northern climes by too much packaging as well as preservatives.'

'I agree.'

They ordered the food and as they were about to leave Ruth stopped and turned back to the shopkeeper. 'Do you have any baklava?'

'Of course.' He pointed at a pastry under a glass counter. 'Made with the best pistachios, honey, lemon juice and cinnamon to be found in Greece.'

She bought half a dozen.

Back on the street Ruth asked, 'Have we given him long enough?'

'Yes.'

'How many did you plant?'

Hunter grinned. 'Four cameras as well as voice recorders. We'll see if he did as he was told or has tried something clever.'

'I take it the visual and voice have been collected by Rosyth?'

'Correct. Someone will be watching and listening.'

'Are you going to leave them there?'

'I'm not sure. If Angelos finds one he'll probably flip. As it is they're not exactly well hidden. There wasn't time for that.'

'So what are you going to do?'

'This evening I am going to insist he comes with us to a restaurant for dinner. He looks like he enjoys his food. I'll have Don and Dave go in and hide the bugs properly. The chances of his finding them will be remote.'

'Remote but not impossible.'

'Of course not. However, we'll know if he looks. Which will mean he's just as guilty as if he actually betrayed us.'

'He can do that anytime from outside his apartment. A burner phone will do it or an internet café like the one I am looking at right now across the street.'

'I appreciate that. It's not perfect but it's the best we can do. We're not going to put a watch on him. No, we'll have to rely on the analysis of the information he passes to us. We'll be able to tell quickly enough how good it is.'

They paused outside the apartment building while Hunter phoned TIFAT and asked for Isobel.

'Anything?'

'No, as good as gold, and the information we're getting looks pretty useful.'

'Useful in what way?'

'Contacts. Our friend has been very clever. Each time he agreed a commission, as he likes to refer to them, he tracks down who it is he's working for. Some interesting names have appeared. We are now certain that a number of attacks using both the exploding balls and weapons are due to take place in about ten days.'

'Where?'

'France, Germany, Spain and the UK.'

'How many people are involved, do we know?'

'It appears the attackers will be in teams of three or possibly four.'

'Do we know the precise targets?'

'No. The EUROPOL officer will say where and when.'

'Is he the leader or just a conduit?'

'We think he's the conduit though we don't know who's issuing the orders. The way we read it, hang on a sec, Malcolm has just walked in.'

Hunter could hear a mumble of voices then the General came on.

'We were wrong. The conduit isn't the man at EUROPOL it's a woman. She's hacked into the man's computer and is using it somehow. Gareth has all the details.

'From other reports it seems ever more women are embracing Jihad.'

'You're right. And as they're wearing the burqa it makes stop and search virtually impossible. If we tried it in the West, we'd have lawyers screaming human rights, freedom of religion and whatever else the politically correct come up with.'

'Sir, you know as well as I do that the problem we have is that the majority of Muslims are decent, law abiding citizens who contribute a great deal to our societies.'

'I know. By the way, Angelos and Leo have been talking continuously. Our friend has amassed a mine of information. And not just about Islamic terror attacks but cyber attacks arranged by Russia and North Korea, and also by Pakistan.'

'Why doesn't that surprise me?'

It didn't take much to persuade the Greek to go for dinner. Masters and Hughes effected entry to the apartment and planted video/audio bugs in strategic points throughout, even in the bathroom. To do the job properly took a good hour but eventually they were satisfied.

29

'What do you want to do, Nick?' the General asked.

'Go to Iran, sir. My parents and Louise will be safe enough with you. We need to stop the bomb factory. I can take care of the other matter when we've done that.'

'Fair enough. I take it you've seen the details Ruth has been sent.'

'Yes, on the edge of Kavir National Park. A bit surprising as they normally hide any clandestine operations amongst the general population in the belief we won't blow it up.'

'They're not always right.'

'I know. Mossad and Tehran proved that. Anyway, I've been checking our options. The Park is 80 miles south of Tehran and about 65 miles east of Qom.'

'I've also been looking,' said Macnair. 'It's nearly 700 miles north of Dubai.'

'Yes, I've checked that also. The only way I can see is a high/low jump. Our chances of going both ways overland are pretty remote.'

'There's another consideration,' said the General, 'we're pushed for time.'

'Have they said when the attacks are kicking off?'

'No, but according to Leo, from what he's gleaned, during the next week.'

'I've searched the area on Google Earth and there's an option that may work.'

'What's that?'

'We go in fast in a C130, deploy and get the hell out of there the same way.'

'Nick, a fast entry is one thing. Landing and waiting for the team to do your job and getting out is something entirely different. You'll have the Iranian Air Force on you like a ton of bricks.'

'Presumably their nearest base is Tehran?'

'Correct. Give them time to scramble and they'll be there in about an hour. Where would you land?'

'There's a good road running north south that goes all the way to the factory. It's obviously used to ship materials and men in and out. If we can have some detailed photos of the area, we might be able to work something out. Google maps are useful but we need up-to-date info as well as accurate pictures of the terrain.'

'I saw the road,' said Macnair. 'Okay, we also need to know the situation as far as personnel are concerned and whether there are any armed guards or troops.'

'To do that we need a couple of days surveillance using the satellites. I don't think we have time. If the attacks are due soon, we need to act as quickly as possible.'

'The balls could already have been distributed.'

'You're right, sir, but in that case why not attack now instead of later? My gut is telling me they're waiting for the balls to be delivered.'

'Let's hope you're right.'

'I need to brainstorm my ideas with the others. A couple of them might work.'

'Okay. Whatever you want you'll get. What's our Greek friend up to?'

'He played some sort of computer game for a couple of hours before turning in around 02.00. He was up again at 06.00, played some more of the game and then spent the morning conferring with Leo.'

'Good.'

On that note they broke the connection.

The team met for breakfast around 10.00. The buffet was excellent, the coffee mediocre. They sat together at a couple of tables they had pushed together. Nobody was within hearing distance but they still kept their voices low. Hunter brought them up to speed with the job they were facing and why he thought it was urgent.

'Any ideas?'

Bletchley said, 'We've been looking at the photographs of Kavir Park and the factory. The compound is walled with what looks like three metres of stone topped with three strands of barbed wire. There are watchtowers at each of the four corners and a substantial looking guardhouse at the main gate. We think we've identified the factory, an accommodation block and a smaller self-contained unit close by. Maybe it's for the guards or maybe they share a single accommodation block and the third building is a communal area. You know, some sort of canteen or games room.'

'I doubt that,' said Masters. 'The Iranians aren't known for looking after their people's welfare. Quite the reverse.'

The others nodded. Imprisonment without trial was a common occurrence in a state that owed more to fanatical fascism than spiritual tolerance.

Bletchley continued. 'Iran has a powerful military including a highly experienced airforce. At the last count it had over 700 helicopters and aircraft and over 50,000 personnel.'

'What's your point?' Hunter asked.

'We need to get in by stealth but getting out won't be so easy. They could scramble planes and helicopters and be down on us in no time. We then either take the north road or go some other way.'

'Talking with the General, we estimate we'd have just over an hour max.'

'The nearest road is a 50 mile yomp southeast. They'd have the area saturated with troops and helicopters before we'd gone ten klicks,' said Bletchley.

They all nodded. Putting their lives on the line was one thing, committing suicide was something else entirely. If they had to go down they'd go down fighting.

'We've been checking routes and distances,' said Bletchley, 'and think we have a way in and a potential way out.'

'Only potential?'

'Best we can do, boss,' said Badonovitch.

'Okay, let's hear it.'

'Better up in the bedroom,' said Bletchley, 'we can explain on the laptop.'

'No, I'll get a meeting room,' said Hunter. 'Leave it to me.'

Ten minutes later he was back at the table. 'Okay, we've got a meeting room. It has 12 seats, an Internet connection and a wide screen TV we can plug into.'

It took them a while to connect up and get things the way they wanted. The wide screen TV was connected to the satellite imaging system used by the FVEY countries and was part of the ECHELON system. The satellites GCHQ at Cheltenham controlled had been repositioned to ensure 24/7 coverage of the target area. Not that much repositioning was required when Iran was in the west's top five "states of interest". A close eye was being kept on the country virtually nonstop.

Isobel controlled the screen.

'Isobel, you want to kick off?'

'Thanks, Malcolm. You can see the layout of the whole compound. We are sure the big building is the main factory and this one,' she indicated another building, 'is the accommodation block. You see the smaller building here,' she pointed, 'we think it's the power generating station and the large tank nearby holds diesel.'

'How can you be sure?' Hunter asked.

Isobel smiled. 'Ah, we had a stroke of luck. About an hour ago a tanker arrived and filled the tank. They've only just finished. See the tower alongside it? That's for water and we think it's also a tanker job. Which is good news.'

'How's that?' Ruth asked.

'The area is relatively dry and warm. Hence we suspect all water has to be tankered in and that implies a limit on how many people can be there. And if there is a minimum number of people required to manufacture the balls, it also means there are fewer guards. Also, when it comes to the guards, what are their duties?'

'What do you mean?' Masters asked.

'This is the middle of Iran. Who is going to attack them?'

'They thought that about the Tehran factory,' said Hunter.

'The logistics are entirely different,' Macnair came in. 'In and out of Tehran is relatively simple compared to having 100 miles of virtually open territory to cross.'

Nodding, Hunter said, 'We appreciate that, sir.' There was no sarcasm in his voice. This was a planning meeting where everything was on the table to be discussed, dissected and turned into an action plan. Even the most obvious statement was welcome.

'Ideally,' said Hunter, 'we want into the compound without being seen, set the charges and get out again without being seen.'

'That's a tall order.'

'Yes, sir. We've come to the conclusion that getting out quietly will be impossible. Hence we go for maximum destruction. But we'll come to that later. Sir, Ruth has an update on the military situation.'

'Sorry, General but I received a text a few minutes ago. It seems the Iranians keep a rapid response unit on standby 24/7 at the airport in Tehran.'

Macnair didn't bother asking how Mossad knew. He was well aware that their intelligence gathering was second to none.

'Okay. If they can embark into helicopters in say 10 minutes, make it 30 minutes flying time and we have a whole different situation,' said Hunter.

'Do we know anything about the guards?' Masters asked.

Isobel replied, 'We can see from the satellite photographs there are two in each of the watchtowers and two at the gate. Assume eight hour shifts, that means thirty guards at least.'

'Nick,' said the General, 'we figure they're relying on their location for protection. National Parks in Iran would be considered a disgrace anywhere else in the Western world. The accessible areas are rubbish strewn picnic sites. There are 16 officially designated national parks and over 130 protected areas. There are no fences, few if any rangers, no maps, no guides and no facilities. Even finding some of them is difficult, as they don't appear on any maps, there's no public transport and few if any signs. In conclusion, Kavir National Park is an ideal site to manufacture explosives.'

'Basically,' said Badonovitch, 'to be on the safe side, once we go in we have 30 to 40 minutes to do the job and get away.'

'I agree,' said Macnair.

'One good thing,' said Masters, 'we won't need to take any explosives with us. A few timer detonators will be more than enough.'

For the next four hours they brainstormed what they should do. Gradually, as options were examined a plan began to emerge. When they had finished, they all sat back and for a few seconds, were silent.

Then the General said, 'Considering the timing and distances involved I guess that's the best we can come up with.'

'It's prayer and seat-of-pants,' said Hunter, 'but you're right, sir. It's about as good as we'll get it.'

'Kick-off,' said Macnair, 'will be in a couple of days, depending on how quickly we get the gear together. Most of it we have here. Burg, you okay with this?'

'Yes sir.'

They had settled on a Lockheed C130 Hercules, one of the most robust transport aircraft ever built. Although a military aircraft, it was available for sale by Lockheed to civilians. TIFAT had bought one a few months ago, second hand with a full service history. The Hercules had been in production for over 60 years, the one TIFAT had bought was 30 years old and had cost $20 million. It had been paid for by the funds liberated from the criminals and terrorist organisations they had encountered over the preceding few years. The aircraft was based at Prestwick airport near Glasgow and had only been used for routine maintenance flights.

'I want you back here asap to collect the Herky Bird. Okay, let's get to it.'

Hughes collected their weapons while Masters and Schwarzkopf packed their bags. Hughes drove them the short distance to the private sector of the airport. The Gulfstream checks were completed in record time and they were soon in the air.

Meanwhile Hunter booked them through to Cyprus where they would meet the plane when it arrived from Scotland.

Flight time to Larnaca was 1hr 45mins. They left Athens at 09.00 the following morning after a brief visit to the Greek. Leo had assured Hunter that the hacker was behaving himself; he was co-operating fully and willingly.

'He said something interesting,' said Leo when Hunter called him from the airport before departure, 'and that was he was relieved.'

'Relieved? How? Or more importantly, why?'

'He reckoned he was trapped into doing what he did and wanted out. We gave him that opportunity to get out.'

'Sounds like a leopard changing its spots which is as rare as hens' teeth.'

Ruth had overheard Hunter's side of the conversation and smiling said, 'Two clichés in a short sentence is a record even by your standards.'

'I try.'

'I know and you're very trying.'

Though it was infantile joking it helped to relieve the tension.

30

Macnair was at Prestwick to meet the plane.

'Good flight?'

'Yes sir. Smooth and fast, just the way I like it,' said Schwarzkopf.

'Good. I appreciate that normally the C130 flies with two pilots, a navigator, a flight engineer and if needed a loadmaster. In this case it'll be just the two of you.'

Schwarzkopf nodded. 'I appreciate that, sir. It's not a problem.'

'The C130 has been loaded and there's a pot of green paint in number one container. Here's the manifest.' Macnair shoved a list of items at Masters. 'Have we forgotten anything?'

Masters scanned the list before passing it over to Schwarzkopf. 'I don't think so, sir. Burg?'

The pilot glanced down the sheet of paper before shaking his head. 'Everything is as we planned. How did Leo get on?'

'It took him a little while to understand how it worked but once he did it was plain sailing. Your flight is registered with the Iranian authorities as a military training flight involving their air force and special army units. The flight path is as we agreed. The remote auto-pilots have been programmed to within a hundred metres. The weather is calm and warm so there shouldn't be a problem hitting the target. We checked the track fifty miles to the south and it appears suitable for the Hercules. Do you need a few hours rest?'

Both men shook their heads. Schwarzkopf said, 'We took it in turns to sleep and anyway the plane flies itself so we're fine. It'll be the same going back.'

'Good. I've spoken to Colonel Cozzi who is in command at Aviano and he'll be ready for you. Turn round time should be less than an hour. Distance to go is 1,370 miles so should take just about four hours depending on the wind. Aviano to RAF Akrotiri is another five.'

The General was referring to Aviano Air Base in northeastern Italy in the Friuli-Venezia Giulia region. It was jointly used by the Italian Air Force and the US Air Force. It was now home to two fighter squadrons and two rescue squadrons plus an Air Control Squadron.

'Okay, sir,' said Schwarzkopf, 'then we'd better get going.'

In spite of the plane being ready they still completed their own pre-flight checks. Then they flashed up the four engines and taxied to the runway. At 97mph Schwarzkopf pulled back on the yoke and the plane rose gracefully into the air. Thirty minutes after take-off the plane was cruising at 26,000ft on autopilot.

Masters went aft to a cot and was asleep in minutes. Schwarzkopf sat at the controls reading an Alistair Maclean wartime thriller, *Where Eagles Dare*.

They landed at Aviano on time where they refuelled. After a steak meal with all the trimmings, as good as any sold in a first class restaurant, they were back in the air. This time Masters sat at the controls and Schwarzkopf slept. Only this time Masters was listening to language tapes, brushing up on his Farsi.

'Burg, Akrotiri on the radio. They've sent landing instructions. We're to taxi to the southeastern corner and into the hangar waiting for us.'

'ETA?'

'Fifty minutes.'

The Hercules landed on Cyprus and taxied away from the main reception area. They pulled into a hangar to be greeted by a Major General, who was in command of the two British military bases on the island.

'Malcolm phoned and explained the situation, this place is out of bounds except for Sergeant Jones and Corporal Smith. They'll help with the roundels. They're in the mess having an early dinner if you care to join them.'

'Thanks, sir. What about Nick and the others?'

'In a hotel in Larnaca. You can go there or there are rooms here.'

The two men exchanged glances, Masters shrugged and Schwarzkopf spoke.

'We may as well stay here, thank you, sir. I'll phone Nick. He'll want to go over the plans either tonight or tomorrow morning.'

'When are you leaving?'

'In the early evening. It's three hours to Kuwait. We don't want to hang around too long. A C130 with Iranian colours is too noticeable.'

'Here's Smith and Jones. They'll give you a hand.'

The General nodded and headed for the door, returning salutes as he passed the two NCOs.

While Masters found the three pots of paint, Jones stood a stepladder under the starboard wing of the plane while Smith did the same under the port wing. Sergeant Jones had the delicate task of drawing a three-circle roundel on the wing. When he'd done so, Smith began painting the inner circle red. Jones drew the same roundels on the port and starboard belly of the plane while Smith followed him with the paint. The middle circle was painted white and the outer circle green. The plane now sported the colours of the Iranian Air Force.

Hunter and the others arrived at the base mid-morning. They arranged the use of a classroom to go over their plans once again.

'First of all,' said Schwarzkopf, 'I want to look at distances again. The range we have to play with is 2,300 nautical miles. If we had external fuel tanks we could stretch it to 4,500 nautical miles but we don't have any. From here to the target is 1,000 miles, flying direct over Syria and Iraq. That doesn't leave much in the tank to get away again. However, there is an alternative. From here to Ayn al Asad Air Base in Iraq is 520 miles and is controlled by the Iraqis and Americans and where we could refuel. From there to the target is a further 510 miles. Bearing in mind our range that leaves us with another 1,790 miles plus, with some in the reserve tank.'

'Sounds good to me,' said Bletchley.

'I haven't told you the best bit. You probably don't know but a Herky Bird at 20,000ft will glide for over 60 miles. If you guys jump out over the target, I can glide to the second drop zone, unleash the cargo and continue to the third where I'll drop the other canisters. Ruth, I need you in the plane. I've talked to Nick and you're coming with me.'

She was about to argue when she saw the fixed looks on the faces of the others. 'It goes against the grain but okay.'

Hunter knew Ruth and had been expecting an argument.

'I'll go a fair distance before I restart the engines and I will land where we said. From the detailed photographs of the terrain it's easy to see the route is just about impassible for any vehicles until the other side of the escarpment where we find the track. It looks solid enough, long and straight and should work.'

'If it doesn't?' Badonovitch asked.

'Then I'll let you know and you head north to Tehran just like we discussed. We'll make a beeline for Cyprus, a distance of 940 miles.

The others nodded.

'I like it, Burg,' said Hunter. 'For the record, last night I had a word with the General. Let me spell it out. The civilians at the factory are the real targets. They are the people who created the explosives, designed the bombs and are now manufacturing them. If we let them live, they could have another factory up and running in months, even weeks. And this time we might not know where they are for some time. Enough time for them to manufacture enough explosive and balls to sell to enough of our enemies to cause the death and injury of an awful lot of innocent people. So take note. These are not innocent civilians. They are the driving force behind the manufacture and sale of a pretty nasty weapon aimed at us.'

'And the guards?' Hughes asked.

'Our enemies. Okay, that's us. I'll speak to the General and see if he can arrange for us to land and refuel in Iraq.'

'What about the roundels? Masters asked.

310

'We'll be landing at night,' Hunter replied, 'so we'll leave them. They are red, white and green while ours are red, white and blue. The chances are nobody will notice. And if they do, they'll do nothing about it.'

They quit the base at 20.00 for the two-hour flight to Al Anbar Govemorate, 100 miles west of Baghdad. Arrangements had been made for them to land, refuel and depart again at midnight.

Sunset in Iran was 19.55, the weather was overcast with an occasional shower. There was no moon and the wind was a gentle 10 knots from the southeast. It meant a dark night. They couldn't have wished for anything more.

Like the seasoned campaigners they were, they had prepped the plane for such a journey. Flying time was 1hr 30mins, camp beds were quickly assembled and to the comforting drone of the engines, the team was soon asleep. Schwarzkopf and Hunter manned the cockpit.

Wajeeh Soliman understood the English saying 'on the horns of a dilemma'. Or even better, 'between a rock and a hard place'. He knew he had to make a move but when?

He paced his office. The Prince was holding on and Soliman was sure it was only the thought of Hunter's pain at his family's death that was keeping him alive.

If the Prince died in the palace then the chances of Soliman getting out alive were slim. The Prince's offspring would see to that. When the Prince's sons and daughters got together, they often spoke in whispers. That had set alarm bells ringing; he was convinced they knew the part of the palace they inhabited was bugged.

At that moment he had a flash of inspiration. The super yacht - *The Star of Medina*. She was berthed in a marina on the edge of Jeddah.

She had been designed and built for the Prince a decade earlier. It was fitted with eight staterooms and a dozen cabins for the crew and any servants the Prince took with him. Plus there were public rooms ranging from a lounge that stretched the width of the boat to a cinema and plush dining room.

There were four permanent crew members who were loyal to him. He had made sure of that when he had hired them. They were well paid and did virtually nothing except have a party that teetered on being an orgy, once a month. From time to time he attended. The whores from Russia were particularly inventive and he always returned to the palace satisfied.

Getting away from the yacht would be a simple affair compared with escaping from the palace. Then he had another thought. He wouldn't have to. Why not leave onboard her? The thought took him in another direction. What if he were to own the vessel? If he remembered correctly, it had cost over \$60 million to build.

Whenever the Prince arrived he had his palace entourage with him from his butler and chef to the dogsbodies who waited on him full time

The first thing he required was a capable lawyer and more importantly, a willingness to create a deed gifting him the yacht. He would register his ownership in the International Register of Shipping. He didn't even need to ask the Prince for his signature, with his blessing, he'd been forging it for years. In fact, if the Prince tried to sign his name, it would be illegible and unrecognisable. He could barely hold a pen.

He needed to persuade the Prince to visit the yacht for a few days, but how? Then he smiled. It would give him the greatest pleasure to see Hunter die. If he told him the man had been captured and would be delivered to the yacht, the Prince would insist on being there.

Everyone knew the Prince had only days maybe a couple of weeks to live. If his oxygen was turned off he wouldn't live long. The Prince's stateroom was virtually soundproof. He could gasp for breath and try and call out but nobody would hear him. He could even put a pillow over the Prince's face if he was taking too long to die. It would be an act of kindness.

He could then arrange for the doctor, the nurse and the remainder of the staff to accompany the body back to the palace. In the meantime, he would put to sea. The chances were it would take the family a day or two to realise he had gone. The more he thought about it, the more sure he was that it would work.

The Israelis owed him big time and now it was time to collect.

The C130 landed at Al Anbar and taxied to a corner hangar. General Macnair had done a good job. The plane was refuelled and the team supplied with sandwiches and flasks of coffee. They were ready to go at 23.00. Flight time to the national park was 1hr 30mins, target time was 03.00.

The American Officer commanding the post arrived to say goodbye and to wish them good luck. It turned out he and Macnair had been at Staff College together and knew one another pretty well. When it came to fighting the good fight as the American put it, they were on the same page.

Schwarzkopf completed his preflight checks and the great beast rolled out of the hangar. At 80 knots and after rolling 2,000ft the C130 lumbered into the air.

Like all good soldiers, the team checked their equipment once more.

Ruth sat in the co-pilot's seat, her stomach in knots. The next few hours would be one of the most dangerous TIFAT had ever faced.

The plane was equipped with a radar detection unit tuned to the frequency used by air traffic control. After takeoff they flew south of Baghdad and headed directly for Arak.

When they hit Iranian airspace, flight control called them up demanding to know who they were. The automatic translation program was already fitted and had been carefully tested.

'Unknown aircraft identify yourself.' The question was in Farsi and instantly translated into English.

Schwarzkopf replied. 'This is an Iranian Airforce C130 on a training flight as promulgated in a NOTAM. You should have details of the flight.'

Leo had done a good job hacking into the Iranian air-traffic control system. The C130 was acknowledged and they flew on at 28,000ft and 350 knots.

'According to the satnav,' said Ruth, 'we're just west of Arak and should be off flight control any minute. Kavir National Park is now 100 miles further east. Haftad Qolleh Protected Area is coming up. Apparently it's a place of outstanding beauty and interest and visited often by tourists who risk entering Iran.'

'A risk?'

'Check out the number of Iranians who have emigrated, settled in other countries with full citizenship rights and visited family back in Iran only to be arrested on spurious charges.' Ruth paused and then added, 'You know the Iranians are a highly educated people who helped to civilize the world when the west was still living in caves. Look at it now! It's going backwards thanks to the Mullahs of Islam who have wrecked not only their country but also their religion. I hate the swine. Sorry, I'm sounding off.'

'That's okay. I agree. Nick,' he spoke into his mic.

'Yes, Burg.'

'Less than twenty minutes.'

'Okay. We're hot to trot.'

A short while later Schwarzkopf said, 'Feathering now.'

He turned the variable pitch propellers so that their mid-to-outer sections were aligned with the airflow to create minimal resistance. This created minimum drag when the engines stopped, which they did 30 seconds later. Silence engulfed the plane. They were only 20 nautical miles from the factory.

31

They had debated whether or not to use a paramotor or a parasail for the first part of the attack. As silence was vital, they had decided on the sail. The paramotors could easily clatter as they hit the ground and that could lead to disaster.

The team were dressed in mottled grey cameo suits over new kevlar based body and arm armour. They had two transmitters strapped to their waist and an earphone in each ear. One allowed them to speak to each other, the second was connected to the plane. They all wore grey war paint to hide their pale faces and had silenced Glocks on their hip and a K-Bar knife held in the sleeve of their jackets.

From their cruising height of 28,000ft, they knew the C130 could glide for about 70 nautical miles, so a distance of 20 was nothing. The plane swooped down to 3,000ft before leveling out. Now they were only three nautical miles from their target.

Schwarzkopf announced, 'Opening rear door in two.' The plane heeled and turned hard to port as they turned away from the factory and into the light wind blowing from the north.

The rear door opened and suddenly, the wind was howling outside the belly of the plane.

The light above the door changed from red to green and they pushed the canisters out.

'All gone,' Hunter told Schwarzkopf.

The plane banked again and glided for 10 nautical miles. Schwarzkopf unfeathered the props, pressed the ignition buttons on each of the four engines and was relieved when they burst into life.

A quick glance over the panel in front of him assured him that everything was running correctly.

'Check their location,' Schwarzkopf told Ruth.

'I'm watching them. The canisters are together south side of the track by about five metres as programmed. Did you hear that?'

'Yes, thanks, Ruth. Okay, take us to 8,000ft and we'll get going.'

'Good luck,' a sentiment echoed by Schwarzkopf.

The pilot repeated the performance with the engines and when the green light came on, Dave Hughes jumped. His parasail deployed and he drifted down towards his landing spot. Unlike the others, he was headed for an escarpment 200 metres from the nearest wall. The steep slope gave him a bird's eye view of three corners as well as the main gate.

He was carrying his British army L115A3, part of the Sniper System Improvement Programme, the same weapon he had used in Germany.

Exactly three minutes after he had left the plane the others followed, their wings deploying smoothly.

Unlike an ordinary parasail wing these were unique to TIFAT. They were made of the same non-rip reinforced nylon, but rather than being brightly coloured they were a dark grey and difficult to see at night. Instead of keeping their shape due to air pressure entering vents in the front of the wing and the aerodynamic forces of the air flowing over the outside, these also had helium pods inside the wing. This meant the wing was smaller and had more lift enabling the flyer to carry more gear. On this occasion, the team was travelling light. They expected to find what they needed at the factory.

The helium pods were controlled by two buttons, one released the gas into the wing, the other dumped it. Flying them took a great deal of practice. The team now had a few years of experience without mishaps.

'Okay, Dave,' Hunter broadcast, 'we are at 1,000 feet.'

The night was dark, the sky overcast and masking the moon. There was virtually no wind, which meant complete control of the sail.

'All set. I have the main gate and three of the towers covered. All preps complete.' By that he meant he had taken accurate distances between his position and his targets using a range finder accurate to a few centimetres. The nearest watchtower was 211.4 metres away, the furthest was 1,423.6 metres. Assuming the team landed where expected, then the danger came from the third target at 756.39 metres.

Badonovitch and the others were now directly over the compound and dropping quickly. The area was in darkness apart from the lights in the guard booth at the main gate. Thanks to their NVGs, they could see the layout and guards clearly.

They were entering the window of greatest danger. The main weapon each carried was a Heckler & Koch MP7 fitted with a suppressor and the 40 rounds magazine, which fed into the grip. The weapon was made mostly of polymer so was lightweight at just over 5lbs. Even with its foldable stock extended, it was only 25 inches long. The suppressor added a further 4.5 inches. It could be fired single shot or as a machinegun at a rate of 950 rounds per minute. The bullet had been designed especially for the HK7 and was armour piercing. In effect it meant that at 200 metres, the effective range of the gun, body armour would not stop it.

If circumstances were different, Hunter would have enjoyed the flight. It would have given him a sense of freedom and peace, not mayhem and death, which was what they faced. Killing so many people didn't sit well with him even if they were the enemy. They had to know what they were doing and why – trying to kill innocent men, women and children all over the world. The General had been right when he'd said they must be exterminated, otherwise the factory would be up and running again in no time.

The guards would be casualties of war. It was a case of them or the team. There was only going to be one outcome.

David Hughes was watching the compound through high-viz nighttime binoculars. The walls of the compound were three metres high, about 0.5m thick and topped with three strands of barbed wire.

The watchtowers were a further three metres higher, the top half of each being open to the elements.

'Nick, in the three towers I can see one guard standing and the head of another one who is either just sitting or probably asleep. At the main gate are two guards, one standing and one sitting. The one sitting has his head resting on his chest and also looks to be asleep. No, hang on, he's just stood up and is coming outside. He's out. He's headed in your direction.'

'Roger that. Have you got him?'

'Yes.'

'If he looks up take him.'

'He's looking up. Straight at you. He's turning.' Hughes pulled the trigger. There was a faint sound and the guard went down. The bullet had hit him in the sternum throwing him backwards.

'He's down.'

'Any reaction?'

'No. Nobody is looking. As we thought, they're bored out of their minds in the middle of nowhere in a country that's almost as buttoned up as North Korea.'

'Good. Landing in 30 seconds.'

'Roger that.'

The controls held in each of the pilot's hands connected to the trailing edge of the port and starboard sides of the wing. These were the brakes and by pulling down, the wing could flare for landing. There were three methods of making a fast landing. They had the quaint tags of Big Ears, B-line Stall and Spiral Dive. The latter was the fastest controlled descent, at a rate of 25 metres per second. The manoeuvre halts forward progress and brings the flyer almost straight down. The team was well grounded in the Spiral Dive technique, following a great deal of practice.

Hunter pulled the brakes on the left side and shifted his weight to create a tight turn. His flight path was now a corkscrew. His wing pointed directly at the ground and at the correct height he slowly released the inner brake shifting his weight to the right side and braking again. This ended his spiral dive in a couple of turns. The G-forces involved could induce blackouts and required skill and nerve to master. The team had both in spades.

Hunter touched down first and unshackled the parasail letting it drop to the ground. He took up a position covering the team as Badonovitch, Bletchley and Masters landed gently, just seconds apart and quickly collapsed their wings.

'All's still quiet,' Hughes transmitted, 'nobody is taking any notice.'

The dead man was about 50 metres away and Hunter crossed the packed earth of the compound, grabbed the back of the man's collar and dragged him back to the wall of the factory where they had landed.

After the cold of the flight the temperate 15°C was welcome.

'Dave?' Hunter whispered.

'Here, Nick.'

'There are no windows this side of the factory. We'll check the other walls.'

Slowly and silently Hunter and Badonovitch went one way while Bletchley and Masters went the other. They met on the other side of the factory outside the only door into the building. It was big enough to allow a lorry in but had a postern door next to it.

'Burg?'

'Yes, Nick.'

'The factory has no windows. We still need to examine the accommodation blocks. Where are you?'

'We're lining up to land. Need to go. Out.'

Schwarzkopf and Ruth had glided from the team drop off point across rugged terrain to the track they had identified from satellite pictures in Rosyth. The track looked flat and straight with low bushes either side. They had their underwing cameras operating and Ruth was looking intently at the picture on the screen in front of her.

'It looks good, Burg.'

Banking the plane, Burg turned her around and headed into the light breeze now coming from the west. Just before touchdown he started the starboard inner engine to flash up the hydraulic systems, lowered the wheels and increased the angle of the flight path five degrees skywards. As they neared the ground, he increased the angle until they were at 30 degrees when the rear wheels touched down and the front wheels dropped onto the track with a heavy thump. He braked hard and the lumbering beast came slowly to a standstill.

'Nice one, Burg,' Ruth croaked before clearing her throat.

'Thanks. Nick, down and waiting.'

'Roger that.'

'Ruth how about a cup of coffee and a sandwich? For some reason I feel dehydrated and hungry.'

'You and me both.'

The accommodation block did have windows although no lights showed and the curtains were drawn. Masters tried the front door, which opened with a low squeak. Badonovitch and Masters went inside and closed the door behind them.

Meanwhile, Hunter checked the small outhouse, which proved to contain a heavy-duty diesel-powered generator.

Masters and Badonovitch began searching the place. The entrance hall was a large open space with a staircase on the left and a swing door on the right. With silenced Glocks in their hands the two men went through the door and into a corridor. Without their NVGs they would have been in total darkness. The first door on the right opened into a large canteen with a serving hatch and about 30 tables with four uncomfortable looking, plastic backed chairs at each.

The next room was a recreation room with a TV set, a couple of dozen easy chairs and an incongruous looking table for playing table tennis.

There followed another three doors on the right each with half a dozen shower cubicles, sinks and toilets.

They started back up the corridor checking the other doors. Each one was an occupied room. They were well furnished with a single bed, table and chair, an easy chair and a TV, wash basin and a curtained window. Each of the beds was occupied.

Upstairs were rooms on both sides of the corridor though not all were in use.

Back in the foyer Masters transmitted, 'We've counted 42 people. All asleep.'

Meanwhile Bletchley and Hunter had searched the other, smaller block. Bletchley said, 'There are twenty-three asleep over here and all military. They are armed with rifles as well as automatics.'

Hunter transmitted. 'We take out the guards, put the generator out of use and then enter the factory. 'Dave, you ready?'

'Sure, Nick. I suggest I take out the one on the right first, then the left and then the nearest.'

'Okay. You take the ones standing, we'll deal with the sitters. I'll take the furthest, Chris to the left, Jan to the right, Don the closest. Dave you take your three in that order. Chris, as soon as you're done take the guard at the gate. Let's go.'

They moved out. Hunter had the furthest to go by about 30 seconds. Once he reached the base of the steps to the watchtower he stopped and waited as the team checked in.

'Okay, Dave. Take the first when Chris tells you.'

'Roger that.' Hughes already had his first target in his sights.

Bletchley went quietly and slowly up the steps until his head was at floor level to the tower. He whispered, 'Now, Dave.'

The guard who was standing flew backwards as the bullet hit him in the chest. Bletchley fired into the head of the guard who was seated and obviously asleep. The Heckler and Koch barely burped.

'Both down,' transmitted the marine softly.

Hughes said, 'Ready, Jan?'

'Now,' said the Russian.

Hughes fired at the same time as Badonovitch. Both shots were identical to the previous ones.

Still the compound was silent.

'Hughes said, 'Ready, Don?'

'Now,' said the REME.

The same again meant both guards died without knowing it.

Hunter was at the floor level of his tower. He shot the guard who was leaning on the parapet looking towards the sky and a second later he killed the seated guard.

'Clear,' said Hunter.

Bletchley followed the wall of the compound to the guardhouse. The guard had his back to the door and didn't even bother to look around. Bletchley's bullet hit the man in the back of the head, exited his forehead, leaving a small hole both sides.

Already Masters and Badonovitch were opening the door to the generator and turning off every valve they could see. Masters identified the feed for the diesel and broke it off. The smell of diesel grew more powerful and they quickly left the building closing the door behind them.

So far everything had gone according to plan.

The team crossed the compound to the postern door to the factory. Hunter opened the door and they trooped inside. It was as dark as the devil's armpit.

The door opened on to a single space stretching the length and breadth of the building. The factory was lined with aisles of shelves reaching to the ceiling three metres high. On the shelves were boxes of different colours. Masters lifted down a red box, about two foot square and a foot deep. There were two clips holding the lid down and he flicked them open. Inside he found two 10 by 10 layers of explosive balls. It meant 200 to a box.

Hunter and Bletchley had walked the length of the room and at the farthest section found the site where the explosive was being manufactured. It appeared to be an automated system for creating the explosive to manufacturing and filling the balls.

'This is a major industrial setup,' said Hunter.

'Nick,' said Masters, 'it isn't just the balls. In the black boxes there are one kilo packs with timers. The green boxes have two pencil thin strips, each a foot long. They are flexible with a timer attached, ideal for opening doors or blowing a hole in a wall. Hello, this is interesting. The orange boxes contain blocks of explosives operated by a transmitted signal. I've seen this type of transmitter before. The power to create the signal is made by a small windup key. It means the explosive can be transported safely and be ready to go in seconds. It's a little gizmo designed by the Israelis. All you need to do is flick the switch on the explosive itself and it's set to go.' He slipped a transmitter into his pocket.

'There must be hundreds of tonnes of explosives here,' said Bletchley. 'I'd say this lot is ready for shipping to the customers. We're only just in time.'

'Okay guys, let's move it. We stack the boxes against the walls of the accommodation blocks as well as the generator house and the diesel tank.'

The team grabbed a couple of boxes each and hurried through the door. They made 10 trips stacking the boxes against the walls of the buildings. They ran the thin thread of explosive from box to box and set the timers for 04.20.

While the other two continued moving boxes, Hunter and Masters set more timers in the main room.

They had been at it for nearly 30 minutes when Hughes transmitted, 'Nick, get out now. Incoming, two helicopters. Look like Bell 214s.

The Rapid Response officer was a captain. He shared the duty with a Major who was also the CO of the unit. They had been put together only weeks earlier as backup for the factory, 80 kilometres south at Kavir National Park. Like the others in the unit, he was bored out of his mind. Their duties had been extended recently to include protecting Tehran's airport following a series of online threats by terrorists who wanted a more secular way of life. A group who wanted religion to be kept in the mosques and not rammed down the throats of ordinary citizens. He snorted. Stupid swine! May they rot in Jahannam.

He amused himself by enumerating in his head the different levels of punishment for wrongdoers as stated in the holy book, the Qur'an.

First came fire and flames that crackle and roar. Then came being immersed in boiling water, swept by scorching wind and forced to breath black smoke. That was four. What followed? Oh, yes. The inhabitants of hell had their skin scorched off their bodies only for it to be replaced and the torment to start again. Was that a new torment or the result of the actions already taken? He decided it was a new one. Then there was the forced drinking of festering water. He liked that idea and amused himself further by trying to imagine what was used to infest the water. He glanced at his watch and groaned 04.09. He was on duty until 08.00.

What came next? Yes, the wrongdoers were linked together with chains, wore clothes made of pitch and had fire on their faces. He pondered that one but it made no sense. However, it was written in the Qur'an and so was true. He made a mental note to ask an Imam about it. Next they had their insides melted and should they try to escape then punishment hooks of iron dragged them back.

How many was that? Of course, not everyone was subject to such torment. It depended upon how many of the seven gates a wrongdoer passed through. A non-believer was subject to them all, minor transgressors only to a few with the possibility of a pardon after a certain number of years. How many years he wondered?

His head drooped onto his chest. The need for sleep slowly seeped through his body. He awoke with a start when his sergeant burst into his office.

'Sir, we have not had the 04.00 radio check from Kavir.'

He was suddenly wide-awake and looked at his watch. It was 04.17.

'The 04.15 check call?'

The sergeant shook his head.

'Have you tried to call them?'

'Yes, sir. There's no reply.'

The Captain was in a dilemma. Should he call the Major and let him decide or should he respond immediately? A rapid response unit was precisely that. By the time the Major was called and the situation explained, many minutes would be lost. Besides he was on duty. It was his responsibility to follow orders and react.

It could be a faulty radio, which would surprise nobody. On the other hand it was an excuse to go into action and alleviate the boredom of the next four hours.

'Let's go. Full kit and ready for action.'

The Sergeant grinned and saluted. 'Yes, sir.'

The Captain stood and stretched. He was 6ft 3ins tall, fit and tough. At 32 he expected more promotion in the army, which would make his parents proud of him. He was wearing green cameos and had an Iranian made polymer framed pistol, a Striker, strapped to his waist.

His 15-man team used the Iranian made Zulfiqar Modular Rifle, a weapon subject to jamming if fired for too long on full automatic. He snorted. This was for all of three to four seconds and so the soldiers practiced short bursts when they were allowed to use the firing range. The last time had been six months ago.

The pilots were already running to the Bell helicopters in their hangar.

The helicopters carried 14 troops and so he required both. He was in the first one along with seven Special Forces operatives and two pilots. The second Bell carried the remaining eight troops. The irony of flying the Bell 214 was lost on the Captain. It had been a military project specifically for manufacture in Iran, designed by Bell and funded by the Iranian government. The contract between Bell and Iran was cancelled in 1979, after the overthrow of the Shah.

The Captain was plugged into the onboard communications system and he made contact with the pilot. 'Give it all you've got.'

'Captain, we will cruise at 140 knots.'

The Captain gritted his teeth and held back the retort that had sprung to his lips. He knew it was pointless.

He used his mobile phone and called his CO. He had been in two minds when to call him. If he had done so before they took off, he would probably have been told to wait for him. That would have delayed things for as much as 10 minutes.

The assignment to the airport was for six months. Special quarters, basic but adequate, had been built outside the airport but only minutes away from the helicopter hangar. They were in their fifth month since the Kavir compound had been opened. In the beginning, there had been a great deal of speculation about the place but the bottom line was the troops had no idea what was going on there. They had also been told in no uncertain terms to stop speculating. The regime under which they existed ensured the subject was quickly dropped.

'Sir? We are en-route to Kavir.'

'What for? What's going on? What time is it?' Major Rostami sounded less than half-awake.

'It's 04.37 and there has been no radio contact since midnight.'

The Major was rapidly coming to. 'No 04.00?'

'No sir. Nor was there a 04.15 check call and so I've scrambled the squad.'

'You should have called me!' There was no disguising the anger in his voice.

'Sorry, Major but there wasn't time.' He didn't actually believe what he was saying and he was damned sure the Major didn't believe it either. However, there was nothing his CO could do. The glory would be his. He relished the thought. He hated his CO for his lack of piety, his non-observance of the Qur'an and his secularism, which would damn the man's soul for eternity.

'I'm coming now. Wait until we join you. Understand?'

'Sorry, Major I can't hear you. Say that again.'

'I said do not take any action until I get there.'

'Sorry sir, say again.' He switched off his phone and smiled. 'Distance to go?'

The pilot replied, 'Thirty kilometres.'

'Time to go is what I want!' He didn't add imbecile though he wanted to. As his tension mounted, he ignored the fact that he had asked for the distance. This was the first time he hadn't been on a planned and formulated exercise. This was for real. His mouth was dry and he could feel the sweat on his brow. He looked around the cabin. The others looked as though they hadn't a care in the world but then all of them had seen action of one sort or another. He envied them.

'The compound is ahead,' announced the pilot.

'Good. Straight in and…'

His orders were cut short. The explosion was huge. He looked at what was happening in utter shock. This couldn't be! It was impossible! Bricks, stones and other debris flew into the air, some of it smashing into the helicopters. The pilot of his craft was killed while the co-pilot was frozen in shock. The helicopter's engine cut out and it went into a dive straight towards the spreading fire.

This couldn't be happening!

He screamed as the craft hit the ground and was engulfed by the flames.

The second helicopter swooped down into the factory smashing through what remained of the roof. The avgas it carried exploded killing those who had survived the impact.

32

'Good work, Don,' said Hunter.

Masters hadn't left it to the timers on the detonators but instead had used the remote control.

'Dave, get the hell out of there.'

'Already on it.'

Hughes spread out his aerofoil and began to strap himself in. He was ready to go when he heard the sound of helicopters.

'Nick, two more in-bound Bells.'

'Copy that. We're three kilometres from the drop.'

The team wasn't yomping but running as though the hounds of hell were on their tail. Hunter looked back and saw that the fire was raging. In the glow cast into the cloud leaden sky, he could see the helicopters circling like huge vultures.

The Major looked at the still burning fire and the devastation of the compound. He did not know what had been produced there but he'd had his suspicions. It looked as though he'd been right. An explosives factory! But why the secrecy? The country had the right to manufacture any explosives it liked. Unless they were for illegal purposes.

Fighting a war and defending your country was one thing, committing acts of terrorism something else. Then he had another thought. What if the explosives were being manufactured for use by other countries and other organisations? He made the connection. Sell whatever had been made there to terrorists, get hard currency in return and promote and instigate attacks on the West.

He realised the idea wasn't beyond the bounds of possibility. That was the sort of ludicrous thinking the political leadership under the control of Ayatollah Shahbazi would indulge in.

The Major was highly intelligent and was aware that his chances of further promotion under the current regime were infinitesimal. It was partly his fault and partly his family's lack of connections. He had been overheard criticising the regime and disparaging Shahbazi. He knew that the man who reported him had been his second-in-command, now dead.

The Major was a dedicated officer sworn to protect his country, an oath he took seriously. His dilemma was the fact that the enemy was within and many of his colleagues felt the same. The hardships the Iranians were suffering stemmed from the obduracy of the Supreme Leader, the man who talked to God whenever it suited him. It usually started "I have been steered to the Qur'an by the word of God" and went on from there. It was all nonsense of course but it appealed to the masses. The West was to blame was the mantra.

What had happened? An accident or an attack? One of the watch-towers was still intact and he ordered the pilot to fly closer. He focused his binoculars on the structure and saw the body of a guard leaning back against the wall.

'Closer still.'

'This is as close as we can get.'

'Okay.'

The bullet hole in the man's head was plain to see. 'The man in the watchtower has been shot. This is sabotage.'

He licked dry lips and pressed the speed dial on his phone. He had never used it before and he was suddenly very nervous. The Brigadier was an idiot but was the man in command of the military in the region.

A sleep filled voice said, 'This had better be good.'

'Sir. This is Major…'

'I know who you are you idiot. Your name has come up on my screen. What do you want?'

'Sir, the compound at Kavir National Park has been destroyed!'

'What?' There was no disguising the shock in his CO's voice.

'The premises in Kavir have been totally wiped out.'

'Oh my God. How? Who? I don't believe it. It's impossible!'

'Terrorists sir. We don't know who they are. However, the level of devastation is huge. It must have been an overwhelming force. Everyone appears to be dead.'

'Never mind them. I want the terrorists caught alive if possible, dead if not.'

'Sir, two of our helicopters are down and the teams are dead. We are the off-watch team. I need back-up as quickly as possible. I suggest we find the terrorists and follow them keeping a safe distance. They are bound to be heavily armed. They can't get out of the country so all we need to do is watch them until you get here.'

'All right. I'll mobilise now. Just make sure you find the swine otherwise…'

He left the sentence unfinished but the Major knew what he meant. Someone was going to be blamed; it was the nature of things in Iran. The saying that crap rolled downhill was true and he was at the bottom of that hill.

They hadn't seen anything coming south from Tehran. A convoy of vehicles would have been all too noticeable. The only way was for the terrorists to head east though how they thought they were going to escape was beyond him. They couldn't head south because the terrain was too rough for vehicles and walking would take forever, besides which, where would they be going? The more he thought about it the more convinced he became that he was dealing with a bunch of amateurs. Possibly even home-grown terrorists who wanted the regime to fall.

'Sir!' The pilot yelled. 'Helicopter 2 just broadcast Mayday.'

The craft suddenly turned on its axis and he yelled in alarm. 'What the…!!' He stopped and watched in horror as the second helicopter with half his team spun out of control and crashed into the raging fire.

He didn't have time to order the pilot to move it. They were already turning and accelerating away.

The Major kept his wits about him. 'Pilot, follow the track east as quickly as you can.'

'Yes, sir.'

David Hughes shook the straps of his aerofoil and unfolded the two legs on the front of his L115A3. He was using the .338 Lapua Magnum ammunition that was capable of penetrating armoured glass. The effective range of the rifle was 1,500 – 1,700 metres though kills had been recorded as far as 2,475 metres in Afghanistan.

The two helicopters had just dipped their noses and turned east. Hughes aimed, made adjustments for a target at 1,600 metres and fired at the second one. The bullet hit the tail rotor and sent the machine into a tailspin. From a height of about 300 metres it smashed into the ground and exploded.

'Nick, one down, one coming up fast.'

'Roger that. Good work. Now get out of there. Head for the drop zone and start getting the kit together.'

'Roger that.' He quickly climbed into the foil and walked off the edge of the cliff pumping helium into the wing as he did. He soared into the sky and turned 90 degrees to starboard and swooped skywards, following the helicopter. There was no way on earth that he'd leave the others and head for the drop zone. He knew how valuable his rifle would be in a gunfight. Especially when he wasn't expected.

The pilot said to the Major, 'Sir, I can see four men running down the track about one kilometre away.'

'Are you sure?'

'They're showing up on the infra-red signal of the new radar.'

'Good, get to within 800 metres and land.'

The Iranians weren't short of highly intelligent and highly trained engineers and weapons designers. The radar had been designed by the French and stolen by an Iranian employee of the Toulouse-based manufacturer. The man still had 10 years to serve in prison in France. His sacrifice for the Iranian cause was ignored by the regime as though he had never existed. His family now lived in poverty in Tehran, after being deported from France.

A small team of men he could handle. If he could capture or kill them then he still had a chance to redeem himself in the eyes of both the General and the regime.

'The chopper is coming fast,' said Masters.

'Okay, take cover,' Hunter replied.

Hunter and Bletchley took cover to the right of the track, Masters and Badonovitch to the left. There were boulders on both sides that offered some protection but if the troopers were carrying RPGs it would be a different story. They put some distance between themselves, ensuring the Iranians had to split their fire.

'Wait until we see the colour of their eyes,' Hunter called out.

The Heckler and Koch MP7's effective range was 200 metres.

They had expected the chopper to fly past when they would open up with a withering rate of fire. It didn't happen. The helicopter suddenly began to hover and then it landed. Troops piled out and quickly took up positions either side of the track.

'Nick?'

'Yes, Dave. Where are you?'

'I've just landed about 150 metres behind the 'copter. We can't let them follow us. We need to put it out of action.'

'Concur. Seven armed soldiers just emerged. The pilot will make eight if he joins the fight. Also I'm pretty sure one of them is carrying an RPG.'

'It'll be an old RPG2, a gift from the Russians,' said Hughes.

Iran and Russia were military allies in the wars in Syria and Iraq. Due to Western sanctions against Iran, Russia had become an important trading partner in oil and military equipment.

'Nick, the pilot is getting out.

'Can you take him?'

'No problem. I can also damage the helo. Maybe even set it off.'

'Okay. Pilot first.'

By way of an answer, Hughes took aim and fired into the back of the head of the pilot. He went down without a sound. By this time the Iranians were at least 200 metres closer to their targets and hidden behind boulders front and back.

'Nick,' said Bletchley, 'two are about 400 metres away.'

'Roger that,' whispered Hunter. 'I can't see anyone.'

'Dave, can you see anybody?'

'One guy comes into view and vanishes again behind the rocks.'

'Put five rounds into the helicopter. We might get lucky.'

The mag held five rounds and Hughes had already replaced the spent bullets. He took aim at the housing between the main propeller and fired. Three shots ensured the helicopter wouldn't fly again. His next two were aimed at the underbelly where the highly combustible avgas was stored. He fired twice and had the satisfaction of watching the helicopter explode in a fiery ball.

Hughes ejected his magazine and swapped it for another. In those couple of seconds, the man he had been watching stood up and looked at the burning helicopter. Hughes fired and the man went down.

'One ugly on the south side of the track.'

'By my reckoning,' said Bletchley, 'that leaves six.'

'Nick, they are hidden by a large scattering of boulders. I'd be more useful assembling the gear.'

'Agreed, Dave. Do it piece by piece on each one.'

Hughes knew what he meant. There was no point putting one together followed by a second and so on. It was possible he wouldn't get the job done in time and although the first one or two could get away, the others could be left to do their own. Better to have them all at the same stage of completion.

He climbed back into his aerofoil and pumped as much helium into the wing as it would take. He walked forward and felt the wing lift. He broke into a stumbling trot on the uneven surface and then he took off, aiming up, soaring into the night sky. Sometime during the last hour or two the clouds had cleared and the stars filled the sky. It was then he realised it was gradually growing light. He looked down. The landscape was still dark but dawn wasn't far away.

The Major looked at his helicopter in shocked horror. He hadn't noticed one of his men being killed as the corpse now lay on the far side of the track behind a massive boulder. He called in his team on the communications system and that was when he realised the man was dead.

They were six against how many? He still couldn't be sure. He thought about his options and realised he had none. If he couldn't follow the terrorists, he had to attack. Otherwise he'd be arrested for cowardice, tried, found guilty and hanged.

'Listen all of you. We need to attack. To let them escape without doing our best to stop them is tantamount to suicide.' He didn't have to spell it out. They understood what he was saying all too well.

He deployed his men, three each side of the track and moved out. The NCO carrying the RPG went to the south of the track, he went to the north.

David Hughes was high in the sky by this time and looking down at what was going on. He knew he needed to get to the drop zone but from his vantage point he could survey the scene.

'Nick, look up at twelve o'clock. Can you see me against the sky?'

A few seconds later Hunter said, 'I've got you.'

'I'm at 1,000ft and I can direct you. There are three each side of the track. I'd say about 350 metres from your positions. Whoever is on the south side, if you head further south for about 50 metres I think that's a shallow gully I can see, though it's difficult to tell from this height and angle. If I'm right it stretches about 100 metres then turns 90 degrees to the right. Whoever takes it will come up behind the three southern targets. I will be able to tell when you're near them.'

'That's me and Jan,' said Hunter. 'We're on our way.'

Hughes watched the two men moving south and at the same time he kept an eye on the three targets.

'Where's our deliveries?' Masters asked.

'I can't see them. They appear to have gone to ground.'

Like a giant bat the aerofoil circled the area. Thanks to his NVGs, Hughes could see clearly but still only had the three men in sight. At that moment he regretted not having a hand grenade to drop. He knew he could put one hand in the middle of the steering bar and hold the kite steady though steering wasn't an option. He could then use his Glock and hopefully get away.

'Nick, are you okay?'

'Affirmative. It is a gully. Underfoot is pretty smooth. Where are the uglies?'

'Come round the bend. They've just reached the gully, heading your way.'

'I see them.'

Hughes watched as Hunter and Badonovitch hit the deck, their Heckler and Kochs ready to fire. Only there was nobody to fire at. The Iranians were Special Forces and had been in combat on numerous occasions. They knew what they were doing and they did it well.

'Nick, one of them appears to be holding an RPG. They're about 150 metres away and worming towards you. There's a large boulder right in front of you, 100 metres away. They'll reach it in about two minutes. You guys are out in the open.'

'Tell us about it,' was the droll reply.

'I'm going to close and shoot at them without my silencer. It might distract them long enough for you to get to the boulder before them.'

Hughes moved his left hand to the centre of the control bar to steady the foil and pulled out his Glock. Awkwardly, he unscrewed the suppressor and dropped it near the Iranians. The sound must have distracted the three men because they stopped and looked behind them. Hughes aimed at the three with his Glock18 on automatic. He opened fire just as the Iranians hit back.

The Iranian with the RPG knelt down, put the weapon to his shoulder and fired at the boulder.

At the same moment, Hughes opened fire as one of the targets looked up. The target dropped to the ground, rolled onto his back and started firing into the sky.

The RPG2 rocket hit the boulder and blew it to bits, scattering pieces of rock while the Iranian and Hughes exchanged automatic fire. The Iranian's bullets stitched holes in the starboard wing of the foil and the final bullet hit Dave Hughes in the leg, scraping a deep gouge of his flesh from his knee to his waist. The TIFAT warrior held his nerve and emptied his 33 round magazine around the Iranian, two bullets blowing the man's head apart.

Hughes was already losing height and beginning to spin out of control. A glance at his instrument panel showed he was at 350 metres and descending rapidly. He opened the valve on his helium bottle as far as it would go, pulled down on the starboard control lines and stopped the spin and his rapid descent. He was still on the way down but not as rapidly, thanks to the pods in the wing. He was aware that if he landed anywhere on the rough terrain, there was a better than even chance he would suffer serious injury from breaking a leg to breaking his neck. His only chance was to land on the track and he aimed for it now about 10 metres away. He hit the ground with a thump and rolled to one side, hitting the quick release catch as he fell.

It was just as well. An automatic pistol opened fire and a line of bullets stitched a pattern along the track missing him by inches. His rifle was of no use and his Glock was empty. Even so he kept his head and crawled behind a boulder while dropping into a shallow ditch. The next string of bullets traversed the ground and scraped along his back. His Kevlar vest saved him from serious injury but left him bruised.

He reached into his right leg trouser pocket and extracted a hypodermic needle ready for use. He pulled off the plastic cap and thumped his right thigh with it, close to his wound, which was bleeding badly. The morphine-based painkiller kicked in within seconds and allowed him to think more clearly.

He remembered the RPG explosion and whispered, 'Nick? Come in, Nick. Are you okay?'

He looked up. A man in uniform was standing over him with his pistol pointed at his head.

There was no reply from Hunter or Badonovitch.

33

The two TIFAT men were about 50 metres away from the boulder when it exploded. They had been bent over as they headed along the gully and dropped to the ground when they heard the initial whoosh of the rocket being fired. It was a split-second warning but it was enough. The rocket hit the base of the boulder and lifted it a few inches off the ground while at the same time blowing it to bits. Pieces of rock as big as a man's fist flew in all directions.

One chunk landed on Badonovitch's right shoulder breaking his collarbone. He dropped his Glock but snatched it up using his left hand. He was in agony but he gritted his teeth and opened fire. When it came to a choice between pain and death, there was no competition. He had his pistol on fully automatic and sprayed the gully.

Without the boulder the two Iranians who were hurrying towards Badonovitch and Hunter were in plain view. The Russian's first two shots went through the face of the lead fighter while his next two hit the other man in the top of his right shoulder, practically severing his arm. The remainder of his bullets missed. He saw the soldier fall and then get to his feet. The man swayed for a few seconds and then collapsed heavily.

Badonovitch ran towards the two bodies. He needed to make sure both were dead. He didn't want any surprises. The first body had almost no head left while the second man groaned. Badonovitch knelt by the man to check his wound. He was torn between helping him and going to see to Hunter first. Even as he knelt there, the loss of blood proved too much and the man gasped and died. He noticed the gold

337

sun-like pip on the man's shoulders and knew he was a Major. He hurried back to Hunter who was now groaning softly.

Badonovitch could see the blood on the back of Hunter's head as well as blood seeping down his right arm. He took out his morphine hypodermic and rammed the needle into his own left upper arm. Next he reached into Hunter's right leg pocket, extracted his hypodermic, removed the plastic cover and injected Hunter's right arm. He cut Hunter's sleeve away. A bullet had hit the seam of his Kevlar vest and ricocheted across his upper arm causing a deep gash. It was bleeding but not too badly. He took out a tube of medical cyanoacrylate adhesive and squeezed the glue along the gash, which stopped the bleeding. He used a plaster to cover the wound to prevent irritation from Hunter's clothes.

Masters and Bletchley had moved quickly going from boulder to boulder, each one covering the other as they did so. They hadn't seen the enemy but guessed there were three or four of them.

They suddenly saw one about 50 metres away standing up and pointing his automatic at the ground.

'Is that Dave on the ground?' Masters whispered.

'Yes.'

Both men opened fire simultaneously. Both were head shots.

They ducked back down in time to avoid withering fire coming from a small number of large boulders. The shots ricocheted around them like angry wasps. Most of the rounds missed but one scraped along the left side of Bletchley's head causing him to drop to the ground unconscious.

Masters reached into a pocket and extracted two of the cricket balls he had taken from the factory. These weren't operated by pressure but by a timing device. He gripped the first ball in two hands and twisted the two halves around the seam. They clicked twice. He threw the ball as hard as he could and was gratified to see it land behind the boulders. There was an explosion followed by silence. He now had to decide whether his enemies were dead or not. He had no choice other than to go and find out. Time was becoming vital and they still had a couple of kilometres to go. He paused for a moment, trying to decide whether to take care of Bletchley or the enemy. The Royal Marine groaned and that convinced him.

Masters darted forward about 20 metres and threw the second ball. It landed where he had hoped and exploded. At the same time, he threw himself to the ground just as a man from behind the boulders stepped into view and aimed his rifle at him. The Iranian was carrying a KL-7.62 assault weapon, made in Iran, but designed by the Chinese. The banana shaped magazine gave more than a hint of the Russian-made AK74, except the Iranian weapon was more reliable.

Masters began to aim his gun when the Iranian fired and the bullet hit the Royal Engineer in the top of his right arm throwing off his aim. The Iranian began to walk towards him as Masters tried to take his Heckler and Koch in his left hand in spite of knowing he was too late. What a lousy place to die was his thought as the Iranian staggered forward and began to turn as a second bullet hit him in the face. Hughes came into sight and limped towards Masters.

'You okay?'

'I guess I'll live but a bullet went through my arm. I think the bone is broken or at least chipped.' He spoke through gritted teeth. 'Help me get my syringe.'

Hughes found the hypodermic, removed the protection cap and injected Masters in the arm.

'You're bleeding,' said Masters looking at his friend's bloodied trouser leg.

'Yeah.' Hughes took out his K-Bar and cut a slit along his trousers. It was bleeding quite badly and he knew he needed to do something about it asap before he bled to death. He took out his tube of medical glue and squeezed it along the wound. Next he pressed the palms of his hands either side of the wound and pushed the gash together. In seconds the bleeding had stopped and he wrapped a bandage around it. 'Let me look at your arm.'

'No. Take a look at Chris.'

Hughes stayed bent over and hurried along the gully to Bletchley who was now groaning and trying to sit up. The RM Captain put his hand to his head, felt something wet and sticky and groaned again.

'Hang on, Chris.'

Hughes began first aid with the painkiller and the glue but without trying to pull the scalp together. Instead he wrapped a bandage around the wound.

'How are the others?' Bletchley asked.

'No idea. I can't raise Nick or Jan.'

Bletchley swore before saying, 'Thanks, Dave. I can get up.' He climbed to his feet and swayed slightly before recovering his balance. 'What about you, Don?' The REME had rejoined them.

'Bullet in the shoulder.'

'Dave, you take care of it and I'll go and look for Nick and Jan.'

Masters sat down while Hughes cut open his sleeve. The bullet had gone straight through without hitting a vein or artery.

'Jesus, Don! Talk about luck.'

They heard a noise and looked along the track in time to see Hunter and Badonovitch walking towards them. Neither man looked to be in good shape.

Hughes repeated his first aid work with the glue to stop the bleeding and covered it with a plaster. Next, he used a bandage to strap Masters' arm across his chest to give the glue time to set. He would need the use of his arm soon enough.

'Are you okay, Nick?' Bletchley asked.

'My head took most of the damage but I think I'll live. What about you guys?'

They described their wounds in a nonchalant, off-hand manner, which didn't fool Hunter for a moment.

'We'd better get going. This must have been an advance party. Rapid Response probably. The main force could arrive any time.'

While the team changed their magazines Bletchley asked, 'Any Iranians left?'

Hughes replied, 'Not that I could see. None alive, that is.'

Badonovitch confirmed the fact. 'I think we would have either

Vendetta

seen them or heard them by now.' He was down on one knee facing back the way they had come, watching for any trouble that could still be out there.

They checked their communication systems. A bullet had hit Hughes' equipment and it was wrecked but it had saved him from a bullet in his left hip.

Each took long drafts of mineralised water and finally started down the track. In spite of their wounds, they yomped quickly and made reasonable time.

The General was beside himself with rage. As the senior officer in the region, he was responsible for all security matters, whether it was a threat from a foreign country or home-grown insurgents. Nowadays the latter was considered more likely. He took deep breaths and tried to calm down. The idiot Major had said the compound had been devastated but what did that mean? Surely it couldn't be as bad as he said?

He knew how the regime thought because he was one of them. They would want someone to blame. He would do his utmost to make that someone the Major. It would all depend on what he found. How much damage had been done? How many attackers had there been and were they now dead or captured? The latter was preferred, the former was acceptable.

He knew what the factory in the compound was being used for and heartily approved. Hard currency and attacks on the West, especially the Great Satan, was a combination too good to miss.

He harangued his officers mercilessly in an effort to get them to hurry up. Panic was in his voice and stress mixed with fear brought out the natural bully in him. He had two Boeing CH-47 Chinook helicopters at his disposal and although they were left over from the 1970s, they were still capable of 170 knots with 50 fully kitted troops onboard.

At 06.23 he received a phone message from the Captain in charge of aircraft maintenance. 'Sir, one of the helicopters is not in working order. It is being used for spare parts on the one that is operational.'

341

'What? How long has this been the case? Why didn't I know about it?'

'Sir, with all due respect, I delivered the memo a week ago.'

'Then send 50 men by truck and the other 50 will go in the helicopter. Do I have to think of everything myself?'

He was in his quarters at the barracks and walked out the front door to stand on the veranda. Finally, a car arrived to pick him up and drive him across to the other side of the military camp where the helicopter hangars were located.

The Captain greeted him with a routine salute, which he barely acknowledged.

As he climbed into the helicopter he asked a Colonel, the next most senior officer, 'The pilots know where we are going?'

'Yes, sir.'

'Is the convoy on its way?'

'Yes, sir. Fifty men in each of five trucks, all heavily armed.'

'What are we waiting for Colonel? Get this load of crap into the air.'

'Yes, sir. Straightaway, sir. Let's go, pilot.' He spoke on his inter-com and seconds later they took off.

The Colonel looked across the cabin, fighting back the urge to say something that at best would result in his court martial and dismissal from the service, or more likely a firing squad for insubordination. General Rostami had always been proud of his surname and was known to boast about it. Back in the time of the Parthian Empire, Rostam had been known as the mightiest of Iranian paladins or holy warriors. The General claimed his name came from that time and he also claimed to be a direct descendant of the mighty hero.

The General had never been in combat in spite of the troubles Iran had faced starting with the Iran – Iraq war in the early 1980s. There had been many incidents all across the Gulf and the Middle East, but somehow he had managed to avoid them. Like the Colonel sitting opposite him, those in high office who knew him, knew him to be a loud-mouthed coward. But that description would fit many of Iran's hierarchy.

They were the inheritors of Iran's privileged and wealthy class who were too ignorant to do anything other than cower behind their army uniforms giving each other meaningless medals they did nothing to earn.

So what was going on now? He knew about the compound at Kavir National Park but he didn't know what it was being used for. There were plenty of rumours but he did his best not to listen to them. They were inevitably exaggerated. He did the speed distance calculation and decided they would take 40 minutes. The time was then 06.39. The sun had risen 19 minutes ago. Visibility would be good

The convoy would take at least to two hours, possibly two and a half.

Hunter and the others had reached the drop zone and found the five canisters. Quickly they slipped the parachutes and then unclipped the lids.

They laid out the sail and ropes and placed the seat and motor on the ground. It didn't take long to hook each machine together. They had practiced often enough. They helped each other into their back-up parachutes and were ready to start the motors of their paramotors only 23 minutes after arriving. This was at least 10 minutes longer than normal but it was the first time they had done the job when wounded. Tough though they were, they were all approaching the limits of their strength and determination.

The canisters they hid in a gully and buried under rocks, stones and dust. If the Iranians found them it was possible they could figure out the team had somehow left at that point which would mean only one thing - they were flying out. There was still the dilemma as to which direction they had taken but the Iranians had enough military resources to cover all directions. With nothing to show they had been there it was more than likely that the Iranians would continue down the track hoping to catch them.

Their means of escape was by powered paraglider. The propeller was behind the pilot, enclosed in a strong cage. The single blade was five feet in length and could push the parasail at a speed over 35mph.

343

It was ideal for crossing rough terrain littered with large boulders and rocks. They had 50 miles to go to the track where the C130 was waiting for them. The estimated travel time was 90 minutes.

When they were just about ready to go, they drank the last of their water and swallowed two caffeine based energy pills.

They put on safety helmets equipped with a communications system that was voice activated so there was no need to operate any buttons. The foil also had the helium lift, which helped takeoff and finally, it had a built in location transponder attuned to the location of the C130.. The glider would steer itself to their destination. All they had to do was watch their height.

They started their motors and stepped forward into the breeze. They opened up the helium valves and one by one, they sailed gracefully into the air. At 1,000ft their foils turned towards the south. Their transponders showed they had 47.9 miles to go and that their speed was 38.2mph.

Sunrise had been 32 minutes earlier. Time was 06.52. The sky was cloudless and blue while the air was clear with visibility as far as the horizon. These were not the conditions the team wanted.

The Chinook circled the compound. The General looked down in a mixture of shock and dread. The whole place had been wiped off the face of the earth. The only part left standing was a single watchtower. He suddenly felt the urge to use a toilet though whether to sit on or be sick into it was debatable.

'Should we land, sir?' His Second in Command called out.

There was no response.

'Sir,' he yelled louder, 'do you want us to land?'

'What? No! No! Pilot, radio the convoy and tell them to get a move on.'

'What do you want us to do, sir?' The Colonel could see the man didn't know. Or was unwilling to say and hence take responsibility for their next move.

'What do you suggest?' The General licked dry lips, already seeing his court martial in his mind's eye.

'Logically the only way that makes any sense is east. I have checked the map. To the west there's nothing but a deteriorating track for about 100 kilometres when it becomes impassible. To the east, the track runs for about 60 kilometres before hitting the main road to Nein, 100 kilometres distant. Once there, they can lose themselves.'

'Colonel, this attack must have taken a large force of insurgents. A couple of lorry loads anyway. Easily 30 to 40 men.'

'Hence their need to get to the city to hide. It's the only place they can go.'

It made sense to Rostami and reluctantly he nodded. The decision was taken. He had committed his forces and now all he could do was pray to Allah that he had chosen correctly. No, his Colonel had chosen correctly. Any mistakes would be on the Colonel's head. He would see to that.

'Give the order.'

'Yes, sir. Pilot, follow the track as fast as you can.'

The helicopter turned and picked up speed. A minute later, they passed over the site where the team had assembled their parasails.

Twenty minutes later the Colonel said, 'Sir, they can't have come this far. It's impossible.'

'Then where are they?' Rostami snarled.

'They must have gone south. It will be hard going but there's the main road from Nein to Kashan. They could have vehicles waiting there.'

'But how will they cross this wilderness? It will take them forever.'

'I don't know. Grow wings and fly I suspect.' There was no disguising the ridicule in his voice.

'Don't be ridiculous. I don't like your tone, Colonel.'

'Sorry, sir. There was no intention...' he trailed off.

'No intention of what?'

'Sir, that's it! You've got it.'

'Got what?'

'If we are correct and they are heading south across this hellish landscape then the only way will be to fly.'

'Insurgents aren't that well organised or equipped to have helicopters at their disposal. And a suitable large force would need two the size of a Chinook. And that's impossible. The only ones of that size belong to us.'

'Yes, sir, you're right. But what about motorised parasails?'

'Colonel, what in Jahannam are you talking about?'

'They are collapsible wings with a small motor. You can buy them for less than $10,000 each. Thirty attackers, price $300,000 dollars as opposed to a helicopter costing tens of millions. And like you said, the only ones big enough are military.'

The Colonel let the idea percolate through the General's brain.

Finally the General nodded. 'You could be right. So what do you suggest?'

The Colonel had removed a map of the area from a satchel and was studying it. '60 kilometres south is a track that leads to the Nein/ Kashan highway. That's where I'd have the getaway vehicles.'

'All well and good but where do we start looking?'

By way of answer the Colonel said, 'Pilot.'

'Yes, sir.'

'Head south until you come to this map reference,' he read out the co-ordinates, 'and then head west following the track as fast as you can. Keep a look out for parked lorries or cars. Sufficient to carry at least 20 or 30 men.'

'Yes, sir.'

34

'Nick! Nick! Wake up, damn it!' Bletchley yelled into his mic.

Hunter groggily lifted his head and looked down. He was swooping towards the earth. The safety alarm went off telling him he was falling below 200 feet. He jerked into full consciousness and opened the helium valve.

'Nick, are you okay?' Badonovitch closed on his boss to take a better look.

'I'm fine, Jan. I went under for a few seconds but I'm back again.'

'It must be the wound to your head,' said Bletchley. 'Luckily it's so thick otherwise you might really have been damaged.'

They were in a V formation with Hunter in the lead, Bletchley followed by Masters to his left, Badonovitch was to Bletchley's right followed by Hughes. They were making 30mph over the ground due to an increase in the wind. The clear skies were clouding over from the west and it was obvious that thanks to an anti-cyclone from the same direction, a storm was on its way.

The transponder showed they had 25 miles to go and it would take 52 minutes.

Hunter transmitted, 'It'll be touch and go whether we get to the plane before the storm.'

The parasails were robust and normally safe to fly. However, in a storm with updrafts and downdrafts they were hard to control as they neared the ground. That was at the best of times. In their wounded state, it wasn't the best of times.

Hunter said, 'Switching to Burg.'

'Burg, copy?'

'Yes, Nick loud and clear.'

'We're 50 minutes out.'

'We'll be ready to go when you get here. The weather isn't looking too good.'

'Nothing we can do about it except hope for the best.'

The General looked at his watch. He needed to report to the Military Council at some point but knew if he called before 09.00 he wouldn't be able to reach anyone. He dreaded the imminent conversation. The Army was represented on the Council by a four star General, and was an exception to the rule that Iranian officers were promoted at least a couple of levels above their competence. The General was tough, ruthless and efficient. He was tipped to be the Marshal of the Army, a promotion that would occur soon. He was also a hawk who detested the West with a passion equalled only by that of the Ayatollah Shahbazi.

Rostami knew that if he didn't kill or capture the people who had carried out the attack he had no doubt he would be facing a firing squad in the near future.

Fervently he prayed to Allah that the Colonel was correct in his assessment of the situation. Otherwise...Otherwise...his stomach rumbled ominously.

'The pilot came over the intercom, 'Sir, there's a C130 on the track ahead.'

'A what? What are you talking about man?'

The Colonel replied, 'A Hercules C130 has landed on the track.'

The General looked out of the window, his jaw dropping in surprise. 'What's a C130 doing there?'

Neither the pilot nor the Colonel bothered to answer.

The pilot said, 'I'll call Channel 12 and switch to another frequency.'

'Hercules this is Chinook, do you copy, over?' The message was repeated and then a clear voice came back in Farsi, 'This is Hercules. Going up, channel 23, over.'

Schwarzkopf spoke slowly to give the computer time to translate his words though technically it wasn't necessary.

'We are on a training exercise. Please contact air traffic control and check your Notices to Airmen.'

The helicopter stopped its forward flight and hovered a few hundred metres short of the plane. The pilot radioed the Tehran ATC and received confirmation that the flight was a training flight.

'We had better keep going,' said the General. 'I'll wait until we get back before I create holy Jahannam. How dare the air force hold an exercise in my territory without telling me.' His indignation helped him to forget his troubles for a few seconds but then they washed over him like a deluge of cold water. He had to find the people responsible.

The Colonel didn't point out that a NOTAM had probably been issued and the General hadn't bothered to read it. Like so much, it was typical of the man.

'What do you think, Colonel?'

The Colonel looked down at the plane as they flew past, 300 feet above the ground. Then he saw it. Or rather he didn't see what should have been there.

He looked at the General and said, 'They are not from our air force.'

'What? Don't be stupid. You heard air traffic control.'

'Take a look at the plane's markings.'

'I can see them clearly. The roundels are Iranian Air Force. Besides where would a bunch of insurgents or terrorists get hold of a Hercules?'

'Look at the tail fin.'

'I can't see anything.'

'Precisely. The roundels are clear enough but where is the tail flag?'

'By Allah, you are right. Pilot land ahead of the plane and prepare for us to attack. We'll take these terrorist scum alive.'

'Sir,' his Colonel spoke wearily as though teaching a child a few basic manoeuvers, 'the plane would have left by now if the attackers had already returned. I respectfully suggest the plane is waiting for them. If we go down the track and over the hill we will be hidden from the pilot. We can then establish a lookout position and watch for the enemy returning. Incidentally they are not terrorists.'

'What do you mean?'

'No terrorist organisation is capable of pulling off an attack like this.'

'Then who are they?'

'Either the Americans or the Israelis. Nobody else would dare attack us.'

A few seconds later the General said, 'You are right. It makes sense.' He began to feel excited. Either would be the answer to his prayers. It would save him from a firing squad. 'Pilot, land quickly when we are out of sight of the Hercules.'

Schwarzkopf said, 'I'm sure the helicopter has landed on the other side of the hill.'

'I think you're right. What gave us away, I wonder?'

'God knows. Whatever it was, I think they're waiting for the others to get here. They'll want us all, not just the two of us.'

'As soon as we start up they'll hear us and be over the hill in no time.'

'Then we'll play chicken,' said Schwarzkopf. 'Nick?'

'Yes, Burg.'

'We've got a problem.'

'Yeah, we know. We can see it. We're landing behind them and see what we can do.'

'Incapacitating the helicopter would be a great help.

'Roger that.'

They flew a wide dogleg until they reached a position a couple of kilometres away from the helicopter. They switched off their motors and drifted a bit further before dropping silently to earth. They shook off their harnesses and took up positions each side of the track. They moved forward carefully, their silenced Heckler and Koch's ready to fire.

They rounded a bend to see the helicopter about 400 metres away. The troops hadn't bothered to deploy but stood or sat in groups along the sides of the track.

'Nick there must be upwards of 40 men,' said Bletchley.

Masters said, 'At least. We need to get a lot closer if we want to take out some of them but I doubt we'll get them all.'

'He's right, Nick,' said Badonovitch.

They knew the assessment was accurate and they weren't into suicide attacks.

Hunter said, 'Okay, here's what we'll do. We dump the motors behind those rocks then we'll launch as usual. As soon as we're ready to go, Dave you fire at the helicopter. Try and hit the main rotor or the cockpit. We'll empty our mags in their direction. I doubt we'll hit anyone but it might encourage them to keep their heads down for a few minutes. We'll go behind the C130 and straight in.'

They unhooked the motors and dumped them in a narrow ravine a few metres back from the track. By now the effects of the painkillers were wearing off and they each injected themselves with a second dose. The glue was holding and none of them had any fresh blood.

'Okay, open fire.'

They fired on fully automatic, their weapons pointed at the enemy. A few bullets grazed some of the soldiers but did no real damage.

David Hughes fired five rounds in rapid succession to more effect.

The Colonel moved the quickest, throwing himself at the ground and yelling, 'Get down all of you! Get down!'

He saw a bullet strike the helicopter's cockpit and shatter the glass, killing the pilot. A second round hit the forward rotor where it connected through the hull putting the helicopter out of action. Two soldiers were killed and the General was hit in the arm. He was lying on the ground, writhing and groaning, in tears.

351

'Help me, Colonel. In the name of Allah, help me.'

The Colonel lay where he was, wondering what he should do. Where had the bullets come from? How many had been shooting at them? Were the enemy coming closer? His men were looking to him, waiting for orders and he was cowering like a coward in the dust.

'Sorry, sir, we have to stop the attackers. Get to your feet and let's go.'

The men stayed where they were. They'd been having the same thoughts as the Colonel.

Hunter and his men walked and then trotted along the track, injecting helium as they went. After less than a dozen paces they were airborne. They stayed low, sweeping around in a wide circle. It was then the storm that had been threatening finally arrived blowing them high into the sky in a sudden updraught. It took all their skills to control their parasails as a moment later they were plummeting earthwards. Rain hit in a heavy deluge hindering their vision.

Another updraught sent them skywards. They dumped helium as fast as they could, steadied their flight and fell towards the ground. Now they opened their valves and let in more gas. The rain came down even harder and made visibility even worse.

'Burg?'

'Yes, Nick.'

'According to the satnav we're about 500 metres away and coming in fast.'

'The ramp door is open.'

The rear of the plane was suddenly plain to see and Hunter lifted his feet to go through the door. As he sat on the ramp he hit his quick-release catch and the foil floated away. Badonovitch was five seconds behind him, which gave Hunter time to scramble out of the way. Bletchley managed the same followed by Masters. Hughes missed the ramp and hit the track. He came to a halt seated on the ground with his feet jammed against the rim of the ramp. He hit his release button and scrambled into the cavernous belly of the Hercules.

'Any joy hitting the helicopter?' Hunter yelled.

352

Vendetta

'Yes, Nick. I don't think it will be going anywhere soon.'

'Good. Now let's just hope they don't have any Stingers.'

Hunter was referring to the portable air defence system found in the military of many countries. The 3kg explosive warhead might not bring a Hercules down but it could do a lot of damage.

The four engines were roaring but the plane stood still while Schwarzkopf kept his foot on the brakes. The ramp closed, he lifted his foot and the plane began to roll towards the summit of the hill about 1,500 feet away. The plane accelerated and was doing 60 knots with the hill a mere 500 feet away. Schwarzkopf pulled back on the control column and felt the wheels lift a few inches before dropping back down. Their speed reached 72 knots; he hauled back again and willed the plane to lift.

The C130 appeared over the hill and the Colonel turned his attention to the threat it posed. He saw someone leaning out of the window and immediately recognised the tube pointed in their direction to be a rocket propelled grenade.

'Fire at the plane,' he yelled. 'Fire!'

Some of the soldiers looked up and began to fire their automatic rifles, not bothering to aim.

Ruth had the starboard window open. She was holding a Russian made surface to air missile launcher known as a 9K333 Verba. It was a powerful weapon with a shaped warhead of 3.3lbs of high explosive. As the plane cleared the hill and clawed its way into the sky she aimed at the helicopter and fired. Bullets stitched along the port wing just as the RPG launched. The rocket hit the helicopter's fuel tank containing highly combustible aviation fuel. It blew up with a massive explosion, killing or injuring all the occupants.

Burg turned sharply to port, away from the helicopter. He was too slow. Debris hit the starboard outer engine causing it to burst into flames. Automatically, an extinguisher bottle in the engine compartment released the HFCs – Hydrofluorocompounds – dousing the flames. They'd have to fly on three engines but that was no problem.

'Good work, Ruth, now get back inside.'

There was no reply.

'Ruth! Ruth!' That was when he saw the blood soaking into Ruth's jacket. 'Nick, you'd better get up here now. Ruth's been hit.'

Hunter was in the cockpit only seconds later. He took in what had happened and gently eased Ruth back into her seat.

'Ruth!' He held her gently in his arms as her eyes fluttered and opened.

'Hello, Nick,' she said softly.

'Take it easy. We'll soon get you fixed up,' he lied, his hand covering the wound in her neck. Blood was seeping between his fingers and her eyes were closing.

'You're a liar Nicholas Hunter but I want you to know I love you and always have.'

'I love you too, Ruth. Hang in there.'

Masters arrived at that moment with the first aid box. Hunter looked at him and shook his head.

Ruth closed her eyes, breathed out and died.

Masters and Schwarzkopf exchanged gutted looks. Not only had they thought highly of her as a colleague but counted her as one of their friends.

Hunter opened the first aid box and extracted a wide bandage wrapping it around Ruth's neck. With the blood no longer dripping onto the deck he picked her up and carried her aft. The others looked on in glum silence as Hunter placed her body on the deck and wrapped it in a blanket.

With three engines, the cruising speed of the aircraft had dropped from 320 knots to 270.

Hunter got a bucket of cold water and a cloth and went back into the cockpit. He wiped away the blood as best he could before sitting down. That was when he let loose with a long string of profanity. After a couple of minutes he tailed off.

'Feel any better?' Burg asked.

'No.' He sighed and said, 'We'd better concentrate on where we go from here. The last thing we want is the Iranian Air Force knocking on our door with a couple of air-to-air missiles.'

'Want to give the General an update?'

'I guess I'd better.'

Hunter opened up a secure radio channel to TIFAT and called in.

'Nick, we've seen the footage from the satellites. The job you did to the compound was exemplary. We couldn't see any of the details but it looked as though you got into a hell of a fight. Anyone hurt?'

'Sir, we all have wounds of some description but I have really bad news. Ruth has been killed.'

Macnair swore, something he did only rarely. 'I'm truly sorry, Nick. She was one hell of a woman.'

'Yes, please tell Mossad will you and let them know we're bringing her home. We'll go straight to Israel. Suggest we land at Hatzerim Airbase. It's Air Force only, no civilian planes and nice and quiet in the Negev Desert.'

'That's a good idea. I'll get on to the Israelis straight away.'

Hunter acknowledged the conversation and then broke the connection. He fiddled with the satnav screen in front of him. 'As near as dammit, 1,200 miles. Less than five hours' flying time.'

'Agreed. Only one little problem and that's us flying over Iraq and Jordan with Iranian colours.'

'Yeah, I know.'

'So what do we do?'

'I'm working on it.'

Hunter leant back and closed his eyes. He hadn't injected himself with anymore painkiller but had taken a couple of Paracetamol. They hadn't done much good but he still fell asleep for the next hour. He woke up when Bletchley offered him a mug of coffee.

35

'Any ideas?'

'Sorry, Burg still thinking.' He sipped his coffee.

'You'd better think soon, Nick, I've bamboozled the Iranian ATC but I'm not sure I'll manage it with the Iraqis as well.'

Hunter glanced at the altimeter – 28,000ft the promulgated maximum flying height for the plane.

'Can you get anymore height out of this bucket?'

'Sure. Probably as much as another 5,000 or possibly 7,000. You know what the promulgated specs are like. There's always room to manoeuver.'

Hunter contacted Rosyth and asked to speak to Leo. 'Leo, I have a few things I want you to do.'

'Sure, Nick fire away. By the way we're all sorry about Ruth.'

'Yes, thanks. Okay, I take it you've squared us away with Iran?'

'Yes. Just like we discussed. I kept it until the last moment so they won't have time to check too far. You're on a secret reconnaissance that is so hush-hush no NOTAM has been issued. You know how paranoid they are. They'll believe anything that has the Ayatollah's name attached to it.'

'And this does?'

'The General's idea. Nobody questioned it. The story was sent to the ATC HQ in Tehran, FAO the Director General. It was marked for his eyes only and he was told to instruct ATC on the border to ignore you. No alert and no interception and he was being held responsible if anything went wrong. It was a threat couched as an order but there was no mistaking the underlying message. So you should be okay.'

'Should be but not guaranteed?'

'Best we can do. Get to the border, any interception then get Burg to wind the old crate up and head for the deck.'

'Thanks, Leo. I'll let him know though he may have worked it out already.'

'I'm sure he has. Sorry, just being flippant. No offence.'

'None taken.'

'Hang on, Nick the General wants to talk to you.'

'Yes, sir?'

'Where you cross the border is the back of beyond.'

'That's affirmative.'

'I've spoken with the American SecDef and he's agreed to my proposal.'

The Secretary of Defence was the chief executive officer of the US Department of Defence, the executive department of the armed forces of America. His authority over the armed forces was second only to that of the president.

'Which is?'

'He's instructed the CO at Al Anbar to have an exercise near the border with Iran and just where you'll be entering Iraqi airspace. He'll have a couple of Martin F-35 Lightning II. As you know, they are stealth fighters with amazing properties. They'll cover you should the Iranians come after you. They've been instructed to give one warning and then to shoot down any plane that tries to take you.'

'I doubt the Iraqis will go for it.'

'They won't know until afterwards. Also we will be releasing the footage we have of the destruction of the compound and explain what was being manufactured there. I have it on the highest authority that the West is intending to use every propaganda tool in our armoury to show up the rogue states all across the globe. At last our political masters are waking up to reality. Sanctions on their own aren't enough as I've been saying all along. Teddy Roosevelt was right when he said

America's foreign policy was to speak softly and carry a big stick. It's time the West stopped talking and used the damned thing.'

'Thanks for that, sir. Let me check when we'll be at the border. Burg?'

'An hour fifteen.'

'You got that, sir?'

'Yes. I'll let the CO at Al Anbar know.'

'Sir, don't forget to explain about the roundels.'

'I won't.' Macnair broke the connection.

'Trust the General to come up with something,' said Schwarzkopf.

'He's a wily old devil and no mistake. I'll go back and tell the others.' He unclipped his seat belt, stood, stretched and left the cockpit. A glance showed him that they were all fast asleep. He couldn't blame them, he wanted to do the same. Instead, he made his way to the galley next to the bulkhead to the cockpit and made a couple of cups of coffee. Strong, milk and no sugar for both of them.

Back in the cockpit he sat in the co-pilot's seat sipping his coffee and thinking about Ruth. She had been a very special lady. She would be sorely missed by the international anti-terrorist organisations worldwide. She'd had the knack of engaging with disparate groups to get them to work together. The West's enemy was tens of thousands of fundamentalists who blamed the West for every problem they had. But the problem was those tens of thousands operated in small groups, in different countries, and were like wisps of fog. Finding and eliminating the threat they posed was a mammoth task, needing maximum cooperation and joint effort.

Ruth's strengths were particularly useful even when dealing with her own organisation, Mossad. They operated secretly to the point of paranoia and although aggravating on the one hand, on the other it was understandable. They were surrounded by enemies with their backs to the sea, an uncomfortable position at best. The Saudis were the biggest financiers of terrorism in the world while at the same time, pretending to be bosom pals with the West. If anything 9/11 showed what a duplicitous nation they were. The fact that it was a Saudi

Prince who had put a price on Hunter's head because of the death of his terrorist son was no surprise to anyone.

He placed his mug in the holder, closed his eyes and promptly fell asleep. It seemed like only minutes later Schwarzkopf was shaking him by the shoulder in an effort to wake him.

'Nick! Nick! Wake up! We've got company.'

Normally Hunter snapped awake, this time he came to groggily, lack of sleep and his injuries had taken their toll.

'Okay, Burg I'm awake. What is it?'

'Over the radio. There are a couple of Iranian jets at six o'clock insisting we land or we will be shot down.'

'Have you seen them?'

'Yes. They circled us. I didn't wake you earlier as I hoped they'd ignore us and foxtrot oscar.'

'Have you spoken to them?'

'I acknowledged them and told them to contact ATC Tehran.'

'And?'

'And they said they had done so and that we were to land immediately until the situation was resolved.'

'I'll talk to them.'

'You're on the right frequency. Press the red button and talk.'

'This is Hercules. Are you aware that we are on a top secret mission for the Ayatollah?'

'We have no such information. You must turn and land now or you will be shot down.'

'How far to the border?'

'We crossed it five minutes ago.'

'No sign of the Americans?'

'Not so far.'

'What armament do they carry?'

'They're old Russian built MIG-29s. They're carrying dogfight air-to-air missiles known as Archers. Their range is about 20 miles and they go faster than mach 2. If I remember correctly they're heat-seeking. To summarise we haven't got a dog's chance.'

'We'll have less of a chance if we land.'

'I agree.'

'Can we survive a hit?'

'Into one of the port engines then possibly. The second starboard engine doubtful. And don't forget there's a second plane with a second missile ready to take us out. If it's any consolation, as long as they don't hit a fuel tank we won't be blown out of the sky but if they follow up strafing us, then it's all over bar the shouting.'

'So what do we do?'

'This.'

Burg pushed the control stick forward and opened up the revs. The Hercules picked up speed and dived down, Passing 30,000ft at 350 knots.

The sudden change brought Masters to the cockpit. 'What's up?'

'A couple of Iranian fighters have arrived to spoil our day. Get parachutes on. If they hit us we're out of here though it's one hell of a drop.' That was an understatement. They knew they would have to free fall for as long as possible, reaching terminal velocity after 12 seconds or 1,500 feet. They would then be dropping at a speed of 122mph. But at least there was little chance of the fighters shooting them down until they deployed their parachutes. If they kept their nerve that would be as low as 150 feet or thereabouts. It would mean dangling on the end of their lines for a few seconds only, which gave them a chance to survive the attack. The big question was when to abandon ship.

There was a repeat of the orders to turn and land and then a warning that a missile would be fired if they didn't obey. The next thing they heard was the announcement that a missile had been launched.

They had about 10 seconds to impact.

They heard the explosion in spite of the noise the C130 was making. At the same time, an American fighter shot over the C130 and told the Iranians that they were in Iraqi airspace and to return to Iran.

'F-35 Lightning IIs,' announced Schwarzkopf a great big grin on his face. 'Probably the finest stealth multirole fighter on the planet. Their modified AMRAAMs are just what we needed.'

The Aim-120Advanced Medium Range Air-to-Air Missile was the world's most popular beyond-visual-range. Fire-and-forget meant the pilot could concentrate on flying and not firing, as they liked to say.

'Listen up,' Hunter announced, 'the USAF has arrived in the shape of a couple of Lightnings. They just shot down the missile that was about to hit us.'

'Herky Bird, head for Al Anbar, we'll deal with the attackers.'

'Roger that,' said Schwarzkopf, 'willco.'

They listened to the drama unfold as the Americans threatened the Iranians with a deadline of 60 seconds.

'You are 60 miles inside the Iraqi border, turn immediately and we will escort you out of Iraqi airspace.'

There followed a few seconds of silence and then a heavily accented voice said, 'We demand the Hercules return to Iran. Onboard are criminals who have attacked us and killed many people.'

'That's not the way we understand it. Now leave.'

There was more silence. That's a second missile we have had to shoot down. You have had your last warning.'

'Good one leader. Strike one. The second plane is turning.'

When the Iranian missile had exploded the plane had flown into the debris and plummeted to earth as its engine shredded.

'Damn it all to hell!'

'What's up Leader? You gave them enough warnings.'

'Think of the paperwork,' was his reply, satisfaction in his voice.

The Hercules landed safely at Al Anbar and taxied over to the American side of the base. Schwarzkopf shut down the engines and sat there for a few seconds savouring the peace and quiet. He opened the rear door, dropping the ramp. The team trooped out, too tired and with too many aches and pains to hurry. Each one took a look at the blanket-covered body near the rear.

'There's always a price to pay,' said a voice halfway up the ramp.

They saw the one star and straightened their backs, a natural, ingrained reaction when faced by a General. Then Masters broke into a grin, followed by Hughes and Badonovitch.

'Sir!' Masters called and saluted. The other two did the same and then so did Bletchley thinking he had better follow suit. He was perplexed. He'd never known them to salute anyone apart from Macnair and that was only occasionally.

Hunter appeared from the cockpit and started down the hold. When he saw who was waiting to greet him he also broke into a big smile.

'Hiram, by God it is you!' As he approached he noticed the star and he also saluted.

'Cut it out you clowns,' Hiram B. Walsh said. 'Let's go to my office and you guys can fill me in.'

Walsh had been General Macnair's deputy at TIFAT when it was first established. He had been a Colonel from Delta Force, a tough, resourceful officer who got things done. He had no choice other than to leave when offered promotion to a one star. It was on the cards that he could rise to three stars in the next five or so years. That would mean Brigadier General to Lieutenant General, followed by an honourable retirement.

'What are you doing here?' Hunter asked Walsh.

'I'm CO. I wasn't here when you arrived and didn't know what was going on until I got back. I've had a long chat with Malcolm so I'm abreast of affairs. I know about Ruth, she was unique. Never known a lady like her. Who are you?' He looked at Bletchley.

'Sorry, Hiram this is Chris Bletchley, ex-RM now one of us.'

'How are you enjoying being with this crowd?'

'One thing for sure, there's never a dull moment.'

'I can believe it.'

'Burg piloting?'

'Yeah. He's checking the plane.'

A sergeant saluted as he walked past. Walsh acknowledged and called after him, 'Sergeant Patt!'

'Sir!'

'Please tell the pilot of the Hercules to report to my office. Have you brought out the new engine?'

'It's on its way, sir. I've had a look. It'll take about 12 hours and she'll be as good as new.'

'Excellent, thank you. How are the cartoons coming?'

The sergeant grinned. 'The ones of the officers are, shall we say, very funny?'

Walsh laughed. 'Good. I look forward to seeing them.'

'What's this about an engine?'

'I knew what happened so I had a new engine brought out of storage. We have C130s in and out of here all the time. Regular engine checks are needed and we've found it best to remove the engine, replace it and carry out the checks in the workshop. We'll try and repair the damage as well. Here we are, my luxurious office.'

They went into a low brick, thick walled office block. The first door on the right had a sign, "CO, Brigadier General Hiram B. Walsh" and Walsh pointed at it. 'I still can't get used to that even after five weeks.'

'Is that all the time you've been here?'

'It seems longer but that's all. It's a six months' posting but I don't think I'll be here much longer.'

The room was large with a row of hard-backed chairs around a table capable of seating 10 each side.

'The last time I saw you guys was on Sicily.'

'You were CO of SEAL Team 6,' said Masters.

'That's right. The powers that be figured I'd be of more use as CO here. In reality it's a stepping stone to greater things.' He shrugged. 'Certain jobs are recognised for what they are…'

'Grooming you,' Hunter interrupted, 'for higher command.'

'Correct.'

Walsh opened a cupboard and pulled out a bottle of malt whisky and slid it along the table. It stop in front of Hughes who grabbed glasses and handed them around. He poured a hefty measure for himself and then passed the bottle.

'Just a quick one then you guys are going to the infirmary for checking out. Beds have been arranged along with a line of credit at the base PX store. It's got everything you need.'

Hunter picked up his glass and took a drink, savouring the peaty flavour of the malt whisky.

'Thanks, Hiram but we have plenty of gear.'

Walsh looked at the tired faces around the table. He'd been on enough operations to know what it was like and what was more significant, to lose a comrade.

'You said you won't be here much longer,' said Masters.

Walsh grinned. 'That's right, Don. I had a very interesting conversation with Malcolm. He said Nick here is okay but he'd rather have an experienced second-in-command.'

That raised a few chuckles.

Grinning, Hunter said, 'And?'

'And I'm seriously thinking about it. At least I can have the family with me in Scotland. The more I think about it, the better the idea sounds.'

'Please do,' said Hunter seriously. 'I don't want the job. I'm happiest in the field.'

'That's what Malcolm said. Right you guys, finish your drinks and I'll have you taken to the infirmary. It's as well staffed and equipped as any field hospital in the US military.'

They all knew what that meant, damned good.

'You've got rooms in the infirmary for the night...Ah, Burg, come in.'

Another discussion followed accompanied by more measures of whisky.

Finally, Walsh sent for his assistant, a female Major in the Catering Corps. The men thought how attractive she was until she turned and they saw she was pregnant. Walsh watched their faces and grinned. Typical Special Forces he thought.

The infirmary proved to be as well staffed and kitted out as Walsh had promised. A couple of doctors checked them over as well as having them x-rayed.

Don Masters' bullet wound wasn't as bad as they had thought. The bullet had grazed his humerus and would heal quickly enough.

David Hughes came in for some praise from the surgeons for the work he had done on his own leg. It would heal though he would have a scar for life.

Chris Bletchley's head wound wasn't serious. Nothing was broken though it had bled quite a bit. A typical scalp wound was the way the surgeon put it.

Jan Badonovitch's collar bone was the most awkward to fix but after surgery, the doctors were satisfied and assured him the bone would heal in a few weeks.

The gash on Hunter's arm was not serious and would heal quickly. A small patch of hair on the back of his head was shaved to allow for a closer examination. He was assured his head would be okay as luckily, the flat side of a rock had hit him and not a sharp edge. Otherwise it could easily have been a different story. His eyesight was also checked before he was given painkillers and told to take it easy.

They were allocated a room each in the infirmary and told to rest. It was early evening and they were all knackered. Sleep came easily.

Hunter woke at 19.45 and after showering and changing into clean clothes, felt able to go to the officers' mess for a drink while the others slept the night through. Before he left his room he phoned his sister.

'Lems? How's Dad?'

'He's fine, Nick. He's being let out in a couple of days. He'll join us in Rosyth though both are kicking up about the idea.'

'Tough. Tell them they're going there until I give the all clear.'

'When will that be?'

'Don't know, perhaps a couple of weeks. There are some people I must trace.'

'I hope, whoever they are, that you kill them.'

Hunter smiled. 'I'll do my best.'

'Good. Then that ought to do it.'

'Your faith in me is touching.'

'Nick, these people have to be stopped whatever it takes. Otherwise Mum and Dad will never live a carefree existence again. Not that they do with you as their son.'

'I'll retire one day.'

'Yeah, sure, in a pine box.'

'I keep telling you, a cardboard box and a burning fire is all I need. Then scatter my ashes anywhere that's convenient.'

'Yeah, yeah. I'll let them know you called.'

'Okay, thanks. By the way, I need to tell you,' his voice suddenly dropped from banter to sombre, 'I've bad news.'

He heard Louise take a sharp intake of breath. 'Oh my God, Nick, don't tell me its Chris. Please don't tell me that.'

'No, Chris is okay. He has a slight wound along the side of his head. But he's okay, I promise. He'll phone later. It's Ruth, she was killed.'

Louise was silent for a few seconds before saying in a subdued voice, 'Oh, Nick I'm really sorry to hear that. I liked Ruth. I didn't know her well but what little I saw of her I liked. I'd thought a couple of years ago, you and she…'

'Yeah, I know.'

'Are you okay?'

'Sure. We're in a dangerous world and these things happen. We have to live with it or get out. Look, I need to go. I'll see you in a couple of days.'

A short while later Hunter was sitting at the bar in the officers' mess finishing a whisky and soda with ice when Walsh appeared.

'Same again,' he told the barman, 'and I'll have a Jack Daniels. Make it a double with ice, please.'

'Yes, sir, General, you got it.'

Hunter smiled at Walsh as the barman turned away. 'A quaint form of acknowledging an order or a request.'

'That's us Americans for you. One of the two great nations and a common language.'

'Shaw or Wilde?'

'Etymologists are still arguing about that one.'

'Trust the Irish,' said Hunter. He raised his drink and they clinked glasses.

'Here's to Ruth,' said Walsh. 'She was a lovely lady.'

'She was that.'

'There was no chance you and she...'

Hunter took a sip of his whisky before shaking his head. 'It was long gone. Speaking for myself, life had moved on. I guess you fall in love and build on it. Take away the foundations and you're building on emotional quicksand.'

'Have you been reading love poetry again?' Walsh tried to lighten the mood.

Hunter chuckled. 'No. Kipling is more in my line with a bit of Tennyson added. Kipling always seemed to encapsulate the military mood of the time.'

'Just about any time,' said Walsh. 'Anyway, enough of the morbid atmosphere. One final thing then we can drop the subject. I've had Ruth's body placed in a coffin. We've got plenty here though luckily, we haven't had to use them too often this past year.'

'Thanks, Hiram. I appreciate it.'

'What say we finish these drinks and adjourn to the dining room? I can promise you one of the best steaks you'll ever eat.'

'Iraqi cows?'

'American imported stuffed full of hormones and steroids.'

'Excellent. Sounds like just what I need.'

36

The following morning Hunter met up with the others in the dining room where a lavish breakfast buffet was on offer. He and Walsh had spent too long drinking too much but neither would ever admit to feeling hung over.

'Good evening, boss?' Badonovitch grinned.

'Yes thanks, Jan. Hiram and I had a lot of catching up to do.'

'I bet.'

The team exchanged looks and smiles.

'The engine change and repairs will take longer than we've been told so we're staying another day, so I suggest we enjoy it.'

Around 11.00 they were seated in a quadrangle, lying on sun loungers enjoying the sunshine when Hunter received a call from Macnair.

'Have you spoken to Hiram this morning?'

'No, why?'

'He's coming back at the end of the month.'

'So soon?'

'Yes. There's hell to pay over the attack in Iran and the C130 crossing into Iraq and arriving in Al Anbar. There's also the question of the shooting down of the Iranian plane. The Iranians are demanding your return and the Iraqis are making noises that they'll comply. The Iranians are also insisting their plane was in Iranian airspace and shooting it down was a criminal act.'

'That's rubbish.'

'We know it's rubbish and film and positional navigation info is being put together right now for transmission to Iran and every news outlet in the world.'

'What about the Yanks?'

'They're procrastinating and assuring the Iranians that a full investigation is taking place with regards to the C130.'

'So how does that affect Hiram?'

'He's falling on his sword. He'll admit lack of judgement and will retire with full honours.'

'Sir, that's unfair. That is so wrong.' Hunter said angrily.

'Nick, it's what Hiram wants. He wants back and I want him back. This is an ideal opportunity. In the meantime we will also be releasing the film of the explosion and incorporate any of the shoulder camera film from you guys that we see fit to use. We are going on the offensive with the propaganda. Iran and Russia have had it their way for too long. The West will acknowledge the reasons and justification for the attack while those countries that support Iran will scream blue murder.'

'It's not only the countries that support Iran, sir, but those that are anti-West.'

'Agreed. But before things get out of hand, which is always a possibility, I want you away asap.'

'Does Hiram know all this?'

'Affirmative. He's in the hangar right now chivying his crew to get the plane ready for flight. He told me they'll be a few hours at least.'

Hunter stifled a sigh. He was beginning to unwind and enjoy the sunshine. 'Okay, sir. We're on our way.'

'One other thing. The roundels have been painted over.'

'Understood, sir.'

The others had heard his side of the discussion and sat up.

Hunter brought the team up to date then they all went to lunch. As they ate, General Walsh joined them.

'Relax you guys. Everything is a go. I can't stop, I've got work to do. Curiously enough, you'll not be surprised to learn, connected to recent events.'

'Sorry to put you to all this trouble, sir,' said Bletchley.

Walsh waved his hand across his chest as though brushing away a pesky fly. 'Please believe me I'm delighted. I'll be back with you in a couple of weeks, which is what I was angling for. I'd been told I had to see out a minimum of six months before being considered for retirement. So it suits me. TIFAT is taking the war where it needs to go and I want back in.'

'What about the shooting down of the aircraft?'

'We're on the offensive with satnav info and films from both our aircraft. The Iranians have suddenly stopped screaming about it.'

'Thanks for all you've done,' said Hunter and held out his hand.

They each shook hands with Walsh and then filed out of the mess.

When they took off an hour later they were escorted by a couple of American jets in case anyone had big ideas to attack them. Nobody did and they passed smoothly across the border into Jordan with the Jordanian king's blessing. A private chat between Abdullah II, King of Jordan and Macnair had helped to oil the wheels of diplomacy, not that they needed much oiling.

Jordan and Israel had been at war from 1948 until1994 when they signed the Israel-Jordan peace treaty. There had been tension between the two countries from time to time. However, it had never deteriorated into a hot war.

The American jets peeled off at the border and went RTB.

The Hercules crossed Jordan, flew over the Dead Sea and landed at Hatzerim Airbase. The base was situated in the Negev Desert on the western outskirts of Beersheba near Kibbutz Hatzerim. It was a vital part of Israeli Defence. It had helped to protect a country that had been at war since independence, declared in May 1948.

'Pragmatic people, the Israelis,' said Schwarzkopf.

'In what way?' Hunter asked, sitting alongside the pilot.

'If it suits them they're close friends of the West, if it doesn't they give us the cold shoulder. And that's putting it mildly. The number of times they've spied on the West are legion and that's the ones we know about.'

'Such cynicism in one so young,' quipped Hunter.

The base was home to the IAF Flight School as well as their aerobatic team.

They were waved across the airfield to a hangar where a group of uniformed personnel were waiting to greet them. Hunter noticed that standing to one side were two men and a woman in civilian clothes who he guessed were from Mossad. Burg lowered the tail door and a gurney was rolled up the ramp.

The Commanding Officer of the base, Brigadier General Yosef Elyasaf greeted them with a curt nod.

No welcome and no greeting, just, 'Where is the body?'

'In the coffin,' said Hunter.

'You call me sir when addressing me.'

Trust us, thought Hunter, to be dealing with an idiot. Just then the three civilians walked up the ramp and identified themselves as Mossad.

They shook hands with Hunter and as the coffin was being placed on the gurney the older man said, 'I was Ruth's manager. You must be Commander Hunter.'

'I am.'

'Do you care to tell us what happened?'

'Certainly. Let's take a seat.'

'Yes but not for long. I want you off my base as soon as possible.'

The Brigadier General walked stiffly down the ramp and out of sight.

'What's his problem?'

'I've no idea apart from the fact he didn't want you landing here but was overruled. It seemed to put his nose out of joint.'

'We would like to refuel.'

'Not a problem, it's been arranged.'

Even as he spoke a bowser came around the corner and carefully approached the Hercules. Schwarzkopf was already on the tarmac waiting to greet the driver.

They sat in the canvas bucket seats on the aircraft and Hunter told the agents what had happened and how Mossad would have known about the operation. Some of the story they already knew, having seen the video of the explosion, the rest was new to them.

'Unfortunately, we do not bury our agents with any form of military honours. A quiet funeral in a peaceful graveyard is the best we can offer. She was one hell of a woman.'

Hunter nodded. 'I know. I'm sorry I can't stay and pay my respects but I need to return to Scotland.'

'We understand. Ours is a never-ending war. We appreciate all the help you have given to us during the last couple of years.'

'We're on the same side.'

'One last thing. Our man in Saudi has given us a name, it is Michael Gunther.'

'I've heard that name before somewhere.'

'He arranges specialised attacks. Usually single assassinations.'

Hunter nodded. 'I remember. He was involved in some job in Germany a year ago but nothing came of it.'

'The Germans wanted to arrest him and put him on trial. He had a string of witnesses that proved he couldn't have had anything to do with it.'

'Wasn't it the death of a Public Prosecutor?'

'No, a judge. The job was done on behalf of an Albanian drugs lord after the judge sentenced the Albanian's brother to 50 years in prison for mass murder after selling bad cocaine. A lot of druggies died as a result.'

'A lot of people would say tough on the druggies. They shouldn't have started with the drugs to begin with.'

'And you, Nick? What do you say?'

'The addicts are more to be pitied than censured. They need help and one way is to cut off the drugs but we both know that's impossible.' Hunter sighed. 'I never thought I would ever say so but it seems to me that legalising the narcotics would make all the difference by taking them out of the hands of the criminals.'

'I agree. Worldwide the trade in illegal drugs tops $400 billion. Think of the tax revenues for countries, particularly the poor ones where most of the drugs are either grown or manufactured.'

'I read the report at the time. Gunther is a real piece of work. What can you tell me about him?'

'He organised the attack on your family paid for by the Saudi Prince.'

'Thanks for that. I'll get TIFAT to find the s.o.b. and we'll take care of it. How sure is your man in Saudi?'

'Or woman. He or she hasn't led us astray yet.'

'You don't know if it's a man or a woman?'

Shaking his head the Mossad agent said, 'No. Not even Ruth knew and she was the contact. With Ruth dead we don't know what will happen with our informer. The person has insisted all along to deal only with Ruth. If we learn anymore, we'll let you know. Meanwhile,' he held out his hand, 'good luck on the Gunther front.'

'Don't worry, I'll find him,' Hunter said grimly, shaking the Israeli's hand.

'I'm sure you will. Don't let him have a pleasant death.'

'Oh?'

'We know he's responsible for the deaths of three of our agents and we were about to mount an operation against him as soon as we found him. We'll keep looking and if we learn anything, rest assured we'll share any information with you. 'You can do the work and take the glory.'

'The work yes, the glory no.'

The Americans had supplied the team with prepacked chicken sandwiches, apples and oranges, a couple of large flasks of coffee and cans of cola.

When the refuelling was complete the bowser driver appeared with a clipboard and a form. 'Can one of you sign this?' He held it out and Hunter took it.

'What is it?'

'A receipt for the fuel. The General said somebody had to pay for it.'

Hunter would have told the General to go to hell but not a junior rank doing as ordered. So much for cooperation between countries with a common enemy, he thought.

Hunter joined Schwarzkopf in the cockpit for take off. They were soon taxiing and eased gracefully into the air. It was a beautiful day, sunshine, few clouds and the kind of weather that made a person feel it was good to be alive, but not for Hunter. Anger boiled through his veins and he felt his jaw clench. He wanted to kill every member of Iran's Majiles starting with Shahbazi, the Ayatollah who conversed with God on a daily basis.

'Have you decided the route?'

'Yes. We'll refuel in Ramstein Air Force Base at Kaiserslautern, Germany. It's 1,900 miles away and will take just under six hours.'

'You okay for that?'

'If I was flying legit civvie then no. As it is, I'm well over my time and it doesn't matter. Once we're cruising you can watch things while I sleep on the cot next to the flight door. How's the head by the way?'

'It's okay, a slight headache but nothing serious. I'll take a couple of painkillers,' he said and reached into a pocket for the Paracetamol and took two.

At a cruising altitude of 28,000ft and speed of 350 knots, Schwarzkopf fiddled with the display in front of him and up came the distance and flying time.

'That's all the info. The autopilot is operating nice and steady so over to you.' He quit the flight deck and went into the main cabin, stretched out on the cot and was asleep within minutes.

The remainder of the team had been sleeping since take off.

It was 03.29 when they landed in Germany at the NATO airbase. Kaiserslautern was a picturesque town and very popular with NATO forces as a posting. The accommodation was better than adequate, the local schools were first class and the welcome was warm and friendly. Hunter knew all that, as he'd been there several times. He also knew the warm and friendly attitude had more to do with dollars and other currencies flooding into the area than anything. The Americans no longer brought supplies but bought locally, which was a huge boost to the economy.

Refuelling took 35 minutes and they were in the air again. Distance to go was 662 miles, on a heading of northwest. This time Masters sat in the cockpit while Burg and Hunter got some sleep. Time to Prestwick was just under two hours. Their speed was adjusted for them to land at 07.00.

They taxied to the private side of the airport and into the hangar. There the plane was handed over to ground staff while the team collected their gear and packed it into their cars.

It was about 70 miles to Rosyth and though it was now only 07.55, rush hour was well and truly in progress.

It took the best part of two hours to get back to TIFAT HQ. They had been told to report to the Ops Centre at 10.00 where they would hold a full debrief of the operation. Hunter returned to his boat to get showered, shaved and changed into fresh clothes. Before boarding he carried out his checks to make sure there were no unwelcome surprises waiting for him.

The weather was warm and sunny with just a thin layer of broken cloud and a light breeze from the southeast. Walking along the wooden pier he telephoned his sister.

'Nick! Where are you?'

'Rosyth. Where are you?'

'On our way. We stopped off to pick up some stuff Mum decided she couldn't do without. It required half a dozen suitcases packed with what she calls a few things. We should be there in about half-an-hour.'

'Good. How's Dad?'

'He's okay. Mum is fussing over him like a mother hen and he's enjoying ir.'

'I take it you're not travelling in the same car?'

'Are you kidding? There wasn't room. I've got the suitcases.'

'Anyone with you?'

'Tam is riding shotgun with me and Clive with Mum and Dad.'

'Good. They're specially trained close quarter protection officers so you're in good hands. See you later this morning. Bye for now.'

'BFN, Nick.'

Hunter arrived at the Ops Centre and swiped his card to allow him through the security door. As with the main gate, nothing was left to chance. There were armed guards in various locations around the establishment. A couple of years earlier TIFAT had been attacked by a contingent of armed criminals from Glasgow. It wasn't much of a fight but since then Macnair had kept the establishment ready for anything. All weapons were kept out of sight but in places that were quickly reached.

The team sat with the General, Isobel and Leo and reviewed events in detail.

'What are the Iranians saying?' Hunter asked.

'Nothing. They've gone quiet. We've blasted the Internet with reports, photographs and video showing what the Iranians had been up to. The Americans are spitting blood along with the Europeans led by the UK. More sanctions are to be imposed and God alone knows what that will mean.'

The team left the room apart from the General, Leo and Hunter.

'We've been looking for Michael Gunther,' Macnair began, 'with varying degrees of success. We're still looking for a way for you to get to Prince Abdul-Hameed Saud. You can't go into the palace, he's protected about as well as the President of the USA.' It was a slight exaggeration but not much. 'We've heard he's on his last legs. If that's the case, then all we need do is wait for him to die.'

'I want to be there when he does. Don't worry, sir, I won't do anything stupid. If it isn't possible then so be it. But I will get to Gunther.'

'Nick,' said Leo, 'we've put it out that we're looking for him with $1 million for the information. Something will come of it. He can't hide forever.'

Wajeeh Soliman knew that it was time to make his move. He had drawn up the deed gifting him the ship, he had forged the Prince's signature and the lawyer had registered his ownership with the International Register of Shipping.

Vendetta

He had liquidated his assets and moved the cash offshore and at the same time purloined a further $10 million from the Prince's ready-use account. This was the account Soliman had control over and an examination of the transactions would show payments to various people, none of whom existed except on paper. He left a couple of million plus change in the account in case anyone accused him of stealing the money. However, once the family got hold of him he wouldn't be in any position to argue his innocence. It wouldn't matter. The best he could hope for was a quick death.

The joys of being in charge of the Prince's security were lost on him and had been for a couple of years, ever since he had been ordered to spy on the family.

He entered the Prince's study where the old man lay, propped up in a bed.

'Sir, I have some good news. Our German friend has succeeded beyond our wildest dreams.'

The Prince had the facemask permanently on as his breathing became more laboured each day. He waved his hand at Soliman to continue.

'Sir, I have just had word that Soliman has killed Hunter's parents.

That brought a flash of strength to the dying man and he sat up a little, straightening his back.

Lifting his facemask the Prince said, 'How?' he croaked.

'The people he hired planted a bomb in the car belonging to the parents and set it off remotely. And best of all, the daughter was badly injured. It looks as though she will lose both legs and an arm.'

Lifting the facemask again the Prince rasped, 'Excellent.'

'Sir, that is not the best of it.' Soliman had laced his tone with just the right amount of eagerness and satisfaction. He paused while the invalid gestured frantically for him to continue.

'Hunter appeared to have been stricken with grief. He let his guard down. He went to his parents' house where our men were waiting. They have him, sir! They have him!'

377

The Prince was shaking with excitement. He lifted the facemask and croaked, 'Can we get him here?'

'Yes!'

'How?'

'Leave the details to me, sir, but it is by boat and plane. We should have him here within the next three perhaps four days.'

'Good. Good. You have done well, Wajeeh, very well indeed. I knew I could rely on you.'

'Sir, we must be ready to receive him. We cannot bring him here. Too many people will know what we have done. The consequences could and probably would be horrendous.'

'What do you suggest?' He reached for a mug with a straw and sucked down cold tea laced with honey, which was all the sustenance he was capable of consuming.

'We must retire to *The Star of Medina*. We can make you comfortable and you can watch the man die.'

The Prince nodded. 'In agony I hope.'

'My Prince, I think you should be the one to decide what we do with him. You may enjoy your last days on earth, dreaming of the pain you will be able to inflict.'

The Prince nodded. 'You make my last days before I journey to Jannah, days of great pleasure.'

More likely Jahannam will be your destination, his head of security thought. 'My Prince, I will go and make due preparations for your arrival. We need to open up the staterooms and have the chef arrange suitable menus and fresh food.'

'Yes, do that,' he gasped and coughed for a matter of minutes before managing to say, 'we will go tomorrow. May Allah and Mohammed, peace be upon him, give me the strength to see the man die in agony.'

37

Hunter phoned Cathy. 'Are you busy tonight?'

'Nothing I can't get out of. You know, watching Eastenders, washing my hair, a typical evening for us girls.'

Are you working tomorrow?'

'Actually no, why?'

'It's such fine weather I was thinking of taking the Flush for a run out to Inchkeith. Come back tomorrow sometime.'

'What's the Flush? Besides, I thought Inchkeith is an island.'

'It is and the Flush is my boat. I live on it.'

'You live on a boat?' Cathy was incredulous.

'Sure, why not? I've got to live somewhere.'

'I guess. But I can't imagine you roughing it on a boat.'

'Needs must I guess.'

'This I've got to see. Okay. How do I get to wherever you keep it?'

'It's a she. She might get upset if you refer to her as it.' There was laughter in his voice. 'If you take the train to Rosyth I'll pick you up at the station.'

'What time?'

'Text me to let me know what train you're on but if you can arrive anytime between six and seven, that would be great.'

'Okay, see you later. Oh, Nick, before you go, how's your father?'

'You know what happened?'

'Louise told me.'

'He's fine. Or he will be. The family is holed up here in TIFAT

379

until I can figure out what I'm doing. I have some unfinished business to attend to.'

The train arrived on time at 18.35. Cathy was looking radiant in a cream skirt and matching blouse with large printed flowers.

'You're looking lovely,' Hunter greeted her.

'Why thank you, kind sir.'

'Is that all your luggage?' he asked, looking at the bag she was carrying over her shoulder.

'Don't forget I was an air hostess. We're used to travelling light.'

They headed down to the old HMS *Cochrane* establishment, now TIFAT's HQ and went through the main gate. Hunter drove down to the pier and parked the car. He grabbed Cathy's bag and led the way along the wooden structure towards the boat. When she saw it she stopped in utter surprise.

'Is that your boat?'

'Sure, what did you expect?'

'I don't know. Some sort of sailing boat with a couple of berths, but not this.'

Hunter laughed. 'Wait until you get onboard. Stop a minute.' He began his safety checks.

'What are you doing?'

'Making sure there are no unwelcome surprises.'

'Is it likely?'

'No, but I'm in the habit of checking, as you can never be too sure. Okay, all is quiet. Let's get onboard and I'll flash up while you take a look around. The master cabin is in the stern. That,' he smiled, 'is the bit at the back.'

Cathy playfully tapped his shoulder and said, 'I know. I'm not a landlubber. I used to race single-handed dinghies at school.'

'You went to public school?' Hunter asked in surprise.

'A serious misnomer, but yes. For three years until I went to uni.'

'You told me that bit. Where you read PPE but dropped out after a couple of years. Oh,' he added as an afterthought, 'also when you lost your virginity.'

'Huh, trust you to remember that detail.'

'I have a brilliant memory for some things.'

'I bet.'

Hunter flashed up the engines and busied himself at the console, checking everything was as it should be.

When he was satisfied, he yelled down through the door, 'Are you okay?'

Cathy appeared and said, 'I was exploring. My God, Nick, she's fabulous.'

'I'm glad you like her. When you get some leave, we could go for a proper sail, around Scotland and to the islands.'

'I'd love that.'

'How about a cup of tea?'

'I'd prefer something stronger like a G&T or a glass of white wine.'

'Did you find the drinks cupboard?'

'No.'

'It's the globe in the corner. Lift the top and you'll find a few bottles of spirits. Tonic is in the forward fridge along with the white wine. Lemons and milk are in the main fridge in the galley. I'll take the tea.'

'And I'll have the G&T. What are we having to eat?'

'As soon as we're out of here and in the main channel, I'll put on the barbeque. We're having prawns and steak with salad.'

'A barbeque? Where is it?'

'Aft deck under the black cover. It's gas I'm afraid. Charcoal means too much faffing around.'

'I'll wash the salad.'

'No need, it's supermarket ready to eat.'

'You think of everything.'

'I hope so.' He stepped out of the wheelhouse and onto the deck. He undid the berthing ropes, stepped back onboard and pushed the bow away with his foot. Seconds later, the screws were engaged and they moved sedately away from the pier and into the Forth.

Hunter checked their position, course and speed then switched to autopilot and watched it for a few minutes. Cathy appeared with a mug of tea and handed it to him and said, 'Cheers.'

They sat in silence for a few minutes before Hunter asked, 'How's the new job?'

'Okay. It's different to cabin crew. More settled.'

'Settling down, huh?'

'Not yet, but you never know.'

Hunter set the approach alarm to 0.5mls and took a last look around. 'If anything comes too close an alarm will buzz and warn us. Care to sit in the sun?'

'I brought my bikini to do just that. It's still warm enough.'

'You don't need a bikini on my account and there's only the birds to see us.'

Cathy smiled. 'Where do we sit? Down aft?'

'No. There's a flybridge.' He led the way out on the port side and indicated a ladder fixed to the bulkhead. 'The controls are a replica of the wheelhouse controls.'

They climbed the ladder.

'This is heavenly. Even cushioned bench seats. I'll just go below and change. I'll not be a minute.'

Sitting at the controls, Hunter manipulated a switch and took over. He had a momentary pang of sadness thinking about Ruth but then brought his mind back to the here and now. They operated in a world full of rotten people and there would always be danger with their job.

He heard Cathy behind him and turned his head. She was wearing only her bikini bottoms. Standing up, he took hold of her hand and led her to the seat at the back of the flybridge. If the alarm had sounded he doubted he would have heard it until its tone increased to maximum.

'What's this scar on your shoulder? Cathy asked. 'It wasn't there when we were in Tenerife or I would have noticed.'

'Just a small accident. It's nothing.'

'What happened? You can tell me.'

Sighing, Hunter replied, 'A bullet grazed my shoulder. It's no big deal.'

'Is it something to do with what happened to your father?

'No, that was personal, this was business.'

Cathy snapped her fingers. 'Were you in Iran?' Did you blow up that factory?'

'What makes you think that?'

'Because it's the sort of thing TIFAT would be involved with.'

'That's very astute of you. And yes, but you can't tell anyone.'

'I won't but if I can work it out, so can the powers-that-be.'

'Let them. The Western world is on our side as is most of the rest of the planet. And our enemies will never believe anything we say, even if we do deny it, which we will. They supplied the explosives that blew up the plane and were manufacturing a lot more to sell on the open market.'

'Good. I'm glad you destroyed it and I hope a hell of a lot of them died.'

'They did. Now, where were we?'

The buzzer sounded and took his attention.. He climbed to his feet to see the island of Inchkeith half a mile away. He took control of the boat and steered to a small cove. He brought her to a stop and released the handle that allowed him to drop the anchor.

Switching off the engines he said, 'Now it's time for our barbeque. Let's get the meat prepped.'

'Prepped?'

'Sure. Coat it in English mustard, add a few herbs then on to the grill.'

They sat on the flybridge enjoying a bottle of red wine with their meal, and watched the sun go down.

Gunther's mobile rang, he saw who was calling and answered. 'Michael.'

'It's Edith. I thought you didn't like using the phone or any other form of electronic contact.'

'This won't take long. Jacob had another stroke a few days ago and died. I am returning to the town of my birth and am re-evaluating my life. I am only 56 and hope I have many more years ahead of me. I have left the business now and forever.'

'I'm sorry to hear about Jacob,' he said, not meaning a word of it. He hadn't known him apart from the odd professional contact. 'What else did you want to say?'

'You've heard about TIFAT and the bounty they've put on your head?'

The blood drained from Gunther's face. 'What did you say?' He croaked, his mouth suddenly dry, the hand holding his mobile beginning to tremble.

'The word is out. I've asked a few of our contacts and they have confirmed it, $1 million but only if you're alive. If you're killed, there'll be no payout. Michael, you'd better start running though where to, I've no idea. Where are you now?'

She was speaking to a dead phone. Gunther had dropped it into the canal where he stood. He was in Venice. There was a bench behind him and he sat down as his legs suddenly began to buckle. His plans were now in chaos. He didn't think a plane would be a smart move. Someone at an airport might recognise him. It was unlikely but there was a risk. Flying anywhere was not an option.

He could drive and lose himself in Europe. Some isolated town or village where nobody would know him. But for how long? Some dump in the middle of Hungary or northern Finland?

He knew such a life wasn't for him. The more he thought about it, the more attractive the idea of a cabin cruiser appealed. He could lose himself in the small towns and villages along the coast of the Adriatic and the Mediterranean.

He didn't know much about boats but did that matter? They went forwards and backwards and you steered them using a steering wheel. He would soon master it.

He searched a bookshop that also sold magazines and found one specialising in boats for sale in Italy and France.

He entered a coffee shop and began to leaf through the magazine. That was when he hit his first snag. The size of the boats, even with photographs and diagrams of their layout meant nothing to him. How comfortable was a five metre, twin berth, twin engined cruiser? It didn't sound big enough.

He left the coffee shop and took a taxi to the marina at Sacca de la Misericordia, where there were four dealers in second hand boats. He entered the first one.

Hunter and Cathy were late getting up and when they did, it was to another sunny day.

'You know,' Hunter began, 'in Scotland, it's either raining, just rained or about to rain. I'm not used to this sunshine.'

'Anyone tell you that you're a cynic, Commander?'

'Who, me?'

'Yes, what shall we do today?'

Hunter smiled and Cathy said, 'And you can take that smirk off your face.'

'I wasn't smirking. I was anticipating. I'm going down to see if I can catch dinner. We can stay here or go further south but this is about as good as it gets.'

'Where are you going?'

He pointed to the sea. 'There may be a lobster or two.'

He quickly pulled on a wetsuit jacket, scrubbed around the trousers and checked his bottles. They were full and ready to use. He armed himself with a plastic bottle containing an inch or two of washing up liquid with a 12 inch tube of plastic attached. In his webbing pouch, he checked he had a small fishing bag. Cathy watched his preparations with a puzzled look on her face.

'What on earth...'

'I'll explain when I get back.'

He climbed down into the small inflatable he had launched earlier, took a few breaths with his mouthpiece, adjusted his goggles and, without any fuss, slipped into the water.

He flipped over and headed down. In seconds he was on the bottom. It was sandy with mounds of rocks dotting the seabed. He saw one outcrop of rocks and swam slowly towards it. He had hit the jackpot on his first try. In a narrow gap in the rocks he could see a lobster looking out at him. He knew that trying to hook it out was a waste of time and effort. The creature would flex its claws and muscles and make it difficult to shift.

He fixed the fishing net over the hole and threaded the tube on the bottle into the hole and behind the lobster. He then squeezed the bottle and the washing up liquid squirted out and the lobster shot out of the hole and into the net. It was a decent size and would be enough for two.

Back on board they spent the day lazing in the sun and did very little. Cathy read a book she'd brought with her while Hunter dozed. Around 18.00 Hunter opened a bottle of white wine which they sipped sitting on the flybridge. It turned out they both enjoyed word games and Hunter brought out something called Upwords. The game was like Scrabble but the tiles could also stack on top of the other. They played the equivalent of "dirty word Scrabble" and almost forgot to cook the lobster.

That night Hunter lay awake thinking of Cathy. He really liked her. Was she the one? Maybe, he thought as he drifted off to sleep, it was time to grow up.

He awoke early, went up top and dived into the sea. It was cold and snapped him wide awake as he fast-crawled to the island and back a dozen times before climbing back onboard to warm croissants from the microwave and strong coffee.

His phone rang as he was finishing his second mug. 'Sir?'

'Mossad have been in touch. It seems Prince Abdul-Hameed Saud will be on his yacht *The Star of Medina* in three days' time. He will be on board for a few days before returning to the palace.'

'Ideal,' said Hunter. There was no emotion in his voice.

'There's more information I'll pass on when I see you.'

'Okay and thanks, sir. Will tomorrow be soon enough?'

'Yes, but don't leave it too late. You'll want to get to Saudi in plenty of time.'

'Roger that.'

38

Prince Abdul-Hameed Saud was clinging to life by a thread. Soliman was convinced the only thing keeping the man alive was the notion of watching Hunter being tortured to death. The Prince was going to be a very sad man when the time came.

'My Prince, the man Hunter will be with us in two days. I suggest we go to the yacht in three days' time.'

Lifting his facemask the Prince said, 'Good. You have done well.' He coughed, spat blood into a handkerchief and discarded it on to the floor. 'Have my cook and doctor there...'

'My Prince, leave the details to me. I will take care of everything.'

'I know you will, Wajeeh. You have been like a son to me.'

'It has always been my pleasure to serve you, Your Highness.' To himself his thoughts were, 'so much like a son yet you have treated me like a serf.'

'Tell me,' the Prince asked, gasping for breath, 'is the man Hunter in good health? He hasn't been injured?'

'No, Your Highness. He is in good health.'

'Good. Then he will live a long time in dire agony. You will see to that Wajeeh, won't you?'

'Yes, Your Highness, I will see to that.' Again he thought to himself, 'and have TIFAT looking for me for the rest of my life while you are resting wherever it is the dead go. In your case to Jahannam with the other hypocrites. He showed nothing of the contempt he felt for the Prince with his avowed piousness and prayers to Allah five times a day. At the same time, he had more than 20 men and women held in bondage working for peanuts, slaves in reality. They were whipped if they didn't quickly do as they were told. In the past before he became ill, the man had enjoyed deflowering young virgins and God help them if they didn't perform as he wanted.

Soliman knew that after the Prince's death, he would be in danger, unless he took action. He knew too many family secrets. In fact he knew a great deal more than the Prince. There was some information he had acquired that he kept to himself.

The Prince's three surviving sons were mere playboys and two of his daughters were twittering magpies. They made stupid remarks to their husbands in a manner he found nauseating. The eldest daughter was the one he feared. She was ruthless and hated both her father and her dead brother with a passion.

She would be the one who ensured he didn't live long. The others would go along with her. Provided they lived in luxury, they wouldn't care what happened. Even the brother who would become Prince, would leave matters in her hands. He was incapable of running the organisation created by the Prince, whose wealth had doubled in his lifetime. The sister's name was A'shadieeyah, meaning princess, cute, perfect. Her husband had died three years' earlier from what was said to be a heart attack but Soliman knew he had been poisoned. The death certificate recorded a heart attack but the doctor who had issued it, had been paid $1 million to ensure secrecy.

A'sha, as she was known, didn't remarry. Her preferences had changed.

While Soliman made preparations to take the Prince to *The Star of Medina*, the rest of the family were planning a lavish banquet to be held a week after the Prince's death to celebrate the passing of the title.

'Nick,' Gareth Scarlatti greeted him when Hunter walked into the Ops Centre, 'we have more information about the Prince and the yacht.'

'Let me get a coffee and I'm all ears.'

Mug in hand, Hunter crossed the room to where Scarlatti sat in front of his computer screen.

'It came in half an hour ago, encrypted, from Mossad. It seems the Prince will be arriving in three days and staying four possibly five. He'll have a group of helpers, including nurses and a doctor. The reason for him being there is very interesting.'

'Oh? What's that?'

'To see you die in agony.'

'What makes him think that will happen?'

'Someone told him that you had been taken and would arrive on the yacht in a few days. He wants to be there to welcome you. It appears the staff will be sent ashore, the yacht will put to sea and you'll not be returning.'

Hunter's smile wasn't pleasant.

'A clever way to get the Prince out of the palace.'

'I wonder who's arranged all this?'

'Mossad assures us they don't know only that the info they've received from their source has proven accurate in the past.'

'Does the General know?'

'Yes, he's on his way. Of course this could be a double bluff to get you there.'

'That's occurred to me but somehow I don't think so. It's like Mossad said, the information we've been getting has been very useful.'

The General arrived and greeted the two men with a question. 'Who do you think it is?'

'Someone high up in the Prince's entourage otherwise he or she wouldn't know the sort of detail Mossad has been getting,' Scarlatti replied.

The General nodded. 'Most likely a man. The Arabs aren't very welcoming to women in high positions.'

'I agree,' said Hunter looking at Macnair, 'You know I'm going to Jeddah?'

'Of course I know. I've sent a box of goodies to the British Consulate. The MI6 officer there is an old acquaintance of mine from our army days. It went in the diplomatic pouch so there shouldn't be

389

any problems with its contents. The box is marked for his use as personal items. The so-called pouch can be 24 inches long and 40 lbs in weight, so there was plenty of scope.'

'Thanks, sir. There's a flight at 18.45 that gets in tomorrow morning at 05.50. There's a brief stopover at Heathrow.'

'I know. Your tickets are booked. I made them first class. Standard class leg room on BA flights is too small.'

Hunter grinned. 'I'd better get going.'

'Good luck, Nick. And if possible, make sure the Prince knows about TIFAT.'

'That's my intention.'

'Good. We'll make sure the word goes out that we're responsible. I want it to be a warning to other groups who think they can attack us with impunity.'

Hunter made the flight with time to spare. It was a personal rule that he never drank when he flew. It was just one of his many idiosyncrasies that Ruth had enjoyed pointing out when she was teasing him. Ruth, damnation. He hadn't seen her in over two years but she had been there and he had intended meeting up with her some day. Not for any romance but as a friend.

He brought his mind back to the job ahead. A middle of the night entry, a quiet search of the yacht, a day hidden onboard and a visit to the Prince about 03.00.

The question was whether or not he was being set up. It was a conundrum he'd know the answer to soon enough.

The BA flight was only 90 minutes late arriving at Jeddah. He passed through immigration and customs without any difficulty and was on the concourse when his phone rang. A glance at the screen showed it to be TIFAT HQ.

'Hunter.'

'Ah, Commander, I have some new intelligence for you along with an addition to your op.'

Hunter didn't like the sound of that but said, 'Yes, sir. What are they?'

'First Chris is on his way to join you.'

'But…'

'No buts, Nick. First of all Chris has made it clear that he is a part of the family in all but name, which will change in a couple of months. And he told me to tell you if you thought he would be spending his life with Louise if something happened to you, then you can think again. He added that she would probably marry him just to spend her life making his a misery.'

Hunter smiled. 'I guess he knows my sister pretty well.'

Macnair chuckled. 'I guess he does.'

'When will he get here?'

'He's in the Sabreliner. Burg is piloting. Flight time is eight hours plus refuelling in Cyprus. So he should be landing about half an hour behind you. There's a second diplomatic pouch onboard.'

'Thanks, sir. What's the info?'

'Ah, it's what persuaded me to send Chris. Mossad has been informed that Princess A'shadieeyah will be there along with four bodyguards who are loyal to her. She won't be leaving when the others in the entourage disembark.'

'Any idea why not?'

'None. Except we know what an evil bitch she is. Maybe she thinks there will be enjoyment watching you being tortured to death.'

'She's in for a grave disappointment in that case.'

'I sincerely hope so.'

On that note Macnair broke the connection. Hunter crossed the concourse and bought a coffee at a Starbucks.

Bletchley sauntered through only minutes later. The two men shook hands.

'Did the General tell you what's up?'

'Yep. Truth be told I'm glad to see you.'

'I guess he told you what I said?'

Hunter chuckled. 'You read that right.'

'Do we know where the yacht is berthed?'

'Yes, at the Samaco Marina. There's a hotel called the Sofitel

Jeddah Corniche that practically overlooks the berth. I've booked a suite on the 20th floor so we can take a good look at the yacht and the surrounding area.'

'I know. I'm in the room next door.'

'What about Burg?'

'He's in the Sheraton at the airport. Right now he's clearing customs with the diplomatic bag.'

Minutes later Schwarzkopf appeared with a box on a trolley.'

'Any problems?' Hunter greeted the pilot as they shook hands.

'No.'

They took a taxi to Umm Al Muminin Zaiynab, Ash Shati, where the imposing consulate building was sited. They disgorged from the taxi at the main gate where they were checked off against a list of visitors. At the front desk they were greeted by the Head of Security for the consulate who introduced himself as Clive Johnston. He had a military bearing, tall, slim and fit. He was their MI6 contact.

Johnston nodded at the box they were carrying. 'A second box arrived about 20 minutes ago. Don't tell me what's in it but I can guess. How's Malcolm?'

'Fine,' Hunter replied, 'he sends his best.'

The two men followed Johnston down into the bowels of the building. They arrived at a lower room with a table and four chairs. A box sat in the middle of the table and they dumped the one they were carrying alongside it.

'Welcome to the silent room. Whatever is said in here can't be overheard.'

'The consulate is bugged?' Bletchley asked in surprise.

Johnston shrugged. 'There's an apartment block across the road from where a directional microphone is sometimes aimed our way. It's not there at the moment but we don't take any chances. Anything sensitive is discussed down here.'

'How come you ended up with MI6?' Hunter asked.

'I'd had enough. Three tours in Afghanistan and one in Syria as a special advisor and a failed marriage convinced me it was time to get out. Add on lousy pay, the potential for PTSD, then include the possibility of being charged with murder or manslaughter for killing the enemy, who would cut your head off if they had the chance. I speak Arabic and Hebrew, which led to a job offer with the firm.'

'Enjoy it?' Hunter enquired.

'Yes. It's not so much cloak and dagger as paperwork. My wife is with me plus our two kids and so it's not a bad posting. This is one of the safest countries in the world as long as you obey their restrictive rules. And they're getting better now that women are allowed to drive. The kids go to the European school where they're having a damned good education as well as learning a couple of useful languages. My daughter has a talent for languages while my son seems to favour engineering. So all in all, I made the right choice. Do you want me to leave you guys to open the boxes?'

The two TIFAT officers exchanged glances, Bletchley shrugged and Hunter shook his head.

'I've no doubt you can keep a secret,' said Hunter, 'and I don't mean that in a patronising way. We may need some help before we're through here but I hope not.'

Johnston smiled. 'Good. I was hoping you'd say something like that. So what's it all about?'

'Do you know Prince Abdul-Hameed Saud?'

'That scumbag. I've never met him but I know a great deal about him.'

'How come?' Bletchley asked.

'He's up to his neck in funding attacks on the West. The rumour is he's dying and that his eldest son was killed in a fracas in Germany.'

'Correct,' said Hunter. 'The Prince has only days to live.'

'So what's your interest?'

'I'm going to kill him.'

'Why bother if he's as good as dead?'

'Do you know anything about a terrorist attack on a bowls club in Glasgow?'

'Yes, why?'

'The attack was to kill my family and then me. It was in retribution for the death, in Germany, of his eldest son.'

'Did you do that?'

'Yes, we stopped a major terrorist attack and saved many lives that day,' said Bletchley.

'I know. I read about it in my daily briefing notes.'

'Do you get many of these notes?' Bletchley asked.

'Yes, they take me the best part of an hour to read there's so much terrorist activity all over the world. Most of it is of no interest but some is and so I'm kept abreast as to what's going on. So why kill the Prince?'

'Malcolm is going to put it out that anyone who tries to harm a member of TIFAT or their families will have no hiding place. No matter who they are or where they live.'

'That's a bit risky, isn't it? The politically correct aren't going to like it one bit.'

Hunter smiled. 'That's the good part about working for the General, he doesn't give a damn. TIFAT's mandate is clear and he intends operating it to the full. We have proof the Prince is involved with terrorism so we are taking the fight to him.'

'What are you going to do?'

'We have a highly placed mole amongst the Prince's staff who has been keeping us informed of developments. I say us when I should say Mossad. They've been passing us information.'

'You trust Mossad?'

'We know we can trust them only as long as it suits them. Still,' Hunter shrugged, 'they've called it right so far.'

'You'll never get into the palace. It's like a fortress.'

'You're right,' Bletchley replied, 'but we don't have to. The Prince will be onboard his super yacht, *The Star of Medina*, the day after tomorrow.'

'I know her. I think I can help.'

'How?' Hunter asked.

'Let's take a look at the yacht first then I'll tell you.'

39

Wajeeh Soliman knew he was in serious danger with Princess A'shadieeyah on board the yacht. When her father died his own death would quickly follow. The crew may be loyal but they worked for money so their loyalty would be lost. He knew from spying on the family that Princess A'shadieeyah was determined to take control of the vast businesses they owned. She planned to encourage the eldest brother, the future Prince, to enjoy his life and leave everything to her. He'd soon be persuaded.

The other two brothers were just as indolent and Soliman hated them all.

Hunter, Bletchley and Johnston were standing at the window in Hunter's suite, looking down at the yacht. *The Star of Medina* was berthed starboard side to with her stern pointing at the hotel. Beyond her bows was another mooring space.

'It's as I thought,' said Johnston. 'I own a four berth, 30ft sailing boat. We use it a fair amount so the authorities as well as other boat owners know us'

'What's your idea?' Hunter asked, observing the yacht through binoculars.

'We berth opposite the Prince's yacht and you two swim underneath the pontoon and climb up the stern ladder.'

'That might work,' said Bletchley.

'I'm not sure,' said Hunter.

'Why not?' Johnston asked.

'I'm not sure you should be involved. I appreciate diplomatic immunity extends to your family but if anything goes wrong, your family could be in danger.'

'There's nothing to worry about. It so happens my wife and kids are back in England visiting the parents. If they weren't, they would be on the next plane out of here. We can't trust the Saudis to honour the letter and spirit of diplomatic immunity.'

'Killing one of their own isn't exactly in the spirit,' said Bletchley dryly.

Johnston chuckled. 'You're right. But I can stay on my yacht as backup in case the worst comes to the worst. Think of me as coming to the rescue like the US cavalry dealing with a tribe of Apaches attacking a wagon train.'

'The mind boggles,' said Hunter, 'but I take your point. I can see street lights along the pier. Pity we can't extinguish them.'

'Oh, but we can.'

'How?'

'There's a junction box at the beginning of each pier. They're all on separate circuits so if one has a problem, the whole marina isn't affected. The box is child's play to open. A flick of a switch and out go the lights. Time it for say 10 minutes and I flick them back on.'

'Right,' said Hunter, 'that should be long enough. We've studied plans of the yacht and know there's a hatch to the tiller flat right aft. There won't be a lock so we should be able to get in quickly enough. The flat is connected to the engine room through a watertight hatch. What do you think, Chris?'

'I think it's a goer.'

'Okay Clive, you're on. Let's go sailing.'

The boat was a Westerly 33 ketch and well maintained. All three were seasoned sailors and it didn't take them long to get Johnston's yacht ready for sea. They proceeded slowly down the estuary with a following breeze of three knots.

They tacked twice, rounded a bend and came into the section where the Prince's yacht was berthed. Compared to their Westerly she appeared huge. They headed out to sea while Bletchley surreptitiously took a video of the yacht. There was no doubt she was a hugely impressive craft.

They saw a number of people on the deck who ignored the small Westerly. If there were any armed guards they weren't in evidence.

The yacht reached the open waters of the Red Sea and they headed up the coast for a few miles. Then they went about and headed back south. They were soon berthed opposite *The Star of Medina* and sitting in the cockpit drinking non-alcoholic lagers and eating cheese sandwiches. One man walked along the deck of the Medina and stared down at them. All three stared back and the man walked away.

The deck of the super yacht loomed above them where they sat.

All three then retired below and slept until 02.00 when Hunter's watch alarm awoke them.

Johnston was dressed in a white thawb that reached down to his ankles and on his head he wore a red and white chequered keffiyeh with a black band known as an agal. He looked every inch a Saudi Arabian. Under the thawb around his waist he had a holstered Glock 17 with silencer. It was on his left side with the grip pointing across his stomach. Access was through a vertical slit in the thawb. If he was challenged he wasn't going anywhere quietly. He knew of too many stories where people were stopped by private contractors acting as guards and never seen again.

'You guys ready? Got everything?'

'Yes,' said Hunter. 'Time to get this show on the road.'

'I'll fix the electricity. If you need more time let me know.'

Johnston stepped onto the pontoon, walked openly towards the gate and stopped at the junction box. Taking a screwdriver from under his thawb, he pushed it hard against the narrow gap between the side of the box and the door. A quick shove and the door flew open. He flicked up the main switch and instantly the lights on the lampposts lining the pontoon went out. The clear sky and quarter moon meant it wasn't as dark as they would have wished but it was an improvement.

Johnston knelt by the box with a pencil torch as though looking to find a fault.

Hunter and Bletchley wore bathing trunks with silenced Glock 40s strapped to their waists. The remainder of their clothes and gear were packed in waterproof bags slung over their shoulders.

The boxes of gear they'd brought with them had been superfluous to requirements. They wouldn't need the re-breathers, wet suits and heavy armament.

They slipped over the side of the boat and swam under the pier to the other side and then along the hull of the yacht to the stern.

Hunter went up the ladder first, taking each step slowly. He reached the deck and cautiously looked over the edge. There was nobody about. He wormed his way the couple of metres to the tiller hatch and quickly undid the butterfly nut holding the hatch closed. He opened the hatch and climbed down. Bletchley was right behind him. As the hatch was closing the pontoon lights came back on.

Inside the yacht the air was warm and oppressive with a faint smell of oil. The tiller flat contained the hydraulic pump that operated the rudder and nothing else. There was plenty of room to lay down though they needed to bend over when standing up. The compartment was about four metres wide by three deep. On each side was a vertical watertight door that led to storerooms with spare, unused coils of berthing ropes and fenders. They dragged out some of the rope and laid it flat on the deck, winding it to make a mattress. It wasn't comfortable but it would be a lot better than the steel deck. At the front of the compartment was another vertical door leading to the rest of the yacht.

They quickly dressed in dark clothing and added their silenced Glocks, ankle revolvers and wrist knives. They slipped on their Kevlar body armour vests and adjusted them to fit comfortably. They had the latest in NVGs which were more like diving masks that protruded from the eyes for a few inches. They also gave a much clearer picture and were effective in the pitch dark as well as semi-darkness. In the pockets of their webbing they secreted small, electronically operated powder puff shaped containers. Inside was a gas known as Kolokol-1. It was opiate-derived and made up of fentanyl and the highly potent carfentanyl. It rendered a person unconscious within a second or two and was effective for 10 minutes or so.

Hunter's phone vibrated and he answered. 'Yes, General?'

'Where are you?'

'In the yacht's tiller flat.'

'Good. We just heard from Mossad. The Prince, his daughter and both their entourages are arriving tomorrow evening.'

'Good, that gives us plenty of time. We're about to search the yacht.'

'Good luck.'

Wajeeh Soliman had finished his preparations. The doctor, a nurse, the chef, the butler and two maids were ready to go. Unfortunately, so was Princess A'shadieeyah. Thanks to the bugs he'd installed in her rooms in the palace, he now knew more about her plans for him, all of which frightened him to the core.

She would be arriving just after her father with her own retinue of maids and two bodyguards. The guards had made it clear to the Princess that they would be willing to kill Soliman. She would claim that Soliman had been killed in self-defence, blaming him for the death of the Prince. Her claim wouldn't be questioned. The Prince and his family controlled the judiciary and the police. Both would do as they were ordered. It was no surprise that the Prince and his family were held in contempt by most of the world for their sheer hypocrisy concerning Islam and terrorism.

Soliman needed to get away at the right time, which was after the Prince's death. He'd received a message from the Israelis telling him on no account was he to kill the Prince. Somebody was coming to do just that and Soliman had a good idea who that someone would be.

TIFAT's reputation as a ruthless organisation not to be trifled with would be made known to all those who needed to get the message.

* * *

Hunter and Bletchley opened the watertight door slowly and entered the engine room. It was spotless which showed the engines weren't used very often.

Hunter opened the door to the corridor and peered out. He could see the knee-high safety lights stretching along the corridor.

'Chris, lift up the master switch on the electricity distribution panel.'

'Will do.'

The safety lights went out. The corridor was pitch black, stretching into the distance. Without their NVGs they would have been unable to see anything.

Hunter stepped over the lip of the doorway and into the corridor. Bletchley followed. Both men had their Glocks drawn, suppressors fitted, safety catches off.

The carpeted corridor was lined with wooden doors about 10 paces apart. Hunter opened the first door on the port side slowly and quietly. They found a cabin that was well fitted out with a double bed, wardrobe, chest of drawers and an en-suite shower and toilet. There were two portholes that looked out on to the pier.

They made their way cautiously along the corridor checking each cabin in turn. As they progressed, they stuck a powder puff under each bed and a listening device next to the hinge of each door. There were eight cabins on each side, all identically fitted out. For crew's quarters they were high on comfort and all were unoccupied.

They came across a series of large storerooms holding everything from fresh linen to tinned foods. One room contained racks of high quality wines and liquor.

'So much for their devout abstinence,' whispered Bletchley.

'Could be for non-Islamic guests.'

'I suppose so. Pity we're on a job otherwise I wouldn't mind trying some of the red. The French premier cru probably cost more than I earn in a week.'

There was a walk-in fridge packed to the gunnels with fresh food. There were also cartons of orange juice and milk. Halfway along on one side was a TV lounge and on the other was a well-equipped canteen.

At the end of the corridor they came to a wide staircase, which led to what they assumed was the Prince's quarters.

The corridor was highly polished mahogany with non-slip rugs scattered along its length. The bulkheads were lined with paintings of Islamic scenes.

There were four doors each side of the corridor and one behind them. They checked that one first, slowly and carefully opening the door.

The crew's cabins were as good as those found on a passenger liner and the whole area displayed luxury and extravagance.

'Jesus Nick, look at this place,' Bletchley whispered. 'Ever seen anything like it?'

'Nope.'

The room was massive. There were no portholes but all-round reinforced windows stretching from the deck to the overhead bulkhead. The view was panoramic and showed the world to port and starboard as well as ahead. The city lights could be seen in the distance. The rest of the cabin's fittings were in keeping with the impression the Prince wanted to portray – that he was rich and powerful. Here they left two powder puffs.

There was a second door leading to a large en-suite bedroom with a bed that could comfortably take four people.

They returned to the corridor. The first cabin on the port side in the corridor was occupied. When they opened the door they were greeted with the gentle snore of its occupant. Bletchley stayed in the corridor while Hunter slowly and silently crossed the room towards the bed. As he did he slipped a facemask out of his leg pocket and put it on. When he reached the bed he gripped the powder puff tightly and then twisted the top. He held it under the nose of the sleeping occupant who grunted, twitched and fell into a much deeper sleep. An alarm clock wouldn't wake him.

The cabin could also be described as opulent though not on the scale of the one they had just left. The first one was obviously the one used by the Prince when he was onboard.

They found three more cabins occupied and in each one put the occupants into a deeper sleep. They also planted powder puffs under each bed. The cabins were identical in size and layout only decorated differently. All eight had a masculine feel to them with the paintings depicting heroic action by Saudis vanquishing the non-believers.

Interspersed with the cabins were ready-use cupboards stocked with items required for a few weeks at sea.

There was a third upper deck that held a dining room, a lounge, a superb kitchen and a cinema. A bar was well stocked with expensive liquors and wines, similar to those stored below.

Everywhere they went they hid the gas filled powder puffs.

Finally they reached the bridge. As was expected it was like something from the space age. The two men studied the layout and identified the various switches, knobs and levers. There was no steering wheel but electronic buttons to alter course.

'We'd better go below,' said Bletchley, 'it's getting light.'

They went below after raiding the food store and fridge. Helping themselves to blankets and pillows, they returned to the tiller flat.

The atmosphere was still oppressive and they opened the door wide. The powerful air conditioning was operating and the atmosphere began to freshen.

'Pity there are no punkah louvres in the flat,' said Hunter.

They ate a meal of smoked salmon, liver pate and high-baked biscuits. They drank orange juice and wished for coffee.

Settling down to sleep, Hunter took the first watch. He found staying awake challenging and fell into a doze only to wake up with a jerk. He let Bletchley sleep for four hours before shaking him awake. It was just coming up to 10.00 and the crew were beginning to stir. Hunter closed the tiller door.

The microphones were voice activated and could also be isolated if necessary. It was clear that when the crew realised how late it was, they went into a panic to clean the cabins they had been using, making the beds and replacing the linen. Eventually they got things under control and repaired to the canteen. There followed an argument about why they had slept so late but found no satisfactory answer.

The voice they identified as the master of the vessel announced he was going to the bridge with his coffee to keep a lookout for the Prince. There followed a tirade of invective aimed at their employer.

Hunter settled down to sleep while Bletchley amused himself listening to what was happening amongst the four crew members.

At noon a squad of 20 servants arrived to clean the yacht from top to bottom. They worked non-stop for nearly four hours until a man who sounded as though he was the overseer announced he was satisfied with the yacht's cleanliness. The squad of servants could be heard stowing away their gear and leaving the vessel.

Late in the afternoon they heard the master say repeatedly in Arabic, 'Alqarf, alqarf, alqarf. Here he comes.'

Another voice said, 'Labeeb, that is no way to speak about our Prince.'

The two TIFAT officers smiled.

'Somehow,' said Bletchley, 'I don't think Prince Abdul-Hameed Saud is very popular with his crew.'

40

'As-salaam alaykum. Peace be upon you.' The master bowed his head to Soliman and offered his hand.

Shaking the proffered hand, the Prince's head of security responded, 'Wa alaykum as-salaam, Labeeb. Peace be upon you also.'

Soliman had made it a point to be friendly with the master at every opportunity. He did so with most of the Prince's staff. It ensured that any bits of information he missed was brought to his attention. When it was, the informer received a generous gratuity. It was an arrangement encouraged by the Prince.

Soliman stood on the bridge wing and looked down at the pier and then across to Johnston's yacht. He could see nobody so he decided it was of no consequence.

'Is the yacht ready for His Highness?'

'Yes, sir. The cleaners have just left. We have had a delivery of fresh food and the Prince's quarters are filled with flowers.'

'Good.' He didn't bother to add the last thing the Prince would be interested in was bunches of flowers. The Prince had agreed that they should put to sea before their plans for Hunter were carried out. His screams would be heard across the marina was the way he explained it to the Prince. It had brought a rictus grin to the dying man. The idea appeared to have invigorated the Prince to such an extent that only hours earlier, the doctor suggested the Prince would live possibly as long as a week. Which didn't suit Soliman for a moment.

The Princess had learnt of Hunter's capture and had announced that she would be staying onboard and going to sea with them. She had claimed she would enjoy seeing her brother's killer suffer for what he had done. The Prince had been pleased with the notion and so Soliman had been forced to go along with it.

'You know what we are going to do?'

The master nodded nervously. 'Are you sure?'

'Yes. There is something you do not know. The Prince has bequeathed this yacht to me. It has been registered with the International Register of Shipping making me the legal owner. When the Prince dies we will arrange for his body to be taken ashore and as soon as we have done so, we will put to sea.'

'But I thought we would be at sea.'

'No, you imbecile. He will die before we set sail.'

'I am confused. I thought the man His Highness wanted killed would be onboard. That we would put to sea to ensure nobody knew what was happening.'

'Is there such a man here?'

'No. I thought you must have arranged for him to be brought here later.'

'There is no man. It was a ruse to ensure the Prince would come. Do you understand?'

'And the Princess?'

'She will be going to sea with us.'

Just as the sun was setting, the Prince was brought onboard. He was on a stretcher and hooked up to an oxygen tank. He was carefully placed on his bed and propped up with pillows. He looked frail but there was determination written on his face.

'Wajeeh my son, is the man here?'

'Not yet, Your Highness. I have just received word that he will arrive in the middle of the night. It is safer. We must not let anyone see what we are doing.'

'You are right as always.' The Prince gasped and sucked oxygen into his lungs. It took a few minutes to bring his breathing under control before he said, 'I have been looking forward to this day for a long time.'

405

At that moment, the Princess swept into the cabin followed closely by her two armed bodyguards.

Under his thawb, Soliman held a Smith and Wesson Chief's Special semi-automatic pistol. The weapon was small and compact but had stopping power. It wasn't much use at distances greater that 50 metres, but for close work it was ideal. If either of the guards reached for a gun he would shoot first and hang the consequences.

He was also wearing body armour, which according to the blurb that came with it, could stop a bullet at 10 paces. He didn't want to test the product's claims.

The Princess was wearing a black burqa that not only covered her body and hands but her head and face. There was a mesh window for her to see through. She pulled the head covering away and stared at Soliman. She was an attractive woman with black hair, almond shaped dark eyes, a straight nose and an oval face. However, Soliman knew her to be cold, callous, calculating, devious and totally evil.

He had long speculated what was to happen to him but now he had confirmation. She would never show her face to someone who was not a member of her family or very close staff – like her bodyguards. But she would to someone who hadn't long to live.

She approached the bed, 'How are you, father?'

The Prince lifted his mask and spoke in a husky voice. 'I am happy to see you.'

'I you. I wanted to make sure that you have the best of care.'

Hunter and Bletchley listened to what was being said.

'You can practically taste her hypocrisy,' said Bletchley.

'That's for sure. If Soliman now owns the yacht what would you do?'

'Tonight I would ensure the Prince died of what appears to be natural causes, put the body ashore along with the rest of his entourage and get the hell away to sea.'

'That's what I'd do as well but what does he do about the Princess?'

'Probably kill her. He's ruthless enough.'

At 03.00 they prepared to move out but before they did, Hunter sent the signal that activated the gas in the powder puffs. Slowly and quietly the gas began to fill the sleeping quarters of the crew and staff.

This time in the engine room, they left the electrical distribution board alone. They wanted the Prince to see what was happening to him and who was responsible.

Their NVGs weren't needed as the emergency lighting showed them the way. The yacht was as silent as the grave as they entered the Prince's stateroom. Dim lights created a soothing ambience through-out the room. They crossed to the bedroom and opened the door. The Prince was propped up on his pillows, wide awake, his eyes staring at the two men as they entered.

'I'll stay here,' said Hunter.

He didn't need to spell it out. They didn't want to be disturbed.

Bletchley crossed the room in time to grab the Prince's hand as he reached for an emergency button. Not that it would have done any good. The gas in the rest of the yacht would have done its job by then.

Looking down at the Prince, Bletchley hesitated. The man looked pathetic.

Lifting his face mask, the Prince stammered, 'Who...who are you?'

'My name is Bletchley, the man with me is Commander Nick Hunter. Do you know him?'

The Prince appeared to push himself into his pillows.

'It was the Commander's family you ordered killed. The pilot of the plane you tried to have destroyed was his sister, who I am going to marry.'

The Prince was gasping for breath but still Bletchley ripped the mask from the man's face. He slipped a plastic tie-wrap around the Prince's neck and slid the noose just tight enough to cut off some of his air. The Prince was gasping, staring at Bletchley, his fingers clawing at the thin plastic as he tried to breathe. He began to thrash around, kicking his legs, eating up what oxygen he had.

Bletchley leant forward and put his left hand around the Prince's neck then he bent down and stared into his eyes. 'We killed your son. We will kill every member of your family as a lesson to those who attack us. They will not have pleasant deaths. We are going to cut your heart out and feed it to the pigs. When you get to Jahannam you will suffer for all eternity for the crimes that you have committed against humanity. And when you get there you will meet again with your son.'

Hunter stepped into the room. 'Someone's coming.'

Bletchley pulled harder on the tie-wrap cutting off the Prince's air completely. The man stopped thrashing about and was dead in less than a minute.

They drew their silenced Glocks and positioned themselves to welcome the intruders. Hunter knelt behind one of the forward curtains in the main cabin while Bletchley took up a position behind a curtain in the bedroom. If there was any trouble they could cover the enemy front and back.

Hunter looked at his watch and frowned. The knockout gas should have worked. He could only surmise the people heading their way had been out and about and not in their staterooms. The door opened and shut. Whoever had entered the room had stopped moving.

Princess A'shadieeyah and her two bodyguards made their way to the Prince's stateroom. She had been below to the servants' cabins and woken the two men. It was 03.05 and her father was about to die. She made her way along the corridor to be met by the yacht's master. They entered the stateroom. The Princess sat at her father's large and ornate desk. The others sat in silence around the room waiting for one more visitor. They didn't have long to wait. The door opened and Soliman entered, quietly closing the door behind him. As he turned to see who was there, he started.

He stood still looking at the four faces staring back at him. He was shocked to see the yacht's master, his elbows on the dining table, a revolver in his right hand.

'What...' he croaked, clearing his throat to try again. 'What's happening?'

Soliman wore a T shirt and jeans and it was obvious he was unarmed.

The Princess replied. 'I was going to ask you the same, even though it's unnecessary. I know you are here to kill my father and then me. You were intending to put the staff and my father's body ashore. You were going to sea where I would be given a watery grave.'

Soliman looked at Labeeb, fury boiling up inside him. 'You son of a whore.'

The master shrugged.

The Princess opened a cigarette box on the desk, took one and lit it using a gold lighter. She inhaled deeply and blew the smoke through her nostrils.

'Labeeb has been on my payroll for over a year. I have been kept well informed as to what has been happening and what you were intending. We caught you in the act of killing the Prince and shot you. Unfortunately we were too late and the Prince was already dead. There will be a great funeral, the King and many Princes weeping crocodile tears and I will take over the family fortune while you rot in a pauper's grave.'

Silence fell as the four people stared at Soliman. If he was going to die, he would do his best to take the bitch with him.

'I want you to know something before you kill me. I have kept the Israelis in the picture as to what you have been doing. They know all about the purchase of the explosives from the Iranians and are even now planning to take their revenge.'

Sneering, the Princess said, 'What can they do? Nothing. They wouldn't dare.'

Soliman shook his head. 'You don't understand. The Prince targeted the family of a senior officer in TIFAT. Do you know who they are?'

'Yes. I know all I need to, as well as their involvement in the death of my brother. An act I am most grateful for, I should add. They will do nothing. The West needs our oil as well as our custom for arms and armaments.'

409

She stood up and aimed an automatic at Soliman's head. He had left it too late to get to her. Cursing to himself he prepared to launch himself across the cabin and the desk. He would never make it but he was determined to try.

'Now we will go into my father's bedroom where you will disconnect his oxygen tank and we will watch him die.'

Soliman didn't question her but took a few steps towards the door to the bedroom. If he was going to make a move, it was as he went through the door. One of the bodyguards stepped behind Soliman and shoved his automatic against his spine.

When they entered the room, Soliman stopped in shock. The Prince was leaning against his pillows, his facemask was missing and he wasn't breathing.

The two bodyguards and the Princess pushed Soliman further into the room and stopped aghast.

'What is this?' The Princess whispered.

'The Prince is dead.' One of the bodyguards spoke in a hoarse whisper.

'But how?' She walked across the deck and stopped next to her father. In the dim light she could see the black tie-wrap around his neck, the index finger of his left hand jammed under it.

'Who could have done this?' She was whispering. 'Who?'

'I do not know. We must search the ship.'

Bletchley and Hunter understood Arabic and had heard what was said. They stepped out from behind their respective curtains startling the Saudis. The guards didn't have time to reach for their weapons before they were both shot dead. Soliman, the master and the Princess stared at the dying men while Hunter and Bletchley watched them.

'Who are you?' Soliman asked looking from one to the other.

'My name is Commander Hunter. It's my family you tried to kill. This is Captain Bletchley and it was his betrothed, my sister, who was piloting the aircraft you tried to bring down.'

'Did you hear what I said?'

'Yes, you've been passing information to Mossad. For that we thank you.'

Soliman managed a caricature of a smile before saying, 'This is Princess A'shadieeyah, the eldest daughter of the Prince.'

'We know,' said Hunter. 'We also know she intends continuing her so-called war on the West armed with her father's money.'

'How do you know?' There was no doubting her courage as she sneered at them. 'If you think you will escape from here, then I suggest you think again. There will be no escape.'

As she was speaking, she was turning towards Hunter who appeared not to have noticed her movement. Her left arm was across her waist, her right arm hung down by her side. She suddenly started to lift her arm to point the gun she was holding in her right hand, when Hunter shot her through the elbow. She screamed and dropped her automatic. Using her left hand to cover the wound, she sank to the deck, crying and moaning at the same time.

'May I?' Soliman indicated the pistol the Princess had dropped.

'By all means, only don't try any sudden moves.'

Soliman picked up the pistol and checked the safety was off. 'You were telling me that I would be going to Jahannam,' he said in his normal voice. 'If I am, then I shall see you there.'

Placing the end of the barrel against her forehead, he pulled the trigger. She was shot dead. The small hole in her forehead, belied the amount of skull and brain scattered across the deck. He shot the yacht's master in the same way.

'Now what?' Soliman asked, fully composed, as though shooting someone was something he did as a matter of routine.

41

'How were you planning to get away?' asked Hunter.

Soliman shrugged. 'I couldn't leave the master alive but that now presents a problem. With the other three members of the crew we could have sailed to Israel without any difficulties. As it is I am not sure what to do. If you look up the International Register of Shipping, you will find that I am the owner of the yacht. It was given to me by the Prince and that is confirmed in his will.' He smiled. 'I wrote the will, the Prince signed it.' He shrugged. 'I have been signing the Prince's documents for some time. My forgery looks more like his signature than his.'

'What about the other three crew?' Bletchley asked. 'Were they on the Princess's payroll?'

'I don't know. Whether or not they were, I'll offer a substantial sum to stay while I decide what to do.'

Hunter said, 'How can you man a yacht this size with only four crew?'

'We only go to sea once in a blue moon. Keeping a full crew is ludicrous. So far, on the few occasions we have sailed, we have managed with just the four plus some of the Prince's people from the palace as deckhands.'

'What about an engineer?' Bletchley asked.

Soliman shrugged. 'We've not needed one but now, there's a bigger problem.'

'Which is?' Hunter asked.

'There's no one capable of driving a vessel this size.'

Hunter wasn't going to correct him just yet. He still had to decide what he and Bletchley were going to do.

'Why have you been passing information to Mossad?'

'Believe it or not, not all Muslims are terrorists.'

'We know that and we acknowledge the fact, publicly as well as privately.'

'The West cannot stop the fanatics. Only Muslims can do that.'

'We've been saying so for many years,' said Bletchley.

'Then think of me as one of those other Muslims.'

Hunter didn't know what to believe but he nodded. 'So what do you want to do now?'

'Cut the tie-wrap from the Prince's neck, wrap the three bodies in something and shove them in a cupboard. Clean the blood and bones as best we can and wait for morning. We let the doctor find the bodies. I'll order him to arrange transport of the Prince back to the palace. I'll also let it be known that the Princess left the yacht during the night to return home. Nobody will question me.'

'And then what?' Bletchley asked.

'Go to the airport and catch the first plane out of here. Any destination in Europe will do.'

'The yacht will be searched at some point, the bodies found and a warrant issued for your arrest.'

'They won't find me,' Soliman said with conviction.

'They might. I have a better idea,' said Hunter, 'why don't we stick to your original plan and take the yacht?'

'I told you, I can't handle it, neither can the other three.'

'No, but I can.'

'You?'

'Yes. I'm a Commander in the Royal Navy. I can handle a ship. All I need is an hour or two on the bridge to check the controls. We can get rid of the bodies at sea and head for Israel. If you want to go there, that is.'

Soliman nodded. 'I would like to meet my Mossad handler, whoever that is. Why are you doing this?'

'You saved a lot of lives and we owe you our thanks. In particular, you saved the lives of my family, for which I shall always be indebted to you.'

Soliman held out his hand and Hunter shook it. He did the same with Bletchley. He then offered the automatic to Hunter who shook his head.

'Keep it. We'd better hide these bodies and clear up the mess as best we can.'

'There's one more thing,' Soliman offered.

The two TIFAT officers looked at him closely.

'I assume you'd like to meet the man who arranged the attack on you and your family?'

Hunter nodded.

'His name is Michael Gunther and I can introduce you to him.'

'You know where to find him?'

'Yes. At least I know where he was three days ago.'

'How?'

'I've been keeping a close eye on him. Or more accurately I have had a close eye kept on him from the very start.'

'Why?'

I didn't trust him not to take the money and run.'

'So where is he?' Hunter asked.

'Three days ago he was at the Sacca de la Misericordia in Venice.'

'What's there?' asked Bletchley.

'A marina with many boats for sale.'

'How can you be certain he'll still be there?'

Soliman looked at Hunter and shrugged. 'I cannot be certain but my instructions were that I should be contacted only if Gunther moved. I have heard nothing, so it's reasonable to assume he is still in Venice. According to what I've heard, he is planning to buy a boat.'

Bletchley said, 'It's a good way to hide.'

Between them they wrapped the bodies in some of the most expensive shrouds ever produced, woven by some of the finest craftsmen in the world. Cleaning bones, brains and blood was the

414

most difficult job but it was made less gruesome using rubber gloves from the storeroom.

It was nearly 07.00 when Hunter announced, 'That'll do. Wajeeh, we'll go to the bridge and start figuring out the controls.

The bridge was a spacecraft of dials, levers and switches but it didn't take Hunter long to identify what each was for. He began to flash-up various pieces of gear including a sat-nav system equipped with a telephone link.

Soliman arrived on the bridge with a flask of coffee, orange juice, boiled eggs, cooked meats and bread rolls.

As he sipped his coffee, Hunter phoned Johnston and brought him up-to-date.

'Okay, Nick. It sounds as though you have everything under control. I'll stay here quietly until you've left.'

'Okay, and thanks.'

'My pleasure, anytime.'

An hour later, the doctor entered the stateroom. When he saw the Prince he stopped in his tracks. Although he had been expecting him to die he hadn't thought it would be so soon. He hurried out of the room to the stateroom next door to get hold of Soliman.

'Sir, sir, wake up.'

Soliman was feigning sleep and lifted his head with a groan. 'What is it?'

'It's the Prince, sir, he's dead.'

Soliman climbed out of bed, threw on a robe and hurried to the Prince's room. He stood by the bed and said, 'I thought he'd have a few more days at least.'

'You can never be certain.' The doctor drew a sheet over the body. 'We had better inform the Princess.'

'We can't. She left during the night.'

'Why?'

'She didn't say. Perhaps…' his voice trailed off.

'Perhaps what?'

'You don't think she had anything to do with his death do you?'

'No!' The doctor's voice was aghast. 'Why should she? His Royal Highness was close to death and there would be no point in her hastening it.'

Soliman nodded. 'You are right. I'll arrange to have the Prince returned to the palace immediately.'

The doctor nodded. 'I understand that all arrangements for the funeral have been made.'

'They have been in place for months. The Prince will be buried in the family tomb alongside his ancestors. He stipulated the ceremony is to start at four o'clock and in accordance with Islamic tradition, within a day of his death.'

Soliman and the doctor made sure the removal of the body went smoothly. The Prince's staff were silent and apprehensive as they left the yacht. Would they still be employed after the funeral?

Soliman went up to the bridge. 'Well?'

Shrugging, Hunter said, 'I don't see any problems. The fuel tanks are full, the water tanks are full and the batteries are fully charged. Every dial is showing readings I would expect for sailing.'

'Yes, but can you steer it? Do you know what you're doing?''

Hunter nodded. 'I've driven bigger vessels than this.'

'All the staff have left. Only the three crew members are still onboard. They know we're planning to leave Saudi and are happy to go. Also a quarter of a million dollars each, sweetened their resolve.'

'The Prince's family may come after you,' said Hunter.

'I doubt it. Not one of them regrets the passing of the Prince or the disappearance of the Princess. What's more, they don't want any more scandal. They've had enough to contend with as it is.'

'So you're safe enough?' Hunter enquired.

'In a nutshell, yes. I know where the bodies are buried. If I meet any trouble, I'll let the King know what I know and believe me, it's enough to make him call off his dogs.'

'You seem to have it all worked out,' said Bletchley.

'I do. I've been planning this a long time.'

42

Hunter eased the yacht clear of the jetty and aimed her at the harbour entrance. He kept her at the posted speed of four knots but once clear of the harbour walls, he steadily increased the speed to 10 knots.

The sea-lanes showed clearly on the chart screen and Hunter aimed the yacht at right angles to the lanes, to cross to the other side. It didn't take long and he turned the yacht to starboard and headed north. The Red Sea was a busy inlet of the Indian Ocean with boats and ships travelling north and south along the Suez Canal.

Bletchley and Soliman appeared on the bridge.

'Why have we cut across the sea?' asked the Saudi.

'It's called the Rule of the Road. It means we use sea-lanes just the way we use motorways and other roads. We need to decide where we're going.'

Soliman looked surprised. 'I thought I told you I wish to go to Israel.'

'Yeah, I know but with this mega-yacht? I've been thinking it's far too dangerous. The Saudis could just put a fatwa on you so quickly you won't have time to learn what's going on. A big enough price and nothing will save you.'

Soliman frowned and nodded. 'I guess you're right. So what do you suggest?'

'We go to Venice unless you hear Gunther has moved on.'

'I can tell you that as of this morning, he is still there.'

'How do you know?' Bletchley asked.

'I had a text. Apparently he's learning how to handle a boat.'

'Good. Let's hope he stays there,' said Hunter. 'We'll go via the Suez Canal. From here to the southern end is 892 nautical miles.' He programmed into the computer a speed of 25 knots and watched as the digital readout slowly increased. At the same time, they could feel the yacht accelerating. 'We'll be at the southern end of the Suez in 36 hours. There are two transits a day, one southbound, one northbound.'

'What are transits?' Soliman asked.

'You transit the canal in a convoy.' Hunter pressed a few buttons on the computer built into the bridge console. 'Speed through the canal is eight knots and the distance from the Port of Suez to Port Said is 120 nautical miles and takes 11 to 12 hours.' Hunter increased speed by another five knots. 'That should ensure we get there in time to join a convoy otherwise we lose a day. It's almost 30 hours from here. We must take on a pilot as far as Ismailia, where we berth for the night at the Suez Yacht Club. We then fall into line behind the north bound convoy in the morning.'

'And from Port Said to Venice?' Bletchley asked.

'That's another couple of days and some.'

'Gunther may not be there by then,' Bletchley offered.

Hunter nodded. 'I'm aware of that. We could jump ship at Suez and fly to Italy. But that will leave Wajeeh in the lurch.' Hunter looked steadily at the Saudi. 'I said earlier that we owe you, which we do. Thanks to you, many lives have been saved. If we leave you at Suez you could have serious problems. We'll get you to Europe and then you can do as you please.'

Soliman nodded and gave a half smile. 'Thank you. I appreciate it.'

A few hours later, Hunter was sitting in the master's chair, nodding off, when Bletchley appeared carrying a mug of coffee. 'Here, Nick.' He proffered the mug and Hunter yawned, came wide-awake and stood up.

'I see it's pretty busy around here.'

'Yep. Thanks,' he took the mug. 'The shipping is doing around 12 knots so we're overtaking at a pretty good lick. I've gone starboard and port alternatively. You see the container ship up ahead?'

'Yes. She's huge.'

'That's the MSC Gulsun, the largest container ship in the world. She was built in South Korea. I looked up the details. She's 400 metres long, with a beam of 61.4 metres, which is a fraction below the maximum allowed to transit the Suez.'

'I was thinking about the last time we were here, only a few months ago. You and Jan in the small yacht after you killed that Saudi prince for smuggling slaves and Jihadists into Europe.'

'Yeah. That was a close call. If the General hadn't arranged for the helicopter to pick us up when it did, I don't think we'd be here now.'

'What gets me is that we had that private conversation with the King and made it clear he was to rein in his family, which he assured us he would do.'

'According to the General he has. This was personal and comes under a different heading.'

'I guess,' Bletchley said dubiously. 'It does show there are some princes who do as they like.'

'They're too powerful even for the king. You should check out the history of the House of Saud since it was established in 1818. There have been many deaths of kings and princes, killed by other members of their family. The family has over 15,000 members but all the wealth is in the hands of less than 2,000. Inequality is alive and kicking in Allah's paradise known as Saudi Arabia.'

'Such cynicism.'

Hunter grinned. 'It's what keeps us all going. That and a desire to keep people safe. I'm turning in. The master's cabin is directly below. I'll go there.'

'Okay, I have the yacht.'

The two men exchanged grins. It was the standard statement made when handing over a ship to another Officer of the Watch.

'I guess,' said Hunter, 'old habits die hard.'

At 02.00, Soliman with Hunter's help, disposed of the bodies and blood stained rugs over the side.

The Suez Yacht Club was obviously exclusive to the wealthy.

It boasted a number of first class restaurants, a ships' chandlers and a refuelling and watering berth. They didn't need water but they topped up the fuel tanks.

They didn't bother with the club's facilities but ate onboard. One of the crew turned out to be a competent chef and they had a passable saddle of lamb with fresh vegetables followed by cheese and biscuits.

The convoy departed at 08.00 on the dot with *The Star of Medina* in the front. They travelled at 10 knots, the maximum allowed whilst the larger ships in the convoy were held to eight knots. This was to reduce the risk of any pressure waves created by the ships from eroding the banks. There were no locks to navigate and so the passage was pleasant enough although there was nothing of interest to see, the land being flat and mostly desert.

They arrived at Port Said, exited the canal and increased speed to 25 knots. Hunter fiddled with the satnav and then said, '68 hours to Sacca de la Misericordia which means we'll arrive in a couple of days, around 15.00. Any word on Gunther's whereabouts?'

'Nothing new. It's safe to assume he's still there.'

When they entered the marina they were two and a half hours later than expected. Hunter had control while Bletchley and Soliman used binoculars to try and identify the boat they had been told now belonged to Gunther.

'I see it,' said Soliman.

Gunther was enjoying himself. He had purchased an opulent 30 foot powerboat, with twin engines. It had four berths, one double cabin aft, two singles forward, a lounge and dining area, a sophisticated galley and a bar. The boat, *The Paradise*, lived up to her name. The cockpit was open topped but had an awning that covered the area, making it wind proof and watertight. He reckoned she had been worth the $100,000 he'd paid. The price included four hours of lessons on how to handle her, as well as some rudimentary knowledge of the Rule of the Road, the maritime equivalent of the Highway Code.

He passed up on the offer of insurance.

Vendetta

There was one disquieting incident that set alarm bells ringing. The previous evening he saw two men, obviously Middle Eastern, in the restaurant where he ate. He was sure he had seen them before.

Then it suddenly dawned on him that the notion of going to sea on his own frightened him. It was one thing to cruise around the area with someone who knew what they were doing, it was something else entirely to leave for another marina. Then came a further thought. Perhaps it wasn't such a good idea after all. He could just as easily take a train or buy a car and travel the continent.

He was sitting in the cockpit looking at the mega-yachts berthed around him, all with people who appeared to be enjoying themselves. Many of the men appeared to be middle-aged with women young enough to be their daughters.

He liked his women mature and experienced. He grinned. He couldn't understand a Muslim's penchant for 72 virgins who would last a lifetime! On the whole, it said a lot for their manhood. He drained his glass of Pernod and stood up, ready to go below. He felt slightly woozy, having been drinking since the early afternoon. He looked at his watch, bleary-eyed. It was only 17.38.

He watched as a super yacht passed in the main channel. He could just make out the name, *The Star of Medina*. With a name like that, it obviously belonged to an Arab. He hated them all.

Once below decks he decided to lie down on the couch and close his eyes. He woke up three hours later. He sat up, groaned and put his face in his hands. He needed an evening ashore and he knew just the club to visit. It had gambling as well as girls.

He showered, changed and drank an inch of brandy before stepping ashore.

At the club he lost 1,000 euros, the maximum he allowed himself. He drank too much, didn't bother about a girl and headed back to *The Paradise*.

He stepped onboard and opened the door to the main cabin. He went below, turned on the lights and stopped in shock. A black haired man was sitting at the table, a silenced automatic in front of him.

Gunther was standing next to a shelf and grabbed it to stop himself from collapsing. He licked dry lips. He could feel his hands trembling. He had arranged many deaths but had never faced his own.

'Sit down.'

Gunther slid onto the bench seat opposite Hunter. He looked at the silenced weapon and then at Hunter's face.

'I need the toilet.'

'Where is it?'

'Through that door behind me.'

'Then carry on. I don't want you to be uncomfortable during our little talk.'

Gunther slid out of the seat and stepped through the door. Hunter could hear him scrabbling about and smiled. He placed a row of 9 mm Parabellum rounds on the table in front of him and waited patiently.

The door was thrown open, Gunther stepped into the cabin, aimed his revolver and pulled the trigger. He pulled it again and again, panic stricken as Hunter pointed to the bullets lined up in front of him. Gunther sank back down on to the seat.

'Did you actually think I'd let you go to the toilet?'

Gunther stared at Hunter, his hands flat on the table while he tried to stop them trembling.

'What do you want?' he whispered.

'You know who I am.'

'No.' His voice was still a croak and he cleared his throat before saying it again. This time he managed with more emphasis. 'No.'

'You're a liar, Michael. You don't mind if I call you Michael, do you? I appreciate our meeting will be a short one but I think we should at least be civil to one another.'

'What do you mean?'

'Well, you're not going to live much longer.' Shrugging, Hunter added, 'Only a few minutes, though it could be a bit longer depending on how fast you bleed out.'

'Why are you doing this?'

'You know why. You took a contract from Prince Abdul-Hameed Saud to have my family killed and then me.'

'No, I didn't!'

Hunter shook his head in mock sorrow. 'Tut, tut. Lying is most unbecoming. I know you did. In fact the Prince's head of security, Wajeeh Soliman, is on the yacht we arrived in only hours ago and can confirm your involvement. But that won't be necessary, will it? By the way, he's been helping us from the very beginning.'

Gunther's face had blanched a pasty white.

Hunter ran through the sequence of events orchestrated by Gunther and also highlighted the moves he had made to wipe out the people responsible.

'There are a couple of bit players we might have a word with but basically you're the end of the line. Naturally, we will ensure the moves taken against you are known in the right quarters to discourage others from making similar threats.'

'Please! I can pay you, one million euros.'

Hunter shook his head in mock refusal.

'Pounds, dollars, two million!' There was no hiding the desperation in Gunther's voice.

Again Hunter shook his head. 'No can do, Michael. You took the contract. How would it look if we let you off? We'd be seen as a soft touch.' Hunter picked up the gun. 'Incidentally, the scumbag you used to attack innocent people in Crosshall shot my father in the shoulder. You will, I am sure, be pleased to learn my father survived, though whether or not he'll ever be the same again is in the laps of the gods. What do you think of that?'

There was no answer so Hunter asked the question again. Still there was no answer so Hunter casually pointed the automatic at Gunther's left shoulder and fired. Gunther was thrown back against the bulkhead with a screech of agony. He opened his mouth to scream when Hunter stood and stepped up to the man. He casually hit him across his mouth with the bottom of the pistol butt. He picked up a dishtowel and wrapped it around Gunther's mouth, tying it tightly.

Next he pulled the man's arms behind his back and used a tie-wrap to secure them.

He took out a small case from a pocket, opened it and showed the hypodermic to Gunther. The man's eyes bulged and he started to moan.

Hunter took the needle, rammed it into Gunther's thigh and pressed the plunger. He looked at his watch before saying, 'It takes about three minutes before the painkiller kicks in. It's morphine-based and very powerful. I couldn't make up my mind what to do. Whether or not to give it to you, but you've got me on a good day. I decided to save you the agony of having your knees destroyed along with an elbow. You see it's important that people think you suffered a bad death, though I hasten to add that no death can be a good one.'

Hunter looked at his watch again and said, 'Time's up.'

He removed the tie-wraps before removing the gag. 'Try and speak.'

Gunther gargled a noise.

'Now scream.'

The sound from his mouth was just as strained.

'Good. The injection contained not only a painkiller but a substance that paralyses. Russian I'm told. Clever people the Russians when it comes to deadly toxins and viruses. I guess a bit like the Chinese.'

Hunter held the tip of the suppressor just above Gunther's patella, pointing it straight down. He pulled the trigger. The phut of the weapon couldn't be heard outside the hull.

Gunther bucked making a gurgling sound. Tears formed in his eyes and rolled down his cheeks. The bullet had gone in at a slight angle, travelled between the tibia and fibula and exited at the bottom of his tibia, shattering the bone.

'Sorry about that. The painkiller is only effective up to a certain point. After that,' Hunter shrugged, 'I guess you can say it's in the lap of the gods, or maybe just the one god. Who knows? You see, Michael, it is important that when your body is found, people will think you died a terrible and painful death. Only a few others and myself will know it isn't quite true. Oh, you'll know as well of course but you won't be able to tell anyone as you will have bled to death.' Hunter's conversational tone continued. He placed the suppressor into the crook of Gunther's right elbow and fired. Gunther's elbow jerked back into the bulkhead.

Hunter stepped back and looked at his handiwork.

'I have a dilemma. You're bleeding all right but not nearly as fast as I thought you would. Now, if you don't bleed to death in say the next 10 minutes, the painkiller will begin to wear off and you will gradually experience agony, the like of which few people have ever known. If that were to happen, you'll scream and might attract attention, which is the last thing I want. I could gag you I suppose, but what if you work the gag free?'

Hunter looked at his prisoner, shrugged and said, 'You shouldn't have attacked my family. Anyone who does, will die as painfully as I can make it. I'll tell you what. I'll help you by speeding up the process.' He placed the suppressor above the man's other patella. Gunther shook his head violently whilst making a peculiar gurgling noise.

Hunter stared into the man's eyes and pulled the trigger. Gunther arched backwards, his leg shooting out in front of him. This time the bullet travelled the length of his leg and smashed through the bottom of the tibia and his heel. Blood spurted out.

There was now a wide pool of blood creeping ever bigger as it drained from Gunther's body.

'That's okay. You should bleed out in a few minutes. I've got to go. By the way, I'm taking your laptop, three mobile phones and a couple of notebooks. I've left your weapons. We must leave something for the authorities to find, mustn't we?'

Gunther's head lolled forward as he took his last breath.

Epilogue

They were in the mess at TIFAT HQ.

The team was there along with Louise and Cathy but Hunter was still to join them. He had driven to Crosshall with his parents who had insisted on returning home. His mother wasn't aware that his father had been issued with a permit to carry a weapon, as well as being supplied with a Glock 17. He had spent a few hours on the firing range with his son, being reminded of the fundamentals when handling an automatic.

Hunter had assured his parents that there would be no further trouble and that the danger had been dealt with. They hadn't asked how. They trusted his word. However, his father would get the full story the next time the two men took Winston, their dog, for a walk.

The ladies sat at the table with glasses of white wine while the men had bottles of cold, locally brewed beer.

They were being blanketed by lethargy, a common reaction after such an intensive operation. The adrenaline had kept them going flat out but now it was time to relax.

'Here's the boss,' said Badonovitch as Hunter approached them.

They greeted him by waving their bottles.

'Mum and Dad okay?' Louise asked.

'Sure. Mum still isn't sleeping too well but she says she'll get over it. They're planning a world cruise so that should keep her busy.'

'What about your father? Won't he be kept busy as well?' Cathy asked.

Louise and Hunter exchanged smiles at the notion.

'What's everyone drinking?' Hunter asked, 'I'm buying.'